The Falling of the Moon

Moonfall Mayhem, Book One

A. E. DECKER

WORLD WEAVER PRESS

Published by World Weaver Press, LLC
Albuquerque, NM
www.WorldWeaverPress.com

Edited by Laura Harvey
Cover designed by World Weaver Press.
Cover illustration by Cary Vandever.

ISBN: 0692526013
ISBN-13: 978-0692526019

Also available as an ebook.

To Harry, as promised.

Also, to the memory of Terry Pratchett.
Death, we're still waiting for you to bring him back.

ACKNOWLEDGMENTS

Acknowledgments are rather like award shows: basically a litany of thanks, except, unlike awards shows, there's no way to critique what everyone's wearing. I'm rather tempted to follow the example of Hugh Laurie, who, upon winning a Golden Globe for *House M.D.*, simply filled his pockets with the names of all the people who'd helped him and selected two at random. But if I did that, I'd probably end up thanking my African dwarf frog, Fink-Nottle, for singing whenever I watch a musical, and charming though that habit is, it didn't really do much in the way of helping me finish a novel.

So, going with tradition, I must first and foremost thank my family for supporting me in my writing career when I probably could've chosen a field that offered a least a chance of a decent paycheck.

I also must express gratitude to Jeanne Cavelos, director of the Odyssey Writing Workshop and teacher extraordinaire. No one else has ever managed to explain the niceties of POV quite so clearly.

Branching off from Odyssey, I also want to thank my Oddfriends Alex, Karen, Hannah, Loriane, Tanith, Olivia, and Natalie for the support, brainstorming sessions, and lessons in the way of trout-killing. Gerald and Richard, a nod to you too, for your helpful criticism.

Thanks also to the Bethlehem Writers Group for their input and comradery.

Special thanks to Jennifer, for all the years of friendship.

Finally, my gratitude to Eileen, Laura, and Elizabeth of World Weaver Press for seeing a spark in Ascot and helping me send her story out into the world. There were times I never thought it would happen, guys!

Oh, and thanks to Fink-Nottle too, I guess. Why not? I'll put on *Hairspray* and you can sing along, little guy.

For Skyler

Enjoy!

THE FALLING OF THE MOON

A. E. Decker

CHAPTER ONE:
MOURNING BECOME ECLECTIC

Count von Abberdorf was staked, beheaded, and burned by the villagers who lived below his castle on the hill, and there was a strong possibility that he deserved it.

"Then they threw his ashes into the sea," said Igor, the Count's servant, summing up the morning's events to the Count's three children. "I fear there is no chance, absolutely none, of the Master's returning."

Ascot's breath stuck in her throat. She knew she was sitting in the castle's drawing room, just as she'd been before Igor began to speak, but the davenport slammed up beneath her, as if the world had been yanked out from under her and she'd landed hard in another identical, yet fundamentally different, one. *Your father is dead.* The words held no reality; not yet.

"Does that mean we can paint some rooms yellow now?" she heard herself ask.

She knew it wasn't the right thing to say, even before her older brother Vincent let drop his wrist, which he'd just pressed to his

3

forehead, and glared at her. "Is that your only reaction to the death of your dear father?" he snapped.

No. But she suspected that by the time she sorted out her feelings, everyone else would have lost interest in the subject. Besides, she had a point about the yellow walls. At its best, Abberdorf Castle's décor suggested a tastefully appointed dungeon. Velvet curtains black as silence cloaked its narrow windows. All the furniture was upholstered in dusky damask and draped with black lace. Generations of spiders' webs veiled the actual color of the rooms' high ceilings, but they were probably black.

Vincent continued glaring. He had a natural talent for it, with his thin, high-arched brows that gave him a look of permanent outrage.

"Remember, our 'dear' father stopped speaking to me a year ago," Ascot reminded him, plucking at a loose thread on the davenport. It wasn't only Castle Abberdorf's décor that made her feel as if she lived in a dungeon.

"Or listening to you," piped up Vlad, Ascot's twin, from the window seat. "Made for some awkward mealtimes." He brushed back the lock of pale hair that hung perpetually in his face. "Remember when that centipede crawled into his soup and you warned him about it?"

Ascot nodded. The most fascinating internal struggle had played out over their father's face as he wrestled between heeding her warning or continuing to pretend he couldn't hear her. She still recalled the visceral crunch of him biting into the centipede with great satisfaction.

"I'd prefer mauve, though," said Vlad. "The walls, I mean. The library would look fabulous in mauve and silver."

The spiders huddled deep inside their webs as Vincent fixed first Vlad, then Ascot, with a glower. If either of them had whispered "periwinkle," he'd have spontaneously combusted. "Stop being ridiculous," he said. "Come along. We must prepare for Father's funeral."

He marched from the room. Ascot made a face at his back. "Acting like he's lord of the manor already."

Shutting his book of Gothic poetry, Vlad cast her a grim look. "With Father gone, he might well be."

"He can't be worse," said Ascot. She looked up at the spiders. "Can he?"

"Serves you right if they instantly weave a giant 'yes' into their webs," said Vlad.

"No, spiders only write when there's some goat or pig they want to praise." She pinched her nose, stifling a sneeze. Contrary to the drawing room's appearance, Igor must have cleaned it recently, for a heavy, floral odor hung in the air, mingling with the scent of dust.

"I forget." Vlad picked a flake of black lacquer off one of his nails. "Why did Father stop speaking to you?"

"I painted my room yellow."

"Vlad! Ascot!" Vincent roared from the hall. Ascot jumped; Vlad started. Both hastened to join their older brother, but Ascot glanced back. One spider right in the center of the ceiling was connecting a long, straight line to the central point of a V-shaped webbing. Her heart leaped. Was it actually weaving a "Y"? The spiders had done nothing but scuttle, catch insects, die, and fall to the floor in little crunchy, leg-curled bunches while her father was alive.

"Come along, you," said Vincent, grabbing her. Ascot craned her neck over her shoulder as he pushed her towards the garden. Two hours passed before she could return to the drawing room, her fingers throbbing from the black roses he'd set her to picking.

"Well," she said, looking up at the ceiling. The spider had indeed woven a "Y." And a "G," a "U," a "Q," and a "Z."

That settled that. Apparently, spiders *could* write, even when not praising livestock. They just couldn't spell worth a damn.

The following midnight, mourners gathered in the parlor, where every whisper echoed and cobwebs wafted in lieu of curtains. Wineglass in hand, Ascot shamelessly eavesdropped on the surrounding conversations from a spot between the brocaded red wall and a heavy armchair where Moony, the family's Vicardi cat, lay stretched along the back.

"Lovely funeral," said a guest. "A shame Count von Abberdorf isn't here to see it himself."

"Yes, well, of course the whole point of a funeral is that the person it's for isn't present," said another.

"Poor bastard. You must say he had it coming, though."

"Yes, so many pink girls in Abberdorf Village were walking around with pocked necks and glazed expressions that you'd think the hickey plague had struck."

"I heard he was biting two maidens a fortnight."

"Three," said Moony, lifting his head from the chair's cushioned back. Ascot reached out to stroke him.

"I thought you intended to nap through this appalling affair," she said. More guests kept pouring in. She recognized her cousin, Vachel, by his bouffant silver hair, and her dowager Aunt Agathena by her expression of imperious constipation.

Moony grinned. Even for a Vicardi cat he was tiny, dark gray save for a pale muzzle and a white streak above his right eye such as a mad barber might sport. Two bat-wings sprouted from his back, just large enough to allow him to flutter, and his thick, bushy tail crackled with static. Taken altogether, he resembled something that had been left out in the rain to attract lightning.

"I'm just waiting for the opportune moment to hack up a hairball," he said.

Ascot snickered. Off to her right, the guests continued their conversation.

"I'm surprised the pinks didn't stake him sooner."

"Well, you know how it is, once you get addicted to the red stuff. A maiden a month is never enough."

"Yes, like potato crisps."

"What are those?"

"Something they eat—" The suggestion of a shudder. "—in the Daylands."

"Oh!" A sympathetic gasp. "Sounds ghastly."

"What's so awful about the Daylands?" Ascot asked Moony. Her mother had been born there.

"I don't know, but I'd like to visit them." Moony sat up, his orange eyes widening. "Do you know they've invented a light without candles or torches? They do it with gas."

"Gas?" said Ascot, hoping she'd misheard.

"Not that kind of gas." He wrinkled his nose. "They make it from some kind of rock. Isn't that amazing?"

"Where did you hear all this?"

"Oh, the fishmonger wraps my cod heads in newspaper. I like to read while I eat. They have many things we don't in the Daylands. Unicorns! Fairies! Coconuts!"

"Coconuts?"

"I think they're some kind of bat." Moony coughed and began washing his face.

Ascot's father never let her read newspapers; said they'd only give her vulgar ideas. "I wonder why Mother came to Shadowvale," she said, staring down into her wine. Her mother had died before she'd been old enough to ask such questions, and her father . . . Well, it was hard to get answers from a person who developed selective deafness whenever you spoke.

But then there'd been Miss Eppicutt, her last, and favorite, governess. She'd come from the Daylands, too, and she'd told the most marvelous stories—

"There you are!"

Ascot yelped as Vincent grabbed her arm and hauled her from her comfortable nook.

"What's the matter?" she asked, looking up into his face. He was scowling—not unusual—and fidgeting—which was.

"Count Zanzibander's coach just pulled up out front," he said.

"So?" she asked, exchanging a puzzled glance with Moony. Vlad, holding one full wineglass and a second, near-empty one, joined their group.

"Couldn't you have worn a dress?" said Vincent, and actually began fussing with her sleeves and arranging her hair. He'd donned his finest black velvet suit; the one Father had bought for him, with crested cufflinks and black diamond buttons. His equally black hair lay in ruthlessly slicked-back rows from his hard, pale face, shades whiter than hers or Vlad's.

Ascot batted his hands away. "I don't like dresses. What's this all about?"

Vlad leaned against her shoulder, crumpling his extravagant cravat. "I think he wants you to do this," he said, fluttering his lashes.

"Flirt? With Count Zanzibander?" Ascot scoffed. "You're joking."

Vincent's thin lips tightened. The doorbell tolled a morbid note. A moment later, a high, whinnying laugh from the entryway rose above the general hum of conversation.

"There's the Count now," said Vlad, and drained his glass.

Sure enough, Count Zanzibander entered the drawing room, clad in black-and-silver paisley. Beaming, he thrust his pudgy hand around for various people to shake, like a mayor trying to garner votes on election day.

Vincent squeezed Ascot's arm. "Now, remember, if he gives you an umbrella, don't treat it like you did the last one."

"That drainpipe needed unclogging," she said, but he was already walking away to greet Count Zanzibander, who *did* have an umbrella tucked under one arm, she noted unhappily. The last one had been maroon and sparkly and went *"whee!"* when unfurled.

"Why does he keep giving me umbrellas?" she asked Vlad. "Just because he collects them doesn't mean everyone's interested."

"No." Vlad stared down at the purple dregs in his wineglass as if the taste soured in his mouth. "But he probably wants his wife to share his interest."

"But he's not—" Ascot stopped.

Oh, no. Vincent's fussing. Count Zanzibander's marked attentions. They couldn't mean. Surely they couldn't mean . . . ? Her hand trembled, slopping wine over her fingers. "I won't," she said. "Don't be ridiculous."

Vlad swiped her glass and drained it. "Don't hate me for saying this, sis, but what are your options?"

"To marrying Count Zanzibander? Death. Insanity. Training an ogre to eat him on sight."

Moony snickered but Vlad didn't so much as smile. "Father never thought Count Zanzibander was good enough for our family." Vlad set his three empty wineglasses down carefully, one by one, on the small table next to the armchair before meeting her gaze. His dark burgundy eyes displayed not a single spark of their usual mirth. The dimple that generally hovered at the left corner of his mouth had flattened out, and even his wayward lock of hair had been tamed for the night. "But Father's dead."

Vincent approached with Count Zanzibander in tow. Ascot's gaze darted to the latticed patio doors, but Aunt Agathena had planted herself in front of them, and her bosom alone would halt the advance of an entire army. Before she could plot another escape route, Vincent and Count Zanzibander rolled to a stop before her.

"Say hello to Count Zanzibander, dear sister," said Vincent with the air of a man bestowing a great prize on an undeserving victor.

Ascot swallowed. "Hello, Count Zanzibander." She hated the squeak in her voice.

Count Zanzibander beamed. "Zis is for you," he said, presenting the umbrella.

It was plaid; orange and green plaid with a thin crisscrossing of blue. Ascot wore a black silk blouse and pants, but the umbrella still managed to clash with them. Again she considered bolting, but Vincent's prize-dispensing manner had attracted the attention of the entire parlor. A sea of eyes glittered back at her. One old lady in a spangled gray gown had a particularly bright pair, sparkling like brown gems. Her skin stood out too, rosier than the rest of the crowd's. A pink? Here?

Ascot forced her attention back to Count Zanzibander. "Thank you," she said, accepting the umbrella. She ran her fingers over its folds, wondering what to do next.

"*Go on,*" Vincent mouthed over Count Zanzibander's shoulder.

He could have meant kiss the Count, unfurl the umbrella, or burst into appreciative tears. Ascot opted for the second. Braced for another "*whee!*" she released the catch. The umbrella unfurled.

"*Ribbit!*" A large, yellow-green frog popped free of the folds and landed on the parlor carpet. It sat there for a second, amber eyes goggling; then, with a speed Ascot would never have credited any frog with, it dashed to hide under Aunt Agathena's spreading skirts.

She'd never have credited Aunt Agathena with the ability to hit the pitch she promptly did, either. A few of the chandelier's dangling black crystals shattered.

"Zat vasn't supposed to happen," commented Count Zanzibander with mild bafflement.

"Garlic!" Vincent howled, tearing at his hair. The guests flinched at the obscenity. "What have you done now, Ascot?"

"Me?" Her mouth rounded in indignation. "That's rich."

But he'd already whirled off to aid Aunt Agathena, now doing a frenzied yet indignant dance in the middle of the parlor. She'd already kicked three mourners who'd tried to help. Vincent skittered just out of range, shouting words of support.

"I'll get it," said Moony. Before Ascot could grab him, he launched himself off the back of the armchair and slithered under Aunt Agathena's skirts.

More chandelier crystals promptly shattered. "Stop laughing, Vlad," Ascot snapped at her twin, but he slid to the floor, clutching his sides.

Giving up on Vlad, she dashed forward, still clutching the umbrella. She didn't have a plan, just the thought that if the frog normally lived in the umbrella, it wasn't surprising that it found the ruffled spread of Aunt Agathena's skirt inviting. *But it would probably rather be back in its actual home*, she reasoned.

Aunt Agathena's skirts rippled. Her great, creaky assemblage of corsets, crinolines, and whalebone pinged. A desperate *"Ribbit!"* followed an eager *"Mew!"*

"Moony, get out of there," Ascot cried. She dodged Vincent and ducked under Aunt Agathena's flailing arm. "I need your help."

Moony emerged in a flash. "What can I do?" he asked, all eager orange eyes and twitching tail-tip.

Ascot pointed to Aunt Agathena's shoulders. "Jump up there and go into sleep mode."

With a grin and salute, Moony sprang. Aunt Agathena yelped when his claws snagged her immense gigot sleeves, a sound fortunately less ear-splitting than her earlier shrieks. As soon as he found his perch, Moony went limp, instantly gaining an extra fifteen pounds in the mysterious way of all sleeping cats. Aunt Agathena staggered, then stilled, anchored by the sudden extra weight.

"Good," said Ascot. Reversing her grip on the umbrella, she knelt and hooked up the hem of Aunt Agathena's skirt. Amidst the countless layers of frilly black, she was rewarded with a flash of yellow-green. "Here, froggy, froggy, froggy," she called, tilting the umbrella so it could see the inviting plaid bowl.

The frog's throat bubbled a few times. Its amber eyes blinked once. Then it seemed to make its mind up all at once; with two quick hops, it leaped into the center of the umbrella.

Ascot folded the umbrella up, frog and all, and stood. "That wasn't so difficult," she commented to the room at large.

Vincent glared daggers. Black crystal fragments littered the parlor rug. Two mourners nursed bruises and a settee bore the imprint of a high-heeled boot. Her cousin, Vachel, sprawled across the buffet table, cobra tartar dripping off his deflated silver bouffant.

But three people didn't share the crowd's general opinion. Moony smirked proudly. Count Zanzibander positively beamed. Ascot wasn't aware of her third supporter until she felt a smooth cube being pressed into her hand. Her nose wrinkled at the scent of powdery lilacs. Turning, she looked down into the sparkling brown eyes of the little old lady.

"You have spirit, my dear," the old lady whispered. She patted Ascot's hand, a hand now holding a small wooden box. "Open this, should you choose to follow your dreams."

She whisked off, vanishing in a swirl of lavender glitter and floating wisps that looked suspiciously like cat hairs. Before Ascot could adjust her thoughts, Vincent's fingers bit into her shoulder.

"This will be the last time you embarrass me in public, sister," he growled in her ear. "I promise you."

He shook her once and left. Standing alone in the middle of the parlor, Ascot squeezed the wooden box until her knuckles ached.

CHAPTER TWO:
THE HEIR CUT

Aunt Agathena departed immediately. An hour later, having drunk all the wine, the other guests left, still sniggering when anyone whispered "frog." Every one of them had forgotten they were supposed to be mourning.

Half an hour afterwards, at precisely three o' clock, Count von Abberdorf's scaly green lawyer crept up the hill to preside over the reading of the will.

Vincent inherited the castle.

Vlad received Igor.

Ascot got Moony.

≶⧫

"You can't stay here." Still dressed in his black velvet, Vincent paced the parlor, one elegantly manicured hand clasped in the small of his back, the other used for grand gesticulation. "Father let this place go for too long. It needs work."

Ascot sat on the heavy armchair, head bowed, counting the patterned bats on the carpet. At regular, twenty-second intervals, Vincent's feet passed through her line of vision, interrupting her calculations. Moony crouched beside her, motionless save for the very tip of his tail.

"Every spare cent I possess will be needed for the renovations," Vincent continued.

Vlad looked up from the footstool in the corner. "*Every* spare cent?" he asked. "Are you planning to coat the castle in gold?"

Vincent ignored him. "Igor can help with the work, which is why I'm letting Vlad stay. But all you have is your cat."

"I'm my own cat," Moony growled.

"It's impossible for me to support a sister with no income of her own." Vincent reached the apex of his path and turned.

Ascot's nails dug into the chair's dusky upholstery. If she had to listen to one more of his excuses, she was going to lose her cobra tartar. "And just how am I supposed to earn an income?" she demanded. "Father fired Miss Eppicutt just for teaching me how to sew." *That, and for spurning his advances,* she added privately. "He said work was beneath a von Abberdorf."

Vincent waved that off. "I happen to agree with him there. Fortunately, you have another option. One that won't embarrass the family."

He smiled, not in a nice way. At almost the same instant, the doorbell tolled a morbid note. A moment later, Igor entered the parlor. "Count Zanzibander's at the door," he announced.

⚕

Late the following day, Ascot slipped the letter she'd just written into the coffin where Vlad lay sleeping, all rumpled in his favorite purple satin pajamas.

"Good-bye," she whispered. He snored. She stroked his cheek, then went down to the larder, where she took six sandwiches, a wheel of cheese, two hardboiled black swans' eggs, and the can of hash Miss Eppicutt had left behind thirteen years ago and stuffed them into a knapsack. Donning her long black leather coat, she filled its pockets with silverware. As the light drained from the sky, she tucked Miss Eppicutt's white book of stories under one arm and scooped up Moony. Then, without a final glance back, she stalked down the hill, leaving behind the castle that was no longer her home.

§

"Ass! My brother's a complete ass," said Ascot around a mouthful of roast rat on pumpernickel.

"So you told me a couple miles back, miss," replied the coachman.

"My father was an ass, too," she added, in case she'd forgotten to mention it.

Moony looked up from licking the mustard off a leg of roasted rat. "He willed me away, like an object. Can you imagine?"

"Must've hurt like poison," said the coachman. He really was a very nice fellow, Ascot thought. He'd accepted a thin handful of coins—all she'd managed to save over the years—in return for taking her and Moony to the town closest to the Daylands' border, provided they were willing to sit outside so as not to frighten the other travelers, pinks all.

No, not pinks. Humans, she corrected herself. Miss Eppicutt had always frowned when she said "pinks."

In any case, she didn't mind. The scenery provided endless distractions as the coach rolled eastward through Shadowvale, that lonely mountainous country where the wind blew shrill and the light shone murky even at the height of noon. Bats swarmed overhead and wargs and wights came howling out of dark forests in the middle of the night. At present they traversed a glade, turned a weird and wicked place under the silvery moonlight. Each gnarled oak they passed resembled a bearded giant and every mushroom patch might have hid a goblin. Fallen leaves made jagged patterns on the pale earth.

"Have you ever been out of Shadowvale?" Ascot asked the coachman. She took another bite of her sandwich.

"Once, when I was a nipper." He scratched the back of his head with the handle of his whip. "Eh, it's much brighter there. The sunlight's yellow instead of gray. The people are ruddier, too, sometimes brown, even. They don't go about scared of the—" He flashed her a sideways look and fell silent.

Of the noble Shadowvaleans, Ascot finished for him. People like her father. She swallowed her latest mouthful. "My mother was from the Daylands."

"Ah. That explains it." The coachman nodded sagely. "You're naught as pale as most o' the nobles, and your eyes are more brown than red."

A stab of unexpected pride struck Ascot. She sat a little straighter on the box. Of course; that's why she'd never fit in among the languid, dreary Shadowvalean aristocracy. She'd always been meant to go east, to her mother's people.

But go east and do what, precisely? She stared down at her sandwich. The little wooden box, stowed inside her trouser pocket, dug into her hip. Should she open it? But the old lady had said to do so if she meant to follow her dreams. Ascot didn't think "running away screaming from Count Zanzibander" quite counted as following a dream.

The coach jolted over a bump in the road and Ascot's purloined silverware clinked inside her pockets. One thing was certain: she could not return home. Forget the threat of marrying Count Zanzibander; Vincent would have her arrested for theft if she set foot in Abberdorf County now. *I hope Vincent doesn't take out his anger on Vlad.* No, Igor would protect her twin. She'd always suspected Vincent of being secretly terrified of Igor, with his scars and gray skin.

"Have you heard about the light they make from stones in the Daylands?" Moony asked the coachman. "It runs on gas."

"Gas?" said the coachman.

"Not *that* kind of gas."

Mustard oozed between Ascot's fingers. Preoccupied with her thoughts, she'd mashed her sandwich into an unappetizing lump. "What am I going to do?" she asked.

No one answered.

She still didn't know by the following dawn, when the coach reached an inn crouched on the very border of Shadowvale. She couldn't go any farther east without actually entering the Daylands. Ascot's pulse raced at the prospect, but instead of pressing on—the sun was nearly up, after all—she offered the innkeeper a silver cup in exchange for a day's room and board.

That took care of the next few hours. After that . . .

"Moony, what are we going to do in the Daylands?" she asked as they finished up their supper in the inn's whitewashed dining area, alone save for a grandmotherly woman sipping tea in the corner.

"Find a marauding dragon, kill him, and accept half his treasure and the gratitude of the surrounding countryside," Moony answered promptly.

THE FALLING OF THE MOON

Ascot smiled. Feisty little Moony had been her best friend for years. Every day he curled up at the foot of her coffin and every night she'd awaken and tickle his chin until he purred.

"Are there that many dragons in the Daylands?" she asked. And wouldn't all Daylanders be rich if there were?

Maybe all Daylanders *were* rich. But Moony twitched his tufted ears, a sign of embarrassment. "Well, I don't really know how many dragons there are," he admitted. "I was just using Miss Eppicutt's stories for guidance. She was from the Daylands, wasn't she?"

"That's it!" Ascot slapped the plank tabletop. Cutlery rattled. "I brought Miss Eppicutt's book along. Maybe it'll give us an idea of what we should do."

Eager now, she brought out the thick white volume and laid it open on the table. The heavy paper purred as she turned the pages. Moony climbed onto her shoulder. His whiskers tickled her cheek as they perused the chapters together.

After a time, he hopped onto the tabletop, spun round as if chasing his tail, and sat. "Well, it's pretty clear," he said, blinking up at her. "You have to marry a prince."

Ascot ran a finger over an illustration of a blonde girl in rags squeezing her foot into a tiny, glittering shoe. "I left home to avoid marrying Count Zanzibander. How would marrying a prince be any better?"

Moony shrugged his wings. "Well, according to the book, princes are always handsome and charming. Marrying one guarantees that you'll live—what's the phrase?" He squinted at a page. "Happily ever after."

Pursing her lips, Ascot flipped through a few more chapters. Moony was right. Outside of marrying princes, there didn't appear to be many options for girls, unless she wanted to bring a basket of goodies to her granny and get eaten by a wolf. Or vandalize a bears' house, and she couldn't see the point of that. *My hair isn't golden, anyway*, she thought, turning another page.

And there it was. She closed her eyes, shook her head, and looked again. The illustration was still there, laid out before her: a magnificent castle, all tall white peaks, silver filigree, and regal blue pennants, formed a backdrop for a cheering crowd tossing flowers at a gilded carriage pulled by four creamy horses. Inside the carriage, a handsome prince cuddled his beautiful bride. A thick golden aura surrounded the princess, as if artist wished to depict her literally glowing with joy.

Ascot stared at the picture. "Happily ever after." She touched the princess's face. "Think this could be me, Moony?" she asked, forcing a laugh.

But something inside her held its breath. Adoration. Wealth. Eternal happiness. All for her, the restless, half-Daylander girl of Shadowvale. Her pale, curvy cousins would sneer at the idea. Vincent would laugh, derisively. She herself, after a glance in the mirror at her tall, lanky figure and unruly black hair, would probably slink off into the woods for a few hours of throwing rocks at trees until she felt better.

"Why not?" said Moony. "You have spirit. Isn't that what the old lady told you? The one who smelled of lilac talcum powder?"

Smiling, Ascot scratched his cheek. He leaned into her palm, purring. Across the room, the sound of rocking ceased. "What are you reading there, dearie?"

Ascot raised her head as the bent but apple-cheeked granny hobbled over, assisted by an ivory-topped cane. "Tales of the Daylands," she said, lifting the cover to show her.

"Ah, yes." The granny nodded. "Many an unappreciated lass has found eternal happiness in the Daylands." She stroked the book. "It's all in here."

It was all real, then. Ascot stared straight ahead for a long moment, then, with a new determination, dug into her pocket and brought out the little wooden box. Moony propped his chin on her wrist as she set it on the table.

The box opened smoothly, with a whisper rather than a click. Ascot gasped at the sight of the gold ring nestled in folds of black velvet. "Oh, how pretty."

Moony sniffed it. "Kind of plain."

True. Some of Ascot's pleasure faded on second inspection. The ring's single, dull cabochon stone shone a dark red without a sparkle. It was only when she drew it out that she noticed the inscription scrolling over the ring's band. "*'I burn bright in True Love's sight.'* Oh!"

"Yes, pretty lousy poetry." Moony licked a paw.

"No, no." She held up the ring. "Don't you see? It'll glow when my True Love is near. This," she touched the box, "why, this must've been given to me by a Fairy Godmother!" Of course; a kindly old woman in a spangly gown. Why hadn't she seen it before?

Moony's eyes widened. "Oh, I see. I didn't know Fairy Godmothers ever visited Shadowvale. Do you think we get coconuts, too, and just haven't noticed? Ascot?" He butted his head under her arm. "What's wrong?"

Ascot frowned. She'd been just about to slip the ring onto her finger when she'd noticed a second inscription in its inner band, this one etched in harsh, jagged letters. "*'If you light not where I have shone, live out your life unloved, alone,'*" she read aloud. She nibbled a dry spot on her lip. "That sounds . . . does that means that if I put on this ring but don't marry my True Love, then I won't ever find anyone else?"

Chuckling, the granny reached out to pat her hand. "Are you forgetting the stories already, my dear? True Loves are always

21

princes. Why would you want anyone else if you could have a prince?"

Ascot chewed her lip some more. She rolled the ring in her hand, then held it to the light, watching it not-sparkle.

Think of it as arranging a marriage, she told herself. Only instead of the matchmaker being mostly concerned with wealth or status— or just wanting to get her out of the house—they meant to find her someone she truly liked.

The trouble with that way of thinking was that, even in arranged matches, there was usually a way out, a chance to try again.

Then again, a prince . . . True Love . . . Happily Ever After. Ascot flipped to the illustration of the carriage ride again. The literally glowing princess, her joy virtually throwing rays of warmth off the page.

You couldn't ask for better than eternal happiness, could you? How many people were offered such a chance? Looked at in that way, it seemed cowardly and ungrateful not to take it.

"You're right," she said, and slipped on the ring. It slid smoothly onto her finger, without a tingle.

"So what do you do now?" asked Moony. "Go around waving it at princes until the stone lights up?"

Ascot looked at the granny, still leaning on her cane and smiling her apple-cheeked smile. "Know of any available princes?"

"You came to the Daylands at the right time," she replied, settling onto the bench opposite Ascot. "Queen Bettina Anna of Albright is holding a ball next week for her son's birthday."

A ball! Perfect! Ascot leaned forward. "How do we—"

Brrrechkkkktttt!

The belch reverberated off the whitewashed walls of the inn and shook beetles from the exposed rafter beams.

Ascot glared at Moony.

THE FALLING OF THE MOON

He shrugged. "'Scuse me. Eel pie will repeat." Hopping off the table, he went to investigate a rustling under the bench.

Ascot returned her attention to the granny. "How do we reach Albright?"

"Albright's close to the border, a bit south from here. You can reach it in a few days by walking, if you don't mind roughing it." The granny's gnarled forefinger traced a path through a scattering of salt on the tabletop. "Just go east through the birch woods until you find a road of white stones. Follow it south and it'll take you straight into Albright."

"Thank you so much." Ascot closed the book. "I know so little about the Daylands. It's good to know I can trust this—" She held up her ring. "—and have the stories to guide me."

"That's right, dear." The granny rubbed the ivory hook of her stick as Moony emerged from beneath a bench with something gray and wriggling dangling from his jaws. "Be brave and true and happiness will follow."

She smiled and limped out of the inn. It wasn't until the door closed behind her that Ascot thought to ask: "True to what?"

Oh, well. She finished her tea. It was a minor question and probably of little importance.

Moony abruptly sneezed, dropping the gray thing onto the floor. "Do you smell dusty lilacs?" he asked.

❦

That evening, the innkeeper's wife gave her a package of biscuits and some extra cheese for her travel, free of charge. *Daylanders are so nice*, Ascot thought, waving farewell to the woman standing in the doorway of the inn.

She walked fast, eager to reach Albright. In deference to Moony's shorter stride, she let him ride on her shoulder. Details of their journey blurred in the corners of her eyes, remembered only in sleep: the curdled edges of a boulder, like a giant, half-buried sheep; an abandoned caravan, its red-and-blue paint gone weathered and dingy; a herd of deer that stared at her from behind the white columns of the birch trees. Her toes ached from stubbing them against rocks half-hidden by the accumulated fall of rotten leaves. At dawn, she'd remove her boots and soak her sore feet in cooling brooks.

Five nights later, her efforts to reach Albright paid off. The white road cut through a grove in the woods, gleaming like a silver snake under the moonlight, its stones smooth as a collection of eggs.

"Look, Moony, there are flowers planted along one side," said Ascot, bending over to sniff the blossoms. Marigolds and chrysanthemums, their petals tightly folded for the night. "With such a fine road leading to it, Albright must be amazing."

Moony took two steps along the road, then shivered and hunched, wrapping his tail around his paws. "You'll still carry me, won't you?" he mewed, a tiny, helpless ball of fur all alone in the great world. He gazed up at her, his orange eyes huge and beseeching in his pointed face.

"Oh, Moony." Ascot held out for three seconds before giving in. "Just don't pull that trick too often, okay?" She scooped him up and tickled his chin.

"Okay," he purred, eyes half-closed in satisfaction.

Ascot shook her head, hiding a smile. What a shameless liar.

꒰🐾꒱

"Ascot!"

Twenty needlelike claws lanced Ascot's shoulder, awakening her from her nightdream of being carried through Albright's gem-encrusted streets by an adoring throng.

"Ouch! Don't do that," she told Moony, rubbing her shoulder. The last of the huzzahs faded from her imagination with a few final cheers and bleating of horns. "Lucky my coat's thick. What's the matter?"

"Something's stalking us," said Moony. He shifted on her shoulder, his tail brushing her cheek as he peered into the darkness beyond the road. "Some animal. It moves like a predator. Should I go get it?" The fur along his back rose, crackling with excitement. Ascot grabbed hold of a wing before he could whisk off into the night.

"No, just ignore it," she said. "Big predators are cowardly. They'll only attack if you're injured." At least she recalled reading something of the sort in the family library.

Something in the brush rumbled a low growl. Ascot's memory coughed nervously and slunk away, muttering excuses. *Maybe this isn't the best time to rely on half-forgotten books.* She peered into the darkness. Thorny bushes bristled in the shadows beyond the flowers, thick enough to conceal a plow horse with the plow attached. What were they hiding now?

"Maybe it thinks you're injured," said Moony. His fur crackled some more.

Whatever-it-was growled again, closer this time. Keeping her eyes on the bushes, Ascot slid her knapsack off her back and rifled through it. Cheese, biscuits, socks . . . *There must be something I can use.*

Moony leaped off her shoulder and crouched on the road, his ears twisting this way and that. "Can't hear it anymore. Maybe it ran away."

Ascot relaxed. "Told you they were cowards."

Another growl rumbled from the brush. Ascot went back to rummaging.

"It's still there," said Moony.

"Yes, I figured that out." Inside the knapsack, her fingers closed around what she was looking for. She straightened. "Hey, Moony. Remember my favorite game back home?"

"Checkers?"

"No. Fancy a guess, you cowardly brute?" she called to the bushes. The growl, which had never quite subsided, deepened to a full-fledged snarl.

There you are. She smiled, measuring the cool, heavy weight of Miss Eppicutt's can of hash in her hand. It was the easiest thing in the world to cock her arm, aim, and let fly.

She counted two seconds.

Thunk.

The snarling broke off in a squall of pain. Branches snapped under heavy paws as the unseen creature made good its escape.

Ascot dusted off her hands. "The throwing-things-at-other-things game."

"Oh, right." Moony stared into the shadows. "It's gone," he said, disappointed. "I could have taken it."

"You can have the next one." Ascot stepped off the road, meaning to retrieve the hash. The brush pushed back. Thorns hooked into her pants and coat, threatening to ensnare her. She quickly tugged herself free. "Oh, well," she said. "Miss Eppicutt would've approved of the use I put it to."

They resumed their journey, swaggering just a little. The road grew hillier, and more winding. One great rise took all Ascot's energy to surmount. *I'll pause to catch my breath after I pass that beech tree,* she promised herself, panting. The beech tree passed. *No, I can wait until after we go by that turtle-shaped rock . . . that clump of asters . . . that mushroom with the funny flat cap . . .*

She reached the crest. Wheezing, she doubled over, clasping her knees.

"Ascot!" cried Moony from her shoulder.

Ascot straightened and instantly forgot her exhaustion. The kingdom of Albright lay spread out below her.

CHAPTER THREE:
A BONE TO PICK

Even in the middle of the night, light flashed off gilded domes, sparkled over stained-glass windows, and gleamed on marble steps. Albright resembled a huge jewelry box that had been commissioned by someone with a heap of money and absolutely no taste.

"Make sure everyone notices the diamonds," Ascot could hear the rich, fruity voice commanding. *"Add a row of rubies and a few sapphires as well. Big sapphires! Big rubies! Don't forget the opals, and be generous with the golden curlicues and pearl inlay, while you're at it."*

"Look at all the colors," she said. She'd never seen so many put together at once and couldn't decide if she wanted to clap or wince.

"Kind of gaudy," said Moony.

"It's just living up to its name," said Ascot, remembering that Albright was, after all, going to be *her* kingdom. "Daylander aesthetics differ from those of Shadowvale."

"Yes, they're tackier."

Ascot tweaked his tail. He swatted her hand. They proceeded down the hill. The white city wall loomed as they neared.

The wall. From the hill's crest it had looked insignificant; a mere candy shell coating the luscious chocolate center that was the city proper. But once they reached it . . .

"How do we get in?" asked Moony, staring up at twelve feet of smooth, un-climbable stone.

"There has to be a gate."

There was a gate. A shut gate. Unarguably shut by a huge oak door crisscrossed with iron reinforcement. A young man stood beside it, thin and indifferent as a straight line. His hands vanished into the pockets of his light brown coat. His hair, falling to his shoulders, matched his coat's color. If he hadn't been standing in a puddle of moonlight, Ascot might not have even noticed him, so silent and still was he. She only gave him a second glance to compare her black coat to his brown one.

"Good night," she said, reaching for the latch.

"Halt," he replied.

Something in his tone made her body freeze before her brain had a chance to argue. "What do you mean, halt?"

"It means 'cease your forward motion,'" said the man. His hazel eyes narrowed, studying her. The right was swollen, half-closed, and ringed with a dark circle. Ascot could barely make sense of his accent and certainly didn't understand his attitude.

"Why?" she asked.

"Do you have a pass?" he replied.

"A pass? What for?" Her body recovered from its brief paralysis. She tugged on the latch, but she might as well have tried to yank open a mountainside for all the effect her efforts made. "Do you have the key?"

"Do you have a pass?" he countered, with a shard of a smile.

Moony stirred on her shoulder. "There's the pass," he said puckishly, nodding towards the gate.

Ascot doubted the man had ever met a Vicardi cat before, but she wouldn't have known it from his reaction—or lack thereof—to a talking, bat-winged kitty. "You need a pass to pass through this pass," he said. "If you don't have a pass, I can't let you pass."

"That's it." Ascot planted her hands on her hips. "The pass jokes have officially become annoying. Why would I have a pass to a place I've never been? That's ridiculous."

The brown-coated ruffian shrugged. "Farewell, then."

"What?"

"Albright is locked up at night. To keep out thieves and vagabonds and wild women from the hills."

Ascot's hands flew self-consciously to her hair. "But I need to attend the ball," she sputtered.

"Do you, now?" He moved at last, lifting his eyes to the full moon riding overhead. Its pallid light made his face all points and angles. "In that case, I will let you into the city when the moon falls out of the sky into the palm of your hand."

Ascot blinked. "When—?"

"Go home, girl," he said, and closing his eyes, returned to his indifferent attitude.

"Should I bite him?" asked Moony, lashing his tail. His fur started crackling.

Ascot looked from the moon to the brown-coated man. She shook herself. "No, don't soil your teeth. He's outside the city, so I suppose he's a vagabond. Or a thief, more likely."

So much for all Daylanders being kind. She hoped his eye *really* hurt. "Come along, Moony," she said, wrapping her coat—which *was* nicer than his coat—around her and turning with a flourish. "We'll come back when decent people are present."

She had a thought. Instead of returning to the road, she followed the wall as it curved to her left. A wind, smelling of damp dust and dying leaves, kicked up. Ascot turned her collar up against the chill.

"Are you looking for a place to sleep?" asked Moony, huddling close to her neck for warmth.

"No." Ascot peered over her shoulder. She'd half expected the brown-coated man to follow her so he could continue being annoying, but he remained at his post by the door. "There has to be more than one entrance," she said. "Maybe it's guarded by someone less infuriating." She could hardly imagine anyone more infuriating.

Reaching out, she trailed her fingertips over the surface of the wall, as cool and smooth as wet silk. The tap of her boots against the cobblestone path made the only sound to break the night's silence. Long, tattered weeds grew up between the mottled rose and dove-gray stones. Some had been pried up, leaving irregular brown holes in their place. *I'll see to their restoration when I'm queen.*

Queen Ascot. Was it her imagination, or did a few red sparks swirl in the depths of her ring's dark stone? Maybe that meant she was getting nearer. To him: her True Love. Forgetting the faint squalor of the neglected path, she pictured herself in a gilded carriage, its cherry-red velvet cushions smelling of roses and cinnamon. Someone cuddled beside her, someone tall and handsome, smiling lovingly down on her. Outside, the crowds cheered and tossed flowers until the petals covered her lap like a skirt made of blossoms. The carriage—

—hit a bump, flinging her out. Moony yowled as he was thrown off her shoulder and—

Moony? Ascot rejoined reality just in time for the cobbles to rise up and smack her in the face. She revised her opinion about them the instant she hit. They were too hard; when she was queen, she'd have them pried up and flowers planted in their place.

"What just happened?" she mumbled, lying face-down on the ground, the world spinning about her.

"You tripped over something," replied Moony, who had, naturally, landed safely on his feet.

"That would've been me," said a mournful voice from under Ascot.

She leaped. Her heart, by the feel of it, tried to leap in a different direction, but she swallowed it down. "Who's there?" she asked, pressing back against the solid support of the white wall.

In the spot where she'd fallen, a man—maybe—sprawled like a large, partially squashed spider. He only had four limbs, but they seemed as gangly as a spider's legs, and his torso not much thicker. He was clad in the silk tatters of what once, centuries ago, perhaps, had been an elegant evening suit and black cloak. The frayed hems, thin as cobwebs, floated on the faint night breeze.

"Who are you?" asked Ascot. Her heart still seemed to pound in quite the wrong part of her body. She tried swallowing again. "I mean, are you all right?"

"I'm a vagrant, I am," replied the stranger in a thin, sad way. "When the sun sets, they lock me out. No room at the inn for Rags-n-Bones! His bed is the Queen's Highway, and very gracious of Her Majesty it is to provide lodging for such as I."

"They lock you out of the city?" asked Moony, crouching on a loose cobble.

Instead of replying, Rags-n-Bones pulled himself erect in much the same way a puppeteer might manipulate a marionette, watching his limbs closely all the while as if afraid they'd pull a trick on him. The instant he attained his feet, he folded in half, like a book closing up. The ragged tips of his rusty brown hair dusted the ground. Ascot jumped back, her knapsack crunching against the wall, before she recognized the gesture as a bow.

"I apologize for your falling on me," Rags-n-Bones mumbled to the pavement.

"What? No, don't be silly. It was my fault."

"Not much do I claim as my own," said Rags-n-Bones, still bent over, voice beginning to quiver, "but the fault was surely mine."

"But *I* tripped over *you*."

Tears dribbled down the strands of Rags-n-Bones' hair and pooled on the cobbles near his head. His lanky form shook. "Beg your pardon, miss, and I do hate to contradict you, but the accident was completely due to my pig-headed determination to lie in a place where I might easily be trod upon."

"But that's—"

Rags-n-Bones sobbed.

"Give it up, Ascot," said Moony, grooming his ears.

Ascot bit back the first three or four things she wanted to say. Stepping forward, she patted Rags-n-Bones' shoulder. It felt like a collection of twigs wrapped in tissue. "I forgive you," she said.

"Oh, thank you, miss. Thank you." Heaving a sigh of what sounded like genuine relief, he unfolded himself and blinked down on her, taller by more than a head. "Oh, dear," he said, and tried to solve this new problem by slouching.

"Don't worry about it," said Ascot. "Plenty of people are taller than me."

"You are too kind, miss." Still slouched, he took out a roll and began nibbling. *Crunch, crunch, crunch.*

"It's all right. You needn't—" Surely bread, no matter how stale, shouldn't make so loud a noise? "What are you eating?"

Taking the object from his mouth, he peered at it mournfully. Ascot gasped. Not a roll. One of the dove-gray cobblestones. Toothmarks pocked its surface.

"They're not so bad once you get accustomed to the taste," said Rags-n-Bones.

Never try to hand-feed him, Ascot noted to herself. "Why are you eating that? Don't you have anything else?"

He crouched down on his long haunches with a sigh. "Nothing else. During the day I beg by the gate, hoping that someone will pity me and give me an avocado."

"An avocado?"

"Doesn't the very word sound luscious?" He ran a hungry tongue over thin lips. "Sometimes for dinner I repeat it until my belly feels full."

"Does it work?" Moony's eyes rounded with amazement.

"No," said Rags-n-Bones. "But I get such pleasure out of saying avocado. Avocado, avocado, avocado."

Ascot's hands clenched and unclenched. *My life in Shadowvale was far from ideal, but at least I had a warm coffin to sleep in and fish-head stew for supper.*

She took her pack off her back. "I'm sorry, Rags, I have no avocados," she said, rummaging through it. She located one of the remaining biscuits the innkeeper's wife had given her, golden and crunchy with little seeds encrusting the top. "It's a bit stale, but it's better than a rock." She pressed it into Rags-n-Bones' hands before he could demur.

Rags-n-Bones gaped, looking down at the unexpected treasure. Trembling, he clasped the biscuit to his breast. He sobbed once, violently, then commenced weeping so hard that Ascot feared she might have killed him with kindness.

"There, there," she said, patting his shoulder again.

"A biscuit!" Rags-n-Bones cried. "A whole biscuit! No one has ever . . . is it . . . is it really all for me?" he asked, perhaps in the sudden fear that he'd presumed too much and was expected to return half the prize.

"Yes, you may have it all," she hastened to assure him. He exploded in tears. While he wailed and gurgled, Ascot propped her pack against the wall, dusted off some cobbles, and sat. She also broke off a hunk of cheese and fed it to Moony to stifle his snickers. At last, many long minutes later, Rags-n-Bones' sobs faded into sniffles. He hiccoughed once, wiped his nose on a sleeve, and lifted the cobblestone to his mouth again.

Ascot caught his wrist. "No! Eat the biscuit."

Rags-n-Bones regarded it with reverence. "Oh, no, miss. I could never."

Ascot sighed. She'd try offering him some cheese, except he might really die of joy if she did. If he could survive on nibblets of rock, feeding him probably wasn't necessary, but the scrape of his teeth against the cobblestone raised the hairs on the back of her neck.

Then she had an idea. "Do you know anything about the ball, Rags?" she asked.

The long, bony hand holding the cobblestone slowly dropped to the ground. "Prince Parvanel's twenty-first birthday ball?" Rags-n-Bones asked, his voice hovering indecisively between disapproval and dismay.

"Twenty-first?" Ascot set her hand on a thistle growing between two cobbles, winced, and cradled it on her lap. "Why, he's just a child."

"Not if he's human," said Moony, licking cheese off his lips. "I think twenty-one would be around forty in noble Shadowvalean terms."

Ascot herself was in her late thirties; just the age when noble Shadowvalean maidens began searching for a properly pale and lugubrious count to put a ring on their finger and invite them to spend a lifetime terrorizing villagers together. "Can I marry a human?" she asked, looking at her ring. "I mean, the age difference . . ."

"Your father did," said Moony. "Actually, you'd be marrying your own kind, in a way."

True. And besides, what sort of Happily Ever After would it be if it couldn't overcome a small thing like a decade or so difference in age? *Anyway, if Parvanel's not my True Love, the stone just won't glow.* Satisfied, she folded up her hand. "So, this ball, Rags. Is it one of those affairs where all the girls in the kingdom are invited and the prince picks the one with the most impractical footwear?"

Rags-n-Bones scratched his head, evidently confused, but plucked up his courage and replied, "It is just like that, only not exactly. That is, there is to be a ball, but only the maidens who pass Queen Bettina Anna's inspection may go."

"You have to pass an interview to attend a ball?" asked Ascot, astounded. It seemed so cold-blooded.

But Moony looked up from his cheese. "There always has to be some trouble before you get to the ball," he said, nodding. "Your stepsisters ruin your gown or lock you in the attic or something. It's not a challenge, otherwise."

The stories, yes. Order reestablished itself. Ascot relaxed. "The ball's tomorrow night, right? When is the Queen meeting the candidates?"

"This morning, at ten," replied Rags-n-Bones. "Eligible maidens have been arriving for the past week. It's been quite a show," he said wistfully. "Heralds and guardsmen, gilded carriages, shoes so fine you could eat soup out of them. I sit by the gate and watch, but no one has ever given me an avocado."

"This morning," Ascot muttered, drawing her knees to her chest. A cloud covered the moon and a chill breeze whipped the tips of her hair against her face. Some princess-elect she was: grimy from travel, locked out of her own kingdom by a rogue, and about to get rained on.

But then again, in the stories, the harder the heroine had it at the beginning, the grander was her triumph in the end.

She lifted her head. "I can sell some of this silverware to buy a gown. I think I'll have to forgo a carriage, but what about a guardsman? It'll look wrong if I show up all by myself."

Moony's wings flared. "You're not all by yourself." Abandoning his cheese, he hopped onto her knee.

"I'm here, too," said Rags-n-Bones. "You gave me a biscuit." To her surprise, he hugged an arm around her.

Ascot looked from Moony's furry, mischievous countenance to Rags-n-Bones' thin, bleached face with its huge, watery gray eyes. "Oh, that's very kind of you both," she said. Her smile wobbled only a little. "But the other guardsmen will be in livery. They'll have big hats, and swords, and fancy boots."

"Boots?" Moony's nose twitched. He passed a paw over it, wings flicking thoughtfully. "Ascot, fetch out Miss Eppicutt's book, will you? I remember reading something in there that might solve all our problems."

CHAPTER FOUR:
THERE'S ALWAYS A CATCH

"There's Albright Castle." Rags-n-Bones pointed.

Rubbing her head, Ascot hurried up the last few feet of the winding, oak-lined path that led through the park. Every time the breeze raked the treetops, acorns pattered from their branches in a slow, heavy rain. Pleasant to listen to, but not, as she had discovered, to be caught standing beneath.

She surmounted the hill. "Oh."

She'd expected something like the illustration in the book: graceful white towers capped with spiral peaks, a drawbridge spanning a moat filled with blue forget-me-nots, and stained-glass windows as fine-crafted as jewelry. Instead—

It's a giant yellow box, she thought. She blinked, but a second inspection did not improve her opinion. Albright Castle hulked over the hilltop like a toad brooding on a lily pad. Its dun-colored bricks gleamed greasily in the midmorning sun. Far too many stumpy columns bracketed the heavy doors and narrow, plain glass windows. She stared up into an enormous clock face embedded in the blocky central tower and the second hand twitched, as if the clock were gawking stupidly down at her.

"Well, at least it's big," said Moony at her side.

"Yes. It's big." And thankfully someone had surrounded it with ivy-covered walls and marble statues and plots of exotic flowers in an attempt to make it appear less like . . . like . . .

. . . like a great dumpy yellow box. She sighed. She hated to admit it, even to herself, but thus far she'd found Albright something of a disappointment. Upon awakening, she'd found the white wall's pearly luster drabbled to a soapy gray in the cold morning light. She'd been allowed through the gate, yes, but the guard manning it had responded to her "good morning" by belching in her face. Then he'd gone back to gnawing the chicken leg he held without so much as an "excuse me." And Albright's outer streets, at least, were a sad display of missing cobbles and piles of mushy horse dung.

Moony tugged at her trouser leg. "Ascot? It's a quarter to ten."

She shook herself out of her musings. "Right," she said. "Don't want to miss the appointment. Lead on, my guardsman."

Moony's whiskers fanned. Tilting his hat to a rakish angle, he strutted forward, tottering only slightly in his tooled leather boots. His evident pleasure in his new station cheered her.

Two teaspoons and a toasting fork had gone into purchasing those boots and hat plus a small green cape from a doll shop that morning. Ascot had washed her face in a nearby fountain while Rags-n-Bones located a shop with a tiny sword on display. It had been pawned by a dwarf who ran away from the circus to become an accountant, and the proprietor gladly traded it for a pair of silver candlesticks.

Moony had some trouble settling the cape at first; it kept tangling in his wings. The hat fell over his eyes, and as for walking on his hind legs, after he'd toppled for the twelfth time, Ascot had decided that the cat in the story must've been double-jointed.

But he got there in the end, she thought, following him up the path. *Just see him now, walking proudly before me, his paw on the hilt of his sword.*

Looking like a plush toy from the shop where they'd bought his clothes. Had the cat in the story looked half as adorably ridiculous?

The wind shifted, bringing the reek of a hundred perfumes to her nose. A quiet babble, like a huddle of well-fed pigeons, reached her ears. Passing out of the oak grove, the winding dirt path transformed into a straight red brick one leading to a large, hexagonal plaza fenced in by laurels. Here, a crowd of richly dressed people stood waiting before the locked castle gates.

Heads turned as Ascot approached. The tap of her boot heels rang out deafeningly in the sudden cessation of conversation.

Goodness, so many colors! Her eyes watered at the muted rainbow of carnation pink, lemon chiffon, mint green, and sky blue filling the plaza. Jewels sparkled around the ladies' necks and dangled from their ears. Their guardsmen wore long coats of crimson or navy with embroidered waistcoats. Sunlight flashed off the gold tassels on their boots and glinted on the hilts of their swords, rattling in crested sheaths.

Ascot looked down at her own plain black coat and gray trousers, worn from days of travel. She hadn't had time to purchase a dress. But she'd washed, and surely Moony's dashing attire made up for the rest.

Someone in the crowd sniggered. Rags-n-Bones' nerve faltered. Racing to Ascot, he hid behind her, his long limbs poking up at odd angles.

She patted his shoulder. "He's easily scared," she said to a pair of girls wearing such enormous hoopskirts—one fuchsia pink, the other sea-green—that they resembled a pair of enameled bells. "Are you here for the ball?"

The girls stared back, their eyes doll-wide. ". . . es," said one of them after a moment.

Ascot nodded encouragingly, but nothing more was forthcoming. Poor things. She couldn't imagine how they kept their heads erect on their necks under the weight of all their face powder, rouge, and lacquered hair.

I'll ask if their Fairy Godmother made their dresses, she decided, and was about to do so when a new party entered the plaza: four guardsmen escorting an older man with silvery hair and a red-haired girl wearing a gown the exact golden-peach shade of dawn. Chins high, they strode through the crowd, which parted before them, leaving ripples of silence in their wake. A ruby flashed on the man's left hand.

"Who is that?" asked Ascot, but the hoop-skirted girls had shrunk even further into themselves.

"I think we should move to the front of the crowd, too," said Moony, staring after the new party. "There are so many people here that the queen might just choose the first ten girls she sees and call it quits."

"Good idea," said Ascot. She nodded at the hoop-skirted girls. "Nice talking to you."

Completely by accident, she put her foot straight through the sea-green hoopskirt. She wasn't the only one who winced at the protracted ripping sound.

"Sorry!" she apologized, stepping back to pull her leg out of the hoop. Another tearing sound rewarded her efforts. *What the—?*

Wind-milling her arms, she located the source of the problem. The bootlaces on her free foot had come undone and wound themselves into the trailing ruffles of the pink gown. Her step back

41

had just torn several feet of lace off its hem. Rags-n-Bones promptly got tangled in it.

"'Scuse me! Sorry!" cried Ascot, dancing a frantic jig to keep her balance. It was only a matter of seconds before her rump kissed the plaza brick. She knew she wasn't imagining the sniggers now.

The pink-clad girl shrieked, hitting the exact note of a goosed goose, then burst into tears. Her cries drew the attention of her guardsman, an ogre-sized man in incongruous frills. Ascot tried to shrink in on herself as this massive apparition took a slow, deliberate step in her direction.

"No, you don't!" cried Moony, bounding onto the guardsman's chest. He stuffed the end of his tail up the man's nostrils. The guardsman's eyes crossed. His nose twitched. Then his mouth stretched hippopotamus-wide, delivering a sneeze that tore another two feet of lace off the pink-clad girl's dress. As he fell on his rear, Ascot's foot came free of the ruffles.

She hopped twice, regaining her balance, then gingerly pulled her other leg out of the green hoopskirt. "Thank, you Moony," she said.

He bowed. "At your service, my lady." Setting a booted foot on the still-wheezing guardsman's knee, he addressed the crowd. "Anyone else care to stand in the way of the Countess von Abberdorf? I'm a cat. I can instinctively sense who is allergic to me." His orange eyes narrowed, studying the array of colorful gowns. "By the way, I have plenty of fur just waiting to be shed. Gray hairs look dreadful on pastel silk, don't they?"

A moment later, Ascot found her rivals huddled to either side of the plaza, forming an aisle leading straight to the gate. "That will do, Moony," she said, helping Rags-n-Bones to his feet. He peered at her from under a ruffle that had gotten wrapped around his head.

"Is the ball over yet?" he asked.

"No, we're just going to go meet the queen." She took his arm. "By the way," she whispered to Moony as they strolled up the aisle, "I'm not actually a Countess."

"It sounded better." He grinned. "By the way, Countess, there's a piece of lace sticking to your heel."

Ascot tried to pull it off casually.

The clock tower began tolling ten just as she stepped up to the gate. Here, at the head of the crowd, the redheaded girl in the sunrise gown stood a little off to one side, separated from the rest of the candidates, her hand tucked under the older man's arm. Her father? How nice to have a father who took you places instead of forbidding you to leave the castle grounds. A little envious, Ascot gave the girl a cordial nod.

In return, the girl raised her already high chin two more inches and averted her head. Her father cast Ascot one look out of slitted eyes, then turned a cold shoulder.

Well, of all the rude—No. Ascot took a calming breath. They were probably just worried that she'd send Moony to be-fur that pretty gown. *I'll explain later*, she thought, pressing her face against the gate's curlicue golden bars. Oh, much better; she could hardly see the castle from this angle. A white seashell path lined with hibiscus flowers cut through a slope of grass as smooth as plush velvet. Ascot pressed harder, until the bars left imprints on her cheeks, admiring every detail: the elegant bronze sundial standing on a small terrace to one side of the path, the flock of tame peacocks pecking among the pearly shells, the gray-green wisteria clinging to a trellis, even the motley squirrels frolicking through the branches of a beech tree.

Overhead, the last chime faded. As it did, the great square door in the front of the castle opened. An orderly procession of people started down the white path, seashells crunching beneath their feet. A lady walked at the head, her manner as composed as if she'd never known a moment's discomfort. Gems sparkled on her hands and at her throat, and a gold diadem encircled her brow. Her sculpted curls had to weigh at least five pounds and her face was so artfully painted that she should have carried a frame to go with it. She could only be Queen Bettina Anna.

Then Ascot's gaze fell on the man two steps behind the queen. "Oh, no," she said. "No." She pinched the back of her hand, but he didn't vanish: a figure in a brown coat, thin and indifferent as a straight line. "He can't be the prince!" She glanced at her ring. Seeing the stone remained dark, she relaxed.

Rags-n-Bones peered over her shoulder, hunching down to do it properly. "No," he said. "Prince Parvanel never rises before noon. That's Catch, the captain of the guard."

"Frabjacket." Ascot kicked a seashell that had rolled beyond the boundary of the gate. She'd never guessed the brown-coated rogue was a person of any importance.

Bettina Anna halted before the gate, coming to such a precise stop that Ascot pictured wheels hidden under her heavy golden skirt. As two uniformed guards stepped forward to unlock it, Bettina Anna gazed through the bars, head cocked to one side. Her diadem remained fixed in place, as if glued to her hair. The giggle building in Ascot's throat died when she noticed Catch watching her. His brown coat looked quite out of place among the lavender breeches, violet jackets, and white stockings of the guards. Squaring her shoulders, Ascot stared defiantly back.

The gate swung soundlessly open. Bettina Anna stepped into the brick plaza, her hands clasped before her. Despite the flattering cut of her gown, her belly pushed out the fabric like she was hiding a small cake to snack on later. She came to another pinpoint halt a few feet before Ascot, who wrenched her gaze from Catch with a guilty jerk.

How should I greet her? she wondered, as Moony and Rags-n-Bones fell back, leaving the stage, and the decisions, to her. Every drop of moisture had deserted her mouth, but she forced herself to smile. "Good morning, Your Majesty," she said. She didn't have skirts to unfurl, so she bowed instead of curtsied. "I am Miss Ascot Abberdorf." On an instant's whim she dropped the "von." She'd always hated the obsequious little syllable, wriggling like a worm between her personal and family names.

Bettina Anna's head tilted a fraction of an inch further. Swallowing, Ascot rolled her hands into fists to hide the lines of dirt under her nails. She was sure she'd overlooked a scrap of dead leaf caught in her hair.

"I wish to attend the prince's ball," she added, in case that wasn't clear. Now she could *smell* the dirt on her road-worn clothes.

"I told you to go home, girl," said Catch, his voice just as uncaring as it had been the night before. The dark circle ringing his right eye was only a little paler.

"You also said I'd only get into Albright when the moon fell out of the sky," Ascot shot back, and bit her tongue. This was not the right note to hit before the queen.

"I said I would not let you into the kingdom until the moon fell," he replied. "And I did not."

Frabjacket, he was right. Ascot opened her mouth to protest, then decided all at once that she didn't care. What did he matter? He was just a servant. Pointedly, she faced Bettina Anna.

"My recently deceased father was Count Vadim of Abberdorf. My brother, Vincent, inherited the title. Upon our father's death, he desired me to make a proper match. Hearing of your son's birthday ball, I came to seek his hand."

It's a truth, of sorts, she whispered to herself, stifling her conscience's protests.

The slightest crease marred the skin between Bettina Anna's brows. "We do not know where the county of Abberdorf lies," she said. Her voice fluttered and crackled, like a flute that had been played too often and lost some of its sweetness.

"Shadowvale," said Catch. "The county of Abberdorf is in Shadowvale."

This did not go over at all well with the crowd eavesdropping behind in the plaza. A ripple of cries passed among them, accompanied by one or two gentle thunks, as of swooning bodies hitting brick.

Bettina Anna lifted one hand, smooth-skinned and graceful, if plump, and the murmurs fell silent. Stepping up so close that Ascot could smell the lemon and lavender on her breath, the queen studied her. Not with a kindly interest; more the attention one gives a bug one means to squash before it can sting.

Ascot held still under the scrutiny, suddenly all too aware of her pale skin, the crimson tint to her eyes, her canine teeth that were just a bit longer than a Daylander's. All too aware of the stillness behind her that spoke of different stories, ones involving torches and garlic and wooden stakes. The ones in Miss Eppicutt's book, with their promises of happily ever after, seemed far away now, and childish. Perhaps coming east had been a mistake.

Then again, better to risk everything than marry Count Zanzibander for lack of options. The thought restored her courage. Raising her chin, she looked Queen Bettina Anna square in the face.

Bettina Anna drew back, her golden gown's hem rustling against the neat red bricks, her expression utterly blank. Then she smiled a small, iron smile. "Shadowvale. I have heard the people from that region possess unusual talents."

"We do?" asked Ascot. Out of the corner of her eye, she caught Moony making frantic gestures. "I mean, yes, we do."

"Excellent. Captain?" she said, and Catch snapped to attention. "Is that beast still tormenting the woodcutters in the north?"

Catch raised one eyebrow. "Yes, Your Majesty," he replied slowly. "I had a report just this morning."

"Something must be done to rectify this situation."

"It has my attention, Your Majesty."

It was like watching a tennis match. Every word spoken possessed at least two meanings, and Ascot didn't know what dictionary they were using. Bettina Anna looked over Ascot's shoulder, as if seeing all the way down the hill, past the mansions and the shacks, beyond the white wall to the forest nibbling the edges of the kingdom.

"For the past three nights, the northern woods have been terrorized by a large beast," she said. "Tame it and bring it to the castle by nine o'clock tomorrow morning. If you can accomplish this, you may attend the ball."

A test! Just like in the stories. Ascot mentally clapped her hands. What a lucky chance she'd met that granny in the inn who'd told her to look to the white book for guidance.

Catch, she noticed, watched her with an almost predatory interest, probably hoping she'd be too scared to take up the challenge. Turning her back on him, Ascot favored Bettina Anna with her deepest bow yet.

"I accept, Your Majesty."

CHAPTER FIVE:
CANINES AND PUNISHMENT

"I was afraid you were going to botch it there for a minute," said Moony.

"I almost did," replied Ascot, elbows on the sticky wooden counter. Her bowl of barley mushroom soup cooled before her. Beside her, Rags-n-Bones slurped from his. Another teaspoon had gone into paying for the food. "I completely forgot about the testing thing. Blame Catch for distracting me." She scowled into the smudged mirror hanging at a crooked angle behind the bar.

The tavern stood at the corner of a quiet street on the northern edge of Albright. The savory scents wafting out of the open top of its half door had captivated Ascot as they passed, and although she'd normally be asleep at this time of day, she'd suggested they stop in for the midday meal. "Lunch," the Daylanders called it. How quaint.

Moony's pink tongue quit dabbling in and out of his saucer of soup. "You have to keep your wits about you, Ascot," he said, broth dripping off his whiskers. "If you can't tame this beast tonight—"

"I know." She stifled a yawn with the back of her hand. "'Scuse me. At least it will be night. But what kind of a beast is it? The queen didn't say."

"A wolf," said Moony without hesitation. "It's always wolves in the stories. Dayland wolves must be particularly bad."

Rags-n-Bones came up for air. "Wolves are scary," he said. His biscuit hung from a frayed cord around his neck.

Ascot patted his hand. "Don't worry. I won't let it hurt you." She took up her spoon and paused, creamy brown gravy spilling from its edges. "Father used to go out some evenings and play around with wolves. Remember that, Moony?"

"No."

She ate. Moony resumed lapping from his saucer. Rags-n-Bones finished his soup and began racing peanuts along the bar top. Bowls of potato crisps were ranged along the counter, free for the taking. Remembering her father's funeral, Ascot sampled one. They tasted of salt and dirt, but she found it surprisingly hard to stop eating them.

The warm food kindled a fresh burst of energy. "All right," she said, pushing her empty bowl aside. "Let's say the beast's a wolf. Father could control wolves. Do you think I might have inherited that skill?"

Moony sneezed and rubbed a paw over his nose. "Well, your father was a . . . *very* noble Shadowvalean, if you know what I'm saying. He drank a lot of the red stuff, and they say that gives you powers."

Ascot grimaced. Perhaps it was her mother's Daylander influence, but she'd never developed a taste for the red stuff.

"What's the red stuff?" asked Rags-n-Bones, waggling a forefinger. He'd gotten a peanut shell stuck on it.

Ascot and Moony exchanged a glance. "Cherry juice," she said.

"Pepper sauce," said Moony at the same time.

"Cheery juice and pepper sauce? That doesn't sound yummy." Rags-n-Bones tugged at the peanut shell.

Ascot let the relieved breath whisper out of her lungs. A noise from the rear of the tavern made her look around. There, braced against a rough brick wall gone black with age and grease, stood a small raised stage. A young man in a checkered waistcoat had just pulled out the seat in front of the battered piano. Another fellow came on stage carrying a brass horn, followed by a woman in a red dress with skin the rich, smooth color of caramel.

Some kind of performance, thought Ascot as the barmaid brought her a mug of perfectly black tea. On the stage, the man in the checkered waistcoat rattled off a jaunty assortment of notes, and nodded at the horn player. The caramel-skinned woman took a breath.

"Ask the moon to fall right out of the sky," she sang.
"Tell a second to step straight out of its time,
Buy yourself a needle and crawl through its eye,
Or ask the moon to fall . . .
. . . into the palm of your hand."

Ask the moon to fall. Ascot frowned, remembering Catch's words, that first night outside the city gate. For some reason, he was opposed to her going to the ball, perhaps even opposed to her being in Albright. "He's going to be trouble," she said.

"Who?" asked Moony, but the singer began again.

"Dangle the earth on the end of a string,
Wear the sun on your hand in a bright gold ring,
Teach the mountaintop to stand up and sing,
And ask the moon to fall . . .
. . . has it fallen yet?"

The singer's hand swept through the air, rearranging swirls of blue tobacco smoke.

"Catch," said Ascot over the next bar of music. "I believe he means to stop me from going the ball."

Moony licked a paw. "Well, to be honest, he has a fine start. I mean, how do we even plan to find this wolf?"

Ascot meant to respond, but she'd just taken a sip of tea. Its unexpected bitterness shriveled her tongue. Rags-n-Bones pounded her sympathetically on the back as she sputtered.

"Why do you hear 'yes' when I'm saying 'no'?
Why do you linger when I tell you to go?
Build yourself a fire with a handful of snow
Then ask the moon to fall . . .
. . . if you ask the moon, it might fall."

"I'll find the wolf, somehow," Ascot wheezed. Taking up the sugar bowl, she dumped seven spoonfuls into her strange, aromatic black tea.

"What, are you just going to stroll into the woods and start yelling 'here wolf, here wolf, good boy'?" asked Moony. "I'll laugh myself sick if you do."

"I'll search for tracks," said Ascot, banging the sugar bowl back down on the counter.

Moony snickered. "You wouldn't know a wolf's footprint from one of mine."

"We'll ask my friends." Rags-n-Bones sucked the peanut shell off his finger.

Ascot and Moony stared at him.

"So, so long, goodbye, cheerio, farewell.
Should we meet in Heaven, I'll know I'm in Hell.
If I ever say 'I love you,' I'll know the moon fell.
I'll know the moon just fell . . .
. . . onto the top of my head.
Right smack down onto the top of my head."

"You have friends?" asked Moony.

Rags-n-Bones looked hurt.

"Behave," Ascot told Moony, tugging one of his ears. She drained her now-tolerable tea, then hopped off her stool. "I think that's a great idea, Rags. We'll meet your friends, then find a place to nap for the rest of the day. We have a long night ahead of us."

"Last night was long, too." Moony sprang off the counter and onto her shoulder. "After all this, I hope Parvanel lives up to the princes in the stories."

"He won't," said Rags-n-Bones cheerfully. "After all, he never gave me a biscuit."

🐀

Rags-n-Bones led them to the outskirts of Albright, through streets that were little more than streaks of dirt pocked with oily brown puddles. Skeletal houses groaned in the wind. Every so often, a tile would slide off a sagging roof, hit the ground, and crack dully in two.

Who would live here? Ascot's curiosity grew with every step. Maybe Moony was right. Maybe Rags-n-Bones' friends were imaginary. But his step was firm and, for Rags-n-Bones, confident. He guided them to a tin dustbin propped up against the city's encompassing wall, not far from where they'd encountered him the night before. Crouching down on his haunches, he emitted several squeaks.

"Rats," Moony whispered as small, whiskered shapes scurried out of gutters and from underneath rubbish. "His friends are rats."

"Good." Ascot ran an appreciative eye over the little gray flock assembling on the grubby cobbles around Rags-n-Bones' feet. "I haven't had roasted rat in several days."

Moony lashed his tail severely, whacking her in the ear. "You're getting it wrong again. You helped Rags-n-Bones, so now his friends will help you. That's how the stories go."

Oh, right. Ascot grumbled, but before she could turn it into a full-fledged sulk, Rags-n-Bones stood, cradling a rat in the palms of his hands. "This is Nipper," he said. The rat's oil-drop eyes bored into Ascot's as if accepting a challenge.

"Hi, Nipper," said Ascot without enthusiasm.

"And these are Squeaker, Tuft-Tail, Scuttle, and Brownie."

Ascot stared at the swarm. She'd rather call them Morsel, Snack, Dinner, and Yum, but she just couldn't bear to betray Rags-n-Bones' trusting expression. She summoned up a little more energy. "Hi, guys."

"Nipper's heard of a wolf that roams the northern woods," said Rags-n-Bones, stroking the rat's head with a bony finger. "He'll lead us there tonight."

"Thanks, Nipper," said Ascot. "And thank you, too, Rags." Rags-n-Bones dipped his head, blushing.

Finding a comfortable spot against the wall, Ascot wrapped herself in her coat and spent the day napping. Moony snored on her lap. Every so often she cracked an eye open to watch Rags-n-Bones, conversing with the rats. He must've been telling them about the biscuit, for he held it up, chirruping excitedly. The rats seemed very impressed. One or two sneaked a nibble while he wasn't looking. *Good sense on their part*, she mused.

Really, they were kind of cute, with their long whiskers, beady eyes, and little pink feet. Pity they were so darned tasty as well.

§

A slate gray sky crowded with clouds greeted Ascot when she woke. The chill wind gnawed her exposed ears. *Should've stuffed a hat in my knapsack,* she thought, stretching the ache from sleeping against the cold wall out of her shoulders. She laughed when Rags-n-Bones mimicked her, twisting his neck until his vertebrae popped like heated corn.

"Are we ready?" she asked. Moony yawned and hopped onto her shoulder.

Rags-n-Bones conferred with Nipper. "Yes."

"Let's be off, then."

Per Nipper's squeaked instructions, Rags-n-Bones led them away from the city, into a thickening landscape of trees. Twigs crunched under Ascot's feet and a light drizzle chilled her skin. She tugged her coat collar closer, tucking her chin for added warmth.

A shaft of moonlight speared through the clouds, illuminating a narrow path winding through the forest a few feet to her right. "Look there," Ascot called to Rags-n-Bones. "That's better than stumbling through bramble." Eagerly, she pushed between two trees to reach it.

One of them turned its head and looked at her.

She leaped straight up. Moony sailed off her shoulder, yowling. Rags-n-Bones yelped and cowered.

The tree watched with mild interest.

On her way back to earth, Ascot recognized the "tree's" brown coat and straight figure. Terror converted to rage. "What are you doing here?" she demanded the instant her boots touched the ground.

"I came to ascertain if you intended to go through with this charade," said Catch, disengaging himself from the trunk he'd been leaning against. "Means 'to determine.'"

Crossing her arms over her chest, Ascot glared. "Hoping that I'd given up?"

"Indeed. It would save many some trouble, particularly yourself."

Why did he roll his r's in his throat that way, as if he feared their sharp edges might cut his tongue? It distracted her. He didn't seem the least bit cold, either, which was just unfair.

"I'm going to attend the prince's ball if I have to round up every beast in the forest," she said, refusing to shiver as another strong breeze raked the branches.

Catch shrugged. "One will suffice. By the by, I've checked the local menageries. Just in case."

"In case of what?"

"In case you try to pass off a tame animal as the beast."

I never thought of that. She boggled at herself, feeling more foolish than virtuous. She covered it with a snort. "Good at finding ways to cheat, aren't you?"

"You'd better learn," he replied, unruffled, "if you want to marry the prince." He paused, as if searching for something to say—or perhaps he knew what he wanted to say, but not how to frame it. Finally, he shrugged. "I'll leave you to it." He walked off, his footsteps making no sound on the crunchy leaves. "Make sure the beast's housebroken before you bring it to the castle."

"Don't worry," Ascot yelled after him. "I'll leave the peeing on the floor to you."

Of course the wind lulled just at that moment, making her words sound louder and even more stupid than they naturally would have. Moony and Rags-n-Bones stared at her, and even Nipper twitched his whiskers as if to say he thought she ought to be sent to her room without supper.

Clearing her throat, Ascot tugged her coat straighter. "Are we almost there, Rags?"

Squeak, squeak. "Nipper says just a little farther, in a clearing."

"You were right, Ascot," said Moony as they tromped through a patch of late mushrooms. "Catch is plotting something."

Ascot swatted a branch out of her face. "Why else would he be out here? We'd better find the wolf before he does. Is that the clearing up ahead, Rags?"

Rags-n-Bones conferred with Nipper in a series of squeaks, barely audible against the rising moan of the wind and the echoing whisk of branches. "Yes," Rags-n-Bones translated, "and Nipper's leaving now. Wolves scare him. Wolves are scary," he added, as if hoping she might change her mind at the last moment. Nipper was already scurrying away, a black blot streaking through the patchwork of leaves.

The wind whipped Ascot's already tangled hair into knots as she stepped into the clearing. "Don't worry," she said. "I'll tame the wolf, and he'll love us and fetch us avocados."

Rags-n-Bones brightened. "Can they do that?"

"Wolves have keen noses. You can train them to find anything." She steadied herself against a gust that almost blew her off her feet. "Rotten weather. Hope the wolf didn't decide to stay home tonight." Hands on hips, she gazed into an interwoven tangle of hawthorn branches obscuring the far side of the clearing.

"Are you trying to produce pheromones or something?" asked Moony after a couple minutes. "Or is it a silent wolf call?"

"I am trying," said Ascot between her teeth, "to remember the poem Father recited before he went out to play with the wolves. It might have been a charm."

"Let's hear it, then," said Moony.

Ascot scoured her memory. "Wolf, wolf, wolf in the forest wild. Fierce predator you, and much reviled. Come to me this storm-dark night, and we'll give the villagers one big fright."

Moony winced. "Your father had a strange sense of humor."

"I like it," said Rags-n-Bones, and to Ascot's horror, began singing. "Wolf, wolf, wolf, oh, please be nice. Come and I'll feed you peas and rice. Together we'll have loads of fun, so come and howl and romp and run!"

His voice wavered, searching for the right pitch and never quite finding it. But he was pleased enough with his performance to begin a kind of dance in the middle of the glade, flinging his arms over his head and kicking up leaves with his thin, nervous feet. "Wolf, wolf, wolf, I'd like to meet you. I promise I will never eat you. Wolf, please come and be my friend, and I will sniff your rear—"

The hawthorn branches crackled. Rags-n-Bones froze in mid-pirouette, then dashed to hide behind Ascot. Moony's ears pricked up.

"Could it be?" Ascot whispered, nerves tingling. Between the shoddy light and the obscuring vegetation, she could make out nothing. For all she could tell, the sound had been made by a nocturnal chipmunk. *And if it is*, she thought, *ten to one Rags-n-Bones will have it perched on his finger before the night's out.*

Moony sniffed the air. "Smells like wolf."

Success! Her father's silly rhyme must have been a charm after all. More confident, she stepped forward, spreading her hands dramatically before her. "Wolf, wolf, wolf, come to me, now. To my wit and will you must bow. Wolf, come forth from the forest's sway. Hear my words, come and obey."

More crackling from the hawthorn. It swelled and broke apart as a huge wolf pushed through, shrugging off the knotty branches as if they were reeds. The great beast's head was level with her shoulder. Its coat, cream-colored with faint silver markings, looked thick enough for a hand to sink into past the wrist. Amber gaze fixed on Ascot, it padded across the clearing on paws the size of dinner plates.

She wanted to step back. In fact, she wanted to take so many steps back that Albright's comfortably solid wall would stand between her and the huge animal.

The ball. True Love, she reminded herself, and gritted her teeth. "Wolf, oh wolf, of the forest fell, heed well the words that now—"

Reaching out with one of those enormous forepaws, the wolf cuffed her lightly on the side of the head. Ascot went sprawling into a pile of leaves.

"You have some nerve, young lady," it said.

Ascot gaped. A dead leaf clung to her lips. Her fingertips ached from the pressure of mud collected under her nails. The wolf, showing no inclination of bowing to her superior spirit sat, wrapping its tail neatly around its front paws. Its disapproving expression would not have been out of place on Miss Eppicutt's face.

This is not how it's supposed to go, thought Ascot as Rags-n-Bones helped her to her feet and began brushing off her clothes, depositing at least as much dirt as he removed. All the wolves in the stories were sneaky, venal, and, frankly, rather stupid.

Perhaps she'd hit the wrong pitch. Pulling a twig out of her mouth, Ascot cleared her throat, straining for a deeper tone. "Wolf, oh wolf—"

"Dmitri," interrupted the wolf, still favoring her with that severe mien. "My name is Dmitri, and you shall address me as such."

"Dmitri?" The last straw broke. "But you're a wolf, for pity's sake," Ascot wailed. "Your name should be Fang, or Howl, or—" She racked her brain.

"Fluffy," said Rags-n-Bones.

"Big Bad," said Moony.

Dmitri's eyes narrowed. "And I suppose you're Mina or Elizabeta, then, since we're holding to stereotypes. Which would you prefer I called you?"

Ascot's hands rolled into fists. "I'm Ascot Abberdorf." A thumb-jerk in the direction of her companions. "They're Rags-n-Bones and Moony. Now that we've been introduced, you're coming with us."

"Indeed." Dmitri flicked his ears, looking just a bit larger than he had a moment before, and as immovable as if his paws were rooted in the forest floor.

Ascot re-thought her last words. "That is, we'd very much appreciate it if you'd come with us, sir."

"What's my motivation?" asked Dmitri.

"Huh?"

Sighing, Dmitri settled on his belly, forepaws crossed under his chest. "See this?" He ducked his head to display a triangular nick in his right ear. "Only a month ago I was peacefully reading *The Brothers Karamazov* when a bullet—"

"The what?" asked Ascot, catching herself before she added something along the lines of "Shouldn't you have been harassing pigs or devouring grannies?" She sensed he wouldn't appreciate it.

"*The Brothers Karamazov.* By Fyodor Dostoyevsky. You've never read it?"

"No."

"Well, you surely know *Crime and Punishment.*"

"Oh, yes," said Ascot. She couldn't remember all the crimes Miss Eppicutt had punished her for.

Satisfied, Dmitri continued. "With such evidence that the citizens of Albright resent my presence in this region, I ask, what is your business with me?"

Ascot's brain spun. Was Dmitri really the beast that had been terrorizing the woodcutters? What could he be doing to scare them? Using words they didn't understand?

"Well?"

"Hm? What—oh!" Ascot shook herself. "Have you heard of Queen Bettina Anna?"

Ascot's story spilled out. She found herself going all the way back to her father's death and Count Zanzibander's proposal. Moony pounced at leaves and interjected the occasional comment while

Rags-n-Bones never took his eyes off Dmitri, seeming torn between fear of the wolf and a desire to pet him.

"So I need your help to win entrance to the ball," Ascot concluded. Her voice rasped from all the talking.

Closing his eyes, Dmitri exhaled a long, noisy sigh. "And you chose this course of action based on a book? Never let it be said reading isn't dangerous," he added in a mutter. Or something of the sort; Ascot didn't quite catch all the words.

"It's not just a book," she said. "I have a ring, too. It will glow when I meet my True Love." She extended her hand.

Opening his eyes, Dmitri held her gaze for a long moment. "You trust a chip of corundum to select your ideal matrimonial prospect?"

Ascot gnawed her lip. She let her hand drop to her side. "Every girl who marries a prince lives Happily Ever After. The book's very clear about that."

Moony nodded.

"I'm sure they get avocados," said Rags-n-Bones, with a touch of uncertainty.

Dmitri rubbed a paw along his snout.

"You should know I'm not going to give up," said Ascot. "If you won't help, I'll find another beast to take to the queen."

"Pride," said Dmitri. "I can appreciate that, despite the generous leavenings of stupidity."

"Then you'll come to Albright with me?" asked Ascot, deciding to overlook the stupidity comment. "I promise I won't let anyone shoot you."

He focused on her. "How kind. I suppose I should return such magnanimous sentiments by promising not to devour any human who ventures into the forest. That would be jolly decent of me, wouldn't it?" A wolf's expression should be unreadable, but Ascot knew a smirk when she saw one.

Frabjacket. With the night growing fouler, she really didn't want to search out a second wolf. Especially since the next one might be more inclined to eat her than to banter.

And then a positive inspiration burst into her head, so big and so brilliant that she half-closed her eyes in case light gleamed out of them. *Sometimes I amaze myself.*

"It's a shame," she said. She picked at her cuticles, affecting indifference. "I bet Albright Castle has a huge library."

Something of an answering gleam lit Dmitri's eyes.

"Everything Dusty-evvy—"

"Dostoyevsky."

"—ever wrote. If I were queen, you could live in the library and read all day."

Dmitri's eyes glazed. The tip of his tongue lolled out the side of his mouth. "Tempting." He laid his head on his paws. "It seems a small risk for a significant gain."

"Then you'll help?" asked Ascot.

"And you won't eat us?" added Rags-n-Bones, apparently feeling they should be very definite on that point.

Dmitri meditated, nibbling between two toes. All at once he rose and stretched, forepaws gouging holes in the soft ground. "Very well; I'll assist you. And no, I won't eat you. I'd feel guilty if I did, not to mention dyspeptic."

Rags-n-Bones threw his arms around Dmitri's neck. "I like you."

"All right, that's enough, there's a good fellow." Dmitri gingerly disengaged himself from Rags-n-Bones' embrace. He scrutinized Ascot from her toes to her hair while she did her best not to squirm. "You. The princess bride. Even getting you into the ball should prove a considerable challenge."

"No, Bettina Anna promised that if I tamed . . ." Ascot spotted a potential problem. "You *are* the beast that's been, um, upsetting woodcutters, aren't you?"

61

"How would I know? We don't fraternize. But as the queen failed to provide a proper description of the beast, she must accept any large predator you deliver."

Ascot grinned. "You're right. She can't exactly say 'wait, that's not the beast I meant,' can she?"

Moony laughed, but Dmitri shook his great head. "Actually, this challenge smacks of subterfuge."

"A what?" asked Ascot.

"A trick," he said patiently. "No large predators reside in these woods, apart from myself. The humans have scared them all away. If you hadn't encountered me, you most certainly would have failed."

"But we saw a beast," said Moony. "Ascot threw a can at it." He cocked his head to one side. "Of course that was on the south side of the kingdom."

"Really?" said Dmitri. "Hmm."

Ascot waved a hand. "In the stories, everyone expects the heroine to fail. I'm sure Bettina Anna knows this and that's why she tried to trick me."

"She tried to trick you, therefore she wants you to succeed?" Dmitri didn't have eyebrows, but he gave the impression of raising them.

"Well, if I couldn't pass the test, she'd know I wasn't her son's True Love, wouldn't she?"

"This might prove more challenging than I previously believed," said Dmitri. Or something like that; again Ascot didn't quite hear the words over the wail of the strongest gust of wind yet. Rags-n-Bones shivered violently.

Dmitri took note. "Well, let's leave it for now. Your coats aren't as thick as mine. Let's repair to the kingdom and take some repose."

Ascot lifted Moony onto her shoulder for a little extra warmth. The frosty leaves splintered underfoot as they walked back to

Albright. Rags-n-Bones trotted behind Ascot, bumping his chin against her head, never taking his eyes off Dmitri, whose huge paws covered the ground in easy strides. Ascot jogged to keep up with him.

"I forgot to say 'thank you,' didn't I?" she said to Dmitri. "Thank you."

"Thank the woodcutters," he replied. Overhead, the moon emerged from the oily depths of the sky, like a silver coin surfacing in a vat of treacle.

"The woodcutters? Why?"

"Because one of them stole my copy of *The Idiot* and I simply must procure a new one. Do you know where he took it? Into his privy!" Dmitri howled. "I don't believe he intended to read it in there, either."

Ascot covered her mouth with one hand and used the other to pet Moony before he could snigger. "We'll get you a new one. Signed by the author, if you like."

Dmitri sighed. "You really don't know Dostoyevsky, do you?"

CHAPTER SIX:
WINNING FRIENDS AND INFLUENCING PEOPLE

"Strange," mused Ascot, watching Dmitri crunch down four biscuits in one go, "I'm going to marry him, and yet I really haven't given much thought to Prince Parvanel."

Dmitri licked crumbs off his muzzle. "Why does that not surprise me?" he asked. Untapped oceans of snideness drenched his tone. He lapped from a trickle of water wending between two cobbles, then swallowed half a farmhouse cheddar. Dmitri may have labeled himself an intellectual giant, but Ascot pegged him as a glutton.

Upon exiting the woods last night, they'd found the city gates once again locked tight. *Catch's doing*, snarled Ascot, adding another check to the list of grievances she was keeping against him. Someday she'd call for an accounting. Until then, she'd had to spend another night sleeping propped against the wall, with Dmitri for a pillow.

"Does anyone know anything about Prince Parvanel?" she asked.

"He's blond and handsome and likes frogs," said Rags-n-Bones, swinging by his ankles from the branch of a nearby maple.

"Frogs?" Ascot grimaced. She'd had her fill of frogs recently. Besides, it didn't seem right. According to the stories, princes were allowed to *be* frogs, at least until a princess kissed them—but liking them?

"They say he had a special pond dug to house his collection." Rags-n-Bones flipped up onto the branch, long legs dangling. "Of course, I've never seen it with my own eyes."

"But frogs?" she wailed.

Dmitri harrumphed. "Everyone needs a hobby. What do you know about frogs?"

"They're yummy deep-fried and dipped in anchovy sauce."

"Keep it to yourself, then." Dmitri took another drink from the puddle. "Are we ready to proceed?"

Rags-n-Bones slid off his branch. Moony emerged from a clump of weeds with a quarter of an unlucky chipmunk dangling from his mouth; fortunately, he swallowed it before Rags-n-Bones noticed. Cramming the last of her own biscuit into her mouth, Ascot nodded.

Another gray day in Albright. A horse heaved a resigned snort as it clopped past, pulling a cart filled with tin buckets of flowers. Every time the wheels hit a bump, the cans rattled. Pink and yellow petals, like spatters of decorative paint, marked the cart's path.

Ascot blew on her chilly hands. *Frogs.* Perhaps she was wrong to be discomfited. Maybe the whole reason that frog was in Count Zanzibander's umbrella in the first place was because the Fairy Godmother had put it there specifically to point her towards Parvanel. Cheering up, she skipped over a gnarled section of the sidewalk, where old tree roots had pushed up the bricks from underneath. The cutlery in her pockets jangled. "I hope I have enough silverware to buy a decent dress," she said, clapping her hands over her pockets to quell the sound.

"Worry more about gaining admittance to the ball," said Dmitri, padding at her side, feral and furry and utterly incongruous in this neat landscape of pastel townhouses and close-clipped bushes. The few pedestrians out at this hour of the morning skirted to the opposite side of the street, white-eyed and looking ready to bolt.

"Bettina Anna will keep her word." Ascot waved at a pair of matrons in morning gowns. They hiked up their skirts and bolted. Sighing, Ascot dropped her hand.

"She might not if she realizes you didn't tame me," said Dmitri, dragging her attention back to practicalities. "I am a talking wolf, after all."

Rags-n-Bones, who had been loafing a couple feet behind, leaped forward. "I know," he said, beaming. "If Sir Dmitri talks differently, the queen will believe you tamed him."

Dmitri paused, one paw suspended a foot above the sidewalk. "Differently?" he asked, his voice promising nothing.

Rags-n-Bones nodded. "Like: Rello! Ri'm a rulf! That's how dogs are supposed to talk. I saw it in a puppet show."

Moony fell off Ascot's shoulder, laughing. Ascot wrapped her arms around her middle and folded until her head nearly touched the street, stifling giggles.

The faintest suggestion of a growl rippled Dmitri's lips. He set his paw down. "We will not be taking that course of action."

"Perhaps you shouldn't talk at all?" Ascot squeaked.

"I suppose that would be preferable," agreed Dmitri. His tail-tip flicked. "Scrape your cat off the ground and let's get going."

Ascot scooped up Moony, who lolled in her arms, limp as a furry pudding. Rags-n-Bones elected to walk the next stretch of the journey on his hands. As they reached the winding, oak-lined path through the park, Ascot remembered to watch for falling acorns. Over the crest of the hill, the great, greasy-butter cube of Albright Castle loomed. She suppressed a sigh.

"The castle in the book's much prettier," said Moony, echoing her thoughts.

"More important to our purpose, there are guards at the gate," said Dmitri. His claws clicked against brick as they crossed the deserted plaza.

Dragging her gaze from Albright Castle's ugly yellow façade, Ascot focused on the gate. Sure enough, two lavender-clad guards stood at attention outside the golden bars. Six more paraded about inside, hands on gilded sword hilts, buttons polished and gleaming. It should have looked impressive. But . . .

You can't look impressive in lavender, Ascot realized. Maybe that's why noble Shadowvaleans disdained it. "We're here to see the queen," she said, stepping up to the gate.

The guard stared blankly over her shoulder, pretending not to hear. He did this rather well; she almost turned for a look herself, to see what he found so fascinating. *It's all part of the test*, she reminded herself, tapping a finger against her chin.

Maybe she could take advantage of some of the outlandish tales the Daylanders told about Shadowvaleans. Worth a try. Locating a spot on the guard's neck where a blue vein throbbed, she stared at it. Fixedly. Then she licked her lips.

"There's a café in the park if you're hungry, miss," said the guard politely.

Ascot sucked her tongue back in. Blinked. "Actually, I was wondering if you could let me in."

"I'm afraid you'll have to show me some papers before I'm authorized to do that," he replied. "In the meantime, would you mind backing off a bit? My mum says I have issues with personal space."

Aha! Smiling, Ascot stepped up close enough for her coat to brush the guard's leg. Moony circled his ankles, purring thunderously.

Drops of sweat beaded the guard's upper lip.

Ascot laid her cheek on his shoulder. Moony kneaded his knee. Then Rags-n-Bones spread his arms, advancing upon the guard like a giant toddler determined on a hug.

He broke. "Wilkinson," he called. His voice cracked. Clearing his throat, he made a second attempt. "Wilkinson, inform Her Majesty that—"

"Never mind," said a voice by Ascot's ear. "I'll escort them in myself."

This time she managed—barely—not to jump. "Captain Catch," she said, pinning on a smile before turning. He stood behind her, fists stuffed into the pockets of his ubiquitous brown coat. "Got the beast."

Catch contemplated Dmitri. If he'd enjoyed startling her, it wasn't enough to cheer him. "So I see," he said. Dmitri panted gently, wearing an expression suitable for a cow. "It's tame, then?"

"As a puppy." Ascot patted Dmitri's head. She heard teeth grind.

"Can it play dead?" asked Catch.

"Don't try it," said Dmitri under his breath.

"No," said Ascot. "But he can help you play dead. In fact, the play will be so good that everyone will believe you actually are dead."

Catch glowered. She glared back.

The guard cleared his throat. "Should I open the gate, Captain?"

"I suppose you must," said Catch, not taking his eyes from Ascot. The bruise around the right one had turned a splendid shade of sickly green.

"Thank you," Ascot told the guard as he produced a long key from around his neck and inserted it into the lock. She could be polite if Catch couldn't manage it, and anyway, she felt bad about the personal space business.

They started up the seashell path, Catch striding a dozen paces ahead. Big, fuzzy bees busied themselves in the purple asters lining the path. Ascot stopped to sniff the petals of a perfectly spherical blue flower composed of hundreds of other, tinier blossoms. Following her example, Rags-n-Bones instantly broke into sneezes.

"Here." Ascot handed him a kerchief as a colorful butterfly wobbled past. Butterflies. Ridiculous creatures, really. They always looked like they were about to fall out of the air.

Moony jumped and it vanished with a crunch. Ascot quickly glanced away so she could pretend she hadn't seen.

Rags-n-Bones stopped sneezing long enough to tap Catch's shoulder. "Are there any avocado trees?" he asked.

"Yes, in one of the conservatories," Catch replied.

Rags-n-Bones burst into a brief, frenetic, and very silly jig.

"You can have them all once I'm queen," Ascot told him.

Catch snorted.

A stone arch half hidden under a tangle of climbing roses marked the end of the garden. Beyond it, the path cut straight and purposeful through a vista of clipped grass to the great square mouth of the castle's main door. Catch fell back a few steps. "All dressed up to meet Her Majesty?" he inquired, pinching a fold of Ascot's leather coat.

Ascot smacked his hand away. "Yes," she said, staring pointedly at his scuffed boots and well-worn shirt.

He lifted an eyebrow, but shrugged as if to say it wasn't any of his business and he didn't really care, but would enjoy watching her make a fool of herself.

He certainly could pack a lot of meaning into a shrug.

"Come inside, then," he said, opening the door. "The candidates are assembled in the Cupid Chamber."

The small party followed him into the foyer. Blue-and-white checkered marble squeaked under Ascot's feet. "Ugh."

Catch glanced over his shoulder. "I beg your pardon?" he asked in a tone that begged nothing at all.

"I coughed," she said quickly, and waved him to lead on.

Did Miss Eppicutt's book contain any pictures of the castle's insides? She couldn't remember. If it had, the illustration hadn't in the least resembled Albright Castle's interior.

"Look, stars," said Rags-n-Bones, pointing up at the fresco painted on the hall's wide, flat ceiling. The heavy wooden paneling covering the walls muted his voice, lending it an odd, muffled quality.

I hate wood paneling. "Yes, stars," she agreed. Dusty gold stars twinkling against a backdrop of pottery blue, with doe-faced angels giggling in the corners. But the ceiling wasn't the worst bit of décor. Less easy to ignore were the plaster carvings of leaves and flowers that slithered up columns and entwined every doorway, as if some pale, carnivorous plant life was bent on devouring the castle from the inside out.

At her side, Dmitri made grumbling noises in his throat. Ascot suspected keeping silent was just about killing the big wolf.

"I told you Daylanders have no taste," Moony whispered.

"Everything will have to be changed once I'm queen," she whispered back.

"So nice to know you'll spend Albright's wealth on important matters," said Catch, without turning. The man had good ears. He stopped before a door with a carving of a nude, gilded cupid beaming from its surface.

Ascot burned. "That's not what I—"

"Mind you, I do hate this cupid," said Catch. He pushed its pudgy, dimpled cheek and the door opened, revealing a long room trimmed in sky blue. A white carpet stretched from the door to a dais, upon which stood Bettina Anna. Today's gown was silvery and trimmed with pearls. Lace burst from her cuffs like bubbles out of a champagne bottle, covering her small, plump hands.

"Well?" Catch bowed theatrically towards the doorway. "Do enter, Miss Abberdorf."

Ascot straightened. "Thank you, Captain." She brushed past, resisting the temptation to tread on his foot.

Bettina Anna cocked her head as Ascot approached. If she felt any surprise, it didn't show through her expression of regal blandness. The sixteen young women arranged on the blue-and-white checkered tiles like pieces on a chessboard were not so well disciplined.

"Wolf!" shrieked one, pointing at Dmitri.

"Stickman!" squealed another. Rags-n-Bones nervously saluted, prompting a flurry of giggles and a discreet thump as the most enterprising girl of all crumpled to the floor in a delicate swoon.

Ascot reached the foot of the dais. "Good morning, Your Majesty," she said, bowing. "I brought your beast, and he's as tame as a kitten."

Moony dug his claws into her shoulder.

"Tamer," she amended. "Much tamer."

"Ruff," said Dmitri.

Ascot kicked him, a smile fixed to her face. None of the young ladies appeared to notice; they were too busy murmuring and having attacks of the vapors, but Bettina Anna threw a glance to Catch, still loitering by the far door. His answering shrug was no more than a tiny lift of his shoulders.

Before Ascot could ponder the exchange, Bettina Anna addressed her. "Well done, Miss Abberdorf," she said, still bland as high quality paper. "You shall be granted entrance to the ball. Provided that your attire passes muster."

On cue, a small man in a powdered wig stepped forward from the shadows behind the queen. He coughed a self-important cough into his balled hand, flicked open a scroll, and began to read.

"Guests will present themselves in the ballroom foyer at eight o'clock, properly attired in a formal gown, with styled hair, gloves, and appropriate shoes. Makeup and jewelry suitable to the occasion is also required, as is perfume. All unmarried ladies must be accompanied by a male escort."

Gulping, Ascot covertly studied the other candidates. From what she could see, any one of them could spend the day napping, wake, brush off her dress, and enter the ballroom without a strand of hair having to be re-curled.

"The ball will end promptly at midnight. All guests have been furnished with rooms in the Nosegay Wing, to which they'll be escorted after this interview is concluded. Guests are expected to behave with modesty and decorum. Any who fail in civility may be escorted off the premises." He allowed a few seconds for the last to sink in. "So mote it be."

"Thanks you, Pollux," said the queen. Bowing, the little man rolled back into the shadows; a motion so smooth he must have stayed up all night rehearsing it.

"Ladies." Bettina Anna inclined her head to the room at large. "I look forward to greeting you tonight." All the girls spread their skirts in pretty curtsies as the queen's guardsmen escorted her off the dais. Ascot did the best she could, holding up a tail of her coat. The moment the door clicked shut behind the queen, a tall girl whose black hair was secured with a cascade of silver ribbons sprang up.

"It's not fair," she said, stamping her foot. "Why was she allowed to bring her cat when Mr. Nutty had to stay behind?"

"Who's Mr. Nutty?" asked Ascot.

"Her pet squirrel." Ascot recognized the girl who answered: the redhead whose appearance had caused such a sensation in the plaza the day before. She studied Ascot through narrowed eyes.

"Moony's my guardsman, not a pet," said Ascot. She tried chucking him under the chin, but he leaped off her shoulder. His boots slid on the tiles, but he recovered his balance and laid a paw on his sword's hilt.

"Surely you've heard of the legendary cat in footwear?" he said, fanning out his whiskers.

The redhead laughed, false and sardonic. But a girl with sunny blonde hair clapped her hands. "Oh, of course!" she cried, sounding as if it were her birthday and she'd just discovered the world was made of chocolate and had been given a new puppy on top of it all. "Don't be cross, Miss Maverly. He's such a cuuuuttte kitty!"

Moony was too stunned to move when she bent down and tickled his chin. A reluctant purr rumbled out of his throat.

Miss Maverly continued to scowl. "Do get up, Miss Beige," she said, bestowing a few kicks on the swooning girl.

"Wolf," murmured Miss Beige. She pressed the back of her wrist to her mousy brown curls.

Miss Maverly hauled her upright. "Perhaps it'll eat you," she said. The notion seemed to please her.

"Oh, I'm sure he won't," said the blonde. "He looks like such a sweeeeet wolf." She began rumpling Dmitri's ears. "Hello, wolfie! You may call me Scincilla!"

Miss Beige swooned again, perhaps expecting to see Scincilla devoured on the spot. Miss Maverly let her hit the floor.

"Um, woof?" Dmitri offered. Apparently this was a situation Dostoyevsky had never covered.

"I'm Rags-n-Bones," said Rags-n-Bones, but Scincilla didn't hear him over her own cooing.

Just as well, thought Ascot. *She'd probably pet him, too.*

A loud rapping drew everyone's eyes to the back of the room. Catch stood beside the gilded door, beating his knuckles against it and radiating boredom. "If you've all introduced yourselves, perhaps you'd care to follow me to your quarters," he said.

"Of course," lilted the redhead, cherry lips parting in a pearly smile. But as the party followed Catch out into the hall, she leaned over to Miss Maverly. "Quarters?" Ascot heard her whisper. "I would never sleep in 'quarters.' The nerve of the scruffy rogue."

"He goes the day after I marry Prince Parvanel," Miss Maverly agreed. "Honestly, why Her Majesty kept him on after that dreadful scandal—"

"Maybelle, dearest, *I'm* going to marry Prince Parvanel."

Scandal? Ascot's ears perked up. She walked a pace behind them, hoping to overhear more, but their whispers turned to a vicious critique of everyone else's attire. Besides, her nose started watering. One of them was wearing perfume strong enough to strip paint off the side of a building.

"Isn't Albright Castle beautiful?" declared Scincilla, staring rapturously at the furnishings. She pressed her hands to her bodice as if she feared her heart might leap out of her chest from sheer joy.

Ascot looked at a picture hanging on the wall. The painted eyes of a glum child in a starched ruff met hers. He held a blobby orange. Her gaze dropped to the flower arrangement on the table beneath; a pretty assortment of lilies and ivy thrust into a vase with a happy cow painted in blue on the side. Ascot coughed and looked away.

"It's quite a change from Abberdorf Castle," she said, picking up Moony.

"Oh, that's right. You're from Shadowvale." Scincilla's smile didn't diminish an inch. "Miss Ascot Abberdorf, correct?"

"Yes, and you're Scincilla, right?"

The girl beamed as if she'd just been given a pony and an ice cream parlor to go along with her puppy. "Yes, Miss Scincilla Glossmarie Harkenpouf."

Ascot coughed again. Part of her wanted to hug Scincilla, and say something along the lines of: "there, there, it's not that bad." The other part wanted to race out of the castle, find Mr. and Mrs. Harkenpouf, and congratulate them on their creation of the most ridiculous name in history.

"That's pretty," said Rags-n-Bones without a hint of irony. Then again, Ascot doubted Rags-n-Bones knew what irony was, and if he did, he'd probably try to eat it.

"Yes, pretty." Ascot petted Moony a little harder than necessary to stifle his giggles. "Pleased to meet you, Miss Harkenpouf."

"Oh, do call me Scincilla," she said, pressing Ascot's arm.

The group turned a corner, entering a tall, hexagonal chamber with honeybee-patterned wallpaper and squat columns topped with sculpted golden beehives. Catch abruptly quickened his pace. Just as well. The light streaming through the round, yellow-glassed windows turned everyone's complexions sallow.

"Are you ready for the ball?" Ascot asked Scincilla.

"Ooh!" Scincilla clutched her bodice. "I can't wait! My gown's blue silk with ecru lace. Tiny sapphires are embedded in my shoes! What color is your gown?"

"Um, purple," Ascot replied. Scincilla waited and Ascot felt compelled to add more, as if that innocent gaze were sucking lies out of her throat. "Purple satin. And my shoes have amethysts—"

Dmitri nipped her ankle and she shut up.

The journey ended at a long hall lined with open doors, its wallpaper patterned with violets and rosebuds. A purple carpet ran down the center of the pale wooden floorboards. Side tables holding vases of flowers and saucers of potpourri were ranged along the wall. The prickly scents of clove and orange-peel masked, if not entirely hid, a slightly musty, unused smell. And flickering in scalloped brass sconces set into the walls—

"Gaslights!" Moony whispered excitedly. Artfully placed mirrors caught and reflected their glow.

"These will be your rooms until tomorrow," said Catch. By standing with his arms akimbo, he managed to block the entire hall entrance. The group clustered behind him, whispering and peering over his shoulders. "Your belongings have already been moved into them. Please notify a servant if there have been any mix-ups."

At least I didn't make more work for anyone, thought Ascot, who carried everything she owned.

"Maids are available to aid you in your preparations," Catch continued. "But kindly don't trouble them until this afternoon, as they have other duties to perform."

Miss Maverly broke the short silence that followed. "May we enter the hall now, Captain?" she asked, each word razor-tipped.

"If you must." Catch stepped aside and the flood of female bodies spilled into the hall.

"I'll visit you once I'm settled," chirped Scincilla, and skipped off. Miss Beige went from door to door, peering myopically at the names tacked on each. She'd probably end up in the wrong one.

The redhead paused before Catch to curtsy. "Thank you for your guidance, Captain," she said, her rosy skirts rippling and unfurling over the thin purple carpet. Her gown was exceptionally fine, even in this sea of painted dolls, and what looked like star rubies sparkled in her ears.

Catch's expression became guarded. "You're welcome, Miss Roebanks."

He wasn't in a position to see how Miss Roebanks' grateful smile cut off the second she turned around. But Ascot noticed. *What a hypocrite.*

Or was she? They'd mentioned some scandal. Perhaps Catch deserved every bit of censure.

"Well, Miss Abberdorf?"

Ascot jumped at Catch's voice, speaking so close. Frabjacket, she wished he'd stop doing that. "Well, what?" she asked, studying him as he leaned against the corner of the entryway. Was he a villain, or simply annoying? So hard to tell under that mask of indifference he wore.

"I notice you're not retiring to your room," he said. "Have you decided to give up this venture after all? Means 'scheme' or 'undertaking,'" he added, perhaps worried that he hadn't been up to his usual irritating standards recently.

Maybe Miss Roebanks was right. Maybe she shouldn't trust him farther than a kitten with a freshly wound ball of yarn.

"Give up?" She tossed her head, aware she wasn't quite as adept at it as Miss Maverly. On the positive side, she managed to whack Catch with the tips of her hair. Served him right for standing so close. "On the contrary, Captain. I'm going out to buy a ballgown."

Mimicking his earlier ironic bow, she left the hall. Catch watched her walk away. She could tell by the prickling on the back of her neck. "Dmitri," she said in an undertone. "Can you find the way out of this maze?"

"Yes," he said, equally softly. He glanced back at Catch. "You didn't tell me about him. Why not?"

"I suppose I forgot."

"Hmm," said Dmitri, and that was all.

But he said it in a way that made her wonder all the rest of the afternoon.

CHAPTER SEVEN:
MUSICAL INTERLUDE

Seven years passed. Dmitri insisted it was only six hours, but Ascot knew better.

"Interminable," she said as the guards bowed them through the golden gate. Her scalp still burned from a hairdresser's ministrations. He'd disciplined her tangles into a cascade of curls that hung to her shoulders. "Means 'endless' or 'perpetual'."

"You don't have to do that, you know," said Dmitri. "Catch isn't here."

For some reason, Ascot's cheeks began burning to match her scalp.

"Miss?" asked Rags-n-Bones, peering from under the brown paper parcel balanced on his head.

"The shopping. Interminable." Ignoring Dmitri, Ascot resettled her grip on her own double-armful of brown paper parcels. Those had grown heavier, too, as had Moony, draped around her neck like a sleepy muffler. His dangling boots scraped her left cheek.

"It's only five o' clock," said Dmitri. He pricked up his ears at a peacock promenading across the white seashell path, but visibly restrained himself. "You can take an hour's nap before starting your preparations."

Ascot scowled. "It's later than that."

Of course the bells in the ugly square clock tower chose this exact moment to begin tolling. Exactly five chimes rang out.

Dmitri didn't say "I told you so," but there was an extra jaunty swish to his tail as he watched the peacock join its flock under a clump of lilacs by the side of the path. Lips pressed tight, Ascot followed him back to the guest quarters in the Nosegay Wing.

Many of the doors lining the hall were shut. Presumably the other girls were taking advantage of the spare time to nap. Ascot tiptoed down the purple carpet, pausing only to check the names written on strips of pink paper tacked to the doors. *Miss Pettershanks. Miss Cromberfootch. Miss Lootby. Miss Harkenpouf—* Scincilla's room. Each door was painted white and sported a pretty brass knob molded in the shape of a flower.

"This is more what I had in mind," she told Moony. He responded with a vague purr.

Miss Harcourt. Miss Burgoyne. Miss Tumberfelt's door hung open. Inside, a deer attempted to graze on the green carpet. Weren't deer supposed to be noble, stately animals? This one was going to upset its digestion. Shrugging, Ascot walked on.

Miss Tattershall. Three mice in tiny hats and booties slipped out of Miss Whipperly's room and scurried beneath a side table. Moony awakened.

"Don't," said Ascot, holding fast to his tail. "I agree that mice in cunning outfits generally deserve to be eaten, but Rags will cry if you do."

"I will, too," said Rags-n-Bones, who had two bluebirds and a robin perched on his shoulders. A dove pecked at the biscuit around his neck.

Miss Callo. Miss Jutebell. The next door flung open. Ascot barely had time to read the name tacked to it before it hit the wall with a violent bang.

Miss Roebanks.

"You nasty little wretch," cried a voice inside the room. An instant later, a maid in a lace cap scrambled out, hounded closely by Miss Roebanks, her ruddy hair done up in curling papers.

The maid bumped into Ascot, who reflexively dropped her parcels and caught her. A shock of recognition ran through her as their eyes met. "You're—"

Then Miss Roebanks was there, looming over them both. "I'll have you dismissed before supper," she raged.

The maid pulled herself straight. "At least that leaves me free to speak my mind," she said, her voice smoky as fire. "You look like a cherry pudding in that red gown."

Miss Roebanks turned the color of boiled beets. "How dare you address your superiors so!" Her hand lifted.

"Don't!" Ascot flung herself between them. She hadn't meant to intervene, but when it came down to it, it didn't really require thought.

Miss Roebanks' narrowed eyes flew wide. Her pursed lips sagged open. "No!" she shrieked, huddling behind the pitiful defense of her own crossed arms. Shrinking back, she knocked against a side table, oversetting the vase on its top. Pink hothouse roses slopped onto the floor. Water dripped off the table's edge, darkening the purple carpet to indigo.

Silence filled Nosegay Wing. Ascot stood gaping, her arms outstretched. Gradually, she grew aware of the faces peeping from behind half-opened doors.

"What's the trouble here?" asked Catch's unfortunately familiar voice from the far end of the hall. He paced slowly towards her, flanked by a pair of impeccable butlers.

"She tried to suck my blood," wailed Miss Roebanks, pointing a finger at Ascot.

"I—what?" Ascot stared helplessly from Miss Roebanks to Catch to Dmitri. Maybe he could explain. But the big wolf sat silent, and Ascot remembered he wasn't supposed to speak. Moony seemed just as shocked as she was, and Rags-n-Bones trembled.

Miss Roebanks seized the advantage. "She attacked me," she whimpered. "She and that wolf of hers." Dropping her face into her hands, she made sobbing noises.

Catch quit prodding the puddle of roses with the toe of his boot and looked up. He raised an eyebrow.

If he believes her, he could have me dismissed. And why wouldn't he choose to believe, seeing how he wanted her gone, anyway? Ascot's heart slid down her spine and landed with a mushy thump in her boots. Miss Roebanks' shoulders continued shaking, the corner of a triumphant smirk just visible between her fingers.

"Oh, that can't be true," piped up a sunny voice. Stepping out from behind her door, Scincilla approached Catch. "I'm sure there's been a misunderstanding."

Catch's eyebrow did not lower one iota. "Did you witness the exchange?" he asked.

Scincilla twisted her fingers together. "No."

"Well, then—"

"Misunderstanding, my foot." Completely recovered now, the maid faced Catch, her fists balled on her hips. "I know it's not my place to speak, sir, but Miss Abberdorf stepped in to save me from a slapping."

Catch's eyebrow stayed in place a moment longer. Then slowly it lowered. "Ah." He nudged the roses again. "Get these cleaned up," he said to one of the butlers.

Miss Roebanks flounced upright, her cheeks scarlet and perfectly dry. "I've been attacked and you're worried about the carpet?" she demanded.

"Don't want it to mildew," said Catch. Stooping, he picked a petal off his boot and flicked it away. "I'll find another maid to attend you, Miss Roebanks. Kindly refrain from physically correcting her."

Miss Roebanks' eyes widened, then narrowed. Catch turned to leave.

"By the way," he added over his shoulder, "a maid's better than a mirror for an honest opinion. If you don't care to take it, it's your loss."

He paced back up the hall without so much as a nod to the girls gawking behind half-open doors. Ascot took her first deep breath in several minutes. *He didn't dismiss me. Why didn't he dismiss me?*

Miss Roebanks unfroze. "I suppose I should have guessed," she said. Stalking into her room, she slammed the door hard enough to set all the vases on the side tables to rattling. Another fell over.

One by one, the doors to either side of the hall closed. Only Scincilla and the maid remained with Ascot's group. "Oh, dear, you dropped your parcels," said Scincilla, picking them up for her.

"Thank you, Cindy," said Ascot.

Scincilla's eyelids flickered, as if she'd just been startled by something that had been standing beside her all her life. "Cindy? No one's called me that before."

"I won't, if you don't like it."

"No, it's—pretty." She paused, seemingly struggling with a difficult thought, then gave it up in favor of a bright smile. "I'm glad everything worked out. I'm sure Miss Roebanks is just anxious about the ball."

Ascot remembered the smirk half-hidden in Miss Roebanks' cupped hands. She held her tongue.

"Well, I'll let you get ready," Scincilla continued. "Only two and a half hours until the ball!" She squealed, bouncing on her heels. "See you this evening, Ascot. Your hair looks very fetching."

"Bye, Cindy." Ascot watched her skip back to her room. Then she turned to the maid. "You have a marvelous voice."

The maid's caramel cheeks blushed cherry. "I thought I saw you in The Polished Pear yesterday. You're hard to miss." She glanced at Dmitri, then looked up and up at Rags-n-Bones as he unfolded himself.

"But why are you working as a maid when you have so much talent?" asked Ascot.

The blush deepened to pure apple-red. "My parents don't approve of my being on stage," she said. "They say it's not respectable. Don't tell anyone you saw me there, please, miss?"

"Of course not," said Ascot, remembering far too well parents and their odd rules of propriety. "As long as you call me Ascot instead of miss."

"Ascot." The maid grinned. "And I'm Maggie. If you need any help, just ask for me. Might as well, since it looks like I won't be helping Miss Roebanks anymore." She wrinkled her nose, apparently remembering something. "Oh, but I better go fetch the blacksmith first."

"The blacksmith? Whatever for?"

"For Jane's—sorry, Miss Beige's corset. We can't pull it tight enough to suit her mother. Mr. Halloway's efforts will satisfy her, right enough."

"Oh," said Ascot. They'd tried to sell her a corset in the dress shop, much to her dismay. White, but otherwise identical to the black, lace-edged ones in vogue in Shadowvale. *"If my spine needs support, I'll stick a poker down my back,"* she'd said. She didn't think they'd been amused.

"Miss Beige will be lucky if she doesn't pass out in the punchbowl. Keep an eye on her, will you?" Maggie hesitated, rumpling her apron. "We were friends as children, before her papa made such a heap of money. Used to play the piano together."

"I'd be glad to," said Ascot. Really, why was Maggie fretting? Miss Beige was going to a ball, not a battle.

"Thanks. She doesn't really fit in here, for all her parents wishing it otherwise." Maggie untangled her hands from her apron. "I'd better get back to work." She started to curtsy then paused in mid-dip and waved instead.

"What a shame," said Ascot as she trotted away. "Such a fine voice and her parents want her to dust shelves, instead."

"They're probably trying to protect her," said Dmitri.

"Protect her from what? Doing something she enjoys for a living?" Scowling, Ascot took a fresh hold on her parcels. "When I'm queen, I'll appoint her court singer."

Dmitri butted her in the legs. "Then you'd better start your preparations, Your Highness."

All Ascot's fatigue returned. "It's still over two hours to the ball!" she protested. She wanted to sit right down on her parcels, there in the middle of the hall.

"From the sound of it, your rivals are getting ready." Dmitri shoved her again.

"Please, miss," said Rags-n-Bones, catching Dmitri's urgency. His lips trembled.

Ascot gave in. "Oh, all right." She started walking again. "I'd like a proper bath after all the traveling, anyway."

At the end of the hall, she found her name pinned to the very last door, next to a lumpy plaster bas-relief of fruit and flowers. The door possessed only a plain iron latch, not a pretty brass flower knob. She had to bang it with her shoulder a few times before it opened. The moment it did, a ripple of gray-brown fur scurried out over her foot, giving the impression of something fast and twitchy and very much inclined to bite. Ascot gave thanks for her thick boots.

"Mr. Nutty, you think?" she asked as it skittered up the hall.

"Probably." Dmitri nosed the door shut while Ascot surveyed what little there was to survey of her kingdom.

Rough plank floorboards, long overdue a polishing, and dingy plaster walls without a single picture. A battered wardrobe, reeking of mothballs, occupied an entire corner of the room. Curtains the exact color of dead moss framed the one small window. They clashed beautifully with the powder blue blankets spread over the narrow bed. The only chair teetered on spindly, fragile legs, as if daring her to sit on it, while the low table under the window sloped noticeably.

"It's an insult." Leaping off her shoulder, Moony fenced with the air. "I'll make whoever's responsible pay."

"No, it's all right." Ascot set her parcels on the bed. "Remember, the girl in the worst situation at the beginning is the one who wins the prince. This just means Bettina Anna's following the stories."

"Oh, right." The fur along Moony's spine settled.

Dmitri closed his eyes. It looked very like a wince. "Go wash," he said. "You turn the spigots and water comes out of a spout and fills the tub."

"Water?" said Moony. "Why do you need water? Just lick yourself."

Taking off her boots, Ascot closed the bathroom door on whatever explanation Dmitri cared to make.

She tried the handles on the white tile wall and tepid water dribbled into the tub, cooling before there was enough of it to step into. "Happily ever after, happily ever after," she chanted, washing quickly. The waxy yellow soap stank of lye. She scrubbed hard and rinsed twice before getting out of the tub.

Wrapped in two towels and a robe, she opened the bathroom door. While Moony, Dmitri, and Rags-n-Bones watched in solemn silence, she retrieved her biggest parcel, laid it on the table, and tore the paper. Green silk glowed against the rough brown backdrop. Deep green, like emeralds, malachite, or the center of a thriving forest. Darker green embroidery made intricate loops and zigzags around the gown's neckline and hem.

She'd had a fine array of gowns to choose from, ordered by rejected candidates. Only one purple satin gown, however, and when she'd tried it on, Rags-n-Bones had crouched down behind her.

"I can see my reflection in your butt!" he'd proclaimed happily.

She'd turned down all satin after that. As for velvet gowns, they made her feel as if she had an entire horse draped around her neck, with maybe a couple more dragging about the hem.

Nothing wrong with green, she thought. Much better than yellow. She'd discovered that no matter how much she liked yellow on walls, wearing it made her resemble a walking cheese. "Think it'll do?" she asked, fingering the dress's soft folds. She hoped they'd removed all the pins from the quick alterations.

"It's plain," said Rags-n-Bones, pulling a sad face. At the shop, he'd proved helplessly enamored of frills.

"Plain but elegant," corrected Dmitri. "You don't need frou-frous to stand out; the color will achieve that."

"Yes, it might make Prince Parvanel think of frogs and lily pads," said Moony. He giggled and clawed the curtains.

Ascot vowed to cut down on his catnip ration.

She laid out her other purchases alongside the dress: a vial of perfume, smelling of sandalwood. Makeup. Pearl earrings; the sort that pinched your ears, because she'd never gotten hers pierced. She hadn't been able to decide between a pearl pendant and a necklace of crystal stars, so she'd bought both. Silk gloves to match the gown and a pair of high-heeled green dancing shoes. All paid for by exchanging her Shadowvalean silverware for Albright coins. She'd let Dmitri handle the transaction in the pawnshop. He believed his use of the phrase "economic fluctuations" was the key to his success, but Ascot suspected it had more to do with the size of his fangs.

Now she had only a few odd bits of silver remaining, and not many coins, either. *No matter*, she thought, holding up her hand to let her ring catch what little light it would. This evening it would glow. Why, Prince Parvanel might very well fall on his knees and propose the moment she stepped into the ballroom. All her pains would prove worthwhile, even donning the awful, toe-pinching, ankle-turning shoes.

"At least we found everything," she said, fingering the necklace of crystal stars.

"Not quite everything," said Dmitri. He lowered his voice. "You know what I'm referring to."

Ascot nodded. Yes, unfortunately she did.

A male escort—why did they need male escorts? Would some of the girls instantly drink hemlock or launch themselves out the window if left unsupervised? Whatever the reason, it put her in a quandary. Even standing on his hind legs, Moony's head reached only a little above her knee. If she entered the ballroom on his paw—well, she could just imagine the shrieks of mirth. And while no one would dare laugh if she arrived with her arm on Dmitri's back, she'd already introduced the big wolf as a pet. That left—

Rags-n-Bones dove onto the bed, flailing his limbs as if swimming.

"You know it must be him," said Dmitri.

Ascot pinched the bridge of her nose. "Yes."

"Must be him, what?" Moony paused in mid-claw.

"Rags must be my escort."

Moony's ears shot up. "But I'm your guardsman," he said. Climbing onto her lap, he stared into her face.

Ascot swallowed. "Well . . ."

"The escorts are meant to dance with the girls while Prince Parvanel is otherwise engaged," said Dmitri. "You're a little short for that."

"Oh." Moony relaxed. "I don't want to dance with Miss Maverly. She wears too much ambergris. Rags can dance and I'll stay on guard and make sure Catch doesn't try anything sneaky."

Dmitri looked at Ascot. She shrugged, deciding to leave it at that for now. "Is this all right with you, Rags?"

Huge gray eyes peered out from between a tangle of sheets. "What, miss?"

"Will you be my escort tonight?"

Rags-n-Bones leaped out of the bedclothes, snagged a foot in a pillowcase, and went sprawling. "An honor, miss," he said, beaming from the floorboards.

"That's settled, then," said Dmitri. "You'd better wash too, Rags. Try to get some of those . . ." His gaze traveled up and down Rags-n-Bones' lanky form. ". . . cobwebs off. And leave the biscuit behind."

Rags-n-Bones clutched it to his chest. "Must I?"

"I'll protect it," said Moony.

Slowly, Rags-n-Bones took off the biscuit and set it on the bed. Casting it worried glances, he walked into the bathroom and shut the door. An instant later, a loud, ominous thump shook the floor, followed by the watery explosion of a small geyser erupting.

Ascot, Dmitri, and Moony looked at each other. Then Dmitri nosed the makeup kit towards Ascot.

"Shall we make a start?" he suggested.

CHAPTER EIGHT: A STITCH IN TIME

Seven o' clock drew near and still Dmitri clicked his tongue over Ascot's attempts to paint her face. "Don't use so much eyeliner."

She wiped it off for the eighth time. "It's the fashion in Shadowvale."

"Here, it'll make people think someone punched you. You're too pale. More rouge."

The rouge clung to her cheeks like a layer of dust. Even worse was the lipstick, which she kept chewing off. But she picked up the puff again.

"Try the bronze eye shadow," said Dmitri, ignoring another clang from the bathroom.

I'd love to know where this wolf picked up makeup tips. Before she could ask, a frantic knock beat against her bedroom door. Ascot jumped, smearing cosmetics across her forehead.

"Frabjacket!" she muttered, wiping it off as she went to answer the knock. Miss Maverly stood in the hall, clad in a pink robe.

"Oh, Miss Abberdorf, it's terrible!" she cried without so much as a greeting. "Some creature grabbed Mr. Nutty!"

Ascot lifted her brows. "And?"

"It's a big dog or something," said Miss Maverly. "And since you can tame animals, I thought, maybe . . ." Putting her face in her hands, she sobbed. Ascot's mind instantly flashed back to Miss Roebanks.

But perhaps Miss Maverly was truly upset. "All right," said Ascot, stepping into the hallway. Moony followed, likely hoping for a chance to fight something larger than himself. Dmitri came, too, and if she read his expression correctly, he was worried.

"Quickly!" said Miss Maverly, beckoning them towards a room with a pansy-shaped doorknob. Inside, Ascot stifled a sigh of longing at the sight of the soft carpet, cushioned furniture, and the window seat commanding a view of a flower-filled courtyard.

The worse you have it in the beginning, the happier you'll be in the end, she reminded herself. It didn't sound as convincing, looking around Miss Maverly's room. It had to be three times the size of hers. Frills, ribbons, and lace covered the canopied bed's satin duvet, and the vanity sagged under the weight of jewelry and perfume. She hoped Miss Maverly wasn't planning to wear all of it at once.

Miss Maverly darted to the half-open window. "There," she cried, wringing her hands.

Out in the gathering dark, a four-legged shape frolicked through a patch of lavender. Moony jumped onto the sill and quivered with eagerness for all of five seconds. Then he sat back. "It's a red setter," he said, deflating. "Just a puppy."

Miss Maverly wailed. Ascot leaned out the window. "Here, boy," she called into the courtyard. The dim shape loped over, wagging its feathery tail. Something furry dangled from its mouth. "Good boy—"

"Girl," corrected Dmitri. Ascot shot him a look before stretching her hand to the dog.

"Good girl. Come here. That's it." The wet black nose snuffled her fingers. The puppy bathed her hand in doggie kisses as she pried the limp squirrel free. "Good girl. That's a good—ow!"

The "dead" squirrel had just sunk its teeth into the base of her right thumb. Sucking air, she shook her hand hard until Mr. Nutty let go and ran up her arm, its nasty claws prickling through her robe.

"Ooh, Mr. Nutty, you're alive!" Miss Maverly cooed as it launched itself into her arms.

Growling, Moony crouched to spring. "Don't!" Ascot shouted. She couldn't grab him; she was busy keeping blood off her robe. Dmitri put a paw on him and Moony subsided with a snarl.

"I should've let you eat the rotten creature," Ascot told the puppy. It wagged its tail. Ascot shut the window and turned, expecting a thank you. Miss Maverly, fussing over Mr. Nutty, didn't even look up.

"Come along." Dmitri nudged her. Ascot gave Miss Maverly a final glance and started towards the door.

A scream shook Nosegay Wing. It came from the end of the hall.

It sounded like Rags-n-Bones.

Ascot bolted. Doors opened to either side. Miss Jutebell's nearly smacked her in the face. As she dodged around it, she glimpsed a most curious sight. Perpendicular to her room, a dark passage gaped. The rounded shape of the bas-relief had swung aside on hidden hinges, revealing a corridor into which the powerful hindquarters and stub tail of some large beast were swiftly vanishing. Even as she ran, the bas-relief began closing. By the time she reached her room, the decoration had clicked back in place.

Panting, she clutched her doorframe for support. Her eyes took a second to focus, probably because they knew they didn't want to see what they were going to see.

They were right.

Rags-n-Bones huddled on the floor, keening over his broken biscuit, lying in pieces on the boards. But Ascot only had an instant's pity to spare for him. Her attention focused on the swath of green fabric, crumpled up and half-dragged off the table. Even from the doorway she saw holes in the skirt.

"Oh," she choked.

Moony darted in between her legs. "Your gown!" he cried.

Ascot released the doorway, swayed, and grabbed it again. Somehow, she staggered the four steps to her ruined gown. Lifting it like a wounded animal, she pressed her face to its soft bodice.

Less than an hour to the ball.

"Ascot." Dmitri wedged his nose under her arm. "You're getting blood on it."

"It's all right," Ascot mumbled, her tongue thick and heavy. "Something like this always happens in the stories."

Why didn't that knowledge cheer her? And more to the point, what was she going to do? Trusting the stories was all very well, but her Fairy Godmother seemed to have missed her cue, and if a wishing star hung outside her window, clouds covered its twinkling.

You know how to sew, said a voice in her head. It sounded very like Miss Eppicutt. *Stop dithering and get on with it.*

Sew? But that seemed so—

No. She couldn't wait for someone to come and solve her problems for her. Ascot jumped to her feet. Poking her head into the hall, she located a figure at the far end, a load of ribbons in its arms. "Maggie!"

"What's the trouble?" Maggie asked, hurrying over. "Ooh! Is that your gown?"

"Yes. Is there any green thread? Scissors?"

"Of course." Maggie dumped her armload of ribbons on a table and raced off. "Back in a minute."

Ascot ducked back inside her room. Spreading her gown on the floor, she counted the holes. Five large ones in the skirt's front and four in the back. Half a dozen pinprick holes. A foot of trim dangled off the hem, and parts of the fabric were damp, just as if—

As if some large creature had tried to chew it up. "What did this?" she asked Rags-n-Bones.

He sniffled, cradling his broken biscuit. "A monstrous big cat-creature with huge fangs. They hung down, like icicles." He placed his fingers at the corners of his mouth to illustrate.

Ascot shook her head slowly. If she hadn't seen the creature's rump, she wouldn't have believed it. "I'm sorry about your biscuit. We'll get you another one."

Rags-n-Bones scrubbed his sleeve under his nose. "Thank you, miss, but it wouldn't be the same." Going to the bathroom, he fetched a towel and offered it to Ascot. As she pressed it against her wound, Maggie ran into the room, a sewing box in one hand and a jar in the other. Throwing an apprehensive glance at Dmitri, who was snuffling around the table, Maggie knelt beside the gown and began sprinkling powder from the jar on the damp spots.

"For cleansing," she explained. "Can't use water on silk."

"Thank you," said Ascot. She found a skein of green thread in the sewing box. Her fingers shook only slightly as she threaded a needle. To her surprise, Maggie threaded a second one. "You don't have to help."

"I know," said Maggie, starting on the trim. Ascot worked on the holes in the back, thanking Miss Eppicutt with every stitch. Seconds ticked past. Ascot almost heard them cackling as they ran by.

"Your perfume's missing," said Dmitri.

Maggie jumped. "It talks!"

Dmitri's eyes narrowed. "*He* talks," he said. After a moment, Maggie blushed.

"Sorry. He."

"Yes," said Ascot, stitching furiously. She'd already jabbed a finger twice. "He's awfully smart. What else is missing, Dmitri?"

"One of your gloves and an earring—no, there it is. Just the glove and perfume."

No time to scream. Ascot forced her frazzled mind to work. *Will they notice if I'm not wearing gloves? How about perfume? Is someone going to smell me before they let me into the ball?* At this point, she wouldn't be surprised.

"Sweet almond oil," said Moony. "There might be some in the kitchen. Beeswax. We can mix up something that'll work."

Right; Miss Eppicutt used to make her own scents. "But you don't know where the kitchen is."

"I'm a cat," said Moony. "If I can't find it, I need to turn in my membership. Rags, get a beeswax candle. Dmitri, see if you can find the missing glove. I'll return in ten minutes."

Moony darted off, keeping to the shadows. Rags-n-Bones jogged into the hall. Ascot had faith both would return successful. She had to have faith; she had nothing else to keep her going. Dmitri poked his nose under the bed.

A scream shook every door in the hall, followed by a tinkling crash, as of a mirror shattering. Maggie lifted her head. "There's one gone," she said, and returned to sewing.

Ascot forgot her needle a moment. "One gone?"

"Miss Lootby, by the sound of it," said Maggie. "The one with the pretty silver-blonde hair. I expect someone snipped it off while she was sleeping." She sewed the last of the trim in place and looked up. "You about done?"

"Almost." Shaking herself, Ascot bent to her work. Two minutes later, she tied off the last stitch and took a good look at the mended gown.

"Oh, no," she groaned. No one would miss the puckers where the holes had been, or the bloodstains on the right shoulder.

"It's the best we can do," said Maggie. Her tone was sympathetic, but pragmatic.

"I found your missing glove," said Dmitri from near the wardrobe. "The hem's torn and there's a hole in one finger."

Ascot stared at her gown.

"Ascot." Dmitri's cold nose prodded her. "There's only twenty minutes to the ball. Are you giving up?"

No, she couldn't. Her True Love awaited. But . . . *I can't wear this,* she wailed internally. Not with those puckers. They'd never let her in. Unless . . .

Outside, a ray of moonlight fought free of the cloud cover. Reaching into the room, it made an object lying under the table twinkle. The solution jolted through Ascot. Scrambling to her feet, she grabbed up the bit of sparkle and broke its chain. Twenty-six crystal stars spilled into her lap. "We'll sew these over the torn spots and bloodstains," she said.

Maggie brightened. "That'll look pretty." She picked up her needle again.

They bent to their task, and now the minutes positively cart-wheeled past. Moony reappeared, carrying several vials tucked under a wing. Ascot hardly noticed. She'd pricked herself again. Rags-n-Bones dripped beeswax from a purloined candle into a jar and he and Moony bent their heads over the concoction, sniffing and consulting.

"It's twelve to eight," said Dmitri.

Twenty crystal stars covered the flaws. With Maggie's help, Ascot pulled the dress over her head and stepped into her pointy green shoes. She hooked on her earrings and the pearl pendant while Maggie darned the hole in the glove's finger.

"I can't mend the hem in time," she said.

"I'll roll it under," Ascot replied. She needed the gloves to hide the bite on her hand.

"Here." Moony offered a jar of brown balm. "It smells pretty good."

It smelled, in fact, of cinnamon. "Thanks." She dabbed it behind her ears. The scent enveloped her, as if she'd fallen onto a fresh pastry.

Picking up Ascot's makeup, Maggie made a few adjustments. "There," she said, stepping back. "You'll do."

"Five minutes," said Dmitri. "Get going."

Ascot grabbed her gloves. "Rags, we have to run." She paused to tip the last six crystal stars into Maggie's hand. "Thank you so much. I couldn't have managed on my own." Looping her arm through Rags-n-Bones', she picked up her skirts. Moony hopped onto her shoulder.

"Remember your manners," said Dmitri. "And good luck!" He didn't add that she would need it, but Ascot heard the words regardless.

Muffled sobs trickled out from behind Miss Lootby's door as they passed by. Ascot slowed to a tiptoe before racing onwards. The soft sound seemed to follow her all the way to the ballroom foyer.

CHAPTER NINE:
LORDS, LADIES, AND LIVESTOCK

The eighth bell chimed exactly as Ascot, Moony, and Rags-n-Bones dashed into the ballroom foyer.

Rags-n-Bones promptly sneezed. She couldn't blame him. The conflicting aroma of a dozen perfumes turned the air thick and stifling. Ascot looked for a window to open, but there weren't any. Blue-veined white marble surrounded them, floor to ceiling, like they all stood in the middle of some great, hollowed-out cheese. There were more of those dreadful columns, too, adorned with carved vines. They were just a little harder to see, due to the thirty or so overdressed people milling about, waiting for the moment when the huge double doors on the north wall would swing open, granting access to the ballroom.

"There's Miss Maverly," said Moony. Ascot followed his intense stare towards the front of the crowd, where Miss Maverly stood arm-in-arm with Miss Roebanks. As if she'd somehow heard her name over the babble filling the room, Miss Maverly's head turned. Her eyes met Ascot's. A look of disappointment crept over her face.

"She meant Mr. Nutty to bite me," said Ascot.

Rags-n-Bones gasped. "Surely not."

Ascot shook her head, lips pressed tight. Her thumb throbbed under its covering of green silk.

Miss Maverly tossed her hair and began whispering to Miss Roebanks. She wore satin, Ascot noted with satisfaction. Yellow satin. She looked like a well-polished lemon. Sadly, Miss Roebanks' pale gold gown perfectly complimented her ruddy complexion.

Silk rustled behind Ascot. She glanced back as Miss Lootby entered the foyer, tears furrowing her makeup and her frosty-gold locks cropped to shoulder length.

A bitter, waxy taste coated Ascot's tongue. *Frabjacket, my lipstick.* She took her teeth out of her lip. Why was she nervous? She shouldn't be. But somehow the formal white entranceway to the ballroom was beginning to remind her of a mausoleum.

Oh, nonsense. Everything would be splendid once she met Parvanel. She drew her fingers through her hair, checking if her elaborate curls were still intact, and examined her gloves. Her ring made an ugly bulge in the left one. Another snag. How could she tell if the stone had started glowing if it was inside the glove? Could she wear it outside? Taking off her left glove, she experimented.

Inside the ballroom, a trill of music started up, went nowhere, and trailed off. Cutlery jangled, crystal clinked harmoniously, and the smell of warm food and sweet wine seeped through the crack between the doors. Miss Maverly and Miss Roebanks strained discreetly forward.

"I feel sick," murmured Miss Beige, sagging under the weight of a pink velvet dress that might have been inspired by a ballerina colliding with an orchard. Her corset cinched her waist so tightly that Ascot wondered how she could breathe without popping straight out of her gown, like a cork from the mouth of a bottle.

Fortunately, her escort was a burly man who looked well-practiced in the art of catching semiconscious bodies before they hit floors.

"You'll be fine," said Ascot. Remembering her promise to Maggie, she patted Miss Beige's hand. "Take some deep breaths."

Miss Beige attempted to comply. "Are those real cherries?" asked Rags-n-Bone, ogling her gown.

"Don't eat any," said Ascot. There; she'd managed to fit the ring over her gloved finger. Still no trace of a glow, but soon. Soon. She shivered.

Another bar of music started up, with more confidence this time. The tension in the foyer coiled tighter. Miss Beige's escort caught her elbow as she sagged. Ascot exchanged a sympathetic glance with him over Miss Beige's head; the poor man seemed likely to win the "had the most miserable time" award by evening's end.

With a squeak, the doors cracked open. Out stepped Pollux, the little major-domo who had read the rules that morning, sporting an absurd tricorne cap with trailing purple, lavender, and white ribbons.

Clearing his throat, he announced: "Her Majesty bids you welcome to Prince Parvanel's twenty-first birthday fête. When your name is called, step forward and present yourself to Her Majesty and His Highness."

One of the guards handed him a scroll. He unrolled it, coughed—Ascot gritted her teeth—and read out the first name.

"Miss Rhoda Pettershanks."

Miss Pettershanks' name was on the first door in Nosegay Wing, Ascot remembered. If they were going in order, she'd be the last to enter the ballroom.

Miss Tilda Cromberfootch was summoned next. She had the second room in Nosegay Wing. Ascot nodded, satisfied. "Just like in the stories," she whispered to Moony. "The prince's True Love always arrives last."

Yawning, Moony settled more comfortably on her shoulder. "That must make it easy for the prince," he said. "He doesn't have to bother looking at the first few girls."

"Well, no, I'm sure he looks at them, but . . ." Ascot's tongue tripped over an explanation that suddenly wasn't there.

"Miss Violet Lootby."

Miss Lootby stepped forward, lip quivering, but spine straight. Someone sniggered—it sounded like Miss Maverly. Instantly, Miss Lootby crumpled. She scurried inside the ballroom as if fleeing a crime.

"Miss Scincilla Harkenpouf."

"The prince looks at them, yes," said Ascot, watching as Scincilla skipped forward, accompanied by a golden-haired man who had to be her brother. "But the last girl, see, has a special aura about her." Ascot smoothed wrinkles from her skirt, wishing she could so easily clear the furrows in her mind. It was in the white book, so it had to be right. So why did it sound ridiculous when she said it aloud?

Miss Wanda Harcourt had opted for a train on her gown. Peach-colored silk slid over white marble. Something gray and furry stuck out between the ruffles. What an odd decoration. Looked almost like—

—a squirrel's tail. It twitched.

"Oh, dear." Ascot's jaw tightened. Surely Mr. Nutty wasn't allowed at the ball? And did Miss Jeanine Whipperly imagine no one would notice her three coyly dressed mice hiding in her hairpiece?

"Miss Tanya Roebanks," called Pollux.

Holding her head as high as if it already wore a crown, Miss Roebanks entered the ballroom on the arm of the silvery-haired man Ascot presumed was her father. She couldn't help noticing the exquisite tailoring of his waistcoat and trousers. The same ruby she'd glimpsed before, the size of a cat's eye, sparkled on his finger.

"Miss Roebanks will marry Prince Parvanel," said Miss Beige.

"What?" Ascot gaped at her. Miss Beige had, if possible, wilted further.

"Lord Ruthven Roebanks is the richest and most powerful man in Albright," said Miss Beige. "Some people wanted him to be Regent after King Alastor died. I'm surprised they didn't engage Prince Parvanel to Miss Roebanks straight off."

After a moment, Ascot shook her head. "But that's not how it works," she said. Hadn't Miss Beige read the stories? "Princes can only marry their True Loves."

"Miss Jane Beige," called Pollux.

Shaking off Ascot's hand, Miss Beige tottered forward. The silk flowers and fake fruit adorning her skirt swayed in time to her walk; save for a bare-stripped patch at the back.

Ascot whirled. "Rags!"

He swallowed. "They don't taste very good, I'm afraid. Someone should tell Miss Beige."

Ascot sighed. Well, the loss of a few wax cherries honestly improved the gown.

"Miss Ascot Abberdorf," called Pollux, and Ascot's pulse quickened. Tucking Rags-n-Bones' arm under her own, she advanced towards the white doors. Things sparkled through the gap.

But Pollux threw out a hand, stopping her progress. "No pets," he said, favoring her with an expression better suited for a long-dead octopus washed up on a beach.

"I'm her escort." Moony's fur crackled. Ascot hoped he wasn't shedding on her gown.

"One escort apiece," said Pollux.

Ascot frowned. Had he truly not noticed Mr. Nutty or Miss Whipperly's mice?

"Would you have me leave the Countess Abberdorf unprotected?" demanded Moony. Jumping off her shoulder, he put a paw to his sword. Pollux's face screwed tighter.

"Wait," said Ascot. She beckoned Moony aside. His ears flattened, but he followed her into a corner, behind a column.

"I won't abandon you," he said before she could speak.

"I'm not asking you to," Ascot replied, glancing quickly at Rags-n-Bones. He appeared to be making friendly conversation with one of the lavender-coated guards. More worrying were the two bluebirds perched on a carved vine on a nearby column, chirping just a little too innocently.

She turned back to Moony. "Something sneaky's going on. I want you to fetch Dmitri." She lifted a finger as Moony started to protest. "Then slip back here and keep an eye on things from the shadows."

He liked the idea, as any self-respecting cat would. His tail rippled like a snake. "Brilliant. They'll never know I'm there." Giving her a salute, he whisked off.

Ascot rejoined Rags-n-Bones. "One escort," she said, taking his arm.

Pollux scowled. He scrutinized her from head to toe and back again, appearing to search for the smallest excuse to bar her entrance. Evidently, he found nothing. "You may proceed," he said.

So she did. And, once again, nearly tripped over a squirrel that sped across the red carpet the instant her foot crossed the boundary delineated by the white doors.

"Ooh!" She stumbled, her ankle turning in her high-heeled shoes. Drat the things. And double-drat that pesky, irritating, rotten Mr. Nutty. By the time she recovered her balance, it had vanished beneath the heavy linen cloth covering a pair of long tables ranged against the right wall.

"Miss!" Rags-n-Bones tugged on her arm, his rounded eyes pinned on the platters of food, glasses of wine, and crystal punchbowls sitting on top of the tables. "Cakes! Sandwiches! Can we eat now?"

The only ones near the tables were two servants in lavender livery rearranging the sandwiches and adding fresh lemon slices to the punch. "Not yet, I'm afraid," she said. "We're supposed to greet Prince Parvanel first."

The prince! How could she have forgotten? Her gaze followed the crimson line of the carpet as it bisected the ballroom's polished gray floor, ran up six alabaster steps, and ended at a raised area. Here, two thrones had been placed. Bettina Anna sat on one, splendidly attired in carnelian silk. The other throne waited beside her. Its prospective tenant stood at the top of the alabaster steps, casting it longing glances over his shoulder.

Prince Parvanel.

Ascot quickly glanced down at her ring.

The stone glowed! Glowed the rich red of claret, of a fiery sunset, of love itself. He *was* her True Love! Heart thumping in her chest, she looked back at Parvanel, bracing herself. Any second now, their eyes would meet over the heads of the crowd. The spangled light from the great, sun-shaped chandelier would soften to a honeyed glow. Swirling rose petals would wreath them both while the orchestra's insipid background music swelled to something tender yet triumphant.

She waited. Prince Parvanel covered a yawn.

What's wrong? She frowned at her hand, gave it a shake. The stone continued to glow unwaveringly.

Maybe she just needed to get closer to him. After all, an entire queue of guests was waiting at the foot of the steps to present themselves. Parvanel probably couldn't see her over all those heads. "Come on, Rags," she said, tugging him forward to join the line.

As they started down the crimson carpet, something fluttered through the open doorway behind her. She ducked. A whoosh of air raised the hairs on the back of her neck. A moment later, a scream tore free from Miss Saskers' throat. One of the bluebirds' droppings had scored a direct hit on her coiffure. As Miss Saskers ran weeping from the ballroom, Ascot double-checked her nearby vicinity for mice, squirrels, songbirds, or other duplicitous vermin. No animals, only Miss Maverly dancing with her partner. Ascot jumped back as they whirled past; she could've sworn Miss Maverly was actively trying to ram her.

"Keep alert," she said to Rags-n-Bones, starting up the carpet again. She watched the bluebirds. When they circled back, intent on another dive-bombing run, she yanked off her left earring—her earlobe was throbbing anyway—and took aim.

"The throwing-things-at-other-things game pays off again," she muttered as one of the bluebirds let out an unmelodic tweet and sought shelter in a bouquet of lilies arranged in a tall vase.

Reaching the sanctuary of the carpet below the raised floor intact, Ascot looked again at Prince Parvanel. He was tall. His hair flowed in golden waves. His shoulders were broad beneath his burgundy coat and his hips slim, but there was something off about his posture. Standing erect and greeting his guests politely seemed to be costing him an effort.

No. An old memory struggled to the surface of Ascot's mind. A moment later, she had it. Vincent had pulled the same attitude on her and Vlad's birthdays. It wasn't that standing upright was costing him an effort; it was that he wasn't enjoying himself and was therefore going to make it look like it was costing him an effort so everyone would know he wasn't enjoying himself.

"That's the prince," said Rags-n-Bones, pointing. Naturally his voice was the only one the ballroom's walls seemed to amplify. Ascot pulled his arm down.

"Yes, I guessed."

"He likes frogs, you know."

"Yes, you told me."

"Not very impressive, is he?"

He'd be crinkling candy wrappers next. "Rags, hush," Ascot begged, but too late. At the front of the line, Miss Roebanks' head turned with the slow, haughty grace of a lioness espying a crippled gazelle. She held the stare two seconds before leaning to whisper in her father's ear.

Warmth blossomed in Ascot's cheeks. She stared resolutely at Miss Whiske's back. Why couldn't Prince Parvanel simply look at her? Their eyes had to meet in order for the magic of True Love to take effect. She was pretty sure that was in the white book, and the first part of her ring's inscription—*I burn bright in True Love's sight*—seemed to bear it out.

There; Parvanel was yawning again. Maybe he simply didn't realize she was the last girl to enter the ballroom. He might have lost track. Yes, that made sense. She shifted, her toes cramping inside her pointed shoes. Well, she'd reach the front of the line soon enough. Then Parvanel would—

"Miss Abberdorf, I presume?" asked an unfamiliar voice. Starting, Ascot turned.

Smiling urbanely, the yellow candlelight painting his silvery hair pale gold, Lord Ruthven Roebanks stood behind her, offering a manicured hand to shake.

CHAPTER TEN:
SOME DISENCHANTING EVENING

"How delightful to make the acquaintance of one of our neighbors from Shadowvale," said Lord Roebanks. A perfect star gleamed in the center of the ruby ring on the third finger of his proffered hand.

Ascot grappled for a polite greeting. Her thoughts crumbled like dry sand.

"Is this your escort?" asked Lord Roebanks, nodding at Rags-n-Bones.

No, he's my lapdog. I was taking him for a walk in three-inch heels and a silk gown and entered the ballroom by mistake. She bit her tongue. "Yes. Rags-n-Bones, Lord Roebanks. Lord Roebanks, Rags-n-Bones."

Rags-n-Bones executed one of his ungainly puppet bows, then continued quivering.

"An old family retainer, I presume?" said Lord Roebanks, raising one eyebrow.

"Well, no, he's—" Ascot bit her tongue again. Behind Lord Roebanks' veneer of charm, she sensed a less friendly question: *why are you alone, un-chaperoned by a member of your family?*

Her backbone stiffened. What business of his was it? And why did she need a chaperone anyway? She wasn't going to impale herself on a spindle the instant she left some male guardian's sight. "Rags is a dear friend," she said, and squeezed his arm. Rags-n-Bones stood a little straighter.

A black-and-white myna bird flew through the open ballroom doors. It swooped to perch on a garland of white roses adorning one of the columns.

"Miss Tattershall smells like a privy!" it cawed. *"Miss Tattershall smells like a privy!"*

Out on the ballroom floor, Miss Tattershall stumbled over her own feet.

"Loyal friends are vital to one's well-being, are they not?" said Lord Roebanks. The myna might not have entered the ballroom for all the notice he took of it; the noise and motion of their surroundings made not the slightest impact on him. He inhabited the space as calmly and completely as a spider its web.

Now why did that comparison spring to mind? Not knowing what to make of his question, Ascot settled for smiling. The silence stretched uncomfortably, yet still Lord Roebanks stood before her, to all appearances waiting for her to continue the conversation.

Is it permissible to just say goodbye and walk away? Ascot wracked her brain, but if Miss Eppicutt's book had any advice on the matter, she couldn't recall it. In Shadowvale, proper ball etiquette was to act very, very bored, but she hoped it was different in the Daylands.

The orchestra twanged the preemptory bars of a waltz. Ascot jumped, her gaze snapping to the front of the line. Prince Parvanel stood at the base of the alabaster steps, one hand clasping Miss

Roebanks' fingers, the other on her hip. Miss Roebanks' face was one giant smirk of satisfaction.

"Ah, I see my daughter has snagged Prince Parvanel for the opening dance." Lord Roebanks laughed the lightest, lilting-est, and most humorless laugh ever laughed. "Well, I suppose I shouldn't be hurt that she'd sooner dance with a prince than her old papa. You'd better run along with your escort, Miss Abberdorf. Mustn't insult the royal family by not dancing."

Unhurriedly, he walked off to stand at the side of the ballroom, by a row of gilt chairs lined up under a life-sized frieze of elegantly attired people captured in mid-waltz. Ascot gaped after him, gaped at the prince, gaped at the other couples, her thoughts tripping over themselves again and again. Looking across the floor, she met Miss Beige's eyes over her escort's shoulder. *Didn't I tell you?* read her sad expression.

But I never got to introduce myself to Prince Parvanel. He never saw me. And I'm his—

Quit sniveling. Ascot pinched herself. The ball wasn't over yet. "Come along, Rags," she said, perhaps a touch too brightly. "It's time to dance."

"Which dance, miss? I know the chicken one."

"Not that one." She arranged Rags-n-Bones' stance, set one of his hands on her hip and took the other in her own. He flushed carmine red. "Just match me," she said. "Step back when I step forward. Forward when I step back. It's a box-like pattern. Easy."

Easy to say, not so easy to accomplish. His ungainly legs swallowed huge swaths of the floor with every step. He bumped so many people with his elbows that she began to think he kept an extra pair in his pocket for that purpose. But just when she was about to write him off as a hopeless gawk, the pattern took them near the refreshment table and one of those long arms swooped an iced cake off a plate and into his mouth. It happened so fast that the only way she knew it had happened was by the crumbs on his lips.

She said nothing. No one else could have seen it, either, and he deserved a few cakes for his pains.

"Miss Tattershall smells like a privy!" the myna squawked. *"Miss Tattershall smells like a privy!"* No matter where Miss Tattershall danced, the myna changed position to follow her.

A rush of brown fur streaked across the ballroom floor, heading directly for Ascot. She jumped and Mr. Nutty ran straight under her and tripped Miss Callo instead. Miss Callo squalled as she hit the floor. Her partner escorted her off, limping. On the other side of the red carpet, Miss Cromberfootch waltzed into an enormous pile of droppings that Miss Tumberfelt's deer had deposited in her path. The immense width of Miss Cromberfootch's carnation-pink skirts prevented her from seeing the mess until she stood ankle-deep in it. Another squeal echoed off the ballroom walls.

Get here soon, Ascot mentally begged Moony and Dmitri, teeth gritted.

Fortunately, the music trilled to an unnecessarily elaborate halt, ending the dance. Ascot's feet actually lightened as all motion whirled to a stop. The knot between her shoulders eased.

"Can we eat now?" asked Rags-n-Bones, loud enough for all to overhear. Miss Maverly tittered behind a hand.

"Soon, hopefully," said Ascot. Food might calm everyone down. Parvanel was beating a retreat back to his throne, every line of his body singing relief. He hadn't fallen eternally in love with Miss Roebanks, then. *Of course not*, she thought, rubbing a thumb over her glowing ring.

As the low babble of conversation filled the great, gray-marbled ballroom, Pollux scurried to the foot of the steps, carrying a staff bedecked with ribbons to match his ridiculous hat. He beat its butt against the floor. "Honored guests," he announced, "please take refreshment while the orchestra prepares to play the Prince's Waltz."

Rags-n-Bones dove for the long tables, all but wrenching Ascot's arm from its socket. "Oof! Rags!" She wobbled on her heels before righting herself. "Couldn't you—" She gave it up. He was too busy inspecting the proffered delicacies.

"Ascot!" called a voice.

Ascot turned. Scincilla walked towards her, hands outstretched as if bearing something invisible yet precious between them. A flash of blue peeked through a chain of white roses swaying over her head. Ascot swiped off her remaining earring and threw it just as the second bluebird lined up its bottom. The gob backfired. Squawking, and perhaps a trifle constipated, the bluebird fled.

"You look lovely," said Scincilla, passing under the roses un-mucked and oblivious.

Her embrace smelled of jasmine. The lapis blue of her silk gown matched her eyes, and her hair shone like sunlight through honey. "You look lovely, too," said Ascot.

"The crystal stars are such a pretty touch. Ascot, this is my brother, Lordling." Scincilla hugged her escort's arm.

Lordling Harkenpouf? Ascot stifled a groan. Their parents should be shot. "Pleased to meet you," she said.

Lordling's dark blue coat suited him to perfection. He smiled, showing off fine white teeth. "Pleased to make your acquaintance, Miss Abberdorf," he said in a warm, agreeable voice. Ascot suspected Miss Maverly and Miss Roebanks would try to eat him later.

Miss Maverly and Miss Roebanks. Where were they? Oh, right. Follow the sound of sniggering. She located it and there they were: jeering at Rags-n-Bones, who had filled two huge plates with cakes and sandwiches and balanced a bowl of punch on his head.

"Rags," called Ascot, "isn't that a bit much?"

Rags-n-Bones pivoted, the bowl of punch staying perfectly level. "This is for the guards," he said, as somber as if announcing the commencement of a war. "Do you know they're expected to stand there all night without a single sandwich? That's not right." He shook his head, still not sloshing the punch, and loped across the room to the entranceway.

Miss Maverly and Miss Roebanks giggled louder.

"Oh, how kind of him," said Scincilla.

Lord Roebanks didn't seem to agree. His mouth tightened as he watched Rags-n-Bones speak with the guards. The ruby on his hand flashed as he swirled his wine. Bettina Anna also studied Rags-n-Bones, her elbow propped on the arm of her throne. One finger tapped her lips. By her side, Parvanel ate, head bent low over a golden plate.

Rags-n-Bones came trotting back. "They were very happy."

"Good chap," said Lordling. "It must be dull to stand about all night, doing nothing."

"Yes," agreed Rags-n-Bones. He clapped his hands together. "Now, about this food—"

"I adore cucumber sandwiches," said Lordling. "Have they any?"

They fell to examining the table, already great friends.

Arm in arm, Miss Maverly and Miss Roebanks strolled towards the refreshments. They took glasses of champagne and the tiniest slivers of cake Ascot had ever seen, so thin they'd sail away if she blew on them, then stood before the table as if guarding it, sipping their champagne and not eating their cake.

"Those custard tarts look wonderful," said Miss Beige, standing a good ten feet from the laden platters. Nor did she approach any closer. Instead, after a final, longing stare, she sighed and trudged across the ballroom, going to sit in one of the gilded chairs under the frieze.

Hsss-whsss-sss, came a snakish whisper from the front of the table, followed by a titter.

Ascot set her jaw. She stepped up to the table only to find her way thwarted by Miss Roebanks.

"Excuse me," said Ascot as they locked gazes. *She has eyes like a rabid fox.*

"Oh, *do* forgive me." Miss Roebanks took her time moving. She watched Ascot pick up two plates and heap them with sandwiches, cheese, fruit, and tarts. She glanced sidelong at Miss Maverly. Both giggled. "You have a hearty appetite, don't you?"

"Yes," said Ascot, ladling two cups full of punch. "That, and I don't want the 'Girl Who Ate the Least Amount in a Single Year' award. The trophy's just a piece of gilded cabbage." She strode off while their mouths were still hanging open.

"Miss Tattershall smells like a privy! Miss Tattershall smells like a privy!"

Bursting into tears, Miss Tattershall raced from the ballroom, her face buried in her hands. Miss Pettershanks hid her grin behind a glass of punch.

Ascot marched across to Miss Beige, crumpled in a gilt chair, half-stifled under the weight of her gown. "Here," she said, handing her one of the plates. "I'll keep Miss Maverly and Miss Roebanks away."

She re-crossed the ballroom, thinking Miss Beige might be more likely to eat if she were given privacy to do it. Lord Roebanks' eyes followed her. He beckoned to a handsome man in a willow-green coat and whispered something in his ear before sauntering to the raised platform where Bettina Anna and Parvanel sat to engage Her Majesty in conversation.

None of my business, Ascot told herself, rejoining the gathering near the refreshment table. Standing by a rose-wrapped column, she sampled the salty-bitter watercress sandwiches—almost as tasty as tadpole pate—and listened to the chatter.

"I wonder who Prince Parvanel will dance with next," said Scincilla, nibbling a raspberry.

Me, thought Ascot, licking the icing off a cake. Parvanel was still eating busily, ignoring the room at large. Leaning over the arm of her throne, Bettina Anna spoke to Lord Roebanks, who stood on the top step of the alabaster stairs.

"I can't stop staring, either." Scincilla sighed. "He's so beautiful."

Ascot choked on her cake. "Beautiful? Isn't he kind of old?"

Scincilla stared. Ascot stared back. "Oh," she said. "You mean Parvanel. I was watching Lord Roebanks. Isn't he . . ." She hesitated, treading carefully. ". . . kind of arrogant?"

The slightest wrinkle creased the skin between Scincilla's brows. She glanced at Lord Roebanks, then leaned forward, looking for once as if she were about to say something that wasn't idle chatter. But just then, Parvanel snapped his fingers and handed his empty plate to a butler. Instant silence filled the room as he rose, posture stiff, as if braced for an unpleasant duty. His foot came down on the first red-carpeted step.

"Oooh!" breathed Scincilla, patting her hair, her dress, and her face. The berries had tinted her lips a deeper shade of pink.

And Ascot realized that she had crumbs ringing her mouth, had probably licked her lipstick off along with the icing, and was stuck holding a half-full plate. *Where to put it?* She glanced frantically about the room as Parvanel reached the last step.

"Allow me to take that for you."

"Thank you," she said, and was actually in the act of handing it over when she recognized the voice and froze.

"Have you decided to keep it after all?" asked Catch, raising an eyebrow.

Recovering, she shoved the plate at him with all the force she dared muster. He took it as smoothly as if he'd been anticipating her action and passed it to a butler. Turning, he looked her up and down. His right eyebrow crept a little higher. Ascot endured the scrutiny, thinking how she'd like to push him into the refreshment table.

"Satisfied?" she asked when it seemed he was finished.

"A noble effort."

That was probably as close to a compliment as she would ever receive from him. He'd changed outfits, too. In fact—*oh dear*.

He wore a willow-green coat. The same green coat as the man she'd mentally tagged as "handsome" just minutes ago. *Must've been a trick of the light.*

"What?" Catch asked, frowning.

"Nothing," she said, forcing a laugh. She indicated the lace-edged cravat tied about his throat. "Just didn't envision you as the ruffle type."

"Didn't think you were the face-paint and ringlets type," he retorted.

Ascot fingered her curls. His hair was tied back with a copper-colored ribbon. The style highlighted his cheekbones and the slight hollows beneath them. "I had no choice," she said.

"Neither did I. Could you expect Her Majesty to permit me to attend His Highness's ball looking like—"

"A scruffy highwayman?" she finished, smiling sweetly. He flashed her a scowl. "I'm sure you're the same conniving ruffian inside."

"And you're the same impertinent tomboy."

Miss Harcourt ran wailing from the ballroom. Her peach-colored train had been completely nibbled away, revealing a pair of green bloomers.

Ascot returned her attention to Catch. "That'll be princess tomboy, before the night's out." She made to brush past him, but he flung out a hand, blocking her way.

"What?" she asked, stopping despite herself. "Do you want something?"

"I heard you had trouble with your dress earlier."

"Did you. From who?"

"Whom."

"Don't correct me." She tried to sidestep him, but he matched her. "Do you bribe the servants to bring you gossip?"

"No," he said, all seriousness. "They bring it to me freely, due to my winning personality."

Ascot blinked at his deadpan expression for a few seconds before, reluctantly, a laugh broke from her throat. "My gown is fine." She smoothed the skirt so the crystal stars twinkled. "See?"

She looked up just in time to see his brow crease. *He's surprised. But why? Unless . . .*

A small but brilliantly red eruption flared inside her head. "You saw my dress before I sewed the stars on, didn't you?" she demanded, pressing forward. "You needed to be able to recognize it so you could send that creature to destroy it."

He shifted his gaze to her face. "Creature?"

"Don't play dumb. Some beast tried to eat my dress."

Catch shook his head. "I don't own any pets, not even a dog."

"So it wasn't something you set on me?"

"On my honor—"

"Oh, don't."

"Very well. You'll just have to accept my word, then."

His word? She'd bet her last teaspoon that he was a gifted liar. The attack on her dress had been too well timed to be a coincidence.

A burst of music interrupted her thoughts. All the other candidates gathered into a loose circle in the middle of the floor. At the center, under the coruscating light of the chandelier, Parvanel and Scincilla swirled in a dance. Scincilla smiled as if she were awake inside a happy dream.

Just like that, Ascot's second chance to meet Prince Parvanel had vanished.

CHAPTER ELEVEN:
THE LAPDOGS OF WAR

But, but . . . Parvanel had just set his foot on the top step. Hadn't he? It couldn't have been so long—

"You!" Ascot whirled on Catch. "You distracted me on purpose!"

"Of course," he said.

"What was that about honor?" she snarled, prepared to blacken his other eye if he said one condescending word.

He huffed. "Come now, Miss Abberdorf, we both know the game we're playing here. I won this round. Don't be a sore loser."

It was true. All the fight drained out of her. She knew he was no friend of hers, and still she'd stood listening to him instead of meeting Parvanel. *You bloody great idiot.* She rubbed her brow with the back of her wrist and considered drowning herself in the punchbowl.

"Care to dance?" asked Catch, holding out a hand.

She dropped her arm. "What?"

"Dance. Means 'move around the floor rhythmically, in a set pattern, to music.'"

"After that explanation, no."

"Yes, perhaps Parvanel would be more impressed if you moped in a corner. He's pretty good at that himself. I just thought you might find dancing more enjoyable."

"Did you."

"Consider it your opportunity to tread on my toes."

Put that way, it sounded appealing. And one look around the ballroom informed her that everyone else had joined the waltz. Even Miss Beige was dancing, with Rags-n-Bones, who clearly didn't know the steps, but was improvising some truly imaginative ones of his own.

"This isn't another trick?" she asked, taking the smallest possible hold of Catch's fingertips.

"Would you believe me if I said no?"

"Probably not."

Smiling, he led her out to where the chandelier's light refracted into rainbow sparks that skittered across the polished ballroom floor. She stiffened when he set his hand on her hip, alert for any new trickery, but after a minute, she relaxed. Better to share the floor with Parvanel than to watch from the sidelines. Scincilla floated in the prince's arms, oblivious to the glares sent her way, but Parvanel danced mechanically, visibly counting the seconds until he could return to his throne. Clearly, he hadn't lost his heart to Scincilla. *Of course not,* she thought. Her ring still glowed an unwavering red.

"Enjoying yourself?" asked Catch, dipping her at the end of a note. The man possessed a certain grace; she had to give him that. But not much else.

"I'd rather you were Prince Parvanel."

"I can't say I feel the same." He smiled. White teeth, surprisingly sharp.

Bloody predator. He smelled of some herb, sharp, yet fresh, like tea or new-cut grass. Flecks of green speckled his hazel irises. The skin around his right eye was still somewhat bruised and swollen. Sometimes she'd catch him studying her, only to have him flick his gaze away as soon as he noticed her looking.

"Why?" she asked, her eyes tracing the line of his jaw. She suspected he didn't smile often. Not really.

"Why what?" he asked, refocusing on her.

"Why don't you want me to meet Parvanel? Afraid he'll choose me?"

"I don't care who he chooses."

Ascot's snort fluttered a lock of his hair. His sleeve brushed the stars on her bodice. "You're making quite an effort for someone who doesn't care," she said.

Catch pursed his lips, staring across the ballroom floor. Miss Whiske pushed away from her partner and raced off, flailing her arms about her head and howling something about beetles in her hair.

"Perhaps I should say I'd prefer not to care," Catch said, gaze turned inward, as if talking to himself. "If people must fall in love, they should be allowed to do it on their own schedule, not according to some . . . plot. Don't you agree?"

His green-flecked eyes speared hers. Blood raced to Ascot's cheeks. Dropping her gaze to the dark floor, she watched his reflection until his shadow distracted her; it seemed to be the wrong shape, or size, or both. Probably just an effect of the confusing lights.

"You didn't answer my question," she said, after her face cooled a bit. "Why don't you want Parvanel to meet me?"

"Scoundrel I may be, but I have my loyalties. I'll see you wed Parvanel when the moon falls out of the sky. Not before."

It wasn't a proper answer, but it pleased her because it made her angry with him again. "We'll see about th—" He spun her out to the end of her arm and a jolt of pain flared up her wrist.

He noticed her wince. "What's wrong?" he asked.

"Nothing," she said, teeth clamped in her lower lip.

Frowning, he brought her back to him and turned her right hand over. An ugly stain tarnished her glove at the heel of her thumb. Ascot's stomach squirmed; she hadn't realized she was bleeding again. "You're hurt," he said.

"Miss Maverly's squirrel bit me."

His mouth puckered into a grimace. "All these blasted animals, someone was bound to get bitten. This should be treated before it gets infected."

"But—" All thoughts of protest died as a brief, intense vision of Mr. Nutty's foul yellow teeth rose into her mind. "Maybe you're right," she conceded, allowing him to sit her on one of the chairs under the frieze and peel off her glove. The wound, an evil shade of purplish-red, contrasted starkly with her pale skin. Catch studied it, *tsking* between his teeth.

"I'll fetch some ointment," he said, and walked off.

"*Psst.*"

Ascot jumped at the sharp hiss coming from directly beneath her. She pulled back a fold of her green skirt, and there was Moony's mischievous little face, peering up at her from under her chair. "I was beginning to think you'd gotten lost," she said.

"I've been stalking mice in jumpers." A grin bared his fangs. He'd ditched his hat, cape, and boots; likely in favor of greater stealth. "Still haven't caught the third; it's a sneaky beggar."

That explained the orange thread dangling from a corner of his jaws. She opened her mouth to rebuke him for the mice's demise and realized her heart wasn't in it. "Where's Dmitri?" she asked instead.

"Playing poker with the guards in the foyer. He says he's gathering information, but I think he's something of a card shark."

Ascot's hand flew to her mouth. "You mean he's talking to them?" Soon everyone would know she hadn't tamed Dmitri. She'd be dismissed—

But Moony just smirked. "Don't worry. Servants are like cats. They love secrets, especially those they can keep from their masters."

Out on the floor, the waltz came to an end. After favoring the company with a bow, Parvanel took the steps to his throne two at a time, relief rolling off him like sweat. While Miss Burgoyne was bent in a curtsy, Miss Tumberfelt's deer ran up behind her and butted her in the rump. Miss Burgoyne fell on her face and came up with a bloody nose.

Rags-n-Bones escorted Miss Beige to the line of gilded chairs. Miss Beige moved with short, halting steps, her face tight. "What's the matter?" asked Ascot as Rags-n-Bones sat her in one of the chairs.

Tears threatened to spill over Miss Beige's eyelids. "These shoes my parents insisted I wear are destroying my feet," she said. She raised her skirt's hem just high enough to display the tip of a tiny shoe that glittered like a spray of fresh water.

Ascot gasped. "Glass slippers?"

"Is there any cheap trick you ladies won't try?"

Catch's voice made them jump. Moony vanished beneath Ascot's chair. Miss Beige stared down at her hands as Catch knelt before Ascot and dabbed some sharp-smelling liquid over her wound.

Ascot bit into her inner cheek. From the feel of it, he'd dropped a live hornet into her open wound. Just as the pain began fading, he poured a second dose on. By sucking in air until she thought her lungs might burst, she managed not to yelp.

"There." Catch wrapped a bandage around her hand. "Keep it clean."

"I know." She blinked away tears. "I'm not an idiot."

The corner of his mouth twitched, fighting an expression she couldn't recognize. A pause stretched and stretched until it transformed itself into a full-fledged silence.

"My apologies," he said at last. The irony was back. Standing, he sketched a brief bow. "Thank you for the dance."

"You're welcome," Ascot muttered, picking at the bloody spot on her glove. She remained bent over until his shadow moved away.

The instant it did, Miss Beige dissolved into tears. "He's right," she said, covering her face with her hands. A strand of ashy brown hair draggled from her coiffure. "It is a cheap trick."

Dropping her glove into her lap, Ascot put an arm around Miss Beige's shoulders. "No, he just doesn't understand about princes and stories."

She patted Miss Beige while she sobbed. Poor thing. If only Parvanel had a younger brother she could marry. She thought she might like having Miss Beige for a sister-in-law. Of course, first she really had to meet Parvanel so their eyes could meet and reveal their True Love. She glanced up at the raised floor, where Parvanel sat rooted on his throne, gaze locked on the clock on the opposite wall. Perhaps now would be a good time to approach him? She shifted her weight, preparing to stand.

Miss Beige sobbed again. Ascot hesitated, looking from Miss Beige to Parvanel, and resettled in her chair. She'd made a promise to Maggie, and Maggie had helped her fix her dress. True Love could wait a few minutes more. Over Miss Beige's bowed head, she spotted the plate of food she'd given her earlier, sitting untouched on the chair beside her.

"Why don't you eat something?" she suggested, drawing back to arm's length. "You'll feel better."

"Some sandwiches have avocado in them," added Rags-n-Bones encouragingly. "Although I may have eaten all of those." He picked a sandwich off Miss Beige's plate. "Look, yummy cheese and tomato."

"You're right." Miss Beige sat up, sniffling. Quiet desperation laced her voice, as if she'd been driven to her last straw. Ignoring the proffered sandwich, she fumbled in a lace purse, half-hidden by her gown's cascading frills. "I'll do it. I'll eat the apple."

"Apple?" Ascot rechecked Miss Beige's plate. She didn't remember selecting an—

Miss Beige pulled an apple out of her purse, an apple red as paint on a child's brush, red all over without shading or variation. Ascot grabbed her wrist before she could put it to her mouth. "Wait. That doesn't look good."

"It's a wishing apple," said Miss Beige, avoiding her eyes.

"A wishing . . ." Ascot remembered that story. One bite, and you slept until the prince kissed you awake. Then it was True Love and Happily Ever After.

But that's not fair, a little voice protested. *It's too . . . easy. Besides, I have the ring. Parvanel's my True Love.*

The rest of her kept staring at the apple. It sat in Miss Beige's hand, glossy as glass and exuding an overwhelming aroma of apple, as if a thousand apples had been condensed into one.

On the other side of the room, Mr. Nutty reappeared from under a candelabrum. He skittered beneath Miss Jutebell's skirts and ran up her back. Squalling, she spilled bright red cherry juice all down the front of her apricot chiffon dress. Miss Maverly's and Miss Roebanks' sniggers accompanied her out the doors.

"My governess told me a version of that story," said Ascot. A different one than was in the white book—if the stories were true, why did different versions exist? Setting the question aside, she took a sip of punch to wet her throat. "In that one, the prince didn't kiss the girl; just had his servants carry her coffin around. Not particularly charming behavior for a prince," she added, frowning thoughtfully. She shook her head and continued. "She didn't wake up until the servants accidentally dropped the coffin and she threw up the piece of apple she'd swallowed."

Miss Beige's mouth trembled.

"What if Parvanel refuses to kiss you?" asked Ascot.

In his throne, Parvanel took a long swig from a golden goblet and continued staring at the clock set into the wall over the doors.

"I'd kiss you, Miss Beige, but I'm not sure it would work," said Rags-n-Bones, laying a hand on her shoulder and fortunately missing the moment Moony reappeared with a long, thin tail dangling from his mouth.

"What if you never woke up?" Ascot shivered. She found coffins quite cozy herself, but every time she lay down in one, it was with the knowledge that she'd awaken, not to discover that she'd been buried alive.

"I know, I know." The apple dropped from Miss Beige's hand and rolled under her chair. She ran a glove under her nose. "It's just another cheap trick. I don't even want to be here. I hate balls."

Bending down, Ascot picked up the apple. *What now?* she wondered, contemplating the unnaturally heavy piece of fruit. If she left it lying about, someone might chomp into it.

For lack of better ideas, she stuffed it into her soiled glove. "Well, it'll be over soon," she said, tying the glove around her wrist. "Have your corset loosened and eat a slice of cake. Chocolate cake. That'll cheer you up." She gave Miss Beige's shoulder a final pat and stood.

"What will you do with the apple, miss?" asked Rags-n-Bones, following her across the ballroom.

"I'd love to feed it to Mr. Nutty." The pesky squirrel had just taken a flying leap onto Miss Tumberfelt's bosom and piddled.

His eyes widened, threatening to water. Ascot sighed. "I won't, Rags. Don't worry." She marched towards the alabaster steps. The ball *would* be over soon. Really, it was time to meet Parvanel and put an end to this charade.

Glass shattered in the vicinity of the refreshment table. "You did this, didn't you?" Miss Lootby screamed at Miss Whipperly. "You sent your mice to nibble off my hair while I was napping!"

Moony belched and giggled.

Miss Lootby threw a punch at Miss Whipperly. The two went down in a tempest of sky blue and lilac silk skirts.

Ascot hesitated in mid-step. How curiously empty the ballroom looked. At the foot of the raised platform, Lord Roebanks swirled his drink and smiled. What a long stretch of space there was between her and him, open and undefended. Small, beady eyes glittered around the perimeter of the room, watching from flower arrangements, under candelabra, and peeping beneath the heavy folds of red velvet framing the frieze.

Spinning on her heel, Ascot went to the double doors and poked her head out into the foyer. "Dmitri?"

Dmitri looked up from where he sat amongst a circle of guards in loosened lavender uniforms. Cards lay scattered about the white marble floor. Apparently, they'd been using truffles, macaroons, and gingerbread in lieu of poker chips. Dmitri's pile was the largest by far.

"Has Parvanel proposed yet?" he asked, tail swishing. Ascot suspected he was fighting a wolf-smirk.

"No, I haven't even met him," she replied. "Every time I try, someone's pet attacks."

Guffaws and knee-slapping amongst the guards. Not a single one seemed surprised.

"Yes, we've been keeping track of casualties." Dmitri rose, stretching fore and aft. "How many did we make it, Will?"

The guard captain tugged his brown mustache. "Nine, so far."

A butler appeared in the ballroom's doorway, Miss Lootby and Miss Whipperly in tow. Red scratches marked their cheeks. Miss Lootby bore a split lip and Miss Whipperly's hair straggled out of its ribbons. "Consider yourselves dismissed," said the butler, giving them a push.

"Eleven," said Captain Will as Misses Lootby and Whipperly fled, whimpering, down the hall.

"Leaving six. Including Miss Roebanks," said Dmitri.

All the grins slipped off the guards' faces. The foyer's atmosphere chilled by several degrees.

"Miss Beige says Parvanel's sure to marry her," said Ascot.

"She's probably right." Captain Will heaved a sigh.

"We'll see about that," said Dmitri before Ascot finished summoning a protest. He strode through the ballroom doors. Ascot followed. The sounds of discreet vomiting, mixed with a familiar malicious giggle, met her ears. They came from the area near the refreshment table, where Miss Pettershanks was heaving into a vase.

Ascot located Scincilla, standing beside a tall silver candelabrum, hand pressed over her mouth. "What's wrong with her?" she asked, nodding towards Miss Pettershanks.

"She discovered odd brown lumps in the bottom of her punch glass," said Scincilla through her fingers.

Odd brown lumps. Miss Maverly stood by the refreshment table, tickling Mr. Nutty's chin. A poorly concealed smirk played over her lips.

As a butler guided the green-faced Miss Pettershanks out of the room, Miss Roebanks made her move. Crossing the room with precise, clicking steps, she joined her father at the foot of the alabaster stairs. A flicker of candlelight made her hair gleam almost as red as her father's ruby. Her eyes settled on Ascot.

Five left.

CHAPTER TWELVE:
IN THE MIDNIGHT HOUR

Ascot held herself straight. It took effort. There was something detached and calculating about Miss Roebanks' appraisal. As if she'd already labeled a stone slab with Ascot's name and was only determining the right moment to bury her. Above and behind her, Prince Parvanel sat in his throne as if glued.

Look at me, look at me, Ascot chanted silently. Couldn't he see the ring on her finger, burning brighter than Lord Roebanks' ruby? He would if he'd only look at her! But his eyes remained fixed on the clock. Ten minutes to twelve, and the ball ended at midnight.

Somehow, she had to attract his attention. Should she wave? Or yodel? Or—her inspiration gave out. The white book hadn't been very forthcoming in this regard.

"Shouldn't we be dancing?" asked Scincilla, twisting a curl of golden hair around one finger.

"I doubt Parvanel would notice," Ascot muttered as Miss Maverly went to stand with the Roebanks. Like sentinels, the three of them, protecting the prince. Except what they were protecting him from was her, his True Love. *Think! What does Parvanel like?*

Frogs. Maybe if she started croaking—

She ended that thought before she grew desperate enough to try it. "Did Parvanel say anything to you while you were dancing?" she asked Scincilla instead.

Scincilla blushed. "He hardly said three words to me. I think he's shy."

"Like me," said Rags-n-Bones.

Dmitri sighed. "Maybe he doesn't want to get married."

"Oh, but he must," said Scincilla. "That's the law of Albright. He can't be king until he is." Her head spun in a double-take. "Does your wolf talk?"

"Yes," said Ascot. "All the time. Don't ask him about Dustyevsky."

"Dostoyevsky," said Dmitri.

"Oh, I loved *The Brothers Karamazov.*" Scincilla clapped her hands. "I wanted to marry Alyosha."

Dmitri's eyes glowed. To avert an epic conversation of staggeringly boring proportions, Ascot stepped on his paw. "You can discuss literature after I wed Parvanel. But first, I have to—"

A darker shadow moved in the shadows beside the white staircase. As it came into the light, the chandelier cast rainbow flecks over shoulders covered in willow-green velvet and a copper ribbon tying back pale brown hair.

Catch, resurfacing again. Their eyes met. One timeless second passed; then, raising a brow, he bowed so deeply it had to be mockery. Ascot dipped in an ironic curtsy.

"Flirt with Catch?" asked Dmitri.

"Ascot danced with him," said Moony brattily.

Ascot straightened so quickly her ankles twanged. "It was only to see what he was up to."

"They looked good together," said Scincilla. She wore the smile of a girl watching her baby sister enjoy a scoop of ice cream.

From warm, Ascot's cheeks heated to flaming. "Probably because we're both wearing green."

"If I marry Parvanel, maybe you could marry Catch," said Scincilla. "Then we'd both have a friend living at Albright Castle."

Marry Catch?

Marry *Catch?*

Even putting aside the fact that her ring didn't so much as sparkle in Catch's presence . . . what kind of Happily Ever After could she expect if she married a scruffy, dishonest rogue like him? Why, the stories didn't even mention such a possibly; apparently such a fate was too ghastly to contemplate.

Something inside Ascot snapped, like a heavy book had slammed shut inside her chest. Her chin went up. She started walking.

"Ascot, where are you going?" called Scincilla.

"I didn't come to Albright to marry a scoundrel," she replied, marching towards the alabaster steps. "Keep an eye out for attackers."

She'd taken five steps when Miss Tumberfelt's deer charged, head lowered, from behind the curtains framing the frieze.

Dmitri growled. The deer's rush changed to a frantic attempt to brake, tiny hooves slipping on the polished gray floor. It crashed into a column, sat stunned for an instant, then leaped up and fled the ballroom, Dmitri in pursuit.

"Thanks, Dmitri," muttered Ascot. Her heels clacked against marble, then shushed on the plush red carpet, thick as Moony's coat. Lord Roebanks, Miss Roebanks, and Miss Maverly stood at the end of it, at the base of the beckoning alabaster stairs.

The myna bird swooped overhead. "Miss Abberdorf stinks—"

Leaping, Rags-n-Bones caught it gently by the feet. "Don't be naughty," he chided, cuddling it.

A bluebird dared peep its head out of an arrangement of chrysanthemums. Taking to the air, Moony rousted both it and its mate with a swipe of one paw and chased them out the doors.

Ascot smiled, sensing victory. Her ring glowed brighter with every step she gained. Miss Roebanks drew herself up as she approached, as if trying to avoid a foul smell. Lord Roebanks' jaw tightened. Miss Maverly's eyes . . .

. . . gleamed. The corners of her lips twitched upwards.

"Watch out, Ascot!" cried Scincilla.

Ascot whirled as a gray-brown streak launched itself from the top of a refreshment table. Mr. Nutty must have been rolling in a jelly. Purple goo smeared its fur. Spread like a starfish, it sailed straight at her, all its nasty claws prepared to hook into her gown.

A small, glittering object, smelling of hot foot, arced from the right. It hit Mr. Nutty squarely in the side. A *thunk*, then both squirrel and glittering object went spinning away across the polished floor.

"Serves you right, you horrid beast!" cried Miss Beige, limping across the room. Chocolate icing smudged her mouth.

Ascot looked at the glittering thing lying next to the stunned squirrel. It was a glass slipper.

"Mr. Nutty!" wailed Miss Maverly. She dived at her pet, only to notice the goop smearing its fur and check herself. Too late; her cry had roused it. Shaking off its stupor, it leaped into her arms for comfort. Bright purple stains spread in hideous contrast to the lemon yellow satin.

"Ooh!" wailed Miss Maverly, spinning towards Miss Roebanks in an appeal for help.

Miss Roebanks stepped back.

"And serves you right, too," added Miss Beige, yanking off her second slipper and clouting Miss Maverly on the ear. Ascot grabbed Miss Beige's wrist before she could strike her again.

"You made your point," she whispered. Miss Maverly's escort was already leading her away.

A smile swam through Miss Beige's smeared makeup. "I did, didn't I?" she said. Facing the thrones, she curtsied. "Thank you for a wonderful evening, Your Majesty. I'll never forget it."

She strode out of the ballroom on her own two feet, followed by her visibly impressed guardsman.

Something that might have been the hint of a smile bent Bettina Anna's lips. Catch cocked his head to one side. Ascot couldn't gauge Prince Parvanel's expression because Lord Roebanks blocked her view of him.

He can't block me forever, thought Ascot. Only herself, Scincilla, and Miss Roebanks remained now. All the pets dealt with. Taking a breath, she readied herself to sink in her finest curtsy, her ring blazing a miniature, cold bonfire on her finger.

Bong. The first chime of midnight struck.

Prince Parvanel shot upright. "Thank you for a wonderful ball," he said, addressing everyone and no one. He snapped his fingers. Six guardsmen instantly fell into formation around him. Caught napping, the orchestra struck up a departing fanfare half a beat after he'd started trotting down the red carpet like he was powered by tightly wound clockwork. Within three seconds, he'd disappeared through the paired doors.

Bong. The second chime struck. Ascot blinked, caught in an awkward half-crouch, watching the glow from her ring fade and die. Slowly, she straightened. Her knees clicked and Miss Roebanks threw her a scornful glance.

Bong. Bong. Servants unobtrusively cleared away the uneaten dishes—very few of these, with Rags-n-Bones around—and mopped up the various animal messes. Scincilla joined Ascot. They exchanged bewildered glances. On her throne, Bettina Anna seemed to be examining the air. Lord Roebanks swirled his wine glass, his ruby flashing. Catch and Dmitri studied each other from a distance.

The clock *bonged* itself to silence. Silence remained, pooling in the room, several long seconds after it stilled.

Then Lord Roebanks spoke. "Your Majesty, the matter is clear."

"Is it, Lord Roebanks?" asked Bettina Anna, still gazing at nothing.

Tilting back his head, Lord Roebanks finally finished off his drink. Ascot fought the urge to applaud. "His Highness only danced with my daughter and Miss Harkenpouf," he said, handing his empty glass to a butler without looking. "We can therefore deduce that his preference lies with them."

Oh, you rotten warg in a waistcoat. Ascot's fingers taloned her skirt.

"His Highness danced with your daughter as a favor, recognizing your service to the throne of Albright," said Bettina Anna. "We could therefore deduce that his true preference lies with Miss Harkenpouf."

Miss Roebanks ceased simpering. She stepped forward, but one glance from her father stilled her.

"Perhaps it would be best to discuss the matter with His Highness tomorrow," said Lord Roebanks.

"That, I think, would be wisest." At last Bettina Anna stirred, rising from her throne with heavy grace. Her gaze went first to Miss Roebanks, then Scincilla, and finally Ascot. "Ladies. Come to the Cupid Chamber tomorrow evening at eight o' clock. There you will discover what has been decided." She made a gesture and six guardsman leaped to attention.

"All three?" asked Lord Roebanks as she descended the alabaster steps, attended by her guardsmen. His gaze touched Ascot, who tightened her grip on her skirt, hoping it would quench the desire to slap him.

Bettina Anna did not pause in her journey towards the white doors. "Yes. All three."

Pale green flickered at the corner of Ascot's vision. She turned her head just enough to spot Catch, lurking in the shadow of the stairs. Gone still as a carving of wood, he kept his eyes trained on Lord Ruthven Roebanks.

He wore an expression of immense weariness.

CHAPTER THIRTEEN:
THE NOT-SO-SECRET GARDEN

"I'm so sorry about Miss Beige," said Ascot, reaching for another cake.

"I'm not," Maggie replied. Grinning, she poured two glasses of lemonade and refilled the sandwich platter. The six crystal stars Ascot had given her sparkled around her neck, restrung on a length of white ribbon.

The faded blue bedspread made a decent blanket for their improvised picnic. There was roast chicken with a crisp, honey-glazed skin, cold potato soup, creamed herring and hard-boiled eggs. Plus, sharp cheese with mustard, soft rolls, and little iced buns. There were even, briefly, three ripe avocados, but Rags-n-Bones grabbed these up and took them into a corner where he stroked each in turn before slicing them open and scooping out the buttery interiors with his fingers. It was slightly disturbing, so Ascot didn't watch.

"But I promised," said Ascot, accepting the lemonade from Maggie. Rubbing her thumb against the glass's long stem, she glanced towards the window. The long shadows of an early autumn evening tinted her room in shades of pewter gray and dusky violet. Only a little more than an hour until the meeting in the Cupid Chamber. "I said I'd look after Miss Beige, and she ended up throwing a shoe at Mr. Nutty instead. She could've been one of the ones meeting Bettina Anna tonight if she hadn't."

Of course, in the end, it only would've made a difference to my conscience, Ascot added silently. Parvanel would be hers. She had the promise—and threat—of the ring. If she hadn't, she might have pawned her pearl pendant and left Albright before the morning cock crowed. Even with the ring, she'd suffered more than a few misgivings after that farce of a ball, so before going to bed, she'd opened the white book. A couple hours' perusal of the stories assured her that trials and misunderstandings were perfectly standard before achieving one's Happily Ever After.

A tingle squirmed down her spine. Perhaps there'd be candelabras and flowers at tonight's meeting. Even more romantic than a ball, really. Her eyes would meet Parvanel's over the soft glow of candle flames—

"Ascot." Dmitri lifted his head from a whole roast chicken. "Are you paying any attention whatsoever?"

Hurriedly, Ascot dragged herself out of her fantasy. "Yes, of course. We were, er, talking about last night's ball."

"We were talking about Jane," said Maggie. "I'm glad she doesn't have to deal with Miss Roebanks' ilk any more. She's been put through enough."

"Yes, thank goodness she didn't bite into that awful apple," agreed Ascot.

"Apple?" asked Maggie.

"Didn't I tell you?" Uncrossing her legs, Ascot got up to fetch it. "She said it was a wishing apple." She went to the window where she'd hung it last night, still encased in the glove so its smell wouldn't stifle them. Even so, its sickly odor could be discerned over the sharp, briny scents of the pickled herring Moony was gobbling.

Returning to the bedspread, Ascot tried to shake the apple loose, but it stuck. She had to squeeze it out bit by bit, like forcing a snake to regurgitate, until it plumped, shining malignantly, onto the powder blue bedspread.

Dmitri recoiled, making disgusted whuffing sounds.

Moony gagged. "Ooh, it stings my nose."

"Wishing apple, my tail," said Dmitri. "Only if you wish to never awaken."

Maggie's dimples vanished. "I never thought Jane's parents would go so far," she said. "She could've been arrested for possessing that apple."

"Arrested?" One of Ascot's hands twitched towards the apple with the vague idea of grabbing it up and throwing it out the window. "Why arrested?"

"Because Jane's parents could only have gotten it from a rogue member of GEL or MAGI."

"GEL or MAGI?" asked Ascot.

"That's the Guild of Enchanting Ladies and the Magical Association of Gentlemen Intellectuals, respectively," said Dmitri. "They're the guilds for fairy godmothers, witches, sorcerers, and the like."

"They have *guilds*?"

"Of course they have guilds," said Dmitri. "You don't want a bunch of charlatans claiming they're wizards just because they know a little sleight-of-hand."

"That's right," said Maggie. "I hear a couple of hucksters sold this one king what they claimed was a magic robe, only they really had him walking around in the nip." She snorted a laugh. "But GEL and MAGI were banished from Albright soon after Bettina

Anna married King Alastor. A shame, really." Maggie's expression turned wistful. "The monarchs of Albright used to consult magicians all the time. King Alastor had his own personal Fairy Godmother and there was a court Wizard, Galfrandon, who used to delight the court with displays of exploding flowers."

Fairy Godmothers aren't allowed in Albright? Ascot twisted her ring on her finger. Surely it didn't count. She'd received it in Shadowvale, so it wasn't like she'd willfully broken any laws. At least it explained why the Fairy Godmother hadn't come to her aid in Albright. "Why did Bettina Anna banish them?" she asked.

Maggie shrugged. "Don't know. Odd, though. Rumor has it that King Alastor's Fairy Godmother is the one who arranged his marriage to Bettina Anna."

"Whatever the queen's reasons, I think we can assume GEL wasn't happy with the decision," said Dmitri. He pointed his nose towards the apple. "Miss Beige's parents probably made a deal that if she married Parvanel, GEL would be allowed back into the city."

Ascot picked the apple off the bedspread. It burned her hand like an iced rock. "Should I get rid of it?"

"Not in here," said Dmitri. "We'll take it outside the city and destroy it when we have the chance. Put it back in the glove for now."

The apple did not seem to want to return to the glove. Twice it slipped out of her grip and once it dropped entirely and rolled across the floor towards Dmitri, who jumped out of its path. It took no bruising from its fall, but gleamed as spotlessly red as ever. Finally she squeezed it back into the glove. She stuffed it deep into a pocket of her leather coat. Only then did they all relax.

"Only an hour before your meeting," said Maggie, glancing out the window. She leaned back against Dmitri. Either she didn't notice that she was lounging against a giant wolf or she had just

137

become that accustomed to his presence. "I wonder if Captain Catch will be there?"

Surreptitiously, Ascot rubbed her bitten hand. The wound had faded to two small, purplish scabs. In her memories, she'd attempted to minimize Catch's presence at the ball. But the look on his face continued to haunt her. Haunt—yes; he'd looked haunted. Or hunted. A man with few lairs left to bolt to. *Not that I care. He's no friend of mine.*

"Ah, yes, Catch." Dmitri sat up, his nostrils flaring, as if taking in a succulent scent. "What do you know about him, Maggie? That accent. He isn't from Albright. Why does Bettina Anna trust him?"

Maggie pursed her lips. "The story I heard, the court held a riding party to celebrate King Alastor and Queen Bettina Anna's first anniversary. Someone, perhaps King Alastor himself, accidentally shot Catch, who was hunting nearby. King Alastor brought him back to the palace to recover and they became friends."

Dmitri's ears twitched. "But you said King Alastor and Bettina Anna were married over twenty years ago, right?"

"Twenty-three, I believe," said Maggie.

"Meaning Catch has lived in Albright for at least twenty-two years and yet doesn't look much older than Parvanel." Dmitri ran a paw down his muzzle. "Could he be a Shadowvalean?"

"Impossible," said Ascot, jolted into a response, no matter how little she wanted to discuss Catch. "He's not pale enough to be a noble Shadowvalean. And Shadowvalean humans age no differently from Daylander humans."

"Are you sure of that?" asked Dmitri.

"Of course I am." She wasn't. Her father had forbidden her to fraternize with the villagers. "I do *not* share a home country with that rogue. I still think he sent that beast to destroy my gown. He denied it, but he looked surprised when he saw the stars. Maybe we could—"

"Skulk around the castle in hopes of finding his hidden lair where he writes all his secrets in a little red book?" asked Dmitri. "Presumably while emitting maniacal cackles?"

It's what happens in the stories. Ascot choked it down. "We could check out the secret passage the beast came through, behind the bas-relief."

Maggie paused in gathering the empty plates. "That's not secret. You just push down on the grapevine and it opens. We maids use it as a short cut to the laundry and kitchen."

Ascot had registered the occasional sounds of footsteps in the hall, but paid them little heed. Now that she listened, she could tell that they were actually going past her room, beyond the point where the hallway supposedly ended. Curious, she opened the door and peeked out. A maid trotted past, her arms filled with linen. The bas-relief at the "dead end" of the hall was swung to one side, revealing a square passage of dun-colored bricks lit with gaslights; depressingly mundane, not the stalactite-and-spider-ridden tunnel she'd envisioned.

Maggie stepped past her, carrying the jingling tray of dishes. "See?" she said. "I can use it to take this back to the kitchen."

Dmitri paced out into the hall. Moony swiftly donned his cape, boots, and hat and hopped on his back. "Does the passage lead anywhere other than the kitchen and laundry?" Dmitri asked Maggie.

"Yes. If you take the left turn it leads to a garden, one with statues and flowers in big stone urns."

"That's it," said Ascot. "The beast had to come from there. They'd have noticed it in the laundry or kitchen. I could use some fresh air anyway, so let's check it out. Come on, Rags," she called back into the room.

He looked up, green pulp smearing his mouth. "What about your meeting?"

"It's still an hour off. Come on. You can bring your avocado."

Reassured, he followed her into the hall. Dmitri's rear end stuck out of the brick passageway while his nose snuffled along its walls.

"Look," he said. "A tuft of fur."

Leaning close, Ascot saw it: a sandy-brown bit of fluff snagged on the rough edge of a brick. She plucked it free.

"What color was the creature?" she asked Rags-n-Bones.

He tugged his chin. "Pale brown with cream mottling, especially on its back and shoulders. Big teeth. Greeny-gold eyes."

Pale brown. Ascot rolled the fur between her fingers, then tucked it into a pocket. "Let's visit the garden."

Her boots tapped against the passage's smooth floor, sending faint reverberations down the corridor. Thirty feet on, the square passage branched off to the right. The salty scent of soup and the sharp tang of chopped herbs perfumed the air. Pans clattered. Someone shouted for pepper.

"There's the kitchen," said Maggie. "The garden's the next branch-off. Try not to end up in the laundry."

"Do you know if there are any hidden passages?" asked Dmitri.

"Never heard of any," called Maggie over her shoulder. "Good luck tonight!"

Ascot slapped her hand against the wall. The bricks felt properly solid, rough, cold, and in all ways, brick-ish. She tested the mortar with her fingernail and it did not crumble. "Hard to conceal a secret door in a wall like this."

"I agree." Dmitri lowered his head and nosed about. Moony jumped off his back and joined him on the floor. "Can you smell it?" Dmitri asked after a few sniffs.

"It's the same catty sort of scent that was in the room." Moony scratched his ear with a hind foot, hissing when his boot sole clouted his head. "I've smelled something like it before, but I can't remember where."

"Nor can I," said Dmitri.

Rags-n-Bones started to crouch for a whiff, but Ascot grabbed his collar. "Is it the same creature that tried to eat my dress?" she asked.

"Unquestionably. But what it is or why it did it I still can't say." Dmitri sniffed further up the passage. "More traces of it here."

As they left the kitchen behind, the passage grew darker, the gaslights farther spaced than before. The temperature dropped slightly, and a faint breeze tugged the little hairs at Ascot's temples. Twenty steps further, the passage forked to the left. Putting his nose to the floor, Dmitri practically inhaled it. "The beast definitely came this way," he said.

Dim yellow light speared through the cracks around a wooden door at the end of the left-hand passage. Cool air, redolent of greenery and damp stone, brushed Ascot's face as she drew back the door's bolt and descended three chipped slate steps into a hidden world.

"It's beautiful," she said.

She stood in a sunken garden: a box decorated in a thousand shades of green. Three moss and ivy-covered slopes angled gently upwards to meet the high walls which surrounded it, shutting it off from the outside world. The evening shadows that had colored her room pewter and violet painted the garden in smoked blueberry and plum. Tangled morning glory vines obscured the crumbling red bricks of two of the walls. The third bore a gray crisscrossing of climbing roses. A few flowers still bloomed in defiance of the cold, their petals the pale yellow of a tart wine. Between a pair of curved stone benches stood the statue of a woman with folded wings; long and scaly, like a dragon's rather than a swan's. A little quirk to her lips said she had watched the world sweep by for many years and found it all quite amusing.

Ascot took a deep breath of air sweetened with aged violets and crushed moss. "I wish I'd known of this garden yesterday."

"Yes. We might have prevented the attack on your dress," said Dmitri. He stared at the soft ground, gave in, and rolled. Moony leaped at an early moth.

Some of the pleasure went out of her surroundings. "Right." Ascot glanced around, not sure what she was looking for.

Dmitri shook himself, crushed greenery streaking his coat. "The cat-creature's been here, but there's a lot of human scent mixed up with its smell. I suspect half the servants in the castle slip out here for a break."

A brown lump lay in the leaves near one of the benches. Ascot prodded it with a toe, recognizing it as the crust of one of last night's custard tarts. "They sneak out leftovers from the kitchens."

"Seems the only castle staff that doesn't come here regularly is the gardeners. That blackberry needs pruning." Dmitri's eyes narrowed. "And look at those steps."

"Steps?" said Ascot.

His snout pointed towards the ivy-coated wall opposite the door that led into the castle. She walked closer and there they were, obscured by vines, made of the same old red brick as the walls. Some of the bricks had nearly crumbled away, dandelions poking up between the cracks. The steps led to an old iron gate, red-brown with rust and tangled with weeds.

"No one's used them for years," she said.

Rags-n-Bones swallowed his last bite of avocado. "How did the beast get in here, miss? If it jumped that gate, it would have torn the ivy to shreds."

"Could it have leaped over one of the other walls?" asked Moony.

"Even if it did, it would still have to open both the door from the garden into the hidden passage and the bas-relief leading into Nosegay Wing," said Dmitri. "Either it's an intelligent beast like

142

myself, or it has a human master—haha!" His eyes lit up. He waited, reeking of expectant triumph.

Ascot sighed. "What did you figure out?"

Delight in his own cleverness was probably the only thing that stopped him from keeping her in suspense. "Remember Bettina Anna's challenge to tame the beast in the northern woods? She meant for you to meet this creature."

Moony flicked his ears. Rags-n-Bones blinked. Groping behind her, Ascot located the seat of one of the benches and guided herself into it. Two or three notions struck her at once.

"Don't you see?" said Dmitri. "I mentioned that the humans had scared all the other large animals away from Albright. If Ascot had encountered this beast, as intended, she never would've been able to tame it. It may even have attacked her."

Moony snarled.

"Oh, dear!" cried Rags-n-Bones.

"The task would've been impossible, had you not met me by a sheer fluke." Dmitri's tone sharpened. "Bettina Anna set you up to fail. She is not on your side."

For some reason, her father's stupid wolf rhyme kept repeating inside Ascot's mind. *Bettina Anna is not on your side. Wolf, oh wolf—* she shook her head, blushing. Had she really tried to tame Dmitri with that nonsense?

"Ascot?" asked Dmitri.

Yes, she'd recited that silly poem, and then Rags-n-Bones had started dancing, and then Dmitri stepped into the clearing—

No, that isn't it. Something that happened before.

Before. Rags-n-Bones carrying Nipper. The cold wind and the trees. One of the trees turning to look at her—

Oh, frabjacket.

"Ascot?"

Ascot raised her head. "You said this creature either has a master or is an intelligent beast. What if there's a third option?" Her voice, barely rising above the damp wind beginning to ruffle the ivy, rang hollow in her ears. "What if it's both?"

"Both?" said Moony. "What do you—" He stopped. Rags-n-Bones still looked confused, but the flattening of Dmitri's ears told her he'd got it.

Holding up a hand, Ascot ticked off points. "I told you that the crystal stars on my gown surprised Catch, as if he'd seen it before I sewed them on. Then, when we danced, I saw his reflection in the floor. I blamed the confusing lights, but it's actually the wrong shape." Her laugh emerged strangled and high-pitched. "He does have very sharp teeth."

Rags-n-Bones gasped. Moony's eyes went round as coins. "Ascot, do you really think—"

"Catch is a shape-shifter. *He's* the beast."

Even saying it, she could scarcely believe it. Shadowvale was copiously supplied with werewolves, but a were-giant-cat-with-long-teeth . . .

The sky melted into oranges and pinks as the sun sank. Doves cooed, crickets sang, and eventually Ascot managed a laugh, something a bit more natural and unforced. "Well, it wasn't a little red book in a secret chamber, but . . ."

Dmitri groaned. "Gloating is unbecoming."

CHAPTER FOURTEEN:
TESTING ONE'S PATIENCE

But as they trekked back to her room, doubts gathered. What proof did she have? A peculiar reflection, some enigmatic glances, and a chance meeting in the woods. "Maybe Catch isn't a shape-shifter," she said.

Dmitri didn't pause or look around. "Maybe not."

Did that mean he wasn't convinced, either? Brooding, Ascot stuffed her hands in her pockets and touched a wad of softness. That tuft of fur. She drew it out. Did it match Catch's hair? "What if he is?"

"If he is, Bettina Anna already knows, so we can't blackmail—excuse me, bribe him—with the information." Dmitri changed his wording when Rags-n-Bones shot him a scandalized look.

"I could take him," muttered Moony, scuffing his boots against the passage bricks.

"So we didn't discover anything useful after all," said Ascot.

"Excepting that one of your adversaries might be able to transform into a giant cat and the queen wanted you out of this competition from the very beginning? No, I suppose nothing useful at all."

Dmitri could give lessons in sarcasm. Ascot stifled a sharp retort. She feared he might be right about Bettina Anna. *I bet she never let Prince Parvanel read the stories,* she thought. *That must be why he didn't look at me last night. She's kept him from learning how Happily Ever Afters work.*

Well, Bettina Anna couldn't keep Parvanel from looking into her eyes tonight. True Love would finally triumph, as the white book said it always did. "Do you think I should wear my green gown to the meeting?" she asked, pushing the bas-relief wide and stepping down onto the floor of the Nosegay Wing.

"Umm." Moony scuffed his boots again. "It might have some hairs on it."

"Oh, Moony, you didn't sleep on it, did you?" She'd been so careful, laying it across the chair before going to bed hanging upside-down in the wardrobe.

His chin came up. "I'm a cat."

Sighing, Ascot went into her room. The dress *did* have hairs on it—a whole crushed circle lined with gray fuzz, right in the middle of the skirt. She sighed again, heavier this time. Moony looked unrepentant.

"Just wear what you have on," said Dmitri before they could quarrel.

I'm going to look so ridiculous if the others are wearing gowns, thought Ascot, running a hand over her trousers.

Abruptly, she changed her mind. So what if she was wearing trousers? They were clean—Maggie had washed them while she slept—and at least she didn't resemble a polished lemon.

I'll say it's the fashion in Shadowvale if anyone asks. Maybe she *would* start a fashion in trousers, once she was queen.

Once she was queen. A warm shiver shook her from head to toe. "Let's get going," she said.

"You're cheerful," Dmitri observed as she skipped into the hall. Catching the silliness from her, Rags-n-Bones cartwheeled down the length of the purple carpet.

Laughing, Ascot leaped to touch a bundle of dried lavender hanging on the wall. "Why shouldn't I be? I'm about to meet my True Love."

"You're quite certain Parvanel's your True Love?"

"My ring glowed around him." She flourished it. "Besides, True Loves are always princes, according to the stories."

"Not Dostoyevsky's stories."

"He writes the wrong kind of story, then." A sprig of lavender broke off in her hand. Twirling it between her fingers, Ascot regarded Dmitri, who sat in Miss Tumberfelt's abandoned doorway, head tilted to the right, as if her perspective was so askew he had to look sideways just to see it straight.

"Why are you helping me if you think I'm mistaken?" she asked. "Is finding a copy of *The Dunce* all you care about?"

"*The Idiot*," Dmitri corrected with gentle horror.

"Fine, *The Idiot*. You know you'll only get it if I become queen. So for all your grumbling, you must believe I'm right." She spun the lavender victoriously. *Got you there, didn't I, Mr. Smarty-wolf?*

Dmitri peeled back his lips, eyes squinting in a wolf-grin. "Perhaps I'm staying for your scintillating conversation."

Storm clouds rumbled across Ascot's clear horizon. The lavender's stem snapped in her grip.

"Oh, don't pout." He butted her hip gently. "It's not far off the truth. I'm not allowed many chances to—hang on." His ears quirked towards the door marked *Miss Roebanks*. "Who is she talking to in there? Shouldn't she be heading for the Cupid Chamber?"

Moony pressed against Miss Roebanks' door. "Sounds like Miss Maverly."

"Miss Maverly? What's she doing in the castle?" Dmitri snorted. "The rejected candidates left this morning."

"Maybe Miss Roebanks got permission for her to stay." Shrugging off the shivery insect-leg sensation creeping along her back, Ascot started walking again. Dmitri and Moony followed, but not, she noticed, before casting glances at Miss Roebanks' shut door.

Two maids watched Ascot out of the corners of their eyes as she crossed the hexagonal honeybee room. A footman scrutinized her while she walked down the hall with the picture of the child in the starched ruff. So did a butler, when she rounded the corner to the Cupid Chamber.

"What are all the fishy looks for?" asked Ascot.

"They're probably wondering if this is the last time they'll see you," said Dmitri.

Ascot reminded herself—again—not to turn to Dmitri for reassurance. Rags-n-Bones shivered and trod on her heels. Even Moony walked with less of a strut.

Ahead, the chubby, gilded cherub flashed in the light of a candle left on a table outside the door, every bit as hideous as she remembered. *I'll have it chiseled off tomorrow*, she promised herself. For now, she allowed herself the luxury of turning her back on it.

"Don't worry," she told her comrades. "Tonight, I become the princess bride. Then, Dmitri, you'll move into the library. You'll never go hungry again, Rags, and as for Moony," she smiled at her oldest friend, "you'll get a whole garden of big, fluttery bugs to jump at."

"Can I still be your guardsman?" he asked.

"You'll always be my guardsman."

His tail rose to its usual jaunty angle. Rags-n-Bones stopped quivering. Dmitri, she suspected, was doing that thing where he would've raised an eyebrow if he had one, but she hadn't spoken for his sake. Adding another smile for comfort, she pushed open the door.

Darkness shrouded the audience chamber. Ascot stopped in the doorway, wondering if she'd accidentally entered the wrong room. No; there couldn't be two of those cupids. Even as she reassured herself, her eyes adjusted enough to see Queen Bettina Anna standing on the dais in a circle of light cast by six lanterns carried by uniformed guardsmen. Her dress for the evening was a sober, if elegant, dark brown. Every so often, a lantern would flare, creating a momentarily blinding flash as it struck a piece of gilding hitherto cloaked by shadow.

"Do come in, Miss Abberdorf," said Bettina Anna's cracked-flute voice.

Ascot jumped. "Sorry," she said, and hurried inside. She banged her shins on an inexplicable footstool hidden by the darkness, stifled a curse, and finally reached the foot of the dais where Scincilla already waited, dressed, Ascot noticed, in a plain cotton gown.

"Ascot." Scincilla took her hand and squeezed. "I'm so glad you're here," she whispered. "This isn't what I was expecting at all."

Nor I. Ascot returned the pressure. She'd expected—

Movement by the side of the dais. A slim figure moved through the shadows, head held high.

Ascot's heart shot into her throat. *Prince Parvanel!* She glanced quickly down at her left hand, but her ring remained dark.

Cloth whisked. No, not cloth; something heavier. Leather. Ascot's heart dropped. By the time the figure neared the edge of lantern light and his features resolved into Catch's, it had returned to its proper position in her chest.

Catch again. Why was it always Catch instead of Parvanel? She fingered the tuft of fur in her pocket, then looked around as the cupid door creaked and Miss Roebanks and Lord Roebanks entered. Apparently in no hurry, they strolled down the white carpet, a footman in red livery lighting their way with a brass lantern. Miss Roebanks wore plain muslin and her face had been carefully painted to make her look fragile and innocent. A well-tailored black suit replaced Lord Roebanks' embroidered silks, but his ruby still sparkled on his finger.

"So we are gathered," said Bettina Anna without preamble as the Roebanks joined Ascot and Scincilla at the foot of the dais. "The law of Albright states that my son cannot be crowned before he is wed. You three, the last remaining candidates, shall undergo a test to prove your worth this evening."

Ascot winced as Scincilla's grip abruptly tightened.

"The one who completes her task most successfully shall be toasted as the princess bride at a banquet, which will be held tomorrow night. Your tasks all relate to this banquet."

Another test. Oh, Ascot knew what was going on now. Someone—the back of her neck ached with the effort of not shooting a glower at Lord Roebanks—must have guessed the import of her glowing ring and concocted this test in order to get her disqualified before she and Parvanel could meet. And the queen was going along with it. No, she was not on Ascot's side.

Her finger bones ground together. "Ease up, Cindy," she pleaded, but Scincilla seemed turned to stone. Ascot glanced past her to Miss Roebanks. Perfectly composed, as if she'd known precisely what was in store for them this evening. Ascot nodded grimly to herself, suspicions confirmed.

"We should make a start," said Lord Roebanks, patting his daughter's arm solicitously. "I believe there is a time restriction?"

Small muscles along Bettina Anna's jaw jumped. Her brows lowered just a fraction. But her voice remained perfectly modulated as she replied. "Yes, Lord Roebanks. The ladies have until seven o'clock tomorrow morning. If they do not return here by the last stroke of the great bell, they will be disqualified."

Now her lips curled, but only on one side. "Of course, they must accomplish these tasks unaided," she added, looking not-quite-pointedly at Lord Roebanks' hand on his daughter's arm.

"But—" The word burst out of Ascot.

"You have a complaint?" asked Lord Roebanks, still patting Miss Roebanks' arm as if to say: *look how hard this edict is on my poor, delicate daughter.*

"No." Ascot slumped.

Rags-n-Bones' mouth trembled. Dmitri emitted a soft growl and Moony lashed his tail.

"Let us proceed, then," said Bettina Anna, and stepped off the dais. The guardsmen stayed in formation, flanking her, keeping her in the center of the light. Ascot and Scincilla stumbled after as best they could, while the Roebanks followed under the guidance of their lantern-bearing footman. Catch, in shadows, brought up the rear.

"You'd better go back to Nosegay Wing," Ascot whispered to her friends.

Flattening his ears, Dmitri whined, looking from Bettina Anna to Lord Roebanks.

"It might be dangerous," wailed Rags-n-Bones.

Moony was silent.

"Of course it won't be dangerous. Anyway, I'll be disqualified if you come along." She forced a smile. "I'll be fine. Look, Cindy's all alone, and she's bearing up."

Scincilla's attempt at a smile resembled a rictus.

"But what if—" Rags-n-Bones began.

Ascot touched his lips gently, hushing him. "If the task is dangerous, I won't do it."

Sniffling, he wiped his nose on his arm. "Promise?"

"Promise. Go on, now. Sorry you have to wait another night for your avocados."

"I had avocados this afternoon. To receive even a single avocado in one's life is a great thing." He threw his arms around her, half-strangling her. "Be safe, miss."

Scincilla pulled at her hand. The Roebanks cast her snotty looks. "Thank you, Rags," gasped Ascot.

Dmitri took Rags-n-Bones' coattail between his teeth. "Come along, Prince Myshkin," he murmured.

Rags-n-Bones' grip loosened. The trio blended into darkness as Ascot went away with the light. Moony, she realized, had not said a word. Worrisome. Almost as worrisome as the satisfied smirk on Miss Roebanks' face. For the first time since leaving Shadowvale, she was completely alone. She felt as if she'd been stripped before a crowd.

Nonsense. The test won't be dangerous. She squeezed Scincilla's hand.

They climbed a grand staircase, carpeted in midnight blue, and wide enough to accommodate a pair of horses. It terminated in a long hall with ancient weaponry hanging on the paneled walls and suits of armor placed in alcoves. Scincilla walked mechanically at her side, but Miss Roebanks frequently ran her fingers over a sword's hilt or a smooth bit of paneling, as if already tallying up her winnings. Once, hearing a small pattering sound, like a spool of thread bouncing over the floor, Ascot paused. Miss Roebanks lingered by a suit of armor, craning her neck into the shadows. Noticing Ascot's stare, she scowled and retook her father's arm.

At the end of the hall, two guardsmen threw open a blue door. Without pause, Bettina Anna led the party inside. Ascot gasped, finding herself in the largest music room she'd ever seen, larger even than the one that housed her father's pipe organ back home. It contained six pianos, two organs, three harpsichords, and row upon row of violins, cellos, lutes, flutes, and oboes. Bookcases along the far wall overflowed with enough sheet music to keep the most fanatical musicians in chords for the rest of their lives.

"Music is necessary for a successful banquet," said Bettina Anna, having given them just enough time to grasp the enormity of the room. "Miss Harkenpouf, come."

Ascot's sweaty fingers un-cramped as Scincilla released her hand. Bettina Anna beckoned Scincilla down an aisle lined with dulcimers, stopping before a golden case large enough to drown five Dmitris in. The lead guardsman lifted his lantern, illuminating ten harps resting on velvet cushions beneath its glass lid.

"These harps are over a hundred years old," said Bettina Anna. "Some have not been played in decades. It is your task, Miss Harkenpouf, to restring and tune all ten before seven o'clock."

Well, that would have been the end for me, thought Ascot, relieved. But Scincilla curtsied, both resolve and a fragile optimism etched across her face. "As you command, Your Majesty," she said.

Ascot caught her eye. "Good luck," she mouthed. *What an odd thing to wish. I'm going to marry Parvanel, right? But I know she's scared.*

Bettina Anna led the way out of the music room. One of the guards set his lantern on the floor. He and the guard who had left his lantern inside with Scincilla took up positions before the door, making sure no one snuck in to help her.

The party returned to the winding stairs. On the stoop, Ascot's toe nicked a small round object, sending it clattering away. *What was that?* Stooping, she felt around the floor. Her hand closed on a hazelnut. What was that doing here?

Ahead, the party passed through yet another door, leaving her behind. Stuffing the nut into her pocket, Ascot jogged to catch up. Someone's dropped snack, she decided, and put it from her mind.

They creaked their way down a humbler staircase, winding up in a narrow white corridor with a diamond-patterned carpet that rattled when they tread on it. The lingering scents of spice and grease and yeasty dough tickled Ascot's nose. She'd already guessed their destination when the party entered an enormous kitchen. A red-tiled floor, huge black ovens, and what seemed to be miles of slate countertops spread out before them, fortified with armies of chopping blocks and platoons of carving knives. Herbs hung from the rafters in sweet or bitter-smelling bunches.

Could this be my task? Ascot held her breath. Miss Eppicutt had taught her the basics of cooking, mostly candied beetles and saffroned eels. This looked a fun place to explore.

But Bettina Anna beckoned to Miss Roebanks, who sent her father a resentful glower before stepping forward.

"Food is, of course, an essential component of a successful banquet," said Bettina Anna. "Miss Roebanks, your task is to bake a cake worthy of a king. It must comprise at least four tiers and be decorated with sugar flowers and other ornaments suited to the occasion."

A *cake*? All Miss Roebanks had to do was *bake a cake*? Yes, a large, fancy cake took time and effort, but did it really compare to stringing ancient harps?

The tasks in the book are never fair, Ascot reminded herself. Her nails bit into her palms.

"Don't fret, precious." Lord Roebanks chucked his daughter under the chin. "I'm sure you'll do splendidly. And after tonight, you'll never have to cook again."

What was so horrible about cooking? From Miss Roebanks' curdled expression, you'd think this coming night was set to be the greatest trial of her entire life.

"I will do as you command, Your Majesty." Miss Roebanks spread her skirts in a graceful curtsy, but Ascot suspected her bowed head hid a scowl.

A guardsman set a lantern on one of the counters. As the rest of the party moved on, he and another guard took up their posts outside the kitchen door.

Bang. Ascot jumped. Glancing back, she glimpsed Miss Roebanks thumping bowls onto the counter with greater force than necessary.

"She fusses, but she'll do just fine," said a jovial, paternal sort of voice.

Ascot jumped again. Lord Roebanks had moved, unnoticed, to walk beside her.

"I'm sure she will, sir," said Ascot after a pause. Her skin prickled on the side nearest him. *Maybe I'm allergic to insincerity.* She wished she had the guts to give him a good shove.

Catch still trailed, his hands in his pockets. She never heard his footsteps, but occasionally his coat rustled. Somehow, his presence was a comfort. At least he was honest about his lying.

"And you," said Lord Roebanks. "Do you feel adequate to the task ahead?"

"Hard to say when I don't know what the task is." What else did a banquet require? Music, food . . . silverware? Would she have to polish every fork in the castle by hand? It would be ironically appropriate, if she did. A few odd bits of purloined Shadowvalean cutlery still clinked in her coat.

"I believe Her Majesty has designated a very special task for you." Lord Roebanks smiled. His canine teeth weren't as sharp as Catch's, but for all that, he looked more predatory. Ascot discreetly moved a few inches further from him.

"You know what it is, then?" she asked as they returned to the white hallway. The diamond-patterned carpet rattled.

"I do." Lord Roebanks' smile sharpened.

Bettina Anna stopped in front of a small wooden door recessed deeply into the east wall. One of the guardsmen took a key from around his neck and inserted it into the large lock. With a grunt and a tug, he heaved the door open, revealing a worn brick landing and steep slat steps leading downward. A waft of air, damp and earthy-smelling, spilled into the hallway.

"You're not claustrophobic, I hope," said Lord Roebanks. "It's quite a long ways down."

Ascot stared into the narrow, dark mouth of the open door as it exhaled another musty gust of air into the corridor. She shivered.

CHAPTER FIFTEEN:
THE DEAD OF NIGHT

It wasn't the dark emanating from the doorway that made her blood run chill. Like most noble Shadowvaleans, Ascot possessed excellent night vision. But she was also half Daylander. Full-blooded noble Shadowvaleans . . .

Occasionally, full-blooded noble Shadowvaleans grew bored of existence and buried themselves. Alive. Like Vincent's mother. She'd entombed herself in one of Abberdorf Castle's gardens sometime before Ascot's father married her and Vlad's mother. Vincent adored pointing out the somber plot where she lay. *"Some night she'll dig herself back up,"* Vincent would say, grinning spitefully. *"I wonder what she'll think of you?"* Then he'd make a snapping gesture with his first two fingers and thumb.

Throughout her childhood, Ascot had spent long days lying awake in her coffin, imagining the *chuff* of dirt against rock as the muddy, emaciated woman dragged herself out of her self-made tomb and . . .

The first guard stepped through the doorway, vanishing as if swallowed. Ascot gulped.

Don't be a ninny, she chided herself. *You're not in Shadowvale. It's just a cellar down there. Nothing but mold and cockroaches.*

Bettina Anna and the second lantern-carrying guard started down the stairs. Lord Roebanks lingered another moment to give her a smile that wasn't really a smile before following the queen, his footman at his heels.

Gritting her teeth, Ascot set her foot on the top stair and her hand on the raw wood banister. The pool of lantern light shone several feet below her, descending steadily. She forced herself to take the next step. Then another, her soles squeaking on the slippery slats. There. Her chest loosened a bit.

At a small scuffing sound, she looked back. Catch stood in the open doorway, the dim shadow of a furrow between his brows. Abruptly, he puffed out his cheeks, turned, and shut the door behind him. Ascot resumed her own descent.

The staircase folded about itself, twisting into the castle's entrails. The walls, slimed with moisture, loomed closer, as if pushed forward by the weight of earth and stone behind them. *What could be down here that has anything to do with a banquet?* Ascot's shoulder accidentally brushed a wall. She shuddered, trying not to imagine what it would be like if the old stairs collapsed.

Stop dithering. She smacked a fist against her thigh. *Cindy and Miss Roebanks' tasks weren't dangerous, so yours won't be, either.*

The scolding helped calm the shivers. A little.

Twenty feet below her, the lanterns stopped; they must have reached bottom. Ascot hurried to catch up. Behind her came the creak of Catch following—even he couldn't walk silently on these old slats—and a soft skittering sound. A rat?

She rounded the final bend. Dust rose, clogging her nostrils, as she reached the queen's party, gathered on the last flight of steps. Braced for the worst, she took in her surroundings.

They stood in the center of a large, rough-hewn cave, its floor smooth from time and use. Immense wooden racks lined the walls, spanning the space from ceiling—and it was a very high ceiling—to floor. Every rack contained hundreds of square apertures, and out of every one of these apertures protruded glass tubes sealed with black, gold, or red wax.

"It's a wine cellar." Ascot nearly laughed, wishing Vlad was with her. He'd be skipping with delight. A faint echo of her words reverberated off the cavern walls.

"Indeed, Miss Abberdorf." Bettina Anna stepped onto the stone floor. A guardsman followed, raising his lantern. White crescent gleams winked off the rounded bodies of thousands of bottles. But one area gaped like a mouth. Wine racks did not completely surround them, after all. A murky passage in the far wall wafted damp, rot-and-wine soured air into the main chamber.

"Fine wine is necessary for a memorable banquet." Bettina Anna studied her rings.

"And so momentous an occasion requires a special vintage," said Lord Roebanks. He, his footman, and the second guard lingered on the last two steps, trapping Ascot in the middle of the flight. Behind her, Catch's breath ruffled the crown of her hair. Slowly, Lord Roebanks' head turned, revealing a smile of calm, spiteful triumph. "The Moonlight Muscatel."

One of Bettina Anna's guards fumbled his lantern.

"Your Majesty," began Catch, his normally indifferent voice sharp. "The Muscatel—"

"Were you given leave to speak, Captain?" said Lord Roebanks.

"This is the year the Moonlight Muscatel reaches perfection," said Bettina Anna, still examining her rings. "If it is not decanted, it

159

will sour." Her fingers snapped closed. "Alastor would not wish it wasted."

Catch's sigh warmed the outer curl of Ascot's ear.

"It is a fair trial," said Lord Roebanks. "With your aid, Miss Abberdorf, the Moonlight Muscatel shall be served at tomorrow night's banquet." Small crinkles appeared at the sides of his mouth. "Or you shall fail and it shall not."

I really should have shoved him earlier. Ascot folded her arms. "I suppose then I'll take comfort in the fact that Miss Roebanks won't have the best vintage to celebrate with."

"A very small comfort, I imagine," said Lord Roebanks.

Bettina Anna touched her temples, as if pained by a headache. Then, briskly, she strode towards a corner of the cavern, where a section of the wall bowed outwards like a thick stone column. "Here," she said, tracing the outline of a low door sunk into the column's surface. "Aged oak, four inches thick, reinforced with steel. The Moonlight Muscatel lies behind this door. Unfortunately, the key has been lost."

"You want me to pick the lock?" asked Ascot.

Lord Roebanks snorted. "Certainly not. You might damage it."

"Albright's best locksmiths have already failed to open it." Bettina Anna meandered back to the staircase, to all appearances deep in thought. "No, you must find the key, Miss Abberdorf. It was lost in the depths of the Great Wine Vault seven years ago."

Ascot frowned. Had Bettina Anna's flutey voice faltered a little?

Lord Roebanks took over. "The entrance to the Great Wine Vault lies there, to the north. You have until six o'clock to return with the key."

"The others have until seven," Ascot protested.

"All you need do is find a key." Lord Roebanks covered a yawn. "What difference will an hour make? Really, the queen's playing quite the favorite here."

"The favorite?" Ascot's hand tightened on the banister until the splintery wood bit back. "What do you mean?"

"Letting you loose to play in the cellars, I mean," he replied. "You should feel quite at home down here with the ghosts."

The banister snapped, barely audible over the blood pounding in her ears. Ghosts. "You rotten warg-rump, you," said Ascot. "When Count Vincent hears of this—"

The smile vanished from Lord Roebanks' lips as if it had been wiped away. "I do not believe your brother knows or cares that you are here," he said, poisonously soft. "I do not believe he will know or care if you vanish, buried forever in the depths of the Great Wine Vault. Go ahead, Miss Abberdorf. Inform me that I'm wrong."

Ascot's tongue lay in her mouth like a stone.

Inhaling deeply through his nose, Lord Roebanks regained calm. "You needn't accept the challenge, Miss Abberdorf. Do you yield?"

"Yield," breathed Catch, almost as silent as thought. "This task is too dangerous."

If he had only spoken one truth in his life, that had been it.

Ascot bowed her head. Somehow, she gathered a dollop of saliva in her mouth and swallowed it down. The sides of her throat unclenched. "No," she said. "I do not yield." She met Bettina Anna's gaze through the darkness of the cavern. "I'll find your key."

"Then best of luck to you, Miss Abberdorf," said Bettina Anna. Impossible to tell if she meant it or not. "Let her pass, Lord Roebanks."

Lord Roebanks drew back against the banister and Ascot squeezed past, trying hard not to brush him. "Accompany her, Captain," he said as her foot touched the floor.

A strand of tension hung in the air, ready to snap. "Sir?" Catch asked right before it did.

"To the Great Vault's door. It's locked and I'd rather not trust her with the key. A person with your skills should be safe enough."

"With your skills." Frabjacket, did Lord Roebanks know Catch's secret, too? Ascot would've bet her fangs he did.

"Go ahead, Captain," said Bettina Anna. "Accompany her."

Long seconds elapsed. "Very well, Your Majesty," Catch replied, his voice uninflected. "I will take her to the entrance." He slipped by Lord Roebanks without a glance in his direction.

Bettina Anna inclined her head. "Until six o'clock, Miss Abberdorf." Returning to the steps, she began ascending, accompanied by her lantern-bearing guards.

"Come to me after you lock the door behind her, Captain," said Lord Roebanks. Darkness reclaimed the great cavern as he followed the queen, his footman in tow.

Not going to leave me even one lantern? Ascot wondered why this should surprise her by now.

Close by, a match flared, illuminating the pale oval of Catch's face. Taking a small lantern from one of his pockets, he held the flame to the wick of the candle inside. The orange glow touched his tight-set mouth and the hollows under his cheekbones. "Why didn't you yield, fool?" he asked, shaking the match out.

"Would you? After *that?*" She flapped her hand in the direction of the receding light, no more than a firefly spark in the darkness above them.

Catch winced. "Lord Roebanks is curt with his social inferiors. Means—"

"Nasty," said Ascot. She didn't care what Catch's definition was.

"Surely you knew the competition was never meant to be fair."

Of course. The tests were never fair in the white book either. But—"*This* unfair?" she demanded, and Catch flinched, gaze falling to the gritty stone floor.

Why was Bettina Anna letting Lord Roebanks have it all his way? Did Lord Roebanks have some sort of hold over her? And if he did, why had she banished GEL and MAGI when they might've been able to help her? Had he forced her to do it, or was she just one of those evil queens so prevalent in the white book's stories?

Ascot rubbed the heels of her hands against her eyelids. No time to worry about that now. It had to be past nine already. "Let's go," she said, forcing herself to walk towards the gaping maw of the northern channel, away from the lantern's comforting light and warmth.

Light? Comfort? How strange. She liked darkness. Just not this darkness. Somewhere beyond, something malicious waited. She couldn't say why she was so sure, but she knew that she and Catch were not alone in the cellar's dank depths.

For a moment she feared he wouldn't follow. But he fell in beside her, holding the lantern before him. The tap of her boots against stone brought back all those childhood memories of lying awake, listening for the first faltering footsteps that would herald Vincent's mother rising out of her muddy grave.

Ugh. She contemplated whistling just to keep the silence at bay. Fortunately, before she grew desperate enough to try it, Catch spoke.

"I wasn't lying back there," he said, not looking at her.

"Really?" From somewhere in the darkness came a tiny rasping sound, as of claws scraping rock. Ascot rubbed her arms, pretending her shiver was from cold, not fear. "Do you need to sit down and recover from the shock?"

"I'm not lying now, either. You should give up your quest before you regret it."

She tried to study his profile, yellow-tinged by candlelight, but he averted his face. She looked to his shadow, moving along with his steady pace, but the flickering light made it dance and waver over the uneven stone and she couldn't tell if it matched his shape or not. Pale streaks of moisture marked the walls, glistening like the tracks of snails. Away from the relatively clean area near the staircase, dust coated the racks and bottles in a layer a quarter-inch thick. The heavy air reeked of earth and mold and, faintly, underlying the other scents, the acidic tang of wine.

"Is the Great Wine Vault really so dangerous?" she asked. She'd never heard of ghosts harming anyone. They were insubstantial, weren't they?

"King Alastor's grandfather was an oenophile," said Catch, his voice as measured as his tread. "Means 'adored wine.' On his command, the cellars beneath Albright Castle were repeatedly enlarged to house his collection. He even recruited MAGI to magically double the available space beneath the castle. One day, the workmen broke through the wall of the old royal crypt."

"Crypt?" Ascot glanced around, half-expecting to see bones poking out of the walls. Only dust and shards.

Catch clicked his tongue. "It's a ways off, deep in the Great Vault. Anyway, when they breached the crypt, falling rocks struck a nearby cask. It split, and five hundred gallons of Burgundy poured over the floor and soaked into the graves. Magic and wine mingle strangely. The first ghost to rise was Artful Prince Alec, who had been buried at the very back of the tomb in hope that historians would fail to remember him."

"Why?" asked Ascot.

"Artful Prince Alec began life as the thirty-sixth contender for the throne. By the time they figured out what he was up to, he was eighth in the line of succession, and by the time they managed to do anything about it, second."

"Oh." Ascot glanced around, feeling the walls press closer on each side, as if they, too, were listening. "Nice."

"Prince Alec's henchman, Jeck the Chipper, woke next."

"The Chipper?"

"The most cheerful assassin in Albright's history." Catch's lips pulled into something vaguely like a smile. "They beheaded him after Prince Alec, ah, met with an accident. It's not too late to turn back, Miss Abberdorf."

Ascot hesitated. "How many ghosts are there?"

"No one's ever counted, but from the sounds, Prince Alec and Jeck must have awakened everyone in both the royal crypt and the old graveyard for the castle servants. Every night they rise and drink themselves silly."

Ascot's mouth opened.

"Don't ask me how," he said, and she closed it again. "All I know is that if you listen at the entrance, you can hear them carousing. No, I know one other thing. Seven years ago, the Head Butler entered the Great Wine Vault and never returned. He had the key to the Moonlight Muscatel in his pocket."

"How . . . how far did he go into the Great Wine Vault?"

"Far enough that no one has ever dared look for the key, even during the day, and with a dozen lanterns." He drew a breath. "What will happen when Prince Alec runs out of wine is anyone's guess. Everyone hopes they'll sleep, but I have my doubts. Cats don't return to their bags so easily."

Speaking of cats, perhaps she should ask him about . . . No, she had no idea how to broach the subject, and if she asked him straight out, he'd probably lie. Probably not too important, anyway, considering the circumstances. With an entire vault of drunken ghosts awaiting her, one man transforming into a giant cat seemed a trifling concern.

"Listen." Catch stopped abruptly. His breath rose in plumes of white mist.

Ascot stopped, too. Without her footsteps to mask it, faint cheers of raucous delight echoed from somewhere up ahead. Oaths were shouted, glass shattered and wood splintered.

"Sounds like they're very whatever-the-dead-equivalent-of-lively is tonight," said Catch, twirling the lantern. Its light shivered and splayed, sending shadows spinning maniacally across the floor, wall, and ceiling. "Come now, Miss Abberdorf. If you believed I was lying, surely you realize your error now. Give up your quest."

Ascot strode past him. "Thanks, Captain. I can find my way from here."

He grabbed her arm. "Ascot. They will kill you."

"No. I didn't come this far to be murdered by ghosts." She tried to pull free, but his grip tightened. "Let me go!" she cried, flailing at him with her free arm.

Catlike, he maintained both his grip and his balance. The lantern, held high in his spare hand, swung crazily. "I should drag you away," he said through his teeth. She stomped on his foot and he sucked in a hiss of air, but didn't release her. "Even if I must knock you unconscious and tie you up, it would be kinder than letting you continue."

Ascot quit struggling and glared. "So, if you can overpower me, that proves you're right?"

He froze. Then, in two precise, deliberate moves, he dropped her arm, stepped back, and sighed. "Why are you so determined to go through with this? You can't be in love with Parvanel. You've never met him."

Ascot rubbed her arm, glaring and resentful. "And who's to blame for that? You're just like Vincent. You're so miserable you can't bear the idea of me being happy."

He arched his brows. "Are you incapable of being happy without Parvanel?"

Ascot blinked. "It's . . . my ring . . . and it's in the stories." Blinking again, she resaid the words inside her head.

They didn't sound any better.

Catch looked away. "The vault's entrance is just a bit further." He shook the creases out of his coat and began walking.

Ascot stared at his retreating back. "Now you're letting me go, just like that?" she asked, sprinting to catch up.

"Far be it from me to stand between you and your acquisition of happiness. I mean, if it's in the *stories*."

Ascot set her jaw and walked, staring straight ahead. Twenty feet on, the lantern's glow picked out the end of the passage. A door fit for the mouth of a dungeon blocked the way. Thick boards, crudely hewn from gnarled old tree trunks, had been nailed into a plank about four feet wide and eight feet tall, and reinforced with iron bars.

"A dragon couldn't smash through that," said Ascot.

"Let's pray the ghosts can't, either," said Catch, setting a key in the lock. "It's a silver lock and key. They say silver keeps ghosts out, but I think it's just as likely that the wine is keeping them in." The key clicked as it turned in the lock; a small, crisp sound like a fresh carrot being snapped in half.

A sudden silence fell on the other side of the door.

"They heard. They'll be ready for you." Catch was using his indifferent voice again. He pressed the silver key into her hand. "I have its mate. I'll lock the door behind you, but you can unlock it if you need to beat a retreat."

"But the door probably won't hold them back if they're determined."

"Probably not. But a little protection is better than none." He handed her the lantern and dug a second candle out of his pocket. "You might need these as well."

"Thanks. Uh, matches?"

He pulled a box out of another pocket and handed it to her. How many other items did he have stashed away in his coat? *Maybe I should ask if he has some ghost repellant.*

No, now was not the time to break out in hysterical giggles; he might try to drag her away again.

"Well. I'm going in." Grasping the enormous iron latch, she heaved. Sweat popped out all over her body. The door grumbled open an inch. Two inches.

Catch gripped the latch just below her hands, adding his strength to hers. Together they dragged the great door open, its hinges screeching like deranged hags. A wash of air, cold as a fish's breath, gushed out, smelling of old ice and spilled wine and things that had for decades lain quietly in the ground.

"Last chance to turn back," said Catch.

"I won't," she said, and winced. Their voices echoed, overly loud and sibilant, against the eerie stillness. Beyond the door, something held its breath in eager anticipation, awaiting her arrival.

"Then go," he said. "Keep the candle lit. Don't lose the key."

"Thanks for the advice." Despite her resolve, Ascot shuddered on the threshold, more than a little remorseful. This was not at all what she'd promised Rags-n-Bones when she said she wouldn't do anything too dangerous.

"One more piece," said Catch. "Don't die." He clapped her on the shoulder, then pushed her hard enough that she was forced to take a step. Forced to feel how the temperature plummeted beyond the door. Maybe even forced to consider turning back one last time.

Ascot turned the forced step into a series of steps. *It's easier to keep going once you've begun*, she told herself. She concentrated on keeping a firm grip on the lantern, holding it steady. The cavern door was still open behind her. She could still turn back.

"Close the door," she said between her teeth. "Do it now."

For a moment she thought he wouldn't obey. Then the hinges squealed. The open space at her back grew smaller and smaller until, with a final shudder and bang, the great door closed and there was nowhere for her to go but forward.

CHAPTER SIXTEEN:
THE GRAPES OF WRATH

A wave of terror threatened to roll Ascot under as the great door boomed shut behind her. Just as she rode it out, there came the small, dry click of Catch's key in the lock and it rose again.

Alone with the ghosts.

She gulped a few times, concentrating on breathing in through her nose and out through her mouth, forcing her chest to rise and fall with slow regularity. There. Better.

Something brushed her ankle.

Her ears winced at the note that emerged from her throat. *It's just a rat. A rat*, she insisted, stomping wildly at dark patches on the floor. *You're not scared of rats. Smash it and save it to eat later.*

"Mwer! Careful, Ascot! You almost mashed my tail."

Ascot stopped in mid-stomp, her right foot suspended in midair. "Moony?"

"Of course." Close to the floor, two bright orange ovals flared. "I couldn't let you face this alone."

"Moony!" She knelt, setting the lantern by her side. The pale light illuminated the little cat, dressed in boots, cape, and hat, whiskers pulled back in a self-congratulatory smirk. Thick dust coated his fur and an angry spider lowered itself off the tip of one wing. "I thought I heard something a couple times."

"I've been following you all evening," said Moony. "Fancy Miss Roebanks only having to bake a cake."

"Well, when I'm queen, I'll have my cake and eat it, too," Ascot laughed, knowing it was ridiculous to feel so much more confident now. Just seeing Moony lifted her spirits. Picking up the lantern, she brushed off her knees and stood. "Let's get going. I'll lecture you later on how you shouldn't have come."

"Of course I had to come. I'm your guardsman." Moony fluttered his wings to keep pace with her.

"Oh? And what did Dmitri say about that?"

"I didn't wait long enough to find out. Listen!" Moony froze at a sudden, discordant jangling from beyond the curve in the wall. "Something just shattered."

"Sounded like a bottle breaking."

"Sounded like several bottles breaking."

Ascot strained her eyes, trying to pierce the darkness. Which, she realized with mounting dread, had changed at some point into not-entirely-darkness. The wall's curve hid the source of an eerie green glow that played along its smooth surface, puddling at the bend, transforming the wine racks into emerald-tinted skeletons, and making the bottles glitter beneath their coating of dust. Ghostlight.

"Maybe they'll be so drunk they won't even notice we're here." Ascot began walking again. Really, what else was there to do? It wasn't as if avoiding the light and sticking to the shadows made sense. Ghosts probably loved shadows.

Another drunken whoop echoed down the narrow passage. *I could still turn back*, she thought, hating herself for it.

"Ascot?" asked Moony, brushing against her leg.

With an effort, Ascot bent back the cold fingers of panic squeezing her heart until their grip loosened and she could breathe again. "We have to mark our path. Sooner or later, these passages will branch off." She scratched a wall. Solid stone; forget about gouging a mark into them. "Maybe I have something we can drop," she said, searching her deep pockets. Her remaining bits of silverware. That inexplicable hazelnut; too bad she didn't have a whole sack of them. Oh, dear—the apple-filled glove. A piece of string.

Her left fingers encountered something smooth, heavy, and tubular. "Hm?" She pulled it out and a flash of silver caught the light. "Oh, Moony, look."

Miss Eppicutt's can of hash was a bit more battered than when she'd taken it from Abberdorf Castle's larder. A corner of its brown paper label had peeled off, exposing the tin beneath.

"How'd that get in your pocket?" asked Moony, standing on his boot-tips, his eyes round.

"Catch must've slipped it into my pocket while we were opening the door," said Ascot. "I was right. He is a shape-shifter. No wonder he was angry when we met him by the gate. He was the beast in the bushes and I'd just chucked this can at him."

"Why'd he give it back now?"

Ascot ran a finger along the can's raised rim. "I don't know. His way of confessing? Maybe an apology?" Shaking her head, she tucked the can back in her pocket. "Still, it doesn't help us mark our trail. If only I'd brought some pebbles. It's—"

"What they do in the stories." Moony's nose wrinkled. "And the next time they scatter breadcrumbs, which the birds eat. Let's forget the stories for now." Baring his claws, he tore a strip of green cloth off the corner of his cape.

Ascot caught her breath. "Moony—"

He let it spiral to the ground. "There, that should do," he said, avoiding her eyes. "Let's get going." He tromped off, leaving the scrap of cloth lying on the gray floor like a fallen summer leaf.

My first action as queen will be to buy him a red velvet cape with silk lining. Ascot checked the candle in the lantern, double-checked her pocket to make sure the spare candle and matches were still there, then bounced on her heels to limber up. "All right," she told herself. "There are ghosts ahead. Ready?"

She wasn't. But it would have to do. She crept forward.

Tension amplified every sound. The accidental scrape of her heel against the cavern's side rasped like sandpaper over glass. To her ears, at least. The ghosts, presumably involved in drunken revelry, didn't notice, or at least didn't come pouring down the passage in a great glowing mass, eager to induct her into their ranks. The eldritch glow brightened, revealing what shouldn't have been visible and leaving what normal light would have illuminated cloaked in blackness. Strange patterns twisted on the air currents, vanishing before she could decipher them.

Moony waited by the crook in the passage. A circle of wavering green light shimmered on the opposite wall. Moony batted at it tentatively, then met Ascot's eyes. She nodded. Together, they turned the corner. Ten steps on, the narrow corridor opened into a room. Ascot and Moony froze on the threshold. Gone equally quiet and still, the room's occupants stared back.

Two rough plank tables with benches to match formed an aisle down the center of a long, narrow room. A writing desk of more refined construction sagged against the back corner, the ink in its well long dried, tattered quill pens strewn across its surface. Underfoot, a carpet that must once have been a deep burgundy color frayed into threads. Years and dust had faded it to a dingy, raw-liver pink. Cracked clay pitchers lay scattered about the room.

Ascot only dimly noticed the peripheral details. Her eyes were nailed to the ghosts.

Oh, the ghosts! She counted seventeen before her vision blurred. Phantoms crowded the benches along the long tables, thronged the carpet, and lounged against the walls. Some were tall. Some were stout. Some had gray beards, others were mere youths. There were distinguished gentlemen in tights and tunics out of fashion for over a century, and maids wearing low-cut smocks and knowing smiles. Only two characteristics did they share: a flagon in the hand, and eager, glittering eyes focused towards the threshold.

Ascot cleared her throat and instantly wished she hadn't. It was such a warm, *living* noise. Besides, she already had their attention.

Too late for regrets. "Can you tell me where to find the Head Butler?" she asked.

Their responding cheer shot through her eardrums like a squirt of cold water. One enterprising dead lady leaped onto a tabletop and began jigging, flinging her skirts high. Other ghosts pounded their flagons against the tables, or the walls, or one another. Most alarming of all were the half dozen or so who charged her, arms outstretched, their translucent faces lit with ferocious joy. Ascot barely had time to flinch before they engulfed her.

So much for Happily Ever Afters. Well, if there's a next time, I hope I do better. I'm sorry, Dmitri, Rags. I wasn't careful. Moony, run while you can. Catch, you were right. I was foolishly stubborn.

The ghosts swarmed her, hooting in her ears. Their fists pummeled her back, a sensation akin to being assaulted with wads of frozen silk.

"At last!" Bitter cold lanced Ascot's skin as the foremost gentleman seized her hand, shaking it between both of his. A huge, curling mustache and a thin pointed beard took up a third of his face. His attire, consisting of a starched ruff, an orange doublet, pumpkin breeches, and blue tights with a prominent codpiece, would have sent Ascot into peals of laughter under ordinary circumstances. The fact that he was dead made it all less risible.

Then his words penetrated. "At last?" she repeated, surreptitiously flexing her fingers. "What do you mean, at last?"

Thankfully, he released her hand. Stepping back, he swept her a bow of such elegance that any lingering humor over his attire vanished. "You inquired after the Head Butler. That means you seek the Moonlight Muscatel. Is that not true, my lady?"

"The Moonlight Muscatel! The Moonlight Muscatel!" a chorus of ghosts whispered reverently, their voices echoing and overlapping.

"That's right." Ascot's heart, already beating hard, increased its tempo. She hoped the ghosts couldn't hear it; it might excite them.

"Ah!" The mustached ghost clasped a hand to his breast. "Do you understand what this means to us?"

"No." Leaping to the top of a table, Moony shared a puzzled look with Ascot. "Muscatel's a dessert wine, isn't it?"

"The Moonlight Muscatel is the most perfect vintage ever distilled," replied the lead ghost. The others, arrayed behind him, bobbed their heads. "Its grapes—small grapes, not much larger than the pips of a lemon, pearly white, beautiful—only grow in a valley far to the northeast. The vintners feed the vines with spring water mixed with crystallized ginger, and honey made from white jasmine flowers. When the grapes ripen—which only happens every three years—they must be picked the night of the first frost, quickly, before they freeze solid." His fingers clicked with the soft sound of a candle winking out. "The juice is then poured into vats of a rare spicewood and left to age for eleven years."

It seemed like a lot of trouble for little return to Ascot, although Vlad would probably disagree. "It must be delicious," she said.

"Delicious?" The ghost dropped his hand. "It may set us free."

"Free?"

"Were you to taste the Moonlight Muscatel, my lady, your spirit would grow almost light enough to lift out of your body and float away." He raised his eyes to the dusty beams reinforcing the ceiling. "Which is what we hope will happen if we partake of the Moonlight Muscatel. To rise straight through this stone prison and then—"

"And then?"

"Well, who knows? But better than this existence."

"You don't want to stay here?" asked Moony.

"Trapped in a cellar for eternity?" The ghost's laugh dropped from his lips like a rotten apple falling from a branch. "Who would want that?"

"Artful Prince Alec?" said Ascot.

A deep sigh rippled through the ghosts' ranks. "Alas, Artful Prince Alec does not share our view," said the lead ghost. "He relishes his existence in these gloomy cellars, gorging himself on wine and plotting vengeance. One day he'll break past the silver-locked door and . . ."

He didn't finish the sentence. He didn't need to. *This isn't merely another test*, Ascot realized. *Lives are at stake here—and afterlives, too.* Achieving this quest would win not only her Happily Ever After, but these ghosts' as well. That felt good. Better than good. Puffing out her chest, she faced the assembly.

"We'll get the key to the Moonlight Muscatel," she said. "We'll banish Artful Prince Alec and free you all."

Another cheer arose, even more ear-chilling than the last, but this time Ascot didn't mind the pain. Their joy warmed her, despite the cold flowing off their ethereal bodies.

"I am Lord Bentley," said the mustached ghost with another exquisite bow. "Gladly will I aid our savior in any way I can."

"Your words are grace itself, sir," said Moony, copying his bow.

"Yes, thank you," said Ascot. "Could you tell us where to find the Head Butler?"

Lord Bentley's face grew somber. "Alas, he lies in the least accessible region of the Great Wine Vault, deep within Prince Alec's territory."

"Of course he does." Ascot had expected nothing less.

"The way is perilous."

"Of course it is."

"Well, then." Lord Bentley stroked his beard. "I take it you're prepared, my lady?"

"As prepared as I can be, under the circumstances." Which, thanks to Lord Roebanks, was not very.

"Then follow me." Lord Bentley wafted towards the exit at the far end of the counting room. Ascot and Moony fell into step behind him, along with another ghost—a page, judging by his curly locks and lace-edged sleeves.

"Why can't you get the key off the Head Butler yourselves?" Moony asked the page. "How can Prince Alec stop you?"

"We've tried, but they're stronger than us," he replied.

"Why is that?" asked Ascot.

The page kicked an empty wine bottle lying against one spindly leg of the writing desk. "This. You know how people say wine makes for spirited conversation? Well, it gives us more spirit, quite literally, when we ingest it."

"And Prince Alec and Jeck have been consuming the best wine for decades," said Lord Bentley, passing through the doorway. "We've tried to reach the Head Butler countless times. That brave man—"

Ascot gasped. "He's still alive?"

"That brave man's ghost," qualified the page.

"Oh."

"He continues guarding the key to the Moonlight Muscatel," Lord Bentley resumed. "If Prince Alec got hold of it, he'd bury it forever. The Head Butler can't get out. We've never gotten in. But now that you're here, I'm certain of success."

He beamed at her. Ascot's face heated. "I'll get the key," she said, fussing with her lantern.

Moony cleared his throat.

"I mean, *we'll* get the key," said Ascot. "How many followers does Prince Alec have?"

"Around two hundred. But it's Jeck and Alec himself that you must be most wary of."

"And Fritter," added the page.

"Oh, yes, Fritter."

"Fritter?" asked Ascot.

"Jeck's horse. Jeck gives it wine, too. Mean bastard." Lord Bentley scowled. "Bit me on the unmentionables last time we attempted to get the key."

Didn't Catch mention that Jeck was beheaded? Yes, he had. Of course. A headless horseman. Was there some clause stating that if you died of decapitation you had to come back with your rump plunked on a horse's back?

"We need a diversion," she said after a moment of thought. "If we go straight at them, it'll turn into a brawl that blocks up the passages and we'll never reach the Head Butler."

"Ah, strategy!" Lord Bentley chortled. "Good thinking. Allow me to draw you a diagram." He dipped his hand to the ground and somehow came up holding a splinter of wood from an old crate. Ascot tried to figure out how he gripped it, but a tic broke out in her left eye after a couple seconds and she desisted.

Squatting, Lord Bentley began drawing lines in the film of dust covering the floor. "This is the main channel of the Great Wine Vault," he said, sketching. "It's wide and straight, but it dead ends after about a quarter mile, so you'll get trapped if you follow it." He drew a few more lines, then used his splinter as a pointer. "All the doors and passages on the right hand side lead to rooms with the sweeter wines. Champagne, sherry, ice wine, and the like. Prince Alec's territory is here, to the left."

The splinter moved again, sketching a veritable labyrinth of twists and turns. Heart sinking, Ascot tried to commit the various passages to heart, knowing she could never remember them all.

"These rooms contain all varieties of red, white, and rose wine," said Lord Bentley. "Prince Alec can usually be found around the claret, deep in the heart of the Vault." He pointed to a series of rectangular rooms connected by a network of tunnels. "It's near where the wall to the Royal Crypt collapsed."

Next, the hand with the piece of wood pointed to the upper part of the diagram. The chambers here were long and thin. "Jeck the Chipper prefers white wines. There's an opening in the wall that leads outside to the servants' graveyard. Jeck loves to gallop Fritter around the tombstones."

"You mean you can get out there?" asked Ascot. "What keeps Jeck from terrorizing the castle grounds?"

"We can't abide the touch of sunlight, for one," said the page. "Also, the servants' graveyard is surrounded by a wall of silver-laced bricks."

"Technically, you could reach the castle grounds from the servants' graveyard, but they blocked up the gate and the walls are very high." Lord Bentley sketched in a few last details and let his splinter drop.

Gnawing a knuckle, Ascot studied the diagram. "So those are the only two exits? The servants' graveyard and back through the door with the silver lock? We can't escape through the Royal Crypt?"

"No, that exit's been sealed up," said Lord Bentley. "If you enter the crypt, Alec can trap you."

"So we avoid the crypt. Now, the most important question: where's the Head Butler?"

Lord Bentley touched a spot halfway between Prince Alec and Jeck's favorite haunts. "Here, where the rose wines are stored. He was searching for a particular vintage seven years ago when Prince Alec came in. Prince Alec demanded the key to the Muscatel. When the Head Butler refused—" Lord Bentley bowed his head "—Prince Alec toppled a rack and crushed him beneath it. The key is buried with his body, somewhere under the broken bottles and wood."

"And he still guards the key, even in death." Moony stroked his whiskers. "A noble fellow."

A noble dead *fellow,* Ascot amended silently. And if she didn't take care, she'd end up the same. "We need to draw Prince Alec and Jeck away from the Head Butler," she said, taking her knuckle from her mouth.

"Hmm. Prince Alec will be suspicious if we don't try to reach the Head Butler. That's what we've always done before."

"How about you make a show of trying to reach the Head Butler, and then when Alec's gang shows up, you retreat?" suggested Moony. "Ascot and I can sneak past while they're chasing you."

Lord Bentley's eyes glowed like a pair of opals, then dimmed. "But why would they pursue us? They merely wish to keep us from the Head Butler."

Ascot touched her pocket. "What does the key to the Muscatel look like?"

"I only know that it's silver," said Lord Bentley. "There's only ever been one key, and its keeping the privilege of the Head Butler."

"Then Prince Alec probably doesn't know, either." Ascot drew out the vault key and held it up. "Let him catch a glimpse of this. If he thinks you've slipped in and gotten the key to the Moonlight Muscatel, he'll chase you to the ends of the earth."

"But you'll be trapped in the vault, then," protested the page.

Ascot gathered all her courage. "There's still the graveyard exit."

"Oh, my lady." Lord Bentley closed his eyes. "You are a worthy heroine."

She beat down the foolish rush of pride. "Let's wait to celebrate. Can you hold silver?"

"No, but if you wrap it in a piece of cloth I can carry that."

Moony scampered back to the counting room and returned with a scrap of old sacking. Ascot wrapped up the key and handed it to Lord Bentley.

"Now," she said, consulting the diagram. "Here's the plan. Moony and I will wait in this room." She selected a rectangle on the map. "Meanwhile, your party will make towards the Head Butler. When Alec and Jeck show up, let them see the key, then retreat to the Royal Crypt. Keep them there while Moony and I fetch the real key from the Head Butler and escape through the servants' graveyard."

"Some of the rooms have letters on the walls to indicate direction," said Lord Bentley. "Head northeast to reach the graveyard. You'll know you're near it when you find the Riesling."

"Are you sure you'll be able to get out?" asked the page, looking concerned. "The walls are very high."

"I'm a good climber," said Ascot, although she really wasn't sure herself. *I'll worry about that problem when I come to it.* "I might not be able to get the Muscatel to you tonight. But I promise to bring it as soon as possible."

Lord Bentley gave her shoulder a gentle squeeze. "Lady, we trust you."

"Thanks." Pushing back her hair, she stood. "Let's go."

The page held up a palm. "One moment," he said. "Your lantern. If Prince Alec's henchmen see it, they'll know someone living's down here."

Ascot hesitated. The candle's small yellow flame represented a speck of warmth in the wine cellar's frigid gloom; a talisman to keep old fears at bay. *It won't be much comfort if Prince Alec's minions spot you because of it*, she reminded herself.

"You're right," she said. She blew out the candle and the shadows pounced. Only the uncanny aura of ghostlight remained to guide her now, turning the floor into a wash of shimmering green and leaving the ceiling shrouded in impenetrable blackness.

Little puffs of dust rose around Ascot's boots as they started up the long, straight main passage. Every breath flowed into her lungs as moist and substantial as sodden paper. She forced herself to concentrate on her footing. The ground was uncertain here; broken shards and stones, hidden by the pervasive dust, shifted under her tread. *Wouldn't it be awful to fall on my face while Prince Alec or Jeck was chasing me?*

Her treacherous mind had just started toying with variations on that scenario when Moony tugged her coat.

"Do you see that?" he whispered.

A red light emanated from an open doorway on the left.

Chapter Seventeen:
Racking One's Brains

Ascot stared at the ruddy aura, wishing it away. It was a truly ugly color; tainted somehow, like rusty water mixed with clean.

"Confound it," swore Lord Bentley in an undertone. "They've posted a sentry. That room is the quickest path to the chamber where the Head Butler lies." His fathomless eyes went to Ascot. "You'll have to sneak past him to reach the Sauterne room. Unless you'd rather change the plan?"

"No." Ascot didn't hesitate. "I'd rather sneak past one than dodge a hundred." Her heart knocked against her breastbone.

"Give us five minutes to reach our chosen hiding place before beginning your assault," said Moony, ever ready for a spot of daring-do. "We'll slip past after you draw Prince Alec's henchmen away."

With noticeable reluctance, Lord Bentley nodded. "It is best. One moment, however."

He lifted his arms. Ascot shrank back, then, ashamed, steeled herself as he wrapped them around her. Cold soaked her skin, sent frost crackling through her bloodstream, and seeped into her bones until she was certain they'd shatter should she attempt to move. Just as her heart began congealing into a lump of ice, Lord Bentley released her and took a large step backwards.

Ascot sucked in a breath. Her exhale steamed in the air. Compared to that embrace, the vault's chill felt positively tropical.

"Forgive me, my lady," said Lord Bentley. "The sentry would have sensed your living warmth in an instant."

I'd forgive you if I could unfreeze my jaw enough to do so.

"Are you all right?" asked Moony. He kneaded her leg. "You're cold as an icicle."

"Ye-yes," she slurred. Her blood sludged through her veins. A thousand pinpricks stabbed her fingers and toes. If only she could take a moment to rub feeling back into them! But of course that would ruin the effect. She forced herself to take a step, half expecting her leg to snap off at the ankle, leaving her foot frozen to the floor of the channel.

"Are you sure you're all right?" asked Moony.

"I'm ready," said Ascot, knowing it wasn't entirely an answer. She glanced back over her shoulder. "Good luck," she mouthed to the waiting ghosts.

Lord Bentley bowed. A few ghosts raised their bottles of wine in salute before quaffing the contents. Preparing for battle, she surmised. Ascot faced the reddish glow.

"Scout ahead, Moony," she whispered, and he vanished instantly. She bit back a cry she couldn't afford to make. Fortunately, he returned as quickly as he had disappeared.

"You're safe for about twenty steps," he said. "Then there's a chance he could spot you, but he's not very alert."

"Good," said Ascot, eyes on the red light. It really was an ominous color; the kind signs warning people away from the edges of cliffs were painted with. Cautiously, she moved towards it, her boots flopping on her numb feet, the gritty floor beneath them a matter of guesswork. After fifteen paces, she pressed herself against the right-hand wall and sidestepped. Her coat scraped the crudely hewn rock. *Not good; the sentry might hear.* She put one hand to the wall instead and felt her way along, vaguely aware that the rough surface was tearing her cold skin and shredding her nails. Inch by cautious inch, she proceeded.

The sentry came into view around the lip of the rotting doorframe he was leaning against. The Merlot room, according to a tarnished brass plaque set into the wall above the door. The dirty metal gleamed copper-red. She'd have to pass under the sentry's very nose, less than twelve feet away. *How can I manage this without him spotting me?*

Well, she had to do it and that was all. Slowly, she inched along, pinned against the back wall like a collector's butterfly. Across the channel, the sentry, an imposing figure in an ornamental breastplate and a bearskin cape, slouched, eyes unfocused. Like sentries the world over, he looked bored to death—*bored silly*, Ascot corrected. Periodically, he raised a bottle of wine to his lips. Every time he drank, his aura intensified.

It's the wine that gives him that awful color. He must have consumed gallons of the stuff.

But wine didn't make the ghosts drunk, exactly. It gave them energy. All the wine the sentry imbibed made him stronger, not more absent-minded.

She pressed as close as she dared to the wall, listening for the slightest scuff of noise that might betray her presence. *If only I could see where to put my feet. It would be so easy to—*

Crunch. Something snapped underfoot.

Ascot froze, locked as tight as an insect in amber. Instantly on the alert, the sentry straightened. His eyes flamed—only cold, very cold. *It's over. Curse my pale complexion; he'll spot me and then—*

"Squeak, squeak!"

Both Ascot and the sentry's heads turned. A glimpse of gray fur scampered through the shadows. After a few more squeaks, the passage fell silent.

The cold flame left the sentry's eyes. Slouching again, he raised the bottle to his lips. Ascot counted to fifty. She didn't dare wait any longer than that; the prickling in her limbs warned her that her blood was rewarming. The next time the sentry lifted his bottle, she scurried past.

There. In the thankful darkness beyond, she spotted another brass plaque on the right wall, hanging crazily by a single corner. *Sauterne*, it read in elegant, flowing script. Ascot counted her steps towards the door beneath it to make them go faster. *Eighteen. Nineteen. Twenty.* She was sure she'd aged a decade by the time she reached it. Ducking inside the room, she slumped against a rickety rack and let out the breath that had been congealing in her chest for the past five minutes.

"Isn't this thrilling?" Moony appeared in front of her, positively dancing with excitement.

Ascot scraped up a smile. "Thanks for the rat impression back there, Moony. You saved me." Somewhat recovered, she pushed away from the rack. The bottles clinked. For another heart-stopping instant, she feared it would fall over. *I can't afford too many more of these*, she thought, leaping to steady it.

The clinking subsided. Wiping her hands on her pants, she went to the door and set her eye to a crack where the frame had warped, wood pulling away from the stone. Moony poked his head right around the doorway, trusting his small size to keep him unseen.

Not a minute passed before a yellow-green glow suffused the tunnel, turning it as bright as a graveyard with the full moon shining overhead. Ascot caught her breath as Lord Bentley's troops, dressed in their ancient, elegant attire, pounded forward, their feet raising no sound against the channel's floor. Roaring a battle cry, they swamped the sentry. In the space between two heartbeats, the yellow-green light quenched the reddish one. So quickly did it happen that for a moment she could believe the battle won; no need for any action on her part.

The flood of ghosts poured into the Merlot room. Silence and stillness briefly reigned. Then an answering roar reverberated off the walls, rattling the bottles in their racks, and shaking great strings of cobweb loose from the ceiling. Dust rose in clouds as the yellow-green party boiled out of the room, hotly pursued by an army of red-and-gold tinged figures. Ascot easily picked out Prince Alec from the lot. He was the tallest, his towering form suffused with a rich, virtually solid, sheen of red. She never imagined such a fiery color could look so cold. He wore etched steel armor and a long cape that flowed behind him like a stream of wine. His wild dark hair waved around his face and his black eyes blazed with a vicious joy.

But no horsemen rode amongst the throng. Jeck the Chipper was definitely one ghost she wanted out of the way while she searched for the Head Butler.

Maybe he's not riding at the moment, and that's why I didn't see him, she reassured herself. *It's not like he'd be wearing a badge reading "Hello, my name is Jeck, and I'm an assassin."*

The last of the ghosts, both green-tinged and red, disappeared up the far end of the tunnel. Her turn to act. Ascot dug out the matchbox Catch had given her and lit the wick of the candle in the little lantern. For a moment, she basked in its warm, natural glow.

"We go now?" asked Moony, quivering with eagerness.

Ascot took a firm grip on the lantern. "As quickly and quietly as we can."

Moony darted off, easily out-quicking and quieting her, leaping over shattered magnums and slipping around the wine racks' splintery edges. Ascot kept snagging her coat on these and had to stop and tug it loose—gently, so as not to bring bottles tumbling down around them. The bitter scent of old wine thickened the air.

"I hope Lord Bentley can keep Prince Alec occupied," said Ascot. The prince's enthusiasm for the chase had struck her as distinctly unpleasant. She just knew that, in life, he'd been the sort to decorate his walls with the heads of dead animals.

"He thinks Lord Bentley has the key to the Moonlight Muscatel," replied Moony, skipping over the ribs of a rotting barrel. "He'll chase them for miles."

Or he'll stake out the Head Butler's room to make sure he hasn't been tricked. That's what I'd do. But Ascot didn't voice her misgivings. What would be the point? They'd committed to this quest.

An hour passed in the search, perhaps two. Except for their dimensions, all the rooms looked much the same: dust and stillness, worm-eaten racks, and floors littered with the shards of broken bottles. Some of the walls were indeed painted with small, gold *N*s, *S*s, *E*s, or *W*s, but most were not, forcing Moony to tear scrap after scrap from his cape to mark their way. Soon it was reduced to a mere rag hanging around his neck. Ascot hungered for air that smelled of grass and flowers and, well, air, instead of damp earth and vinegar.

"Are we even sure these are the rose wines?" she asked, stopping on the threshold of yet another rack-filled room. "All the bottles are covered in dust, and if you wipe that off, the glass is green or brown so whatever's inside looks like tea."

Moony looked up, his eyes flashing carnelian-red in the sulfurous light. "Read the labels?"

"Of course." Ascot pinched the bridge of her nose. "Ignore that stupid outburst." She pulled a bottle out of a rack, grimacing at its soft, gritty coating of dust. "Someone was in love with their quill," she said, studying the label. "Never saw so many flourishes in my life, but I think it says rose."

"Then we're near the right place." Moony trotted ahead. "I don't think we've been through this door yet."

Ascot set the bottle back in the rack, sneezing when the movement raised another puff of stale dust. "I can see why Lord Bentley doesn't want to spend eternity down here," she said. "Nothing but mold and spiders. No wonder they drink."

No answer from Moony. His triangular nose was twitching.

"What is it?" she asked.

His tongue flicked out, tasting the air. "I smell old wine. Lots of it, concentrated, like it was all spilled at once."

"Like maybe a rack toppled and all the bottles broke?"

"Possibly."

"Let's take a look." Reflexively, Ascot checked her lantern, doing a double-take when she realized the candle was almost burned out. Would her second candle see her through the night?

Only one way to know. Reluctantly, she pulled her spare candle out of her pocket, lit the wick, and anchored it in the melted wax of the first. Four or five inches of light, she estimated.

It would have to be enough. "Where do you smell the wine, Moony?"

"Straight ahead, but I don't see a door." Flattening himself, he crawled under a line of racks to investigate. Ascot followed the sound of his scuffling. Her gaze stopped. One rack stood at an angle, its top corner propped against its neighbor's side. Dimly, through its bars, she noticed a crude stack of old boards blocking what looked like a gap in the wall behind it.

"That looks suspicious."

Moony popped out from under a shelf, covered in dust. "What?"

She pointed to the tilted rack. "Check out the wall behind it."

Moony obliged, squeezing behind it. His wild gray tail buffeted the floor. "Well spotted," he said. "There's another room here. Wait a minute." He grunted. Old, rotten bits of wood pattered to the ground. His tail vanished. Ascot waited for his next report.

Very soon his head popped out from behind the tilted rack. "There's a long, narrow room connected to this one," he said. "There are racks against the walls as well as two rows of free-standing ones. Right up the central alley, near the back wall, one of the racks on the left has collapsed."

"We found it." Ascot shivered, from victory as much as cold. "Can you reach the key and bring it here?"

Moony scrubbed dust out of his whiskers with the back of a paw. "The Head Butler's body is buried in all that glass and wood. I doubt I can squeeze under, and it's too heavy for me to lift."

She bit her lip, disliking the obvious course of action, but . . . "I'll come through, then."

Trying not to think about what would come next, she shifted the tilted rack enough to squeeze past. The bottles clinked, threatening to fall. *Careful. Don't want to make a lot of noise.* She pushed hard with her shoulder, creating a two-foot gap. There. She took a breath.

Visions of Vincent's mother arose as, bent double, she forced herself through the cobwebby opening. A splinter gashed her cheek. Her coat snagged on a rough edge, and that almost undid her. Throat clenched, stifling whimpers, she yanked hard. The leather stretched taut before tearing free all at once. Momentum crumpled her onto the floor of a narrow room. She lay still a moment, panting, the scent of briny mud stinging her nostrils.

"You all right?" Moony brushed her knee.

"Yes." Gathering herself, she raised the lantern. Its light revealed moldering racks and walls covered with crumbling red bricks, but couldn't pierce the shadows concealing the back of the long room. She stood, and glass crunched beneath her boots.

"Who's there?" called a voice from the room's end. "Has a living person found me at last?"

It spoke in the deep, resonant tones of a man who knew where the silver polish was kept, trapped in a place where there was no use for silver polish whatsoever. It could only be the voice of the Head Butler.

"Yes," said Ascot. She began picking her way across the shard-strewn floor. "I've come for the key." As she entered the central alley, she couldn't help glancing at the heavy racks to either side, laden with thick glass bottles. *If one of them came crashing down, I wouldn't have time to scream.*

At the alley's end, next to an overturned rack, an ethereal form began coalescing, taking on the shape of a tall man with a hawk-like nose and thicker hair than butlers were generally advised to sport. He stood erect, his back as straight as if he had an iron rod in place of a spine. All of him—skin, hair, and even his faultless black clothes—was tinged with an overlay of pink.

"At last," said the Head Butler as his mouth settled in place. (*What was he speaking with earlier?* Ascot wondered with a shudder.) "How many years has it been?"

"Seven."

"Seven," he repeated, and sighed. "I had almost lost hope that Her Majesty would send in a party to locate my remains. See all the wine I was forced to imbibe to protect the key from those miscreants." Several dozen empty bottles lay scattered across the floor.

That explained his pink hue. "She didn't send a party," said Ascot. "Only me, and Moony tagged along."

Moony, who had climbed the side of one of the racks to better watch the proceedings, bared his teeth in a grin. The Head Butler's expression remained impassive, but a long pause elapsed before he spoke again. "Pardon my saying so, but you seem inadequate to the task."

"That's the point," said Ascot. "It's a test to see who's worthy to marry Prince Parvanel. I believe Lord Ruthven Roebanks selected this one especially for me." She tried to make light of it, but the words tasted bitter.

The Head Butler stared at the far wall, his gaze abstract. At last, he shook his head. "So, Lord Roebanks is still up to his machinations. Poor Betty Ann."

"Betty Ann?" asked Moony.

"Do you mean Queen Bettina Anna?" asked Ascot.

The Head Butler refocused on her. "I do. Her name was changed after she wed King Alastor. 'Betty Ann' was deemed to lack a certain, hm . . ."

"Snob appeal?" suggested Moony.

". . . elegance," finished the Head Butler as if he hadn't paused in the first place.

"Then she wasn't from some rich family before she married King Alastor?" asked Ascot.

"No, she was a simple country girl." Another hesitation. "From my village, in fact."

"Oh, did she win King Alastor's heart because of her goodness and beauty?" Ascot clapped her hands. "Like in the stories?" That would be wonderful. Then Bettina Anna wasn't an evil queen after all, and all her troubles could be blamed on Lord Roebanks.

The Head Butler's sigh brushed her cheek like the touch of a frosted feather. "Very much like in the stories. Everyone in my village admired Betty Ann for her golden hair and gentle ways. But her stepmother was, if not cruel, occasionally uncommonly hard on her."

"Because her own daughters weren't as pretty, or well-liked, right?" chirped Ascot.

The reproving look he sent her could have come from Dmitri. "More likely because the woman had eight children, was constantly tired, and took it out on her stepdaughter. At least that's how Betty Ann always excused her when I complained on her behalf."

Ascot paused. Something was off here. "You knew her that well?"

"Indeed." Again the Head Butler's gaze grew abstract, seemingly fixed on events long past. "Once, I had hopes concerning her. I had, hmm, recently secured an advantageous post at the castle. I dreamed of saving enough money and then returning home and—hmm, yes."

He fell silent. Frowning, Ascot searched her memory. She couldn't recall the white book mentioning a single instance where the heroine had a beau before she married the prince.

The Head Butler stirred. "I was outside polishing Prince Alastor's boots when he returned from a morning's hunt," he said. "She was riding behind him, clinging to his waist. She looked as if she'd learned she could fly."

Of course she did. She'd just found her True Love . . . hadn't she? Ascot looked harder at the Head Butler. Beneath his very proper veneer, she sensed a chasm of regret.

"How did he meet her?" she asked softly.

"Through his Fairy Godmother's intervention. By Albright law, he had to marry to claim his crown. Naturally, Prince Alastor desired a sweet and loving wife. Unfortunately, Albright's coffers were rather bare at the time, and it seemed as if he had little choice but to wed a, hmm, rather forceful young lady, one Miss Regina Roebanks."

Ascot started. A mew escaped Moony.

Unperturbed, the Head Butler continued. "The then-Prince Alastor's Fairy Godmother disguised herself as a crone and sat by a well."

"I know that one," said Ascot. "It's in the book. The Godmother waited for a girl kind enough to draw water for her, and share her last crumb of bread. That girl was Bettina Anna?"

"Exactly," said the Head Butler. "And for her generosity, the Fairy Godmother blessed her so that precious stones fell from her mouth when she spoke. The gift faded after a year, but that was long enough to refill Albright's treasury."

"So it worked out for everyone." Ascot watched his face, seeing the glimmer of un-concealable pain, deep in the dark eyes. "Except for you."

He dropped his gaze. "It did not work out for anyone. The nobles were outraged, Lord Roebanks in particular. Betty Ann did not find one friend at court."

"Wait a moment." Ascot pushed away from the rack she'd been leaning against. "Are you saying she wasn't happy?"

"Happy?" The Head Butler stared at her down both sides of his aquiline nose. "A dairymaid, ascended to royalty? She was the object of scrutiny, gossip, and contempt. Indeed, someone tried to assassinate her a year after her marriage to King Alastor."

The world's foundations ripped out from under Ascot's feet, sending her spinning into space. "But she married the *prince*," she cried, scraping her throat with the force of it. "She was supposed to live Happily Ever After."

The Head Butler appeared to be studying the glitter of old, broken glass at his feet. "That was her belief as well."

A rush of cold air burned the back of Ascot's neck. "But she loved King Alastor, didn't she?" she asked, rubbing it.

The Head Butler did not reply, and the question vanished into the depths of that silence, gathering weight and momentum, like a jug thrown into a deep well whose fall may or may not be cushioned by water at the bottom.

Snort. Grumble. A second frigid gust frosted Ascot's neck. The Head Butler's head snapped up, an expression of horror gelling on his face.

With small, careful motions, Ascot turned. And found herself eyeball to crimson-rimmed eyeball with the biggest, blackest, meanest horse she'd ever seen; so very black that she couldn't tell exactly where its hide left off and the darkness began. Black as the shadow of a horse made solid and outlined in flaming red light.

It snorted again. Ears clamped flat against its long neck, it lifted its wickedly sleek head and stamped a fore hoof. Sparks scattered across the floor.

"This is Fritter," said a jolly voice from somewhere in the vicinity of the horse's back. "I'm afraid he doesn't like you very much."

CHAPTER EIGHTEEN:
IN OVER ONE'S HEAD

Slowly, Ascot raised her eyes. A glowing, yellow-green boot came into view. Then a knee. Then a hand, holding a head, which smiled at her in a friendly sort of way. Numbly, she continued raising her eyes to take in the rest of the body, sitting quite confidently in the saddle. Its neck ended in a stump.

That wasn't what, finally, shook her from her daze. It was the sight of something far more awful: a little round badge pinned to the left side of the torso's chest. Red, with curly black lettering. *"Hello, my name is Jeck, and I'm an assassin,"* it read.

Ascot groaned with the pain of it. "Hello, Jeck," she managed.

"Ah, you've heard of me." The head beamed.

"Unfortunately." Ascot pulled her glance away. "Couldn't you put that in its proper place?"

"Oh, if you like. It tends to wobble a bit, though." The hand lifted the head to the neck and set it on the stump. Unpleasant squishy noises ensued; Jeck had to be making them purely for amusement's sake. Moony watched the process with far too much interest, climbing a nearby rack for a closer look.

How did Jeck and his frabjacketing horse get into the room without me noticing? wondered Ascot, doing her best to ignore the squelches. The ghosts didn't seem capable of walking through walls; perhaps the gallons of wine they consumed prevented it. *They must have sneaked through the gap while we were talking to the Head Butler.*

A final, repugnant snap. "Is this better?" asked Jeck, his head more-or-less in place.

"Yes, it's better. Thanks."

"Good." Jeck drew a sword from the scabbard at his side. Metal hissed against leather. "Now, let's have some fun!"

He held a *real* sword, not the mere ghost of one! Ascot shrank back against a rack, tucking in her chin and trying to fold all her vulnerable limbs behind her. *Where'd he get a real sword? Did the idiots bury him with it just to show respect for the dead?*

Here she'd thought that if Alec or Jeck caught her, they'd crush her under a rack or freeze her to death. Being decapitated herself was somehow worse.

A rush of cold air swept between her and Jeck. Ascot recoiled as the Head Butler interposed himself, arms spread wide to accept the blow.

Jeck paused, sword upraised. "Aw, I can't hurt you. You're already dead."

"Shame on you, varlet, attacking an unarmed lady," replied the Head Butler.

Jeck lowered his weapon further. "I'll accept 'villain,' but not 'varlet,'" he said with dignity. "Sounds like some twitchy kind of weasel-creature. I can't let her waltz out of here with the key to the Muscatel. Prince Alec would kill me. Well, not *kill* me, exactly, but you know what I mean." Jeck tapped his lip with a gloved finger, easily keeping his seat as Fritter shifted beneath him.

Silver. The ghosts couldn't abide the touch of silver. Ascot's hands crept to her pockets, assessing each of her remaining bits of silverware in turn. Two teaspoons, a tiny fork, a napkin ring, and a butter knife. She wrapped her fingers around the latter's hilt. But—

It's so short. If she wanted to stab Jeck, she'd have to get dangerously close to Fritter, who would happily stomp her to death. *Maybe he can't*—but one glance at the foaming, snorting stallion assured her that he'd do his level best to try. Somehow, she had to deal with the enormous, foul-tempered equine first.

And then it came to her.

"I have it!" cried Jeck. Reaching to the left, he wrenched a crosspiece from a wine rack. Splinters flew. Jeck swung the makeshift club experimentally and nodded in satisfaction. "Here," he said, tossing the nail-studded chunk of wood to the floor. "Pick it up, girl. Then we'll both be armed."

Ascot pulled a length of stained green silk from her pocket.

"But you're a ghost," said the Head Butler. "A stick won't deter you."

Shrugging, Jeck raised his sword. "It's an unfair world."

"Come on," Ascot muttered through her teeth, squeezing.

Moony leaped off the side of the rack and landed on his feet, brandishing his own tiny blade. "I'll cross blades with you, sir," he said, fur crackling.

"Ooh, the kitty's armed." Jeck brightened. "Goody." He touched his heels to Fritter's side and the foaming horse lunged forward—

The object popped free. Ascot turned.

—and Fritter stopped dead, a beatific expression crossing his face as an overpowering apple aroma saturated every corner of the room, driving the scents of old wine and dust before it.

Thank you, Miss Beige, thought Ascot, offering the wishing apple in her cupped hands. She'd never met a horse that could resist an apple, not even her father's carriage horses, which tried to snack on

Igor's fingers every time they got the chance. And Fritter, to all appearances, was a horse good and tired of the strictly wine diet. His big yellow teeth snapped forward. Half the apple vanished in a crunch.

"Fritter!" yelled Jeck as the horse's hide flamed an alarming shade of crimson. Fritter's knees buckled. Grinning a grin of pure equine idiocy, the great horse collapsed, flinging Jeck loose. Jeck's head catapulted through the air. Reflexively, Ascot caught it.

They stared at one another. Ascot's stomach performed a few somersaults. Beneath the yellow-green glow, Jeck's eyes shone a surprisingly mild shade of blue.

His mouth formed a sheepish grin. "I don't suppose you'd consider setting me back on my neck?"

"No," said Ascot, and flung the head as hard as she could into the farthest corner of the room.

"Oh, well, I tried," it said indistinctly. It must have landed face-down in the dirt. It sucked in a breath—old habits, presumably, died hard. "Prince Alec! Intruders in the Head Butler's room!"

Bottles clanked. The words bounced off the rack-lined walls and out into the next room, ricocheting into the depth of the vault. "Frabjacket," Ascot swore. "Someone's bound to hear him."

"Then lose no time, my lady." By the overturned rack, the Head Butler began shifting bottles. "Quickly, now."

Ascot flung herself onto her knees beside him, heedless of the broken glass littering the floor. The overturned rack was old, rotting; with an effort, she could break off pieces. "Once we reduce the weight," she panted, "I'll lift it and Moony can squeeze under and get the key." She flung aside a piece of wood, ignoring the splinters that pierced her fingers. Were those voices already, echoing in the distance?

Jeck's body bumped against her, sending a chill down her side. "Your head's that way," snapped Ascot, giving it a push. Now her hands were cold, too. Well, it made the splinters easier to ignore. She wrenched more wood loose and the Head Butler tossed aside more bottles, and now she was quite sure she could hear the whoops of Prince Alec's party echoing in the corridor.

"Let's do it," she said. Grabbing the edge of the rack, she heaved. The Head Butler added his efforts. Together, they raised the heavy wooden frame three inches. Four. Five. Six. *My back's going to snap.* Seven.

"Hold it there," said Moony. Tossing aside his hat and cape, he eeled under the gap. Sweat popped out on Ascot's forehead. She willed her arms not to shake.

"Eww, nasty." Moony's raspy voice drifted from under the rack.

"Ha-hrmm!" The Head Butler cleared his throat.

"Oh, sorry. No offense meant."

"Just hurry, Moony," Ascot pleaded. Some of her fingernails were bending backwards.

"I'm trying. Mr. Butler, where did you keep the key?"

"The inner pocket of my waistcoat. It's silver with a crescent moon on the bow."

Rustling and a few unpleasant crackles. "Found it. Just . . . get it . . . loose." Something bumped against the bottom of the rack, then Moony crawled out rump-first, a long, thin object clasped in his jaws. Years of lying in the vault had tarnished the key nearly black, but the filigreed moon on its bow still possessed enough spirit to glint. As soon as Moony was clear, Ascot dropped the rack. It landed with a floor-shaking thump, raising a fog of dust and splinters.

"Didn't squash yourself, did you?" Jeck's head called from the corner.

Ignoring him, she took the key from Moony's mouth and stowed it in a pocket of her trousers. "Let's go," she said, picking up the lantern with fingers grown stiff and clumsy. Moony retrieved his hat and cape.

The Head Butler touched her arm. "Take the left door out of the next room. It's the closest route to the graveyard. But, one thing before you go."

"Yes?" She flinched as another, closer cry bounced off the walls.

Kneeling, the Head Butler retrieved a small, rosy pink bottle from the bottom corner of a rack. "This is the last of Betty Ann's favorite wine," he said, holding it up. Gold ink outlined the picture of a red rose on the label. "Seven years ago, I came here the night before her birthday, thinking to gift her with it, and lingered too long. My foolish error." He smiled tiredly. "She may as well have it now." He slipped it into a protective sleeve and handed it over.

Ascot tucked it into her coat. "I'll give it to her. Do you want to pass on a message?"

He shook his head. "She knows it all already. Go now. Escape, and return with the Muscatel."

The cries were very close. Ascot took no further time to pause or look back. Moony leaped to her shoulder and they set off at a jog.

"Until we meet again!" cried Jeck, laughing.

❧

Where was the servants' graveyard? They tried one course, then another. A promising route ended when Moony spotted a strip from his cape on the floor. They'd been that way already. Ascot took a westerly path only to spy another scrap of green cloth, draped across a cloudy bottle. They retraced their steps again. And again. All the while, the jeers of Prince Alec's troops rang out, never seeming to gain nor lose ground; an eternal, maddening, treacle-slow chase through dusty darkness.

"I'd kiss Miss Roebanks' foot for a drink of water," Ascot wheezed, collapsing against one of the ever-present racks. Her throat and sandpaper-dry tongue were the only parts of her that felt warm.

"Have some wine," said Moony, rubbing dust off his ears. His whiskers drooped. "It's better than nothing."

"You're right." She pulled the nearest bottle out of its compartment and broke its neck against a corner of the wall. Taking care not to cut her tongue on the sharp edge, she drank greedily. Why had she despised wine before? Vlad was right; this was fabulous. She cupped some in her hand for Moony. He wrinkled his nose, but took a couple laps.

"That's better," she said, and was about to toss the bottle aside when Moony's ears pricked up so high their tufted tips practically tangled. He licked his lips.

"Could this be Riesling?" he asked.

Ascot's exhausted wits slowly focused. Lifting the bottle, she stared at the label. For a moment, the elaborately scripted words just didn't make sense.

And then they did. Her spirits leaped. "Yes, it's Riesling."

"We're near the servants' graveyard." His wings buzzed. Ascot found the energy to smile.

"So near and yet so far," purred a new voice.

Ascot's grin slid off her face. She pushed away from the wall, dreading what she suspected she would see.

She saw it: Prince Alec, tall and terrible, smiling a mad smile as he slapped the flat of a long, double-edged sword against the armored palm of his hand. *Another real sword. Why must they bury these creeps with those things? When I'm queen, I'll make a law forbidding it.*

When she was queen. She almost laughed. *How about getting out of here alive first, Ascot?*

"Only two more rooms, if you find the correct path, that is," Prince Alec continued, savoring her fear like a rare vintage. "And how do you intend to escape the servants' graveyard? The walls are very high, and I have followers there."

"How did you sneak up on us?" asked Moony, paw on his own sword's hilt; a spindly toy compared to Prince Alec's.

"Did you think you invented the idea of a diversion?" Prince Alec retorted. "I sent troops to scare you in the proper direction while I circled round to intercept you here. Better to catch you by the graveyard than risk you slipping out the silver-locked door."

Catch. That, too, almost made her laugh. If only she'd heeded his advice, she wouldn't be in this predicament now.

But that would've doomed Lord Bentley and his followers to an eternity in the cellar.

Lifting Moony, she set him on her shoulder. Then, holding herself very straight, she looked Prince Alec in the eye. "I won't give you the key to the Moonlight Muscatel."

"Really." Prince Alec did not sound dismayed. "Probably just as well. I meant to make you a deal: the key for your life. But I wouldn't have kept it." He shrugged. "Easier, this way." He raised his sword.

Ascot whirled. *His blade's too long to use in such a confined area.* Sure enough, it struck a shelf. Bottles shattered, spraying her with tart yellow liquid and fragments of glass.

"Moony," she asked, fists pumping at her sides. "Can you smell fresh air?"

"Take the door straight ahead," he answered, riding backwards, claws dug into her coat for balance. "Duck!" he shouted before she had run ten steps.

Ascot threw herself forward. The strike nipped off a lock of her hair and sliced a strip from the tail of her coat. Rolling awkwardly, she recovered her feet and risked a glance behind her. Prince Alec had put enough force behind this last blow to embed his blade in the floor. He grunted, struggling to pull it free.

The next room had a door in every wall. "Which one, Moony?" she asked, not slowing. Behind them, Prince Alec chuckled, low and throaty, relishing the sport.

Moony sniffed the air. "Take the left—duck!"

She did. Prince Alec's sword whistled over her head, raising hairs in its wake. Snatching up a bottle, she hurled it at the prince, but it just hit his armor and slid slowly off, as if he were composed of thick jelly.

"What was that?" he said, smiling like a lion assaulted by a beetle.

Dipping into her pocket, she threw a silver teaspoon.

A sharp, brittle *ting,* as of a fingernail flicking the edge of a wineglass, rang out as the teaspoon passed through his shoulder. For the fraction of a second, Prince Alec flickered and paled. His mirth vanished, replaced by a cold and somewhat insane rage.

"I didn't like that," he said, thoughtfully. "I might kill you slowly now."

Ascot raced out the left door. The clean, natural glow of moonlight flowed through a triangular opening in a wall marked with an *N.* The exit to the graveyard. Fresh air washed away the stink of old wine and dust. She glimpsed grass and sky.

He can't reach me. Prince Alec was twenty steps behind her, and even with his long stride, he'd never catch her in time.

She dashed through the gap. Real air and the smell of overturned earth caressed her. The full moon shone overhead. An actual wind trailed trough her hair. Twigs snapped beneath her boots.

I'm free. I'm safe. I'm—

Her toe snagged on the battered stub of an old tombstone, half hidden by the long, weedy grass. Ascot pitched headlong, tumbling through dead leaves, thorns, and fragments of stone. Flung off her shoulder, Moony struck a grave and yowled. The fall jolted the lantern out of her hand. Ascot grabbed for it, but it bounced away over the lumpy ground, its flame winking out.

Hoof-beats and laughter . . .

CHAPTER NINETEEN:
GRAVE MATTERS

Rolling onto her back, Ascot assessed her situation with quick twists of her head. The graveyard was a sloping rectangle of weather-beaten earth studded with the remains of old tombstones that poked up through grass like broken teeth. Its grounds were very large and its walls very high. And everywhere she looked, she saw ghosts.

It was like a repeat of the counting room, grown sinister. Ghosts lounged against mausoleum walls, leered from behind ugly, wind-twisted trees, or simply stood to the side, observing as Prince Alec approached with arrogant slowness. The hoof-beats grew to a crescendo as Jeck the Chipper galloped out of the vault on the back of a restored Fritter.

"How?" Ascot wheezed. Her overworked lungs seemed on the verge of collapse.

"Oh, I got my head back on and then I kissed him," said Jeck, brushing the matter aside.

She squeezed her eyes shut. *To think those could be the last words I hear.*

But Prince Alec spared her that fate, at least. "You did well," he said, planting a boot on her shoulder. Out of breath, strength, and brilliant notions, Ascot writhed, beating her fists against his shin. How dare he make a spectacle of her defeat?

"I'd ask your name," Prince Alec continued, taking no notice of her struggles, "but we'll have plenty of time for introductions after you join our ranks." He raised his sword. A needle-thin line of moonlight gleamed on its edge, its strike, her death, a mere breath away. "Good-bye and hello, Miss Whoever-you-are."

A flutter of wings.

Ascot turned her head as the tiny figure of Moony rose from a tussock of grass and sailed towards Prince Alec. For an instant, his silhouette hung suspended before the face of the moon, batwings outstretched. Against the pearly backdrop, the object clenched between his teeth shone like a halo. Ascot recognized the napkin ring from her hoard of stolen silverware right before Moony passed straight through the glowing red form of Prince Alec.

A ghastly screech, akin to a thin sheet of metal being torn violently in half, rent the air. Prince Alec stood frozen in the center of a flare of white light, vibrating, eyes bugged.

Then he vanished, simple as a snuffed candle.

Moony fell between two tufts of weeds and crumpled. The napkin ring, gone tar-black, dropped from his mouth.

And Ascot found she had strength left after all. Without trouble or trembling, she stood and walked to where Moony lay. Kneeling, she stroked his fur, white-tipped with frost. The cold burned her hand.

"Your Highness?" Jeck's voice broke the silence that enveloped the graveyard. Every one of the ghosts had stopped sniggering. Fritter reared and Jeck's head tipped off. He snatched it up before it hit the ground. "Your Highness?" A pause. "Oh, well. I never liked him, anyway."

As if sleepwalking, Ascot gathered Moony in her arms and started up the hill, heading towards the far wall, which looked slightly lower than the other two. She could feel, thrumming against her chest, an answering heartbeat from Moony. Faint, faltering, but present.

The ghosts—excepting Jeck, who appeared to have stopped for a drink—followed. "Go away," she told them. "Go away." Her eyes burned. If they advanced, she'd . . . she'd do something that would make them regret that they'd ever lived in the first place, and if Moony didn't—recover—she'd return to the graveyard and dig up their coffins and burn their bones to ash and stamp on what was left and pull down those awful trees with her bare hands—

Oh, Moony!

But the ghosts came closer, chilling her, draining her energy. Cradling Moony in one arm, Ascot rummaged in her pockets. Only one piece of silver remained: a dainty, three-pronged fork such as might be used for fishing olives out of a narrow jar. The rest must've spilled when she'd fallen.

"Get away from me," she said, jabbing at the glowing forms that pressed too near. The sharp *ting! ting!* of silver piercing ghostly ether rang out again and again, but there were so many and her arm was growing so tired and her legs so heavy.

I'll make it to the wall if there are a thousand ghosts between it and me. I'll climb it one-handed if I must. And then—

Her existence narrowed to this moment in this graveyard. She seemed to watch herself from far away, jabbing at angry ghosts with a dessert fork, Moony nestled in one arm. That was all there ever was or ever would be.

A searing flash of white light erupted beside her. As Ascot blinked the red afterimages out of her eyes, it happened again. This time she heard the accompanying torn-metal screech while the crowd of ghosts to her right scattered.

Bony fingers gripped her shoulder. "Miss Ascot, you're alive," cried a voice. "I'm so glad."

Rags-n-Bones. Smoke rose from the blackened ends of the candelabrum he clutched. Even as she gaped, Dmitri stepped to her left side, another candelabrum clenched in his jaws.

They're really here. They came to help me. They—She scrubbed her eyes, swallowing tears. "Moony's hurt," she said. "We must get him out of here."

Rags-n-Bones sucked in a breath, his cheeks hollowing. A moment later, his expression turned as determined as she had ever seen it. "We'll get him to safety, miss." Spinning around, he swung his candelabrum in an arc. Dmitri lunged forward. Two ghosts vanished, but more took their places.

"You get 'em, guys," cheered Jeck, lounging on Fritter's back and swigging wine. Ascot spared a second to wonder who he was rooting for.

Unearthly howls tore the night air as the slow battle progressed. Shoulder to shoulder, leaves crackling beneath their feet, Ascot, Dmitri, and Rags-n-Bones fought their way to the wall and put their backs against it. Its silver-laced bricks glittered faintly.

The army of ghosts pressed forward, spreading out in a semi-circle as they advanced. Ascot exchanged a glance with Dmitri and Rags-n-Bones, wordlessly saying: *we're completely cut off from all other retreats.* They must ascend the wall or perish. Dmitri cast one swift glance upwards, then thrust his candelabrum at Ascot.

"I can leap the wall with Moony," he said as she clasped its warm, saliva-wet stem. "But—"

Ascot handed over Moony's limp body. "Go."

He didn't waste breath arguing. Gripping the little cat between his jaws, he faced the wall and crouched. A tremendous heave of his haunches sent him sailing upwards. His forepaws caught the ledge. With another heave, he pulled himself over the top and vanished.

Ascot already knew what she hadn't allowed Dmitri to say. Moony was light enough for him to carry over the wall. She and Rags-n-Bones were not.

"Rags," she said, holding the candelabrum before her like a shield, "you can grab the ledge if I give you a leg up. Come here, and—"

He shook his head, not looking at her. "Never, miss." Bounding forward, he swatted a ghost.

"Rags, take the key."

"No."

A heavy body crashed to the ground beside Ascot. Yelping, she struck out with her candelabrum, and missed clouting Dmitri by two inches.

"Careful," he said, shaking off the landing.

"Why did you come back?" Ascot demanded. "You left Moony alone."

"If I abandoned you, do you think Moony would ever forgive me?"

"We're all getting out of this," said Rags-n-Bones.

"How?" shrieked Ascot.

"Better figure it out pretty quick," called Jeck. He pointed to the old gravestone where Ascot had tripped. There, a swarm of red particles danced on the breeze, merging, beginning to take on shape. Prince Alec was returning.

"That's it," Ascot cried, knowing all was very near lost. The ghosts facing them roared, energized by their master's reappearance. "Go now, go!"

Rags-n-Bones had already started shaking his head when a sleek, feline shape sailed over the top of the wall and landed lightly beside him. Three feet of silver chain dangled from its mouth.

"Dress monster! Dress monster!" yelled Rags-n-Bones, dancing back. His shoulders smacked the wall.

The creature rumbled a growl. As large as Dmitri, it resembled a panther with a stubby tail and two vicious fangs that protruded down past its lower jaw. It swung its head and the length of silver chain snapped out to harry the encroaching ghosts. *Ting! Ting! Ting!*

Catch? Here? Was it truly him? No, now was not the time for explanations. The great cat's appearance had bought them badly needed seconds and, possibly, an escape.

By the gravestone, Prince Alec's tall, red figure stooped to retrieve his sword. Sighing, Jeck smacked the cork into his wine bottle.

"Back to work, I suppose," he said, taking up Fritter's reins.

Ascot crouched beside the cat. "Can you carry me over the wall?" she asked. *If this is Catch, I'll kick myself later for that desperate note in my voice.*

It fixed her with a greeny-gold gaze for a second before nodding. That was all Ascot needed.

Prince Alec charged, howling, sword upraised.

"Rags, over the wall now," she commanded.

This time he obeyed. With a light skip, he leaped onto Dmitri's back, then, before the wolf could so much as wince, jumped and caught the ledge, swinging himself up with more grace than Ascot would have suspected of him. There he perched like an oversized crow, his thin face tight with worry.

"Now you, Dmitri," she said, flailing her candelabrum to gain space.

Dmitri gathered himself and sprang. Across the graveyard, Prince Alec's long legs ate up the distance between himself and Ascot. His teeth showed in a slash of red-tinged white. Behind him, Jeck held Fritter to a somewhat leisurely trot. Possibly while whistling.

"Come along, Miss Ascot," begged Rags-n-Bones from the top of the wall.

Dmitri pulled himself over the top; safe. The cat swung its chain, driving the ghosts back four feet, then dropped it on the ground, gave Ascot a meaningful glance, and crouched.

"No, you don't!" screamed Prince Alec, shoving aside his minions in his frenzy to reach her.

Ascot hurled herself onto the cat's back. Its muscles tensed to spring.

"Stop!" Prince Alec plowed through the semi-circle of ghosts, his face a mask of fury.

Ascot released her grip just long enough to fling her blackened candelabrum into that face. "Serves you right," she said as a particularly loud *ting!* rang out.

Jeck might have sniggered.

Then the world tipped over. Ascot's rump slid on slippery brown fur; panicked, she threw herself forward, locking her hands around the cat's neck and driving her knees into its sides. Wind rushed past her cheeks, streaming her hair behind her. She could have sworn she'd left half her insides behind on the graveyards' dank earth. A jolt snapped through her backbone as they touched down on the ledge.

Prince Alec's maddened scream was echoed by the hoots and curses of his followers. Ascot looked down. Prince Alec was actually beating his sword against the wall in his rage. Other ghosts brandished their fists at her. But Jeck leaned back in his saddle.

"Oh, poopy," he said, uncorking his wine again. "Looks like she escaped."

Ascot swore he winked.

Then the cat jumped down to the orchard lining the wall's other side. At the bump of landing, Ascot's sore hands lost their grip. She rolled along the thankfully soft earth, bumping over fallen apples

211

and pears, and fetched up at the base of one of the trees. For a moment she just lay there, staring up through the boughs, black in the moonlight, bending under the weight of ripe fruit. The sour-sweet scent of apples scoured the graveyard mold from her nostrils.

"Miss?" Rags-n-Bones' worried face interposed itself. He helped her sit up.

"I'm fine," she said as he brushed her off, lamenting every abrasion he discovered. "Moony. Where's Moony? Is he all right?"

"He's over here," answered Dmitri.

Her bleary eyes wouldn't focus. She wiped them with the inner collar of her shirt, and then she was able to see Dmitri, lying on his belly at the base of an apple tree. A little gray body rested against his side, half-hidden in the thick cream-colored fur.

"Moony!" She scrambled up, toppled onto her knees, and crawled the few feet to his side. "Moony." She reached out a filthy hand. His head felt like a snowball.

"Murr?" he mumbled.

"He needs help." Ascot began struggling to her feet, but Dmitri grabbed her coat between his teeth.

"Calm down," he said. "I believe he'll be fine. Let him rest, and when he wakes he should have something warm to drink."

Ascot chewed her knuckles. Moony looked so tiny, lying there. "Are you sure?"

"He's warmer already. Now stop fussing; you know it'd embarrass him." He jabbed his nose to one side. "By the way, your Smilodon's trying to slink off."

"My what?"

"Your saber-toothed tiger." Huffing, Dmitri closed his eyes.

Ascot looked in the indicated direction, and sure enough, the saber-tooth was skulking away under the black bars of shadow the trees cast over the night-grayed ground.

"Hello, Catch," she called.

The saber-tooth stiffened. Only for an instant, but long enough to tell her she was right. The furtive way he began walking again, pretending that he hadn't heard, only further confirmed it.

"Where are you going, Catch?" she said.

He stopped, one foot in the air. Appeared to debate. Then, heaving a sigh, he turned.

"Cat got your tongue?" asked Ascot, using a pear tree to pull herself erect.

The saber-tooth padded up to her and sat. He looked meaningfully at her before transferring his gaze to the top of the pear tree. After a moment, Ascot followed his stare. Tucked up amongst the branches was a bundle.

"What's this?" she asked, fetching it down. Several soft objects spilled into her hands: a brown leather coat, trousers, shirt, boots . . . and another item of clothing.

From freezing, Ascot's cheeks heated to an inferno. "Oh," she said.

With a little growling noise that just might have been a snicker, the saber-tooth hooked a claw into the trousers.

"Perhaps you'd better turn around," called Dmitri.

Oh. Tossing the clothes onto the ground as if they'd scalded her, Ascot turned. Behind her, a moment later, came a series of strange, somehow liquid, sounds. Pops and crackles. She resisted the urge to peek, and continued to resist it when the crackling changed to the rustle of clothes being drawn on. "Are you decent yet?" she asked.

"One minute." Catch's voice, as plain and unconcerned as if nothing exceptional had happened.

She gave him two more seconds.

"Couldn't wait a minute longer?" he asked, raising a brow. He was still buttoning up his shirt. His coat lay on the ground and he was barefoot.

Stooping, she picked up his coat. "Thank you for saving me," she said, holding it out. "Even if you only did it so Bettina Anna could disqualify me."

His eyebrow lowered. "Is that what you think?"

"Is there any reason I shouldn't?" she retorted.

Air hissed between his teeth. He seemed on the verge of speaking, then dropped his head. A muscle twitched along his jaw. "It's a quarter to six, by the by. I presume you successfully retrieved the key to the Moonlight Muscatel?" He snatched his coat from her.

She'd nearly forgotten her time limit. Perhaps would've forgotten altogether, if he hadn't reminded her. Already, a streak of dawn brightened the eastern sky to a dingy orange.

Fifteen minutes. Ascot massaged her eyelids. "I'll get lost. Lead me there."

Catch's gaze flashed up. "I'm under no obligation—"

"Don't be an ass," said Dmitri. "You won't like yourself later."

That shut him up. A laugh seeped out of his throat, short and rusty-sounding. "All right."

Taking Ascot's arm, he led her through the grounds. Ascot concentrated on moving her feet, letting the scenery unfold around her. Seashell-strewn paths, ivy-covered brick walls, screeching blue peacocks, white marble faces of statues in alcoves—all flashed by like visions from a fevered dream. Time and again her legs sagged beneath her, but Catch raised her every time, his arm a warm bar across her shoulders.

"You'd be right to tell the queen, you know," Ascot said, pushing the words through uncooperative lips. "I did cheat. Moony helped me get the key."

"That's not why I came to your aid."

He lied, of course, even if what he'd just said didn't sound quite like a lie. She puzzled it over for a minute before giving up. "Moony will be all right, won't he?"

"Trust Dmitri."

She nodded. Another timeless, dreamlike instant passed. She watched the knobby white river of the path uncoil beneath them. "You're barefoot," she said.

"My soles are tough."

"Must be inconvenient. The, you know, the stripping." *Ouch. Did I really say that? Those words will haunt me later.*

A faint smile touched Catch's lips. "Depends who catches you in the midst of it." He halted.

"What? Why are we—?"

"We're there," he said.

So they were. She recognized the brown, blocky door Catch had escorted her through the first time she'd entered Albright Castle. Perhaps she really had been sleepwalking, because she couldn't recall reaching it.

"Do you remember the way to the Audience Chamber?" he asked.

She concentrated. "I think so. Follow the blue carpet?"

"Yes. Take the first right and the second left. The door with the cupid."

"Yes, I remember the cupid. But, can't you come with me?"

Ouch. That would haunt her later, too. Nor would she forget the way she clung to his hand. His fingers warmed hers.

Gently, he disengaged her grip. "I'd better not."

"Oh, right." She nodded. "Bettina Anna will think you helped me."

He hesitated. "Yes, that." He gave her a push. "Go on, before the clock starts chiming."

Inside, the gaslights hurt her eyes. She glanced back, but Catch was already closing the door. Bruised, limping, and half-blind, she groped her way down the corridor. *Poor maids,* she thought, noticing the black fingerprints she left on the paneled walls. *When I'm queen—*

She was too tired for the idea to sparkle. Giving it up, she went on.

Turn right. Step around the startled maid carrying a breakfast tray. Keep going. Not the first left, the second. Don't fall. Not yet. *And don't think of Moony or you won't be able to go on for the worrying.*

There, ahead. The awful, beaming, gilded cupid, only twelve steps away. She might make it in time. Of course she'd make it. She was already there, gripping the doorknob. Somewhere overhead, the great clock in the tower struck up a tune, preparatory to chiming six.

The door opened. At the far end of the room, Bettina Anna waited on the white dais, hands clasped before her belly. Lord Roebanks reclined on a cushioned chair at its foot. He shot upright when Ascot stepped inside, his grip throttling the chair's arms.

Yet his voice, when he addressed her, was perfectly civil. Even disinterested. "I fear you are late, Miss Abberdorf."

Ascot looked up at him slowly, then down at her feet again. She had to concentrate on following the carpet lest she take a step off its boundaries and be hurled out into space.

"Late?" Pollux, the little major-domo, stood up. Ascot had overlooked him, sitting in a stiff chair pressed against the room's left side. His clothing and wig were as ridiculous as ever, but his face held something like respect. "How could she be late, my lord?" he asked. "It is only now chiming six."

The first *bong* struck.

"Miss Abberdorf was only granted until six o'clock," said Bettina Anna, staring straight ahead. "Upon Lord Roebanks' advice."

"Ah." Worlds of comprehension, muted disapproval, and diplomatic neutrality in that one syllable.

A second *bong*. Pollux took six steps onto the white carpet. "Do you have the key to the Moonlight Muscatel, Miss Abberdorf?" *Bong.*

Ascot nodded, every vertebra in her neck popping. She slipped a hand into her pocket. *Bong.* For a moment she couldn't find the key and her heart seized up. All she needed now was for it to have fallen through a hole in her pants. But no, it was there at the very bottom, its blade tangled in a loose thread. *Bong.* Working it free, she laid it in Pollux's palm.

Pollux's fingers closed around it. "Miss Abberdorf has given me the key," he said. *Bong.* "And it is now *officially* six o'clock."

"Then she has completed her task on time," said Bettina Anna, with the mien of a statue.

The space around Lord Roebanks seemed to boil. "So it seems," he said mildly. "I suppose a final test will be necessary."

"Tonight, at the banquet," said Bettina Anna. "It has already been arranged."

Part of Ascot roused. "Another test? But—"

"My daughter completed her task over an hour ago." Settling back in his chair, Lord Roebanks toyed with his ring. "Really, she should have been declared the victor then."

"With respect, my lord, the test was to see which of the candidates completed their tasks best, not a race to see who finished first," said Pollux. The quarter of his profile that was turned towards Ascot revealed a pleasantly avuncular expression. Quite a change from his former prissiness.

"Of course, of course." Lord Roebanks waved it aside. "It is probably best that the assembled nobles witness the triumph of Parvanel's proper bride."

"But what about Cindy?" asked Ascot.

Pollux's expression went carefully blank. "Miss Harkenpouf has not yet returned," said Bettina Anna.

Scincilla didn't have a ring from her Fairy Godmother. She wasn't Parvanel's True Love, so she had to fail out of the competition sooner or later. And yet . . . Ascot looked from Pollux to the queen. "She has an hour yet, right? She could still succeed."

Pollux bent towards her, a finger laid beside his nose. "I would not pin my hopes on it, Miss Abberdorf," he whispered. He gave her arm a squeeze and returned to his chair.

"Until tonight, then," said Bettina Anna. "You must be tired, Miss Abberdorf. Retire to your room and rest."

Ascot stared down at her hands. Tired, definitely. And sore, filthy, and terribly worried about Moony. But there was Lord Roebanks, lounging on his chair, twisting his ruby about his finger. Smiling. So sure, so smug that Scincilla wouldn't return. Poor Scincilla, who'd been so scared yet bravely determined the night before.

"No," she said. Locating the inexplicable footstool she'd banged her shins on the previous night, she sat. "By your leave, I'll wait until Cindy returns and announces she's strung all the harps."

"As you wish," said Bettina Anna. Tilting back his head, Lord Roebanks smiled at the ceiling.

Elbows on knees, Ascot waited. The bustle of servants at work in the corridors outside ticked away the time. Sunlight poured through the great latticed window to her right, transforming a pale pink dawn into a cloudy blue day.

The scents of coffee and fresh bread wafted into the Cupid Chamber. Voices could be heard, raised in morning greeting. Still Ascot listened for the click of footsteps outside the gilded door, all the while knowing, deep inside, that they would never arrive.

CHAPTER TWENTY:
LOVE LETTERS

A scream shook Nosegay Wing.

Ascot's eyes flew open. "What?" she said. Blearily, she focused on the two feet in practical brown shoes that stood in her immediate line of vision. Shards of pottery surrounded them, along with a pool of that aromatic Daylander tea, soaking into the warped floorboards.

"Oh, lord." Maggie's voice came from a couple feet above her. A long, quavering sigh followed. "I saw you hanging in there like a side of meat and thought Lord Roebanks had you done away with."

Ascot stared, puzzled, then looked up at her knees, clasped over the wardrobe's bar. "Oh, sorry. Noble Shadowvaleans often sleep upside down." She rubbed grit from her eyes with the sleeve of her robe. Frankly, she didn't trust beds. They didn't have nice, close sides like a coffin. Why, you could roll right out of them!

"No, I'm sorry for waking you." Color returned to Maggie's cheeks. Past the line of her skirt, Ascot saw Dmitri, curled in a makeshift nest of the bedspread. Moony rested between his paws.

Dmitri had pronounced Moony's condition improved when she went to fetch them from the orchard that morning, but it appeared he still hadn't awakened.

"I didn't want to disturb you, but Miss Roebanks insisted I give you this now," Maggie continued, taking a piece of pink paper from the pocket of her apron.

"A letter? From Miss Roebanks?" Ascot gingerly unfolded it, wrinkling her nose at the cloying fragrance of narcissus that wafted up. "She wants me to have tea with her at the gazebo at two o'clock," she said, reading the note a second time to make sure her eyes weren't playing tricks.

"Don't taste a thing she offers you," said Dmitri and Maggie at once.

Ascot pursed her lips, folding and unfolding the pink paper.

"Should I tell her you'll come?" asked Maggie, mopping up the spilled tea.

It had to rank among the last ways she'd like to spend an afternoon, but . . . "I suppose," said Ascot. "I'm sure it's some trick, but if I don't fall for this one, she'll only think of something else."

"Undoubtedly." Maggie's pleasant, round face pinched up into something resembling a gargoyle's. Then she smiled and stood, tray in hand. "I'll bring lunch at one, so Miss Roebanks' *vol-au-vents* don't tempt you."

"Thanks." Ascot yawned. "What time is it now?"

"Ten. You can get three hours' sleep, at least. Sorry for scaring you," she added, bending to address someone under the bed; Rags-n-Bones must have darted under it to hide when she screamed.

But only an hour could have elapsed when the wardrobe door opened again. Snorting, Ascot woke from a dream about facing a dragon armed with only a cheese grater while Miss Roebanks watched from a tower, wearing a crown as large as the ballroom's chandelier.

"I'm sorry to disturb you again, Ascot," said Maggie, pale, her hair locked beneath her crisp lace cap and her uniform seemingly ironed in place. "But this one's from the queen." She held out an envelope sealed with a circle of pale violet wax and stamped with the emblem of a crowned sun.

Bettina Anna? Ascot broke the seal.

"What does she want?" asked Dmitri.

Groaning, Ascot closed her eyes. "She commands me to meet her in the library at half past three. She doesn't say why."

"You can't refuse her," said Maggie.

"No." Ascot let the letter slip from her fingers and drift to the wardrobe floor. What could the queen possibly want with her?

"Maybe it's just something about the banquet," said Maggie. She patted Ascot's knee. "I've washed your clothes and gown, by the way. I'll bring them along with the lunch."

But Ascot wasn't surprised when the door creaked open at twelve. She cracked an eyelid.

"I'm so, so sorry, Ascot," said Maggie, holding out a white card with gold filigree all around its edges. "I can't disobey Lord Roebanks."

"Now it's Lord Roebanks," muttered Ascot, taking the card and flipping it over to read the brief missive scrolled on its back. "Five o'clock, in the heart of the maze. Maze?"

"A bush maze, out in the garden," said Maggie. "King Alastor had it planted. He loved puzzles. But why does Lord Roebanks want to see you?"

"Like he'd tell me." Ascot tossed the card onto the floor and closed her eyes. *Hopefully, that's the end of it.* She couldn't think of anyone else who could possibly need to see her.

But when Maggie arrived at one, a crease was drawn deep between her brows. "I'm not sure I should give you this one," she said.

Ascot looked up from where she was sitting on the bed, buttoning her shirt. A curl of yellowed paper protruded between Maggie's thumb and forefinger. Frowning, Ascot hooked the last two buttons—through the wrong holes, but she'd attend to that later. "Who's it from?" she asked, reaching for the note.

Maggie hesitated a moment before relinquishing it. "There's no signature." She set the lunch tray she carried on the table under the window. "Captain Catch found it and brought it to me."

Catch. Ignoring the flutter in her stomach, Ascot smoothed the faintly musty paper and read the spikey letters aloud. "Miss Ascot. This is very, very important. Come to the orchard at six thirty this evening, or you'll be sorry later, and don't say I didn't warn you." She blew out her cheeks. "Well."

"How very curious," said Dmitri. Moony lifted his head from the nest's blue wrinkles and yawned.

"What's curious?" he asked.

Ascot flew to his side. "Moony, you're awake." She touched his head. Warm. "How are you feeling?"

"Fine." His voice rasped more than usual, but Ascot detected a note of swagger in it for all that. "Taught Prince Alec a proper lesson, didn't I?"

"You were very brave, but—" She summoned sternness. "—also very reckless."

"Pot, kettle, black," rumbled Dmitri.

Maggie stooped to tickle Moony's chin. "Bet you could eat some fish, hmmm?"

Moony licked his lips. "Well," he said in a wee voice, curling into a small, pathetic huddle, "perhaps a little salmon. And some cream."

"He's fine," said Dmitri to Ascot.

Ascot laughed. Maggie joined in. "I also brought avocados," she said to the eyes under the bed.

Rags-n-Bones shot out as if he'd been loosed from a bow. Grabbing up a napkin, he tied it around his neck and looked at Maggie with expectant love. She handed him three avocados, set a dish of poached salmon and a bowl of cream before Moony, then crossed her legs and sat.

"I reckon you two can help yourselves," she said to Ascot and Dmitri. "Eat up, or you might find Miss Roebanks' offerings alluring, and I wouldn't want to know what she spiked 'em with."

Still holding the scrap of yellow paper, Ascot bit into a sandwich. Crisp vegetables crunched and tangy mustard and sharp cheese tingled her tongue. She missed her roasted rat, but . . . "Mmm. I doubt I could muster an appetite with Miss Roebanks sitting across from me, anyway," she said, mouth full.

"Even so, be careful," said Dmitri. He crunched biscuits. "Will you answer the last note? It's very unlike the others."

"I wish I knew who wrote it." Ascot spread it on her knee. Pale brown ink. All the words were spelled correctly, but there was something childish about the phrasing.

Maggie leaned over for a look. "It could be from one of the servants," she said. "They're all on your side, you know."

Ascot spilled lemonade down her chin. "Really? Is it . . ." She hesitated. "Is it because of the stories?" Her own faith in the white book had taken several knocks recently.

"Mm." Maggie selected an apple from the tray. "For some romantic souls, probably, but for most of us, if it comes down to having a Shadowvalean or a Roebanks as queen, it's an easy choice." She snapped off the apple's stem. "The Roebanks already act like they own Albright. If Miss Roebanks marries Parvanel, she'll take it as permission to do as she pleases. Or worse, her father will."

"But Parvanel would be king, not Lord Roebanks," said Ascot.

Maggie's lips pressed into a line. "I think Lord Roebanks can make Parvanel forget that. He'd rather spend all his time playing with his frogs, anyway."

Ascot picked at a bit of watercress. Had she really gotten so distracted by visions of pretty castles and cheering throngs that she'd forgotten ruling a kingdom came with responsibilities? Spreading her hand, she contemplated her ring.

"If you marry Parvanel, you may have us all sleeping upside down and eating rats before long," Maggie continued. "But we commoners believe that's better than paying exorbitant taxes and receiving nothing in return." Dimples bracketed a sudden, wicked smile. "I bet I could concoct some tasty rat recipes, anyway."

Thank goodness Rags-n-Bones had run into the corner with his avocados. This talk of rat-eating would have him in tears. "I bet you could," said Ascot. She dropped her hand. Her ring's stone really was ugly when it wasn't glowing. "But you should be singing."

Maggie's smile vanished. Looking down, she began peeling her apple. "Well. Well, that probably isn't going to happen."

"It will if I marry Parvanel," said Ascot.

Maggie glanced up from her apple, flashed a brief, forced smile, then looked down again.

She didn't believe it. Not really. Maggie lived in a world of pans and brushes and toasting forks; practical things. However much they might enjoy the stories, Ascot suspected that people from Maggie's world never woke up believing they might wed a prince before nightfall.

But I'm not asking her to believe she might suddenly be proclaimed Queen of Albright, Ascot thought, frustrated. *Just that she could do what she wants to do rather than what her family expects her to do. Is that really as impossible as . . . as . . .*

. . . as her own True Love, the one she had to marry or live a lonely, loveless life, being a man who'd sooner frolic with frogs than rule his kingdom?

Sighing, Ascot picked up her sandwich. She'd lost her appetite, but she couldn't risk Miss Roebanks tempting it back into life with poisoned dainties in—she squinted out the window at the sun—only twenty minutes, now. She stifled a groan.

"You shouldn't go alone," said Dmitri, correctly interpreting the sound.

"No," said Ascot, glad he'd brought it up. She'd hated the thought of facing Miss Roebanks by herself. "Would you mind coming with me, Dmitri?"

Moony sputtered into his cream. "But I'm your guardsman!"

Ascot stroked him between his wings. This was an easy choice to make. Despite his bravado, Moony was still shaky on his legs. And she refused to expose Rags-n-Bones to Miss Roebanks' derision.

"I'm meeting Bettina Anna in the library afterwards," she whispered to Moony. "You wouldn't deny Dmitri that opportunity, would you?"

Moony looked at Dmitri, who crunched cheese and biscuits as if oblivious. Yet a certain level of added alertness ran through every line of his body. Ascot wondered if he'd intended to accompany her ever since hearing the word 'library.' Knowing Dmitri, most likely.

Heaving a sigh, Moony licked cream off his whiskers. "All right. Dmitri can go. Miss Roebanks will probably be more scared of him anyway."

Which was quite an admission from Moony.

"Although she shouldn't be," he added.

And that was just like him, too. Ascot gave him an extra pat and stood. Dmitri leaped to his feet, tail not quite wagging. "We may as well get going," said Ascot, hiding a smile. "I don't know how long it'll take to find this gazebo."

"It's in the rose garden," said Maggie. "I'll show you to it and then come back here and make sure these two are behaving themselves."

"Thanks, Maggie." Ascot took her leather coat from the back of the chair. Cylindrical lumps pulled down her pockets on either side. *The can of hash*, she thought, touching her right pocket. The object in the left one glugged when she reached inside to investigate.

"Oh," she said. "I forgot to give this to the queen this morning."

"What is it?" asked Maggie.

"A bottle of rose wine. The—" Should she say? The Head Butler hadn't sworn her to secrecy or anything, but his tale of Bettina Anna spoke of old pain. Private pain. She decided to compromise. "I found it in the cellars last night."

Both Maggie and Dmitri cocked their heads, undoubtedly sensing there was more to her tale. But to her relief, neither elected to press. "You can give it to her in the library," said Dmitri.

She nodded. "I'll bring it along. See you later, Moony, Rags," she said, settling her coat over her shoulders.

"Tell Miss Roebanks that if she bullies you, I'll hack up a hairball on her favorite dress," said Moony.

"Good luck, miss." Rags-n-Bones waved.

"Maybe they can go visit Miss Harkenpouf later," said Maggie as they walked down Nosegay Wing. "She could use some cheering up."

Ascot picked at an errant splinter in her left thumb. She'd tried enlisting Rags-n-Bones' help in removing them that morning, but he'd fainted, and she'd had to finish the job herself. Apparently, she'd missed a twig or two. *I wonder if Cindy hates me now. I might hate her, if our positions were reversed.*

Probably Cindy didn't hate her. But it wasn't a pleasant thought, regardless.

"At least Bettina Anna's letting her stay here until tonight's banquet." Maggie beckoned them down a left turn, through a hall lined with inexplicable paintings of camels. Ascot really didn't want to know. "Maybe she can get some rest before she goes home. I wonder if she'll marry Lord Petterloof now."

"What?" Ascot's head snapped to the right. Maggie kept walking, looking perfectly composed, matter-of-fact-ish. "Who's Lord Petterloof?"

"Rumor says he's been courting Miss Harkenpouf a while now." Maggie shrugged. "He's nice enough. Over forty and a widower, but generous and good-humored. And rich, of course."

Ascot's feet slowed. They might have stopped altogether if Maggie hadn't taken her arm, guiding her through the hexagonal chamber with the sculpted beehives Catch so obviously despised. "What are you mooning at?" Maggie asked. "Well-born ladies marry rich nobles. It's all they can do. You know that. Why else did you come all the way from Shadowvale to marry a prince you've never met?"

Because according to my ring, he's my True Love. Because I thought I could live Happily Ever After in the Daylands. Because if I'd known I'd face the same choices here, I might as well have stayed in Shadowvale and married that good-natured bore, Count Zanzibander.

And never have met Rags-n-Bones, Dmitri, Scincilla, or Maggie herself. Never traded wits with a were-saber-tooth tiger, or fought off a horde of ghosts.

Gently, she slipped out of Maggie's grip. "I'm no longer sure I came east for good reasons, but I'm glad I did."

"So am I." Grinning, Maggie opened a door on the north wall. Damp, green-smelling air rushed inside, diluting the odor of stale honey. "You'll make a fine queen when you marry Parvanel."

"*If* she marries Parvanel," said Dmitri. "Let us not forget that others are eager to prevent that eventuality." His snout thrust forward, pointing.

A neat patchwork of rose plots broken into diamond, circle, and even horseshoe shapes by a network of gravel paths, lay spread beyond the open doorway. In summer, with the roses in bloom, the garden probably resembled a stained glass window when viewed from above. But only a handful of flowers remained this far into autumn. Ascot touched a withered white rose and it fell apart, its brown-edged petals scattering across her boot-tips.

Rather a grim backdrop for an afternoon tea. Dusting off her hands, she surveyed the rows of bare branches, like so many tangles of thick wire.

A flare of red caught her eye. Ascot raised her gaze to where the graceful dome of a latticework gazebo rose above the tops of the bushes, long purple pennants snapping from each of its eight corners. Miss Roebanks sat at a round white table in its center, her hair rippling like a crown of flame.

CHAPTER TWENTY-ONE:
MURDER MYSTERY

"Cream, Miss Abberdorf?" asked Miss Roebanks, teapot poised over an eggshell-thin porcelain cup. "Or lemon, perhaps?"

"Just black, please," Ascot replied. Dmitri, sitting beside her, his head almost level with her shoulder, whuffed softly. *"I won't drink it,"* she mouthed at him.

Across the table, Miss Roebanks' brows lowered over her eyes. As expected, an assortment of dainties in pretty, pink-and-white dishes were arranged atop the lacey white tablecloth. Several of the offerings, particularly the fruit tarts that glistened like a collection of edible gems, strained the limits of Ascot's self-control.

"If that thing needs to *do* anything, it will go off amongst the bushes, won't it?" Miss Roebanks asked.

It took Ascot a moment to realize Miss Roebanks was speaking of Dmitri. And when she did realize, her jaw sagged at the very notion. Dmitri's ears torqued back several inches. "Of . . . of course," Ascot stuttered.

"Some dogs simply can't get over the habit of marking everything in sight," said Miss Maverly, from Miss Roebanks' other side. "My mother insists they stay in the kennel." She offered a tidbit to Mr. Nutty, who was wearing a sparkly collar and sitting primly on the top of the table.

And I suppose your frabjacketing squirrel never craps where it shouldn't. Ascot cherished the memory of Miss Beige hurling her shoe at the rotten creature.

Miss Maverly's inclusion in the afternoon's entertainment had come not as a surprise, but with the dull, stomach-churning resignation of expectations met. They'd greeted each other with false smiles, then taken seats on either side of Miss Roebanks, as far apart as possible.

"Wolves must be even harder to train." Miss Roebanks poured, one hand with its pink-varnished nails gracefully supporting the rose-and-gold teapot's spout, the other curled around its delicate handle. Every movement was precise, practiced, perfect. Her sprigged muslin gown with pink trim matched the porcelain. Ascot pinched a fold of her own gray trousers.

"Still," Miss Roebanks continued, "the brute has a lovely pelt."

"It would make a lovely winter cloak," agreed Miss Maverly, running an eye over Dmitri. Her gaze cut, snipped, divided, and stitched.

Under the table, Ascot buried her hand in Dmitri's ruff. His skin quivered under her touch, muscles drawn tight as wires. Miss Roebanks set down the pot and handed the delicate cup on its saucer to Ascot.

Raising the aromatic liquid to her lips, Ascot pretended to drink. "Mm, delicious," she said. It did smell nice, too; like spicy incense. Pity she didn't dare actually taste it.

"My father imports it especially from Buenovillia," said Miss Roebanks, pouring a second cup for Miss Maverly.

"How marvelous," said Ascot. She'd never heard of Buenovillia. She shifted, wishing Miss Roebanks would get to the reason why she'd invited her to tea. Wicker chairs, she'd discovered, had an unpleasant way of pinching one's nether regions.

Miss Roebanks passed the second cup to Miss Maverly, then folded her hands under her chin, her fingers lining up like so many slats of an ivory fan. "Dear Miss Abberdorf," she said, her amber-brown eyes wide and made to seem larger with kohl. "You're probably wondering why I asked you here this afternoon."

Finally. In reality, probably only a few minutes had elapsed since they'd sat down. It felt like weeks. "I was a little surprised," said Ascot, taking another fake sip of tea. Dmitri yawned, eyes sleepy, but pointed ears alert.

"Yes, we didn't start off well." Miss Roebanks slid a sideways glance at Miss Maverly. The corner of Miss Maverly's mouth twitched and she leaned forward to pet Mr. Nutty. Miss Roebanks' gaze returned to Ascot. "My father has high expectations of me, you see. He's determined that I should marry Prince Parvanel. I'm sure you understand."

"Actually . . ." Ascot bit her lip, then went for it. ". . . I heard that King Alastor was once engaged to a Miss Regina Roebanks."

She'd managed to surprise Miss Roebanks, who drew back, her eyelashes fluttering. She quickly recovered her poise. "That would be my Aunt Regina. There never was an official engagement. Where did you hear that?"

Ascot wasn't about to say "the Head Butler's ghost." And if she said "the servants," she suspected Miss Roebanks would blame Maggie and heap petty vengeance on her head.

"Somewhere in town," she said, stirring her tea. Frabjacket, but those fruit tarts looked scrumptious!

"Oh, I thought perhaps Captain Catch told you." Miss Roebanks tented her fingers again. "That's what I wished to speak to you about."

The spoon clattered noisily against the rim of Ascot's teacup. "Catch?" Of all the things Miss Roebanks could have been concerned about, he was . . . well, fairly low on the list. She hoped she wasn't blushing, but from the warmth flooding her cheeks, she feared she was. "What about him?" By her side, Dmitri perked up his ears.

Another side-wards glance at Miss Maverly. "We can't help but notice he's been courting you, dear," said Miss Roebanks.

Good thing she'd already dropped her spoon. "Courting me?"

Tandem nods. "He defended you that first day, when I mistakenly thought you might bite me," said Miss Roebanks.

"And he danced with you at the ball," said Miss Maverly. "I saw him holding your hand."

Bandaging *my hand because your squirrel bit me.* Ascot scowled at Mr. Nutty, squatted next to a pot of jam, vigorously scratching an ear with a hind foot. It probably had fleas. "We've spoken a few times," she said. "I wouldn't call it courting."

"That's good," said Miss Roebanks. Miss Maverly heaved a theatrical sigh of relief and sat back with her teacup. "You're a stranger in Albright, so you wouldn't know you shouldn't trust anything he says."

"I know he's a liar," said Ascot.

"He's a murderer," said Miss Roebanks.

Ascot wasn't holding her cup, so there was no awkward moment where she fumbled it, spilled it, and burned herself. The breath she'd just taken sat in her lungs, solidifying into lead. *Lub-a-dub, lub-a-dub,* went her heart. The sound contrasted strangely with the cheerful whistle of a gardener working a pair of clippers somewhere off to her left.

With great care, Ascot lifted her hands and settled them to either side of her plate, palms flat on the lace tablecloth. *Murderer.* "But—"

Dmitri jumped as if he'd been stung and began nibbling a spot on his shoulder, seemingly plagued by a sudden itch. "Don't protest," he whispered under his breath. "Press for details."

Swallowing twice, Ascot got her throat working again. "Who did he murder?"

"King Alastor." Miss Roebanks' gaze held steady. Ascot glanced at Miss Maverly. Even she looked serious. Dmitri stopped nibbling and rested his chin on the table's edge.

Ascot's fingertips rat-a-tatted against the cloth. She stilled them. "But how?" she asked. "He would've been caught, surely."

"No one could prove anything," said Miss Roebanks. "He and King Alastor went out one morning, and Catch came running back a while later with some story about an accident. When they found King Alastor's body, his face was all swollen and blackened."

Grimacing, Ascot pushed her teacup and untouched plate aside. At least no one would think it suspicious now if she didn't eat anything.

Miss Roebanks' voice continued, inexorably. "Upon investigation, Bettina Anna found Catch innocent of wrong-doing. Now how could that be, when King Alastor was so obviously strangled? My father," Miss Roebanks leaned forward, lowering her voice, and despite herself, Ascot leaned forward as well, "believes Catch has some sinister hold over the queen. He showed up just a year after King Alastor wed her and insinuated himself into the castle. He's never left her side since King Alastor's death. Maybe he knows some secret about her that she doesn't want revealed."

"You can see why we're concerned," said Miss Maverly. "He could be feeding you all sorts of lies to further his own agenda. Or maybe he just wants to ingratiate himself with you, in case you marry Parvanel."

Ascot stared down into her tea. Fragments of brown leaves clumped on the bottom of her cup. They didn't resemble a heart, or a bloody knife, or a crown, or anything other than a powdery bit of sediment.

Catch. He'd refused her entry to Albright, tried to scare her away in saber-tooth form, and tricked her out of meeting Parvanel at the ball. If he was trying to ingratiate himself, he'd done a lousy job of it.

Until last night. Until she was one of the only three candidates remaining, and the sole remaining candidate who'd never heard the rumors of his past.

Could he be a murderer? What did he really want? If he were exploiting some kind of hold over Bettina Anna, he didn't seem to be enjoying it.

Across the table, Miss Roebanks refreshed hers and Miss Maverly's cups of tea. Having scattered loose hair and dander into the jam and all over a plate of crumpets, Mr. Nutty quit scratching and hopped onto Miss Maverly's lap. Their stares pinned Ascot.

If only I knew someone else I could question. She doodled with a drop of tea spilled on the white tablecloth. "Does Cindy— Scincilla—know the rumors about Catch?" she asked. "She never said anything to me." Nor had Miss Beige, come to that.

"I don't know how much attention Miss Harkenpouf pays to politics," said Miss Roebanks. "She's a sweet creature, but her head's always in the clouds. Of course, if she'd passed last night's test, I'd have warned her, as well."

Ascot added another drop of tea to her doodle. It resembled a question mark. "Scincilla seemed so confident last night. I suppose she just ran out of time."

"I heard that she strung some of the harps too tight and the strings snapped," said Miss Roebanks.

A faint giggle overlapped the gardener's whistle. Ascot looked up just in time to see Miss Maverly hide a smirk behind her teacup.

Miss Maverly. What *was* she doing at Albright Castle? Why would she even want to stay, after she was out of the competition for Parvanel's affections?

And why had the mention of snapped strings amused her? Reflecting, Ascot ran a finger around her teacup's rim. A faint whiff of decayed roses mingled with the scents of tea and pastry. Dmitri's tongue swiped out to wet his muzzle.

"Please make sure that beast doesn't drool on my china," said Miss Roebanks sharply, hugging her embroidered shawl closer about her shoulders as a chill breeze fluttered the tablecloth.

Miss Maverly reemerged from behind her teacup. "You will stop vamping at Catch, now, won't you?" she asked.

Ascot started. Had Miss Maverly just used the "v" word? *Dreadfully* crass in Shadowvale, and from the sly grin twisting Miss Maverly's lips, Ascot suspected she knew it.

She went on, all big-eyed and innocent. "I mean, knowing that he's a killer—"

"Nonsense," said Dmitri.

Miss Roebanks' and Miss Maverly's heads swung around. Their mouths rounded.

Maybe I can quickly pretend to be a clever ventriloquist, thought Ascot. But Dmitri negated that option by reaching out a huge forepaw and snagging a plate of cream buns.

"I don't smell anything untoward about these," he said, dragging them onto the seat of the unoccupied chair next to Ascot. Two buns vanished in a single bite.

Miss Maverly leaped to her feet, Mr. Nutty cradled in one arm. "It's a tame wolf," she cried, leveling a finger at Ascot. "You cheated!"

"Keep spinning tales around me and you'll discover how far I am from tame, young lady." Dmitri licked cream off his chops. "No, Ascot did not tame me. But before you run to the queen with complaints of cheating, chew on this: what she did manage was far more impressive." Lifting his head from the plate of buns, Dmitri fixed Miss Maverly with a cold amber gaze. "She *convinced* me. And that, young lady, is something the pair of you have utterly failed to do."

Chapter Twenty-Two:
Message in a Bottle

"I'm surprised they didn't run to Bettina Anna already," said Ascot. Gravel crunched beneath her boots as she marched back towards the castle.

"You mean, about your not really taming me?" asked Dmitri, utterly unrepentant, padding at her heels. Moisture hung in the air, dampening Ascot's skin without the weather having to go through the bother of actually raining. Behind her, in the gazebo, Miss Roebanks' and Miss Maverly's voices rose in sharp staccato. Ascot's neck ached with the effort of not looking back.

"Of course I mean that." She stopped so quickly that gravel pinged off her boots and into the rose plots lining both sides of the path. "Why'd you have to speak up now? I was so close to meeting Parvanel and discovering if he's really—" She bit the thought in half.

Dmitri sat, curling his tail about his forelegs. "Maybe I feared that you were actually starting to believe their lies," he said. "Maybe I felt that since they'd said their piece, there was little point in listening to further slander. And possibly, just possibly, I grew weary of being treated like a senseless brute whose hide may be claimed by the first person to shoot me."

"Oh, Dmitri." Ascot knelt, heedless of the rough pebbles that scoured her knees. Her fingers sank into his thick fur, softer than the finest plush. "I'm sorry. It's not right that you have to pretend to be a pet just to be here. Or that Rags has to eat cobblestones. Or any of it. If I could just meet Parvanel—"

Dmitri rested his chin on her shoulder. "Hush. I'm sorry for worrying you. Miss Roebanks is not going to accuse you of cheating."

Ascot pulled back to arm's length. "Why not?"

"You didn't consider what Maggie said, did you? The common folk are on your side. Perhaps some of the nobles as well; I gather that the Roebanks aren't universally liked. If Bettina Anna dismissed you at this late hour, there would be rancor."

Ascot rubbed her nose, considering.

"Besides," Dmitri added, "I suspect Miss Roebanks would prefer to stifle accusations of cheating."

"You think she cheated herself?"

"I deem it highly unlikely that a lady of Miss Roebanks' status would know how to bake a cake fit for a banquet, yes. Don't excite yourself. Moony helped you in the cellars last night. Your case will not hold up to scrutiny, either."

"I know." Ascot shivered as the wind picked up. "But did you hear how Miss Maverly tittered when Miss Roebanks spoke of Scincilla? I wonder what she found so amusing." She scowled at the sky. A woolly gray carpet of clouds was rolling in, covering the sky like an ill-knit sweater. "It's strange that the strings snapped. Those harps were so old I'd think their frames would break, if you strung them too tight."

"Particularly since old harps were generally strung with copper wire," Dmitri agreed.

Ascot rubbed her nose again. Something didn't fit.

"Why not think as you walk?" Dmitri bumped her legs with his head. "You don't wish to be tardy for your appointment with Her Majesty, after all."

Laughing, Ascot allowed him to bully her to her feet. "You just want to get to the library early enough to look around."

His tongue lolled. "Guilty as charged."

They started walking again. Gardeners hurried past with armloads of fresh-cut bouquets, presumably intended for the banquet. Another biting wind cut past. Ascot thrust her hands deep in her pockets. The wine bottle sloshed. The can of hash clunked. And something round and smooth as a rain-washed pebble rattled softly.

"Oh." Ascot clenched her fist around it. "Mr. Nutty."

Dmitri glanced over his shoulder. "No, he's still at the gazebo."

"No." Ascot's stomach burned. "Last night, Miss Roebanks kept skulking around at the back of the group. I heard something drop a couple times, then I found this." She drew the hazelnut from her pocket. "I think she was leaving a trail for Mr. Nutty. What do you want to bet he bit through those harp strings?" The nasty creature had good jaws, she knew. The scab on her hand still stung intermittently. "We know Miss Maverly was in the castle last night."

"She probably helped Miss Roebanks with her cake, too," said Dmitri. He prodded the nut with his nose, then looked up at her. "It's not evidence enough to convince the queen."

"No." Ascot yanked open the door to the honeybee room. "But it's enough to convince me. The rotten sneak."

Miss Roebanks had cheated Cindy out of victory, and now perhaps she'd have to marry an old lord she didn't love.

Halfway through the door, Ascot paused. *But if I marry Parvanel, I could invite Cindy to the castle. She'd have her pick of handsome young noblemen.*

Already inside the honeybee room, Dmitri let out an impatient grunt. "Why are you dawdling?"

"I'm coming," said Ascot, and promptly snagged her toe on a fuzzy, black-and-yellow striped rug. Yelping, she grabbed for the back of a davenport upholstered in gold brocade.

Catch was sitting on it.

"Good afternoon, Miss Abberdorf," he said, his gaze fixed on one of the beehive-topped columns.

Ascot jumped back. "Captain."

Well. What *did* you say to a potential murderer who had, by the way, saved your life only just that morning? At least he was fully dressed.

"Good afternoon, Captain," said Dmitri.

Ascot closed her eyes in a wince. *Didn't you hear what Miss Roebanks said, Dmitri? Why are you making friendly with the maybe-mad strangler?*

"Perhaps you can guide us to the library?" Dmitri asked, tail waving in what she recognized as a cordial manner.

"That's why I'm here," said Catch. "Her Majesty suspected you would not know the way." He pushed off the davenport slowly, as if his joints hurt. "I did not wish to disrupt your *tête-à-tête* with Miss Roebanks. Means—"

"Yes, thank you," said Ascot. "Let's be going, then." *You could have interrupted us. It's not like you're averse to rudeness. So why didn't you? Because Miss Roebanks knows about you?*

King Alastor's face was black and swollen when they found his body. Ascot's throat tightened.

Catch opened a door on the east wall, revealing a black walnut paneled corridor Ascot had never seen before: dark, narrow, and somber. Albright Castle seemed to go on and on inside, like some great ugly trick box.

Fortunately, Catch didn't appear to be in the mood for conversation. He walked a little ahead, his brown coat swishing behind him.

Maybe he's afraid Miss Roebanks told me about King Alastor. But then, wouldn't he be better served to act friendly, perhaps remind her of his rescue in the graveyard?

Ascot gave up. Catch's motivations remained a mystery. She wished she could ignore him, but every time she tried, he popped up right where he shouldn't, like a thorn in a pudding.

Catch led them up two flights and halfway down a long hall decorated with portraits of the royal family. Prince Parvanel's picture hung just to the left of the stairwell.

"There." Catch nodded to a heavy walnut door with woodwork scrolling, a gleaming plaque set into its surface.

Ascot stared at Parvanel's portrait. Handsome, yes. Golden hair rippled over broad shoulders. She couldn't help but admire his dimples and blue eyes, but found herself less enamored of the loving smile directed at the small green frog he held cupped in one hand.

"Come along," said Dmitri, tugging her coat. Ascot let him pull her towards the library.

"I'll take you to Lord Roebanks when Her Majesty dismisses you," said Catch. He leaned next to the door and folded his arms over his chest.

Ascot's eyes narrowed. "How do you know about our meeting?"

"He told me. Don't argue. You'd get lost trying to find your way through the maze." Catch stared at the opposite wall, lips pressed as tight as if he meant to never speak again.

With a final glare, Ascot turned the latch. The door opened without the slightest squeak of hinges. A hush spilled into the hall, accompanied by the musty smell of old paper. Dmitri slipped through the gap. Stifling a sneeze that would have broken the silence into a million indignant shards, Ascot followed, easing the door shut behind her. A lush burgundy carpet squished beneath her feet.

"Heaven," murmured Dmitri.

Heaven indeed, if your idea of heaven contained many books. Two whole stories of them, in fact, crammed thick on recessed shelves. Warm, earthy colors greeted Ascot everywhere she looked: chocolate brown, brick red, and sand. Floor-to-ceiling windows on the library's far end provided a view of the gardens that would have been stunning on a sunnier day. For the reader craving more privacy, big squashy chairs were placed in alcoves, alongside small round table with oil lamps providing steady, soft illumination.

"Amazing." Ascot ran a hand along a row of leather spines. "Think we can find *The Idiot* before we meet Bettina Anna?"

"We should ask a librarian." Dmitri walked a small circle of the room, stopping to nuzzle a small, iron staircase on wheels, used to access the higher shelves. "Of course, he or she might be involved in banquet preparations."

"Nonsense," said Ascot. "Librarians don't go to parties. He's probably lurking behind one of the bookcases." She squished off across the burgundy floor, passing under the large archway separating the main room from the smaller one with the window. Someone sat in one of the armchairs, back towards the room. Perhaps they knew where the librarian was. As Ascot approached, the light passing through the beveled windows brightened from lead to silver. A sliver of blue cracked the heavy sky.

"Excuse me," said Ascot, stopping behind the plush brown armchair. "Do you know where the librarian is?"

Queen Bettina Anna turned her head to regard Ascot over the chair's wing. "You're early, Miss Abberdorf," she said. Her gaze dissected Ascot into bite-sized fragments.

Oops. Well, how was I to know? What the blazes was the queen doing here all alone, without a single guardsman? She wasn't even wearing a crown.

"My apologies, Your Majesty," she managed to sputter. "I was looking for a book."

Bettina Anna continued studying her, one small, plump hand propping up her chin. Ascot tried not to squirm. She'd already forgotten to curtsy.

"I knew you were coming," said Bettina Anna.

"You invited me, Your—"

"Not to the library. To Albright. I knew the day I decided to hold a ball." Ascot started and Bettina Anna lifted her other hand off the book in her lap to wave her amazement aside. "Not you, specifically. I expected something more classic: a golden flow of hair and a voice like angels' song. I braced myself for a mysterious coach to arrive the night of the ball, made out of lilies, perhaps, or drawn by unicorns. But it appears GEL has more imagination than I gave them credit for."

The Guild of Enchanting Ladies? Ascot stuck her hands in her pockets, then took them out again. They dangled awkwardly at her sides, so she clasped them in front of her abdomen. "I don't understand, Your Majesty."

"You came in search of True Love and Happily Ever After."

"Well, yes," said Ascot. Dmitri padded to her side. She glanced down at him, hoping he might alleviate the confusion, but he watched the queen.

"Of course." Bettina Anna didn't quite nod; perhaps such behavior was considered gauche for a queen. "I hoped it would not come to this. I prayed you would fail, that first night in the woods." She turned a brief scrutiny on Dmitri. "But those favored by GEL have ways of finding ways. They'll do anything to regain influence in Albright."

"I'm not working with GEL," said Ascot.

Bettina Anna's gaze grew pointed. "Can you truly swear to that?"

Ascot opened her mouth—

—and the face of the old lady from her father's funeral instantly rose to her mind, quickly followed by that of the granny's at the inn. Such sweet-looking old women, both of them. Wise, soft, and wrinkly; the kind you'd feel obliged to draw a drink of water for, if you found them sitting by a well.

Ascot shut her mouth. She hadn't consulted with GEL. Hadn't even heard of them until yesterday. But that didn't mean that GEL couldn't have lined her up like an arrow and shot her directly towards Albright.

Bettina Anna picked up a red leather bookmark from the table next to her chair and marked her place. Setting her book aside, she patted the seat of a nearby chair. Ascot sat on its very edge, feet braced against the floor.

"This is irregular," said Bettina Anna, folding her hands in her lap. "But I feel I must make the attempt. Give over your scheme, Miss Abberdorf. Leave before the banquet commences, and I will reimburse you for any debts you may have incurred."

"It's not a scheme," said Ascot. "Whatever GEL's planning, I—I just want my happy ending."

"And what will *my* ending be, if you achieve it?" asked Bettina Anna. "Shall I be made to dance in red hot shoes at your wedding, or will you roll me down a hill in a nail-studded barrel, if GEL returns in triumph?"

Ascot's breath squeaked in her throat.

"How odd, to turn the page and discover the former heroine transformed into the villain," said Bettina Anna. Her eyes misted, fixed on some horrific vision.

"I would never allow such a thing," Ascot protested.

All the last scenes of the stories crowded into her head. Birds pecking out the stepsisters' eyes. The wicked witch, baking in her own oven. The book related their fates matter-of-factly, implying you weren't supposed to care. But now it struck Ascot—they had stories too. *I even called Bettina Anna an evil queen in my mind,* she thought, and went cold inside.

Bettina Anna sat silently in her chair, waiting. Gray threads showed amongst her carefully arranged golden curls. Small lines traced the edges of her mouth.

"Is that why you've been letting Lord Roebanks take control?" Ascot asked. "So GEL couldn't blame you if Parvanel married someone they didn't approve of?"

"Yes." She looked out the window. "That, and the nobles trust Lord Roebanks. He is not an . . . affable man, but he is keenly aware of GEL's machinations. They will not be able to use him as they have others. His daughter's marriage to my son will give Albright stability."

"Shouldn't it be Parvanel's choice?"

Blood darkened Bettina Anna's face. Both her small, plump hands clenched. "My son has reached his majority. If he does not marry and claim his throne soon, Albright law states that GEL and MAGI will elect the next ruler. Better the Roebanks than them."

"But it's not a question of one or the other," said Ascot. If she'd been just a bit younger, she'd have stamped a foot. "I owe GEL nothing, so if Parvanel chooses me—"

"What is that, there, upon your finger?" demanded Bettina Anna.

Ascot barely kept herself from hiding her hand with its dark, ugly ring behind her back.

"I saw it glow at the ball," said Bettina Anna. "You've met a member of GEL. They've given you one of their trinkets, and even if you accepted it in innocence, GEL's gifts never come debt-free."

Her glare blazed ferociously out the window for half a long minute before its fire finally dimmed. She refocused on Ascot. "I cannot see it as anything other than a choice between GEL and the Roebanks. So, Miss Abberdorf, I ask again: kindly leave Albright tonight." She leaned back in her chair, her hands relaxing on her lap. "There is no point in your attending the banquet, anyway. You will find the last test impossible."

"If it's impossible, then Miss Roebanks can't—" Ascot mentally kicked herself. "It's a trick. You've already told her how to win."

"Yes," said Bettina Anna. Not the slightest trace of apology in her manner. "Hate me if you like, but it is the kindest solution." Now, at last, she softened. "For yourself, as well."

That was Betty Ann speaking. Betty Ann, who hadn't found one friend in court. Who had been scorned, despised, and nearly murdered a year after she married King Alastor.

Ascot remembered. "I have something for you, Your Majesty." With cold fingers, she worked the pink bottle out of her pocket, removed its protective wrapping, and set it beside Bettina Anna's book.

Bettina Anna paled to her hairline. "Duncan," she breathed.

Ascot looked away. She'd never given thought to the actual act of handing the bottle over, or the circumstances in which she'd received it. How to tell a person that the ghost of someone they knew, someone they might have loved, was trapped in the cellars? "He wanted you to have it," she mumbled.

From pale, Bettina Anna went white, so white her blue veins showed, as if her skin were a layer of milky glass. *Dye her hair black and she could pass for a noble Shadowvalean.* Ascot stifled a giggle, wanting to slap herself for it.

"This is too cruel," said Bettina Anna, touching the bottle with the very tip of one finger. "Look here, girl. Look at the wreckage the stories leave in their wake. Lord Roebanks wanted GEL banished because their machinations cost his sister her royal wedding. But I banished them because they are just too cruel, with their insistence on neat, bow-wrapped endings."

She looked at Ascot. "You don't understand, do you?"

"Well." Ascot pursed her lips. Was the whole mess really all GEL's fault? Betty Ann could have refused to marry Prince Alastor.

"I understand, Your Majesty," said Dmitri.

Ascot gulped. But Bettina Anna's only reaction to a talking wolf was to raise a brow.

Dmitri appeared to be studying a flock of starlings pirouetting past the beveled window. "I was human once, you see."

Ascot nearly fell off her chair. "You mean you weren't always a wolf?"

"No." A growl underlay Dmitri's words. "That is exactly what I do not mean. I am a wolf. But long ago, a . . . friend thought I would be happier as a human and paid a wizard to transform me." He ran his tongue along his chops. "I was lucky. Very lucky. After a year, I found someone to change me back."

"But couldn't you read books and go to the theatre as a human?" asked Ascot. "Without anyone trying to shoot you?"

Dmitri looked at her. "Yes," he said. "I could." His head turned back to watch the starlings.

"You were indeed very lucky," said Bettina Anna. She fingered the tattered gold foil around the rose bottle's cork. "You were able to go back. As much as one can."

"What's done can never be fully undone," said Dmitri.

Ascot stared from one to the other. *He agrees with her.* "I'm not leaving," she said.

Any satisfaction she might have felt withered when they both looked at her. Ascot shrank in her chair like a schoolgirl who had spoken out of turn.

"I'm not leaving," she repeated, forcing her chin up.

"I have already told you tonight's test is impossible," said Bettina Anna.

"Everyone thought my getting the key to the Moonlight Muscatel was impossible, too. But I did get it, and after that, after nearly getting killed by ghosts, you want me to give up?" She wasn't going to cry. No, she was a million miles from crying. Her fists trembled on her lap, longing to punch something.

"I did say you would be reimbursed."

"That's not good enough."

"Ascot." Dmitri broke into the argument. "You don't still believe that marrying Parvanel is the key to your happiness, do you?"

"Yes! No." She looked out the window. The blue slit of sunlight and sky was slowly sealing itself up. *I don't know what I believe anymore. I just know it's wrong to simply give up, to hand everything over to the Roebanks because they're powerful and want it.*

And if they were wrong, and the stories were right, what did that bode for her future, should she give up on Parvanel? Her ring ached on her hand. *Alone, unwanted, unloved.*

Something warm and rough settled on her knee. She glanced down. Dmitri's paw. "Don't you think it might be wiser to acquiesce to our experience?" he asked.

Ascot's throat loosened. Placing a hand over his paw, she met his eyes. "If I give up because of what you've told me, I'm still just following someone else's story, aren't I?"

Dmitri's sigh fluttered the left leg of her trousers. "Well, there you have it, Your Majesty. Somehow, she always manages to pip me at the post."

Bettina Anna sighed, too. "I cannot prevent you from attending the banquet, Miss Abberdorf. But neither can I wish you success. The Roebanks might be cold and imperious, but at least their powers are natural."

Ascot nodded stiffly. "I understand."

"Then I shall see you at eight, Miss Abberdorf." Picking up her book, Bettina Anna opened it on her lap. "The banquet is formal attire, so make sure you're properly dressed." She turned a page.

Standing, Ascot bowed. "Come on, Dmitri," she said, squishing off across the burgundy carpet. "Might as well get my meeting with Lord Roebanks over with."

No reply. She looked back. Dmitri drooped, staring at the shelves upon shelves of books. An image of Rags-n-Bones denied an avocado rose to her mind. "Oh. You'd like to stay."

"I didn't really get a chance to browse," he said.

You'll have oodles of chances when I'm queen. But perhaps that wasn't going to happen after all. Even if the stories were true, she could no longer fully trust them.

"Go ahead," she said. "I'll see what Lord Roebanks wants with me. Catch can—"

Oh, right. Catch. Oh, dear.

"You don't believe that rot about him being a murderer, do you?" asked Dmitri, as always divining what was on her mind.

Ascot twisted her fingers together. "We don't know much about him," she mumbled. "And he does lie."

Dmitri sat. When his tail curled around his front legs, Ascot knew she was in for a scolding. "He came to me and Rags-n-Bones last night after you were locked in the cellar. He opened the ballroom so we could get the candelabra we used to save you. After directing me and Rags to the servants' graveyard in case you tried to escape by that route, he then went to check the silver-locked door before arriving back at the graveyard in time to carry you over the wall."

He did all that to help me? Why? Her fingers twisted tighter.

"Who would you rather trust? Him or Miss Roebanks?"

"Catch," she said. "But—"

"Good," said Dmitri. "That's sensible."

Ascot kept staring at the floor. She did trust Catch. Sort of. Enough. So why did she dread walking alone with him?

Because I'm afraid I'll learn I was wrong to trust him. That would hurt more than she could imagine.

But it would be unfair to deny Dmitri a chance to find his book after all his help. And most likely Catch wouldn't say or do anything, anyway. "All right," she said, untangling her hands. "I'll meet you back in Nosegay Wing later."

He stepped towards a shelf, then paused. "Are you going to answer that last missive?"

Ascot pursed her lips, fingering the crumbling strip of yellow paper. "Haven't decided yet. I might, since Maggie thinks a servant might have written it. See you later, Dmitri." She didn't pat his head; it wouldn't be right.

"Good luck, Ascot. And thank you."

Before she stepped out into the portrait hall, she glanced back to see Dmitri rear up and snaffle a green leather volume off a high shelf. His tail wagged.

Smiling, she closed the door behind her. Catch still stood with his back to the wall and arms folded, as if he hadn't twitched a muscle since she'd entered the library.

He raised an eyebrow. "Ready to confront Lord Roebanks? Means—"

"Yes," said Ascot. "I am."

CHAPTER TWENTY-THREE:
AMAZEMENT

Catch flinched.

Ascot looked from him to the doorway of the honeybee chamber. "You really hate this room, don't you?" she asked. His shoulders were hiked almost to his ears. A grimace revealed his eyeteeth.

He uncoiled. "Yes," he said, and, hooking her arm, crossed the chamber in six strides. Opening the northern door, he all but threw her into the brisk and damp-smelling air outside, then slammed it behind them, shutting off the bittersweet reek of beeswax candles.

"Ow," said Ascot, rubbing her arm.

Catch walked ahead. "The maze is to the east. Follow close, or you'll get lost."

The wind sharpened its teeth on their skin. Above, the damp, wooly clouds slowly flattened into a solid sheet of gray. As they entered a green corridor formed by ten-foot hedges, their sides and tops pruned flat, yellow sand replaced the gravel coating the path. *Crunch, crunch,* went Ascot's footsteps. Catch's remained silent as a cat's.

At least now I know why. "Maggie said King Alastor had this maze planted," said Ascot.

A fleeting frown crossed Catch's face. "Yes. He liked puzzles," he said, and took the first left turn.

Miss Roebanks claims you murdered him. Ascot bit her tongue. A fresh wind roared down the alley of manicured greenery, pushing against her chest like a giant, invisible hand. Catch's hair danced about his face, clear of his eyes for once. He didn't look like a murderer. Whatever murderers looked like.

The gale subsided. Absently, Catch took a hand out of his pocket and combed his hair with his fingers.

He couldn't be a murderer. Dmitri didn't believe it. Besides, Maggie would have said something. Cindy would have said something. Bettina Anna would've had him arrested. Ascot forced her shoulders to drop.

"Any idea what Lord Roebanks wants with me?" she asked.

A flash of a hazel eye over Catch's shoulder. The right one, still bruised. "Nothing good," he said.

Of course not. His Lordship was probably going to tell her not to come to the banquet too. Ascot set her jaw. *What a waste of time. I should just turn around and go back to Nosegay Wing.*

And she might have, if she hadn't realized she'd missed several turns in the maze. She'd probably get lost trying to find her way back out. Grumbling, she trudged on as Catch led her through an herb garden, small circular plots of aging lavender and dried sage smelling like a sachet in a sock drawer. White moths wobbled through the air, pausing to flit on spiny, gray-green leaves. Ascot smiled, thinking how Moony would enjoy pouncing on them once she was queen. If she became queen.

What if her ring was wrong and Parvanel didn't fall in love with her tonight? Or if the queen's test truly did prove impossible and the Roebanks banished her from Albright? What would she do then, out of silverware and disowned by her family, alone and unloved, forever?

You think that's bad? What if you succeed and discover the white book's right about everything except the Happily Ever After part? What do you do then?

A mouthful of prickles slapped her from her thoughts. "Ugh!" Spitting, she whacked aside the branch she'd just walked into. During her distraction, the path had grown unkempt. Blades of grass jutted through the yellow sand and sprigs of untrimmed greenery poked out of the hedges.

"Are you sure this is the right way?" she asked, scrubbing her mouth with her sleeve. She couldn't imagine Lord Roebanks risking tearing his fine clothes on the cantankerous greenery.

Catch didn't reply. His brown-clad back disappeared through a slit between two bushes. Smacking branches aside with the blade of a hand, Ascot followed. She squeezed through a final gap and found herself standing in a dingy, weed-infested clearing bordered by a dark pond. Sulfuric fumes thickened the air. A thin gray willow grew by the pond's edge, dipping its branches into the dark water.

Ascot set her fists to her hips. Suspicions confirmed; no Lord Roebanks in sight. "Why did you bring—"

A man stood on the far bank of the pond. Tall, slim, and broad-shouldered, with flowing golden hair. As she watched, he pinched something out of a pouch and knelt beside a collection of lily pads.

Rosy light flickered in the corner of her left eye. A quick glance down confirmed that her ring was once more aglow, blazing on her finger. "Prince Parvanel!" she exclaimed, starting forward. What luck! She lifted her hand to wave.

Click.

A crisp and lovely little sound, as if a thousand bits of well-oiled machinery had all fallen into place at exactly the same moment.

Slowly, Ascot turned and stared into the black O of the pistol's mouth, aimed directly at her head.

The black mouth swallowed the world. Nothing else existed. She couldn't look away, and even if she had, she still would've seen it. The black mouth. Leveled. Ready. Gritting her teeth, she waited for it to swallow her.

Time stretched.

A frog croaked. Across the pond, somewhere; a cheerful sound. A pause, then a second frog joined in, then an entire chorus, singing a throaty madrigal. A man's delighted laugh danced across the dark water. *Parvanel. So he is capable of being happy, then.*

Why hadn't the black mouth swallowed her yet?

Because—*oh! Of course.* Ascot's jaw unclenched. Time returned to its proper cadence. "Well," she said, stretching the tension out of her shoulders. "I should've trusted Dmitri."

The waxy light smudged pits under Catch's cheekbones and sank his eyes in their sockets.

"Did Lord Roebanks put you up to this?" asked Ascot, looking out over the pond. Water lilies, white ones with deep pink centers, floated over the wind-ruffled surface. "Did he tell you to cut out my heart and bring it to him in a box, as well?"

"Perhaps I'm acting on my own volition. Means—"

"Liar."

He accepted the charge with a nod. "Lord Roebanks wants you to vanish quietly, Miss Abberdorf. So, no heart-in-a-box."

She could've pointed out the impossibility of her "vanishing quietly" with Parvanel standing across the water, in clear hearing range of any gunshots. But she forbore, sensing Catch needed to play out this charade a while longer.

"Hasn't he heard tonight's test is rigged?" she asked instead, wandering to the pond's edge. The pistol followed her, fixed as the point on a compass. "I'd think he'd enjoy watching me fail."

"If GEL is aiding you, you may not fail. It's a risk his lordship is unwilling to take."

"How odd to think that murder is less risky than allowing someone to attend a banquet." Ascot stooped for a flat stone. "If you mean to sink my body into the pond, you'd better wait until Parvanel leaves." She skipped the stone across the water. "Is that what you were intending? Because noble Shadowvaleans don't crumble into dust, in case you wondered."

No reply. She glanced back. Catch looked as drawn as if he'd caught an illness in the past minute; possibly a fatal one. His throat worked. "I wasn't."

Ascot laughed softly and walked back to stand before him. "At ease, Captain. You're not going to kill me."

He glared. "You don't know me so well."

"I know that if you meant to shoot me, you'd have done so before I turned around. You certainly wouldn't let me wander around talking." She touched his arm. "I'm glad you're not a murderer."

He made a noise, something between a gulp and a sob. Then he made it again and dropped his arm. "I knew I couldn't do it. What now?" Grinding his teeth, he leaped away from her, the pistol again sighting on her in one fluid motion. "Promise to leave Albright, or I will fire. I will."

A breeze rattled the willow's top branches. Ascot cocked her head. "Well?"

Two stripes of angry red ignited along Catch's cheekbones. "Dammit." Spinning on his heel, he hurled the pistol out into the water. It sank with a single, oily *blurt,* momentarily interrupting the frogs' song. "What now? Dammit." He sank into a crouch, arms folded over his head.

I should probably be offended that he's upset over his inability to kill me. Instead, she knelt beside him and wrapped an arm over his shoulders. "Don't beat yourself up about it."

"I knew I would fail," he said. "I knew it. Dammit, what now?"

She patted his back. "Well, now I suppose you go to Lord Roebanks and say 'sorry, couldn't do it.'"

A wild, harsh noise tore out of his throat. It took her a second to recognize it as a laugh. "If Lord Roebanks was so easily put off, do you think I'd have undertaken this assignment in the first place?" he asked, lifting his head.

"Why did you agree to do it?"

His head fell back into his arms. "I wanted to avoid a trip to the scaffold."

"The scaffold? You mean—execution?"

He nodded.

Ascot sank onto her heels, wishing that, like Moony, she could simply find a spot and groom herself until she was ready to face the world again. "What did you do?"

"I—" He passed a hand across his face, then began again, wearily. "The court held a riding party on King Alastor and Queen Bettina Anna's first anniversary."

"That was you." The wind's drone nearly drowned out her whisper. "That attempt on Bettina Anna's life—that was you."

"I was a lousy assassin then, too." Looking out over the pond, he sighed, one arm hanging limp across his knee. "Bettina Anna never was much of a horsewoman. She stayed behind, picking flowers. I approached her in saber-tooth form. Lord Roebanks ordered—"

Ascot made a small sound.

"Yes, Lord Roebanks was also behind that attempt." Catch nodded. "He wanted her death to seem a random animal attack." He smoothed back his hair and the wind promptly disordered it again. "Until today, I always wondered if I would've gone through with it. Alastor snuck away from the main party and spotted me, skulking behind a rock. He shot me before I made up my mind." He smiled without humor. "Only hit my shoulder. I transformed back into human, swearing at him for a lousy shot, and he insisted on dragging me to the castle to recover."

Lifting a hand, Catch stared into his palm as if reading it. "Anything new and unusual fascinated Alastor. I thought he was a fool for trusting me. Perhaps he was. Yet somehow, we became friends."

"Why didn't you tell him Lord Roebanks was behind the assassination attempt?" asked Ascot.

Catch snorted and dropped his hand. "I did, and Alastor could've guessed, anyway. What of it? I had no proof. Do you think I could just point my finger and Lord Roebanks would say 'fair enough, I'm guilty'?"

"All right, don't raise your voice." Her ring was no longer glowing. Ascot glanced quickly across the pond. Frabjacket, Prince Parvanel had left while she was preoccupied with Catch. Another opportunity to attract his attention, gone. Shouting across a rotten egg stinking pond would not have been romantic, but she could have settled the True Love question for good and all.

She corralled her wandering thoughts. "So you failed to assassinate Bettina Anna. That doesn't explain why you agreed to kill me today."

"It does, actually," said Catch. He stood with great effort, as if lead had seeped into his bones. "Lord Roebanks made me sign a contract. His name doesn't appear on it, of course."

Ascot grimaced. "That was stupid."

"I'm inclined to agree with you, both then and now. But I was hardly more than a boy. Young, desperate. Lord Roebanks caught me poaching on his land. I had no friends, no protection, and Lord Roebanks . . ." Catch shuddered. "Lord Roebanks knows of places in this world where they are, to speak mildly, unkind to shifters. I had no desire to be burned alive, or worse. He promised me safety and employment if I killed Bettina Anna."

Catch fell silent a second. "And give me some credit for wits; MAGI enchanted the contract. It is spelled to destroy itself when I fulfill it."

"Which you never did," said Ascot.

"Of course he never did," said a new, and unfortunately, familiar voice.

Jellied sludge clogged Ascot's veins. Swallowing thickly, she turned in unison with Catch.

Framed against the background of lake and willow, Lord Roebanks stood, clapping his hands in slow, methodical applause.

CHAPTER TWENTY-FOUR:
HEADS OVER HEARTS

"Thank you for being predictable, Captain," said Lord Roebanks. Dropping his hands, he leaned on an elegant ebony cane. His ruby gleamed. "I can always smell the soft-hearted. They have an obsequious sort of stink about them; I think it comes from wanting to be liked. I whiffed it about you all those years ago."

"How long have you been watching?" Ascot demanded. And how had he gotten into the clearing without garnering a single green smudge on his exquisitely white britches?

Lord Roebanks studied her with as much care as if he were looking for the best spot to make his first incision. "Long enough to know the good captain has given you most of the particulars. Now." He twirled his cane. "My offer is simple enough. Come to tonight's banquet."

Ascot gave an involuntary shake of her head. Had she heard that right?

"Yes, come," said Lord Roebanks. "And when the last test is presented, lose spectacularly, even if GEL has slipped you the answer. Make a fool of yourself—" He smiled. "—and when my daughter succeeds, prostrate yourself before her. Call her 'Your Highness.' Do that, and tomorrow I will give you the contract the captain here so regretfully signed."

He still has the contract. Of course he does. That's why Catch runs errands for him. "And if I don't?"

Shrugging, he twirled his stick in the opposite direction. "If you win Parvanel's hand tonight, I do believe the captain's contract will be mysteriously discovered." All his faux-affability vanished. Thrusting the cane's point deep in the soft ground, he leaned on it with both hands. "The attempted murder of a queen is a treasonable offense, punishable by decapitation, Miss Abberdorf. Even if GEL helps you to the throne, you will not be able to pardon him. On the contrary, it will be your duty to personally oversee his execution."

There it was: her dreams of happiness, plus any hopes of future companionship, in exchange for Catch's life. More than that, she'd be essentially gifting Albright to this ruthless warg of a man, and Prince Parvanel to his selfish, overbearing daughter. Her nails gouged her palms.

"You don't have to tell me your decision now, Miss Abberdorf," said Lord Roebanks. Pulling his cane free, he smacked it against the willow to knock the dirt from its tip. The willow's spindly branches rattled.

"In fact, you don't have to tell me at all," he continued. "I know what your answer will be. I can smell the soft-hearted stench on you, as well."

Swinging his cane, he walked off, taking a path half-hidden between the pond's edge and a corner of the maze. His jaunty whistle floated back to the clearing. Ascot waited a full minute after it faded to be sure he was gone.

"I'll leave now," said Catch before she could speak. "If I put enough distance between myself and Albright, he might not be able to find me."

"Oh, shut up," said Ascot. "If you thought that would work, you would've run years ago."

"I was helping Bettina Anna. She needed a friend."

"Yes, I'm sure her life will improve vastly once Miss Roebanks is her daughter-in-law."

When he made to speak again, she waved him to silence. "Look, don't argue. Unless you can think of a way to get hold of the contract?"

He snorted.

"Yes, I didn't think so. Well, then; either I have to lose tonight, or we must find another plan."

"I suppose I could still dispatch you," he said. "Means 'kill,' 'slaughter,' or more politely, 'terminate.'"

Apparently he'd recovered his insouciance, or at least his taste for annoying her. Ascot rolled her eyes. "And maybe I could kill you. Then I wouldn't be tormented by the idea of executing you."

"Would it torment you?" Catch stepped closer, close enough for his coat to brush hers. Close enough for her to smell his scent of supple leather and fresh herbs.

Ascot gulped. The breeze felt suddenly refreshing on her hot cheeks. *This is getting me nowhere.* She looked away, scraping wind-blown hair out of her face.

Nowhere, nowhere . . . Oh, yes, she was supposed to be somewhere pretty soon, wasn't she? She'd lost track of time. "You found this, right?" she asked, pulling the scrap of yellowed paper from her pocket and flourishing it between them.

"Yes." A tiny sigh escaped Catch. "Did you figure out who sent it?"

"Maggie said one of the servants, maybe."

"Well, let's go, then. It's already six ten."

Ascot blinked as the warmth of his presence whisked off and cold air rushed in to wrap her in its place. "What are you up to now?" she demanded, spinning around. Catch was already pushing back through the gap in the maze. She jogged after him. "I thought you intended to run away."

"And as you pointed out, if I didn't know that Lord Roebanks is thoroughly vindictive and has a network of allies, I'd have attempted it years ago. Look."

He turned and Ascot barely stopped in time to keep herself from banging her nose on his ear. "My mess is of my own making." Catch took her hand. "Don't let him hold my life over you. Go ahead and win if you can, and I'll run. I'm good at running."

That, she suspected, was not a lie. Perhaps he'd even gotten too good at running, over the years. "Well," she said, looking down at their enjoined hands. "Well." *I don't know how to win*, she wanted to tell him. *I have no secret agreement with GEL. I'm just trusting the stories to be right. And I could be wrong.*

But her tongue seemed tangled, and before she could unknot it, he began walking again. After a pause, she followed, her fingers tingling. "You really think this note is worth investigating? It almost reads like a joke."

A zig in the path hid him momentarily from sight. "At this point I'm willing to grab straws and call them ropes," he said, reappearing at the zag. "Perhaps one of the servants has overheard something useful."

"Maybe it's something about tonight's test."

"Oh, I know what that is."

"You do?" asked Ascot. They entered a large open space outlined in red brick. Bushes clipped into the shape of chess pieces menaced each other across an immense checkerboard created by alternating squares of grass and sand, like two giants had set up a game right in the middle of the maze and then gotten bored and abandoned it.

Perhaps because they couldn't figure out which pieces belonged to whom, since they're all green. Ascot stared up at an immense rook whose crenelated top needed a trim. "Well, what's the last test?" she asked Catch, as he took them between two hedges and down a sloping path, bare of sand in many spots.

"Bettina Anna has placed a ring of engagement inside one of seven boxes. She'll proclaim that it's a magic box, and only the true bride will be able to pick it."

"When, in fact, she's already told Miss Roebanks which is the right one." Ascot slipped, gliding shoulder-first into the prickly green tangle of the hedge wall. "Frabjacket!" She swiped leaves off her face. "But the box isn't really magic, is it?" He shook his head. "Then it's not an impossible test. I should have a one-in-seven chance of choosing correctly."

"Yes. So there must be some other trick to it, but what that is, I don't know."

Ascot chewed her inner lip. "Maybe Dmitri can figure it out." Or maybe she was worrying for nothing; maybe her ring was right all along. Maybe she and Parvanel would fall in love at the banquet's commencement, and she wouldn't have to bother with the box nonsense.

They exited the maze via a short but steep pitch lined with clattering scree. Catch flung out an arm to prevent her from falling on her rump as she half-slid down the last three feet of the slope.

"Thanks," she nodded. The vaguely alcoholic scents of rotting fruit wreathed her head. They'd returned to the orchard. Moss squished underfoot, soft as the library's carpet. "Where'd you find this note?"

"Near the pear tree where I stashed my clothes," he replied.

Oh, that. Using the cold wind as an excuse, Ascot tugged up her collar to hide her cheeks.

"I came looking for some items that dropped out of my pockets." Catch gestured her down an aisle of trees, their branches swaying perilously low under their burden of fruit. Her left boot mashed a pear into impromptu sauce.

"And you found that note instead," she said, scraping it off on the moss.

"Wrapped around a rock." Reaching up, Catch twisted an apple off a low-hanging branch. He tossed it in the air as they walked along. It made a little smacking sound each time it landed in his palm. *Whirl, smack. Whirl, smack.* She wished he'd quit it.

"Seems an awful waste," she said, just to cover the noise.

"Hmm?"

"All these apples, just lying around rotting." She kicked another out of her path. "They could be collected for cider, at least."

"The servants are terrified of coming here. It's too close to the old graveyard."

Ascot stopped, her foot poised to kick another apple. "They don't come here? Then—" *Oh, frabjacket.* She dove for Catch's pocket.

"Hey!"

Ignoring his protest, she yanked out the yellowed paper and read the spikey words again before lifting it to her nose. Catch raised an eyebrow.

She lowered the paper. "Smells like wine." Glancing up, she noted the gray shades of evening creeping over the sky.

"Wine?"

Ascot was already hurrying towards the wall separating the orchard from the graveyard. "I think we'll meet our correspondent here," she said.

The wall was lower on the orchard's side. Without much difficulty, Ascot jumped and heaved herself up. She let her feet dangle over the servants' graveyard, sunk into the earth like a great square pit. Catch's silver chain glinted amongst the bedraggled greeny-gray weeds. The candelabrum, black and twisted, lay discarded beside it. All still.

Cloth scraped against brick as Catch leaped up beside her. Then, in almost the same movement, he jumped down into the graveyard.

"What are you doing?" Ascot called.

"Retrieving my chain," he said, picking it up. "Cost me two years' salary. Do you want the candelabrum? They're pretty black."

Ascot shrugged. "Leave them. They weren't mine anyway. Can you jump the wall without shifting?"

"Probably not." He grinned up at her. "Lucky you."

She made a face at him. He was handling the threat of imminent decapitation fairly well. *Or maybe he's just that certain that I'm going to fail tonight, so why worry?*

Speaking of decapitation . . .

She already suspected the note-writer's identity. So, when the round, greenish-yellow object came hurtling out of the shadows, directly at Catch's back, she was ready.

"Look out," she called.

The man had a lot of quick. In one flowing motion, he dropped the chain, spun, and caught the whatsit squarely. The lines of his body seized up, turning tight and angular. "Ah . . . urgh . . ." he sputtered.

The object in his hands beamed. "Thanks for coming. We need to talk."

"Hello, Jeck," said Ascot, swinging her legs. She shifted her gaze. The rest of Jeck sat astride Fritter's back, several feet away, concealed in the shadow of a crumbling mausoleum. Only Fritter's fiery red outline gave their presence away.

"You knew it was him?" Only Catch's lips moved.

"Wasn't sure until just now. What do you want, Jeck?"

Jeck rode out of his hiding spot, one hand outstretched to reclaim his head. "First, I have to know if you got the Moonlight Muscatel," he said, taking his head by the hair and swinging it idly. Unfreezing, Catch grabbed up his chain and retreated several steps.

"I got the key to the Muscatel. The Muscatel itself is . . ." She didn't know. She looked to Catch for guidance, found him half-turned away, his face screwed up in a grimace. "Captain?"

"Will you put that back in its proper place?" he burst, jabbing a finger at Jeck.

Ascot stared at him, and he puffed out his cheeks. "Sorry." He swept back his hair. "I have a phobia about decapitation."

"I suppose I would, too, if I'd lived under the threat of it for twenty years."

"Oh, decapitation's not so bad," said Jeck, realigning himself. "It's like getting a nice cool shave in a place you usually wouldn't think of wielding a razor."

Catch paled; Ascot didn't think Jeck's description of the process had endeared him to it. Fortunately, Jeck didn't seem to feel obliged to make all the nasty squelchy sounds this evening. "So, you don't have the Muscatel?" he said, having gotten himself together.

"The Muscatel's been taken from the cellar," said Catch. "It's upstairs, under lock and key, waiting to be served at the banquet."

"Served at the banquet?" Jeck hit an ear-wrenching pitch. His hands shook on Fritter's reins.

"I haven't forgotten my promise to Lord Bentley," said Ascot. She hadn't, although it had slipped a few places in her mind's list, what with all the other things she had to keep track of. "I don't like wine, anyway, so they can have my glass plus whatever's left in the cask after . . ."

Both Catch and Jeck stared at her, with curiously matching expressions of exasperation and pity. "What?" she asked. "Oh, that's right. You don't want to be exorcised, do you, Jeck?" She frowned. "So why do you care about the Muscatel?"

A heavy sigh rattled Jeck's frame, nearly shaking his head off his neck. When it was done, he guided Fritter to stand directly below Ascot's dangling toes.

"Because," he said, looking up at her, "Prince Alec intends to kill everyone in Albright Castle tomorrow night."

CHAPTER TWENTY-FIVE:
DEAD RECKONING

A pit opened in Ascot's stomach. All her insides folded up and dropped out of it. "Kill everyone?"

Jeck plucked at Fritter's mane. "After you escaped, Prince Alec's gang panicked. They feared you'd tell the queen; that when they rose tonight, a swarm of people would be waiting, armed with atomizers of Muscatel."

Prince Alec's gang. From her vantage point, Ascot again scrutinized the graveyard, paying particular attention to the shadows. A gentle mist emanated from several of the old tombs. "Speaking of the others, you'd better make this fast."

"Oh, them?" Jeck dismissed them with a flip of Fritter's reins. "They won't rise for a while yet. I'm always the first up and the last in bed. Guess I just possess more *joie-de-mort* than the others. In fact, I intended to ask you to spare me if you did come down here armed with Muscatel."

"You *want* to spend your existence as a headless horseman?" asked Catch.

"Of course I do! It's great fun, galloping about, whooping, holding your head up high." Jeck smiled dreamily. Fritter danced in place, as if agreeing.

Catch started wincing again. "So, now that you know we don't intend to exorcise you immediately, why'd you tell us of Prince Alec's plan?" asked Ascot.

Jeck's grin fell away. "Because I'm against it," he said. "Who will I scare if everyone's a ghost? And just think of the competition for the best wine. Oh, yeah," he added as an afterthought. "It's kind of not nice to kill people, too."

"Didn't you kill people when you were alive?" asked Ascot.

He raised a palm. "It was a job. And look." He lifted his head off his neck. "I paid for those crimes. I've not killed anyone since I died."

"You—" Ascot began, then revisited last night's memories. Jeck had said: *"Let's have some fun."* Not: *"I'm going to kill you."*

Maybe he'd never meant to harm her. And when all was said and done, his madcap presence did add a certain spice to the grounds. All proper castles needed a ghost or two.

"All right," she said. She shifted; her rump was growing numb on the cold, rough ledge. "If you promise to behave, you can stay when I exorcise Prince Alec."

"How are you going to exorcise Prince Alec?" demanded Catch.

Ascot blinked. "Why, with the Moonlight—" Both Catch and Jeck were giving her those pitying looks again. "What?"

"There is only one cask of the Moonlight Muscatel," said Catch. "And it's only about this big." He mimed a shape in the air, perhaps slightly larger than a well's bucket. The silver chain looped over his wrist clinked as he lowered his arms. "It's served in glasses smaller than egg cups. Your portion would never be enough to banish all the ghosts. In fact, I think you'd need the entire cask."

"So . . ." said Ascot. Dreadful deductions took shape inside her head.

"So, every drop will be consumed at tonight's banquet, leaving Albright completely defenseless tomorrow," said Catch.

Ascot's insides fell out again. "The . . . the silver-locked door?"

"Oh, Alec can get past that," said Jeck.

She licked her lips. "Arm everyone in the castle with silver?"

"Almost all the kingdom's silver went into these bricks," said Catch, sweeping a hand at the graveyard wall. "And most of its gold went into paying GEL to make them. Albright was nearly broke when Alastor married Bettina Anna."

"But everything in the castle's gold," Ascot protested, thinking of the cupid.

"No. It's mostly just gilded wood." Catch dragged his sleeve across his face. "Somehow, we have to keep the court from drinking the Muscatel tonight."

"Good luck with that." Jeck plucked at Fritter's mane again. "Prince Alec knows aristocrats. He said you were more likely to guzzle up the Muscatel than waste it on us."

So nice to know Prince Alec finds us predictable, Ascot thought bitterly. She looked down at Catch. He had the most dreadful cowlick right at the back of his scalp. "What should we do? Can we get to the cask?"

"Not a chance," he replied. "And if you don't mind, I'd like to leave the graveyard soon."

The shimmering mist around the tombstones had thickened, forming almost tangible outlines. "Guess people are getting up a bit early tonight," said Jeck.

"Catch, shift now," said Ascot. Prickles tingled her spine.

He started to take off his coat, then paused. "I have a better idea. Come along, Jeck." He hurried across the graveyard grounds, hugging close to the wall. Jeck urged Fritter after, and Ascot, glad of an excuse to stretch, walked along the wall's top.

Catch led them to the sealed gate. A wall of silver-laced bricks had been erected behind its bars, which were wrapped with lengths of silver chains. Jeck stopped well away from it, but Catch reached through the bars to lay a hand on the bricks. He made a sound of satisfaction.

"As I thought. These are looser than the main wall." He turned to Jeck. "Can you squeeze yourself through small spaces?"

"Oh, yes," said Jeck. "In fact—*hee, hee!*—one night Prince Alec dared Lord Rogan to squeeze himself into a magnum. Then he corked it. I think Rogan's still inside."

"Yes, hilarious." Catch began tugging at bricks. "Ascot, come around and help from the other side. I think we can make a small gap."

"A gap? You want to let the ghosts out?"

"Just one." Taking a pointed instrument from one pocket, Catch picked a chain's lock. "Jeck here can be our spokesman. The queen and Lord Roebanks will never give up the cask of Muscatel if all we have is some wild story, but if we actually bring them a ghost, they might."

Jeck listened to the exchange with growing glee, evidenced by the brightening of his yellow-green aura. He squealed. "You mean I'm getting out? Goody!" Fritter reared in his excitement.

"Only if you promise to behave," said Ascot.

He kept whooping. Ascot grimaced. Jeck still had his sword. And even if he meant well, he was just the sort to, well, lose his head and take a swing at someone.

One of her brilliant ideas ignited. "Give me your sword as a token of good faith," she said, reaching down.

That stopped him. "My sword?" asked Jeck. Fritter's front hooves returned to earth with a flat, defeated plop. "What will I flourish dramatically? How can I scare people if I'm unarmed?"

"You're a ghost, Jeck, you'll manage. Besides, it won't fit through the gap." She snapped her fingers. Sighing, Jeck unbuckled his sword belt and handed it up. Ascot pulled the blade a quarter-length out of its sheath. Red-brown patches covered the dull metal.

Naturally. She kicked herself. *It's lain in a crypt for a century. Of course it rusted.*

"I shouldn't have worried," she said, slamming it back into its sheath. "This hunk of junk couldn't slice pudding."

"Poor Tonker has seen better times," Jeck agreed.

Tonker? I didn't need to know that. Grimacing, she slung the belt around her hips and tried to ignore it. "All right; I'm coming," she said, finding a spot where the orchard ground rose up close to the wall. Jumping down, she went to the gate. Catch had already loosened a brick, creating a fist-sized gap. Together, they worked another two bricks free.

"That'll have to do," said Catch. The portion of his face visible through the gap turned in profile as he glanced behind him. "Something's definitely beginning to stir. Step back so Jeck can squeeze through."

Ascot obeyed. A moment later, a flow of glowing green jelly slugged through the gap. "Owie, owie," it moaned.

Fighting off a wash of nausea, Ascot turned her head. "Tell me when you're through."

"I'm through," said Jeck a moment later. "Fritter's coming."

She didn't want to see that, either. She waited until she heard the clomp of hooves on mossy ground to look around. Jeck and Fritter, large as life, if not entirely deserving of the metaphor, stood before her.

"Ooh, I'm free!" sang Jeck. He swung into Fritter's saddle as the horse shook himself. "Hello, birds! Hello, sky! No, don't eat that apple, Fritter. Remember what happened the last time."

"Here."

Catch's voice. Ascot turned back to the gap. Several items of clothing were being shoved through it. She fought the desire to avert her gaze again. One hazel eye peered through the hole. "I'm going to close this back up and re-chain it," Catch said. "Then I'll shift and leap the wall. Don't let Jeck run off."

Not likely; he and Fritter were too busy cavorting in the orchard. But Ascot nodded and Catch shoved the last brick in place. Rattling and jingling sounds came from the unseen side of the gate.

"Hurry up," she called. The sky had grown progressively darker. Ghostly mumbles rose from the vicinity of the tombstones.

And I still have to prepare for the banquet, she reminded herself. The banquet; yes. Finally, she could meet Prince Parvanel. True Love. Happily Ever After. All that.

If she and Prince Parvanel fell in love at first sight and they never went through with the box test, would Lord Roebanks still "accidentally discover" Catch's contract the next day?

You're not that foolish, Ascot.

The ghostly mumbles grew louder. Fortunately, she also heard the liquid crackling of Catch shifting. Suddenly, it ceased. Ascot held her breath until the saber-tooth appeared on the top of the wall.

"Ooh, neat trick," said Jeck as Catch leaped down.

Ascot shook out her coat and brushed off her sleeves. "I have to get ready for the banquet," she said, stopping herself just before she started playing with her hair. "Can you take Jeck to the queen?"

He cocked his head to one side, but nodded. The mottled, creamy fur on his sides looked even softer than Dmitri's. Ascot thrust her hands into her pockets. "I suppose I'll see you in the banquet hall, then."

"Yes, do enjoy the banquet," called a voice from the other side of the wall.

Ascot forgot how to walk. She would've toppled if her muscles hadn't seized up, locking her in place. *Prince Alec.*

"Particularly enjoy the Moonlight Muscatel," continued the mad ghost prince. "Every last drop of it."

Fur rose in a crest along Catch's back. He snarled. Jeck reined in the stamping Fritter and glared at the wall. "I never did like you, you know that? You always were a right bastard."

"Ah, my treacherous companion." Ascot heard the grin in Prince Alec's voice. "What would be a fitting punishment for you? Perhaps I'll have you stuffed in a bottle, along with your horse. One of those tiny ice wine bottles, I think." He sniggered.

The saber-tooth's form writhed and crackled. Ascot realized what was happening only two seconds before Catch stood up on his hind legs, the last traces of fur vanishing from his face.

"He's bluffing," said Catch, as Ascot practically experienced spontaneous combustion firsthand. Fortunately for her sensibilities, he grabbed up his clothes, covering what needed to be covered. "But we mustn't waste time. You get ready for the banquet and I'll take Jeck to the queen." He began dressing.

Prince Alec laughed louder. "You imagine the queen will sacrifice the Muscatel for some ghost story? You don't know royalty!"

Fingers closed around Ascot's arm. She yelped before seeing it was only Catch, decently clad enough. "Come on," he said, tugging her sleeve.

Prince Alec's mocking laughter chased them out of the orchard. After a rude gesture towards the wall, Jeck galloped ahead.

"Bettina Anna won't be unreasonable, will she?" Ascot asked Catch as they trotted down the by-now familiar seashell path. Jeck's sword bumped against her leg, threatening to trip her.

A bar of moonlight divided Catch's face. Beneath it, his expression was grim. "I don't know. The Muscatel's worth more than its weight in gold. *Well* more. Moonlight Valley has a long list of kingdoms wanting a cask of Muscatel. Albright only received its cask as a consolation gift when Alastor died so suddenly."

Now she could ask. "How did King Alastor—?"

"Bee sting. He took me to visit his apiaries, his latest scheme, when one single bee stung him. His throat swelled up." Catch took a deep, slow breath. "I couldn't help him."

Ascot squeezed his arm. "I'm so sorry." It was all she could offer, and she knew how painfully little it was.

"So am I."

"No wonder you hate that room."

"No wonder. But, you can see why the circumstances in which we acquired the Muscatel might make Her Majesty unwilling to part with it. And with Lord Roebanks complicating the issue—" He shrugged deeper into his coat. The top buttons of his shirt hung open. "Well, we needn't be so concerned. You're going to win Parvanel's heart tonight, right?" Irony crept back into his voice. "As princess bride, you can commandeer the Muscatel."

"You're going to be princess?" asked Jeck, riding past. "Congratulations! Can I be in the bridal party?"

"Jeck, hush." Ascot held a breath in her throat. It was either that or kick Catch. At his words, her mind had split.

Of course you're going to the banquet, argued one half. *Parvanel's your True Love.* (Here she shot a glance at her ring. Dark.) *Besides, there are people who are rooting for you. You can't give up now.*

Why not? asked the other, sounding quite rational. *Albright was getting along just fine before you arrived. Bettina Anna will pay you if you stay away. Lord Roebanks might not be entirely satisfied, but he probably won't be so angry as to "find" Catch's contract. And Parvanel—*

Maybe Parvanel really was her True Love. Maybe her ring wasn't just a cheap trick, spelled to glow in his presence so GEL could reap the benefits of her gratitude later. The truth was, part of her would rather flee screaming than find out for certain. The truth was, the idea of looking into a stranger's eyes and feeling compelled to adore him for the rest of her days now sounded as much a cage as returning to Abberdorf and finding her father come back to life.

They'd reached the castle's front door. Instead of turning the knob, Ascot scraped a toe along the path. "Perhaps I shouldn't go to the banquet," she said.

"Ascot, no." Catch clasped her shoulders, forcing her to face him. A faint trace of the bruise she'd put around his right eye lingered. "I told you not to let my predicament influence your decision."

She made herself snort. "Like I would. But—"

His grip tightened until her pulse throbbed beneath his fingers. "Something must be done to check Lord Roebanks. If Miss Roebanks marries Parvanel, he'll as good as rule Albright."

Ascot stiffened. "Do you want me to marry Parvanel?" she demanded.

His gaze jerked away, wandering the dull stretch of grass, the cloudy sky. Anything, she suspected, to avoid meeting her eyes. "Don't you want to live Happily Ever After?"

Of course I do. But . . . She opened her mouth.

"It would be better for Albright," Catch added.

Jeck dropped his face into a palm.

Ascot stared, hardly believing what she'd heard. He wanted to *use* her? For Albright's sake?

Yes; he'd really said it. "Fine," she said. Her hand snapped out, found the door's knob. With a vicious twist, she flung it open. "You take Jeck to the queen. I'll prepare to meet my True Love."

"Ascot—"

She slammed the door on whatever he intended to say. Her feet slapped marble, carrying her to Nosegay Wing. All around her, servants were hard at work, tacking up wreaths and polishing floors. Many paused to favor her with a quick nod and smile. She forced herself to smile back, although her skin felt as if it had been screwed tight behind her ears. She was so glad to escape to the relative quiet of Nosegay Wing that she didn't notice that her door hung slightly ajar until she was halfway down the hall.

"Maggie?" she called. No reply.

Ascot hesitated a few seconds, then shrugged and continued on. It was an old door. Stiff hinges. Someone had just neglected to shut it properly. Reaching her room, she pulled the door open, and a gust of trapped air breathed into her face.

It brought with it the stinging miasma of garlic.

Oh, frabjacket!

A cramp doubled her over. Her knees hit the floor. Gagging back a rising tide of nausea, she saw the huge wreath of garlic pinned to the wall over her chair. A great chain of bulbs dangled from the bar in her open wardrobe. Garlic juice streaked her window. The white book's empty cover lay open on the floor. It had been shucked like an oyster.

Right in the center of her bed, a wooden stake rose obscenely through a carefully arranged sprawl of words:

STAKE THE SUCKER

The letters had been cut from her green gown.

White sparks spat at the edges of Ascot's vision as the rest of the world turned dark and wavy. She felt herself falling away, perhaps up into the sky where she'd take up a vigil with the cold, solitary moon.

No. She clutched her chest. *Help. I need help.* She drew in a breath to cry out, and it poured into her lungs as tainted, as toxic, as the last.

She fell.

CHAPTER TWENTY-SIX:
SUITABLE OPTIONS

"Drink this."

Ascot's gummy eyelids parted reluctantly. A hand thrust a tin cup under her nose. Droplets of moisture beaded its surface. She blinked, thinking the surface beneath her was far too soft to be the bed in her room. A window nearby—a large one with a view of the courtyard—let in drafts of fresh air that mingled with the scent of roses.

"Where am I?" she asked, and blenched. Her throat rasped like she'd swallowed a beach's worth of sand.

"Drink," repeated the voice, with a note of impatience. Ascot followed the line of slim white arm holding the cup up to the face it belonged to. Blue eyes, sunny hair.

Ascot sipped. Ginger tingled on her tongue, washing some of the sand away. "Thank you, Cindy," she whispered, taking the cup and rolling its wonderful coolness against her burning forehead. Her mind and vision slowly cleared. She lay on a silk bedspread in a room twice the size of hers, its walls papered in pink dotted with innocent white roses. All the furniture—two white-cushioned chairs, a vanity, a wash stand, and the four-poster bed—was carved from glossy, red-brown rosewood, giving the space a look of both neatness and quality.

The bedsprings creaked as Scincilla shook her head. "I've never seen so much garlic," she said. "Even your pillow is stuffed with it. And that stake through your mattress—disgusting!"

"Who did it?" asked Ascot, trying to sit up. Her heels kicked out, feebly seeking a purchase on the slick sheets.

Putting an arm around her shoulders, Scincilla assisted, propping her against the headboard. "Dmitri's investigating, but with so much garlic, I doubt he'll be able to smell anything useful."

Scincilla's fingers felt odd against her back. Fuzzy and lumpy. Ascot took a good look at her. "You've changed."

Scincilla's lips twitched. She held up a hand. Gauze wrapped every finger. "I think it has something to do with pulling on copper wires all night."

Ascot winced. "Ow."

"And then to be cheated, anyway." Scincilla folded her hands on her lap. "Dmitri told me all about it. We were picnicking in the statue garden. Maggie took me there to cheer me up." She picked at a bandage. "Thank you for waiting for me this morning."

"I wish it was you," said Ascot. "If only it could be you meeting Parvanel tonight, instead of Miss Roebanks."

"I'm glad," said Scincilla. "I've decided I don't want to marry Parvanel." She looked up from mauling her bandages, a big smile on her face. "But you'll make a great queen, Ascot. It'll be just like a fairy tale come true when you win tonight."

Ascot's heart plummeted through the floor and kept going. "About the banquet—"

"Ascot!"

Moony, Rags-n-Bones, and Dmitri bounded through the open door. Wailing, Rag-n-Bones hugged her head to his chest while Moony, sans boots and hat, pressed against her side. His purrs vibrated her ribs.

"I'm all right," she said, stroking Moony and patting Rags-n-Bones' back simultaneously.

Dmitri rested his chin on the bed. "I'm sorry for leaving your bedroom unattended. I did not expect so vicious an attack."

"I bet Miss Roebanks is behind it," said Scincilla.

"Or Lord Roebanks," said Moony, hissing the "s."

"No, this mischief is too small-minded for His Lordship," said Dmitri. "Destroying your dress seems more to his daughter's taste."

"I think you're right." Ascot sat up. A headache circled her brow, then settled in at her temples and made itself at home. She massaged her forehead. "Lord Roebanks wants everyone to see me lose the final test to Miss Roebanks. So either he didn't tell his daughter his plan, or she doesn't want me to attend the banquet at all."

"She's probably afraid that Prince Parvanel will fall in love with you if you meet him," said Scincilla. "And he will."

Ascot's shoulders knotted. "About that—"

Distant screaming echoed down Nosegay Wing, muffled by the castle's thick walls. Rags-n-Bones shivered. Dmitri and Moony's ears shot up. Ascot tilted her head as the faint thump of a three-beat tempo grew louder and closer until it became obvious it was pounding its way down Nosegay Wing.

"I know that sound," Ascot muttered, but her tired brain refused to make an identification.

It stopped outside Scincilla's room. Pale, one hand clasped to her heart, Scincilla opened the door. Her scream shook the glass in her rosewood vanity. Rags-n-Bones caught her as she staggered backwards.

Hoof beats, said Ascot's brain as a yellow-green glow flickered into the room from the hall, casting a dancing pool of light over the rose-patterned walls.

"Ascot? Are you there?" asked a voice outside.

"Jeck." Ascot released the bed sheets. Her nails had gouged pinprick holes into the soft fabric. Jeck's sword tried to trip her as she pushed off the bed, but she grabbed it by the hilt, wrenched it around to hang by her hip, and went to the door. "What are you doing here?" she asked, looking out.

Fritter almost filled the hallway, his nostrils brushing the floor, his ferocity transformed into meekness. Jeck hunched on his back, although the ceiling was a good two feet over his head—which, thankfully, was in its proper place. Ascot motioned him into Scincilla's room. Everyone squeezed back against the walls as the great black horse pushed inside.

"We couldn't meet the queen," said Jeck, speaking in a rapid patter. "That Lord Roebanks intercepted us."

Ascot froze. Disaster. "What did he say?"

Jeck drew an unnecessary breath. "The captain told him about Alec, the Muscatel, everything. Lord Roebanks stood there, examining his fingernails. When the captain finished, Lord Roebanks ordered the guards to arrest him."

Intakes of breath all around. Ascot had thought she was already cold. Now she discovered she could drop a few more degrees.

"On what charge?" asked Dmitri.

Jeck shrugged. "Inciting rebellion. Scheming to plunder royal property. Oh, and attempted murder. They clapped chains on him."

He won't have a chance to run if I win tonight. Ascot bit her knuckles. "Lord Roebanks didn't believe him, even with you standing there?"

"Oh, he knows there are ghosts. Everyone knows there are ghosts." A series of cries broke out from somewhere deep in the castle. Jeck flinched and glanced out into the hall. "He just didn't believe the Moonlight Muscatel exorcism part. Refused to believe, unless it was tested." Leather squeaked as Jeck's gloved hands clenched. "On me."

Ascot closed her eyes.

"The captain's a good egg," said Jeck. "He refused to allow it. Perhaps too good an egg."

Ascot opened her eyes. Jeck was staring down at Fritter's neck. "I know I'm not worth the lives of everyone in Albright." He looked up, jaw firming. "Even so, I refuse to be a sacrifice. I bolted, hoping to find you. And I did, so what are you going to do?"

Proving the Muscatel works on Jeck would be the easiest way.

It would also be an execution of sorts. The kind of thing Lord Roebanks would do without blinking. She could never go through with it.

A wet nose nudged her hand. "Could you possibly elucidate the situation?" asked Dmitri.

She'd need a big breath to explain all this. She sucked it in. "There's a ghost, Prince Alec, who means to kill everyone tomorrow, after the Muscatel's drunk up. The Moonlight Muscatel exorcises ghosts, see. Catch and Jeck went to warn the queen, but Lord Roebanks ignored the warning and had Catch arrested. So—"

Her breath ran out. She took another that pained her chest. "If Miss Roebanks gets engaged to Parvanel tonight, they'll drink up the Muscatel, dooming Albright. But Catch—" Static fuzzed in her vision and she had to stop again.

Every hair on Dmitri's body bristled as he spun to face the room. "There's only half an hour until the banquet," he barked. "To save Albright, Ascot must win the last task, but first she has to be allowed in, and we're facing a serious obstacle."

But I didn't tell you about Catch's contract. He'll die if I win.
And everyone in Albright will die if I don't.

"Do you have anything she can borrow?" Dmitri asked Scincilla.

"Borrow?" Then a vision of green shreds kicked Ascot in the gut. "My dress!"

"Yes. Your only dress." Dmitri looked at Scincilla. "Well?"

"Of course. But . . ." Petite, curvy Scincilla looked down at her feet.

"Nothing will fit," Ascot interpreted. She leaned against a bedpost, rubbing her temples as her headache giggled. "They wouldn't really keep me out, would they? I think Lord Roebanks would relish the added humiliation of my attending the banquet in old trousers."

"You've forgotten," said Dmitri. "Bettina Anna doesn't want you there, either. Showing up in trousers would give her an excuse to forbid you entry."

She *had* forgotten. Her headache giggled harder.

"Never fear."

Of all people, Rags-n-Bones stepped forward, thrusting out his narrow chest as if offering himself to a firing squad. "I will find Miss Ascot proper attire." He folded in a jerky bow and loped out of the room before anyone gathered their thoughts long enough to protest.

Everyone blinked at one another. This interesting activity was interrupted by a protracted, squeaky whistle coming from Ascot's room. A moment later, Rags-n-Bones bounded past the door again. Going to the front of the hall, he took Maggie's emergency sewing kit from a cabinet, then jogged back to Ascot's room, pausing briefly in the doorway to flash a salute.

Dmitri shook himself until his ears flapped. "All right. Let's trust Rags to fix your dress," he said. "Cindy, help Ascot prepare. You— Jeck? Tell me everything about this Prince Alec. Go!"

At his stamped paw, people sprang into action. Taking Ascot by the shoulders, Scincilla hustled her towards the bathroom.

"Where's Maggie?" asked Ascot.

"At work, preparing for the banquet," said Scincilla. "You'll see her there." She started to say something else, then her lips clamped.

"If I make it to the banquet," Ascot provided for her.

"You must," said Scincilla. She pressed her forehead to Ascot's. "Everyone in Albright could be killed if you don't."

Ascot gulped. Scincilla pushed her into the carnation-and-cream tiled bathroom. "Wash quickly," she said, and exited.

Ascot did. Murmurs from the bedroom occasionally overrode the sound of her splashing. Too soon to have truly enjoyed the warm, rose-scented water, she pulled the plug, dried off, and wrapped herself in Scincilla's pink robe. Bracing herself, she stepped into the bedroom.

A vision of green and gold silk greeted her. The finished gown hung off a dressmaker's frame, its dagged hem and the elaborate network of lacing crisscrossing the bodice like no style she had ever seen.

"Surprise." Rags-n-Bones waved a pair of scissors. Bits of thread covered him from head to toe. Answering squeaks echoed him.

Ascot's gaze traveled to the floor. Assembled around his feet, carrying needles and spools, were Nipper, Scuttle, Tuft-Tail, Squeaker, and Brownie.

Chapter Twenty-seven:
Boxing Day

"Boxes," said Dmitri as they raced through Albright Castle's halls.

"So Catch said," replied Ascot, clutching handfuls of her long golden skirt, taken from one of Scincilla's gowns. Black leather flapped behind her. Her new gown's bodice, created from the remaining shreds of her green dress, barely possessed enough of a back to deserve the name. To save Scincilla's blushes, she'd donned her coat as well.

What irony. She didn't even like dresses, yet twice her fate had hinged on wearing one. Her green shoes clattered and slipped on the marble floors. Of all the items in her room, they alone had escaped destruction. *Of course they did*, she groused as her pinched toes registered their complaints.

"The boxes might have clues attached to them," said Dmitri. "Don't pay them much mind. Remember, Miss Roebanks already knows the correct box."

"Then why have clues at all?" asked Scincilla, carrying Moony on her shoulder. She'd dressed herself in a puff-sleeved white blouse and a satin skirt patterned in big blue and white diamonds. Ascot thought she'd look very fine standing outside a bakery holding a plate of cherry turnovers. Jeck and Fritter had been left in Scincilla's room with injunctions to behave, which they'd probably ignore.

"It's all part of the show," said Dmitri. Nearby, a butler discreetly coughed and indicated the next turning. Ascot nodded her thanks as they rushed past. "They're going to claim the true bride intuitively understood the clue."

"They're writing a story," muttered Ascot. A maid pointed towards a spiral staircase. The distant fanfare of trumpets sounded from above.

"The banquet's already started." Dmitri accelerated, bounding upwards five steps at a time. Cursing her shoes, Ascot hurried after. Rags-n-Bones took her arm. She smiled up at him.

"Thanks for the dress," she said. "A real storybook gown, made by . . . rats."

He beamed.

Three spirals up, they arrived in a large, white, fruit salad of a room, its floor tiles picked out in two shades of lettuce green. Plaster etchings of apples, oranges, and berries covered three of the walls. Carved grapevines with bunches of jade grapes coiled around the obligatory columns in the corners. Two harp-shaped doors on the third wall led into a long room. Presently, Dmitri stood between the doors, growling at the butlers he'd caught in the act of closing them.

"I'm here," cried Ascot, stumbling up the steps. Rags-n-Bones caught her as a heel turned under her. Biting down the pain, she threw a smile to the butlers as they reopened the doors with more relish than Bettina Anna or Lord Roebanks would likely have approved of them showing.

A smell hit her as she entered the banquet hall. Sickly sweet, yet also bitter and curiously medicinal, its reek cut through the more appetizing scents of baked cheese, buttered herbs, and pears poached in brandy.

Ascot located its source on a sideboard. A cake had been placed there, amongst curls of silver ribbon, as if it were some famous sculptor's masterpiece. Four tiers high, covered with sugared fruit and icing flowers, and clearly listing to one side. A servant stood nearby, bearing a mop and a nervous demeanor.

Miss Roebanks was declared a winner for that? She should be ashamed. With a toss of her head, Ascot started up the stretch of green carpet that ran between long tables draped with fine linen cloth, toward a grand high table, heaped with golden dishes. Miss Roebanks waited there beside her father. Her gaze flicked to Ascot. A fleeting scowl puckered her face; then, like a pair of greedy flies, her eyes returned to Parvanel.

Clearly not ashamed.

Parvanel. The prince also stood by the high table, wearing a splendid smoked pewter coat and a surly pumpkin expression. The faces of the lords and ladies lining the long tables turned as Ascot's party promenaded up the green carpet, but he stared sullenly at his place setting.

"Miss Abberdorf, such attire!"

Ascot nearly stumbled again. Standing behind her gilded seat, clad in silvery taffeta, Bettina Anna glared down at her with what Ascot suspected was manufactured outrage.

But perhaps Bettina Anna had erred. At her exclamation, Parvanel's head lifted. The stormy blue of his eyes lightened to summer sky as they fell on Ascot.

"My dress?" said Ascot. Lifting the tail of her coat, she turned in place at the foot of the high table. Green and gold shimmered in the light from a hundred candles. "It's the latest style in Shadowvale."

Let them try and refute that. Grinning, she curtsied. Jeck's sword, concealed beneath her skirt, snagged her heels, but she kept her balance.

"Charming," said Lord Roebanks, on Bettina Anna's left. He toyed with his ring. Bettina Anna's mouth pressed into a line, but as Ascot had suspected, she didn't know enough about Shadowvalean fashion to refute her claims.

One hurdle surmounted.

"Miss Abberdorf," said Parvanel. His voice was as musical as his mother's, but without the crackling. The hush pervading the long banquet hall deepened as he came around the high table, his attention fixed on Ascot. Miss Roebanks whitened beneath her layer of face paint.

"We meet at last," he said, lifting Ascot's cold, stiff hand.

This is it, she thought. The moment foretold by every tale in the white book. Her ring blazed on her third finger, bright as a burning rose. Inside her chest, her heart curled into a shivering lump and refused to be consoled.

Parvanel bent. His breath caressed her knuckles. His golden hair fell over his shoulders, flowing in perfect, rippling waves. Ascot's memory conjured an image of a cowlick.

Lips pressed against her knuckles. Blue eyes regarded her surreptitiously, under the cover of long lashes. Ascot averted her gaze, gulping as he straightened. By his solemn air, she sensed he had something of great import to say to her. Frantically, she scanned the hall, searching for a chair to dive under.

Stop cringing, you ninny! If the two of you fall in love right now, you can save Albright.

Besides, she had to know. Bracing herself, she met his eyes squarely.

"Have you ever seen a Giant Mung Toad?" he asked.

Warmth and color poured back into the world. "A what?" she asked.

"A Giant Mung Toad," he repeated. "They're native to Shadowvale. The books say they can reach five feet at the crest." Those long eyelashes fluttered, as if this notion were almost too delightful to bear.

She'd never known what they were called. "There's one in my Uncle Varney's water garden," she said. "In spring you can hear it croak for miles."

Parvanel's face broke into an enormous smile, featuring exquisite dimples. "Amazing," he said.

Then bowed.

And returned to Bettina Anna's side.

Ascot's heart uncurled. Droplets of perspiration trickled down her back. It seemed hours since she'd dared breathe. Her ring continued to blaze, even when she slipped it off and dropped it on the green carpet. She toed it aside and it rolled under a table to continue shining alone.

Bettina Anna nodded at Pollux, who stood, be-ribboned staff in hand, off to the side. "Guests, kindly be seated," he proclaimed, and there was a general scraping of chairs.

"Wait, Your Majesty," cried Ascot.

The scraping stopped. Two hundred pairs of eyes lanced her. Part of her started searching out chairs to dive under again, but she forced herself to stand straight. "Perhaps we could attempt the final task before we start eating?"

The idea had just come to her: if she failed, she could excuse herself from the banquet. Maybe they hadn't decanted the Muscatel yet. Perhaps she could steal the cask before they toasted Miss Roebanks.

A murmur rippled through the ranks of nobles behind her. It sounded indignant. Bettina Anna's eyes hardened into stones.

Salvation arrived from the most unlikely of sources. A soft white hand touched Bettina Anna's arm. "Please," said Miss Roebanks in the dulcet tones of an angel.

Bettina Anna stared across the room. Considered. Glanced at Lord Roebanks, who inclined his head. Her bodice rose in the hint of a sigh. "So be it," she said. She clapped her hands.

At that signal, two trumpeters standing on either side of a small door at back of the hall blew a fanfare. A moment later, the door swung open, emitting two cherubic pages, each carrying a cushion in his out-thrust arms. Four guards fell in around them. Seven ornate boxes nestled on top of the azure folds of the first cushion. Six keys glittered against the crimson of the second.

Six?

Soft "oohs" resounded throughout the banquet hall. Chairs again scraped the tiled floor as several nobles stood for a better view. Setting their precious burdens before the queen, the pages bowed before retiring to a corner of the room and the more interesting business of exploring the contents of their nostrils with their forefingers.

Bettina Anna picked up each box in turn, arranging them on the white tablecloth just so. "The last test is simple," she announced. "Inside one of these seven enchanted boxes rests a ring of engagement. Only the true bride will be able to open the correct box. Once she's laid the ring in my son's hand, we shall toast her success with the Moonlight Muscatel."

Applause. At the back of the hall, a velvet curtain was pulled aside, revealing a short golden pillar topped with a small wooden cask. Six men guarded it.

Ascot stopped breathing. The Muscatel. Ready to be served.

"Miss Roebanks. Miss Abberdorf." Bettina Anna's voice snapped Ascot to attention. "Who will make the first attempt?"

Ascot looked at Miss Roebanks. A grin was attempting to run away with her face. "I will," said Ascot, and wished she'd spoken louder, more confidently.

Lord Roebanks nodded contentedly. Putting a hand on his daughter's shoulder, he guided her aside.

"Only touch the box you choose," said Bettina Anna. Then she, too, stepped aside.

Ascot surveyed the room. Scincilla had joined her family along the ranks of tables. Maggie stood with the other servants ranged along the walls, almost indistinguishable in her lavender uniform. Rags-n-Bones and Dmitri watched from the green carpet. Moony, clad in his hat and boots, perched on Dmitri's back.

No sign of Catch. Was he locked in some cell, awaiting execution should she win?

I have to win.

Furious, she scrubbed a sleeve across her prickling eyes and studied the boxes arrayed before her.

Two gold, one silver, one crystal, one alabaster, one onyx, and one lead. Carved flowers and mother-of-pearl butterflies decorated one of the gold boxes. The knotwork borders on the alabaster and onyx boxes matched. The crystal box peppered the white tablecloth with fractured rainbows. Among them all, the lead box hulked; an ugly gray lump.

Ascot turned her attention to the red cushion with its keys. Every one had a scrap of paper tied to its bow with a silk ribbon. A seventh curl of paper lay all alone. Taking up each in turn, Ascot read the words aloud.

The gold key. *"Who chooses me risks their heart."*

The silver key. *"Who chooses me chances their happiness."*

The glass key. *"Who chooses me dares mockery."*

The black key. *"Who chooses me gambles with fortune."*

The white key. *"Who chooses me wagers their future."*

The ugly iron key. *"Who chooses me hazards their soul."*

The solo scrap. *"Who chooses me invites mysteries."*

Ascot set the last down. All her insides seemed to have congealed into a single lump of cold gruel. Just as Dmitri had suspected, the "clues" were a load of nonsense that could be twisted any way.

Waiting off to the side, Miss Roebanks smirked. *Don't be so smug*, Ascot raged silently. *There's nothing clever about being given the right answer.*

She drew a calming breath. It had to be the lead box, so hideously out of place amongst the pretty gleaming ones. Besides, in the stories, it was always—

Bettina Anna knows the stories, too!

Ascot snatched back her hand in the very act of touching the iron key. A fleeting look of disappointment passed over both Bettina Anna's and Lord Roebanks' faces.

It wasn't the lead box. That left six. *Think, Ascot, think.*

All right, so the clues didn't actually indicate what was inside the boxes, but words had connotations. The clue on the box Miss Roebanks chose would be connected to her all her life if she became queen. No proper lady would wish to be associated with words like "wager" and "gamble." That eliminated the black and white boxes. And mockery? Vain Miss Roebanks would never endure the slightest hint of it, so there went the crystal box.

Only the gold and silver boxes left. Ascot's tongue scraped her lips. She wanted to choose the silver. After all her adventures, it felt special to her. But—why two gold boxes when all the others were made of different material? Bending closer, she spotted a discreet "BA" embossed on the bottom corner of both the silver box and the plain gold one. Another matched set. *These all must have come from Bettina Anna's personal collection; probably gifts from her husband—*

Her husband. King Alastor. Who had loved puzzles.

Now, too late, Ascot saw the whole of the scheme arranged against her. Why she couldn't win.

The filigreed box was a puzzle box. It might have three or four or even seven hidden chambers, with different combinations to accessing each. And the test wasn't to choose the correct box—it was to *open* it.

The nobles began shifting along the long tables. Whispered conversations grew into mutters. Riffs of cruel laughter stung her ears.

"Perhaps it's time to yield, Miss Abberdorf," said Bettina Anna. Miss Roebanks, too eager to contain herself, took a step forward.

Ascot stared at the filigreed box. *"You found the right one,"* said a voice in her mind. Catch's voice, as if he were standing beside her, hands in pockets and a look of reproach on his face. *"What's taking so long?"*

"There's no key," she whispered.

"The key's in your pocket."

But there was nothing in her pocket. Nothing except—

Ascot sucked a fold of lip between her teeth. If she touched the filigreed box, she chose it, and if she'd reasoned wrong, Albright was doomed.

She touched the box. Her heart gave a great thump, then eased. "This one," she said.

Lord Roebanks' eyes narrowed. "Very well, Miss Abberdorf," he said. "Open it."

Ascot nodded. With a swipe of her arm, she pushed the other boxes aside. Stepping back, she put her hands in her pockets. Her right fingers closed around a smooth, tubular weight.

Catch. Lord Roebanks will have you executed if I do this.

"And everyone in Albright will perish if you don't."

The scales, with a heavy inevitability, tipped.

"Well, girl? Can't you open it?" Lord Roebanks sneered.

Ascot sighed. "Yes. I can." And, whipping the can of hash from her pocket, she brought it crashing down upon the filigreed box.

In Albright, what looks like gold is usually gilded wood.

The box's top split like a ripe walnut. Its sides splintered, gold leaf crumpling, pearl inlay flaking. One blow was all it took to shatter the intricate layers inside. A thin gold band lay gleaming in the wreckage, its bean-sized diamond breaking the candlelight into multicolored sparks.

"It's open," said Ascot into the ghastly silence.

With an ear-shattering scream, Miss Roebanks launched herself across the floor and tried to claw Ascot's eyes out.

Ascot pushed her away. "Sorry, Miss Roebanks. Nothing left for you."

Around the perimeter of the room, someone, perhaps Maggie, began to applaud. Scincilla joined in, her face shining, followed by Lordling. Then Miss Beige, who Ascot spotted sitting at the corner of the very last table, dressed in defiant scarlet.

Over the applause and the growing rumble from the nobles, Moony hopped onto her shoulder and velveted his head against her cheek. "I never doubted you," he said.

I did it. Ascot stared at the diamond. It winked back at her.

Parvanel's chair's legs scraped over the floor. Silence fell, like the curtain after a play, as the prince stood. Expressionless, he salvaged the ring. Miss Roebanks sank into a chair and buried her face in her arms.

"Miss Abberdorf," said Parvanel, sliding the ring onto Ascot's limp, unresisting finger. "Will you marry me?"

If someone struck her, she'd crack like a sucked egg. *I wager my happy ending will soon be followed by Catch's genuine ending.* She folded her hand and the band's edge bit into her flesh. *So how happy can my Happily Ever After truly be?*

Parvanel waited. Ascot licked her dry lips—

Dmitri woofed softly, deep in his throat. A perfectly normal dog-type noise, but so unlike him that Ascot's head whipped around in shock. He sat by the high table, staring upwards. Ascot's gaze moved from him to Bettina Anna's face. She'd never seen naked terror before.

She really believes I'll make her dance in red hot shoes at my wedding, or something of the sort, Ascot marveled.

Then: *And why wouldn't she? She's lived through one fairy story, and see what it got her.*

Her tongue uncramped. "Excuse me," she told Parvanel. He blinked and the nobles gasped, but she went to Bettina Anna and took her hands.

"Why did you hold the ball in the first place?" she asked in a whisper. "Why not simply betroth Parvanel to Miss Roebanks?"

Tears glittered in Bettina Anna's eyes although she shed none. "I wanted him to have what his father did not," she murmured. "I hoped he'd meet someone at the ball. Someone he could truly love, not a True Love." Her hands shook beneath Ascot's.

Ascot bowed her head. She'd thought herself brave, facing ghosts, but Bettina Anna had risked—she believed—painful death for the sake of her son's happiness. She, out of everyone present, deserved better.

And why couldn't she have it? The white book was shucked, gone. Ascot's chin came up. Her shoulders settled. *I'll write my own frabjacketing ending.*

"Don't be afraid, Your Majesty." She squeezed Bettina Anna's hands. "I'll see that everyone gets what they deserve."

Straightening, she met Lord Roebanks' eyes. "Before we commence with the engagement, there's a matter that requires your aid, Lord Roebanks."

His Lordship looked as if he'd swallowed a pill bug. "As you wish . . . your Highness."

Ascot bent her tight lips into a smile. "No need for formalities. I believe we can work matters to our mutual satisfaction."

"Indeed?" Lord Roebanks brightened. Miss Roebanks lifted her wet face from her arms.

"Oh, yes," said Ascot as her friends gathered around her. "Come along. Sharp, now. And bring the Moonlight Muscatel."

CHAPTER TWENTY-EIGHT:
IN VINO VERITAS

Once the harp-shaped doors shut behind them, Ascot pivoted to face Lord Roebanks. "Fetch Captain Catch."

Lord Roebanks' eyes slitted. Ascot made an impatient gesture. "I'm not asking you to tear up the contract. Just have him brought to the wine cellar door. We're going down."

Still Lord Roebanks hesitated. His narrowed gaze traversed the small crowd that had followed them out of the banquet hall. Moony. Dmitri. Rags-n-Bones, carrying the cask of Muscatel. Maggie. Scincilla. Miss Beige, or rather Jane, as she insisted on being called now.

"Well?" asked Ascot.

He drew her aside, into an alcove behind a grapevine-wrapped column. "You know what I want," he said.

Ascot nodded curtly. "You want me to refuse Parvanel. And I will, if you cooperate."

He flashed a razor-thin smile and went to whisper in the ear of a guard standing before the harp-shaped doors. *He'd better be sending for Catch, not concocting some new scheme.* Ascot kept half an eye on him as she beckoned to Moony.

"Fetch Jeck and Fritter and bring them to the cellar," she said.

"You're not going to exorcise them after all, are you?" he asked, tail curling into a question mark.

"No." Ascot relaxed as the guard saluted Lord Roebanks and left. "I have an assignment for Jeck. One he'll like."

🐌

Frabjacket, I hope this is the last time I have to come down here. Ascot's stomach clenched at the smell of sour wine rising from below.

Then she considered what that wish might entail and tried to take it back. Strangely, however, no visions of Vincent's mother lurched forward to trouble her. Perhaps that old fear could finally sleep in its tomb.

And this time she had lanterns: big, bright ones. And companions. Moony rode on her shoulder, and Dmitri walked at her side. Behind her came Rags-n-Bones, hugging the cask of Moonlight Muscatel like a giant teddy bear. From time to time he nibbled the rim. Maggie, Scincilla, and Jane's chattering drifted down from a turn in the staircase behind her. Lord Roebanks followed them, with Catch and Jeck bringing up the rear. Jeck's chattering eclipsed that of the three girls and most of it seemed directed at Catch.

Dust puffed up around Ascot's green shoes as she stepped onto the floor of the wine cellar's main chamber. *Bother. I should've asked Maggie to bring me my boots. Oh, well, too late now.*

Dmitri snuffled the dirt and sneezed. "You have a plan?" he asked, *sotto voce.*

299

She nodded. "Yes, Dmitri. This time I actually have a plan." She waited until everyone was assembled on the floor of the main cavern before crooking a finger at Catch. He practically leaped forward.

"Of course heads don't really bounce," Jeck nattered on, oblivious. "A little, if you kick 'em really hard, but that hurts your toes."

"Yes?" asked Catch, holding up his lantern. It outlined them in a separate circle of light.

"Do you still have the key to the main vault?"

"Yes."

"Walk with me."

They fell into a matched stride, his lantern's light sometimes swinging a little ahead to illuminate their way, sometimes bobbing a step behind. "So you're engaged to Parvanel," said Catch. "Congratulations."

Ascot stared straight ahead. "He proposed. I couldn't commandeer the Muscatel any other way."

"You made the right choice." One of his boots scuffed the cavern floor.

She slid a glance at him. "I said I wouldn't let Lord Roebanks execute you."

"I remember." His mouth crooked. "So, what is this? Are you buying me one final chance to bolt out through the graveyard after we dispose of the ghosts?"

"No."

"Ah, so you want me to hone my assassination skills on Lord Roebanks." He nodded. "Means 'refine—'"

"Oh, shut up." Shoving her fists in her pockets, she stalked ahead, kicking herself for fretting over him in the first place.

On her shoulder, Moony giggled.

"What?" she asked.

"It's fun watching you two squabble," he said. Scincilla giggled.

Ascot's fists clenched tighter. She spent the rest of the trek to Great Wine Vault pretending she was deaf.

In the bright light of four lanterns, the rough, oaken door barring the passage looked even more formidable than she recalled.

"Ooh, you went through that all alone?" asked Scincilla.

"Well, Moony slipped through, too," said Ascot, rapping her knuckles against it.

"My lady?" called a voice behind it.

"Lord Bentley." Ascot pressed her cheek to the rough wood. "I've brought your relief."

The pause that followed was so long she almost thought that sheer joy might have sent him sailing through the ceiling; no need for the Muscatel. Then: "Ah," he said. His voice quavered. "You have no idea how much . . . thank you. A thousand times, thank you."

Ascot swallowed. "And you're welcome, a thousand times over. Captain, open the door."

A sea of green-glowing faces greeted them as Catch and Maggie hauled the door open. Lord Bentley stood at the front, incandescent tears flowing down his cheeks.

"The Muscatel," he whispered. "At last."

Ascot hugged him, ignoring the chill. "You've earned it."

They went to the counting room. With Rags-n-Bones' help, Maggie set the Muscatel on one of the long benches and decanted it. "I forgot to bring a glass," she said, looking around the worn room.

"Here." Jane pulled a pewter goblet from her purse. "I nicked it from the banquet."

Lord Roebanks, lounging in the corner beside the writing desk, scowled. Ascot hid a grin. Meanwhile, Maggie tipped some Moonlight Muscatel into the goblet. Droplets burst above the surface of the nacreous liquid before bubbling down again, as if the Muscatel were laughing.

One by one the ghosts stepped forward. Raising the goblet in salute, they sipped from the brim. The instant the Muscatel touched their lips, their yellow auras clarified into the transparency of a dewdrop. They wafted up through the ceiling and vanished, their beatific expressions a memory to cherish later.

At last only Lord Bentley remained. He hesitated. "What about Prince Alec? And Jeck?" he added, gesturing at Jeck, who remained a wary distance back in the corridor.

"I'm staying," called Jeck.

"You need concern yourself no longer," said Ascot. Smiling, she extended the goblet. "Ready?"

The stiff set of his shoulders relaxed. "More than words can say, my lady." He clasped her hands a final time. "Thank you. Wherever I go from here, I will always thank you."

He drank. And with a sigh like a drawn-out hallelujah, he ascended, haloed in silvery light.

"Farewell," called Ascot. Was it her imagination, or did his glow intensify for a moment before it faded?

"That was beautiful," said Scincilla, wiping away tears.

"That was stupid," muttered Jeck. Fritter snorted.

A small pool of Muscatel remained in the goblet. Ascot dipped her fingers and sniffed. Spices, berries, and pure, sky-fresh lightning. She brought her fingers to her mouth, then hesitated; she didn't quite trust this wine not to run giggling down the halls and pinch the royal crockery if she spilled it.

"All right," she said, dropping her wet hand. "Word must have spread among Prince Alec's followers. Looks like we'll have to—"

Scincilla gasped a scream. Ascot whirled.

Prince Alec blocked the door to the main channel, holding his sword to Lord Roebanks' throat. The long blade gleamed, sleek and silvery, without a fleck of rust.

"Greetings, Miss What's-your-name." Prince Alec grinned like a wolf that never read Dostoyevsky.

"Was this why you insisted I accompany you?" demanded Lord Roebanks. His hot, terrified eyes speared her. A thin red line trickled down his neck.

"No." Fumbling beneath her skirt, Ascot located the hilt of Jeck's sword and drew it from its sheath. She ran her fingers down its rusty blade. "Leave him, Alec. It's me you want."

"True." Prince Alec threw Lord Roebanks aside. His Lordship bounced off the rough stone wall and rolled into the dust.

Moony whipped out his little sword. Catch vaulted a bench and Dmitri growled. Maggie grabbed up a chunk of wood. Ascot knew none of them could reach her in time. Prince Alec was nearly upon her, the blow meant to slay her already formed and acted upon in his head.

So she struck first. Dropping to one knee, she jabbed out with her blade—a laughable little thrust, just nicking the edge of Prince Alec's calf. Not enough to disable a man of flesh and blood, let alone a mad ghost.

Prince Alec's sword clattered to the floor. His crimson aura paled to purest crystal.

He blinked twice. Slowly his gaze focused on the pearly smears streaking Tonker's blade.

"Moonlight Muscatel." Ascot waggled her damp fingers.

"It's . . . good," said Prince Alec. Then, lifting off the faded carpet, he passed through the ceiling.

"Haha! Pawned!" Jeck yelled after him.

"Clever." Catch bent over Ascot's shoulder. His breath tickled her ear. "But it might have been wiser to let Prince Alec cut Lord Roebanks' throat."

"Blame my stench of soft-heartedness," she replied, re-sheathing Tonker. Standing, she clapped Catch's shoulder. "Besides, Lord Roebanks and I have an agreement."

As his right eyebrow shot up, Ascot refilled the goblet from the cask. Kneeling, she raised the shaken Lord Roebanks to a sitting position. "Here," she said, and pressed the goblet into his hand. "This'll make you feel better."

Ripples of disbelief washed off her companions like heat waves. *Trust me a little longer,* she begged silently, smiling over her shoulder. "Now that Prince Alec's gone, the rest of the ghosts shouldn't be too much trouble. Could you go clear them out while I stay here with His Lordship?"

"I'll lead the way," chirped Moony. He dashed ahead. Hefting the cask, Rags-n-Bones followed with Maggie, Scincilla, and Jane trailing after.

"You two stay," said Ascot to Catch and Jeck, then touched Dmitri's ruff. "Once you take care of the ghosts, tell everyone to . . . celebrate," she whispered.

His eyes narrowed, then widened. "Ah." His ears perked up. "Very good." With a wolf grin, he padded off after the others.

Ascot turned to Lord Roebanks, leaning against the counting room wall, sipping Muscatel from the pewter goblet. Color had returned to his face. "I don't expect thanks for saving your life."

"Good. Otherwise I might be moved to ask why you brought me into this confounded basement to begin with." He took another sip of Muscatel. "This should've been used to toast my daughter's ascension to royalty."

An angry growl from Catch. Ascot glanced at him, both in warning and to make sure he hadn't shifted. "It's being put to better use. You'll have to choose some other vintage if your daughter marries Parvanel."

Catch sucked in a breath. Lord Roebanks' face rounded with avarice. "You're giving us Parvanel, then?"

"Parvanel's not mine to give. However . . ." She held up her ringed hand. Catch's lantern touched its diamond and it blazed like white fire, reminding her of her other ring's rosy glow. *One false light for another*, she thought. *Let's make it three. That's the magic number in the stories, isn't it?*

She managed not to laugh. "I'll swap you this one for that." She nodded at Lord Roebanks' ruby.

"My ring? Why?"

"If you want me to leave Albright, I'll need some traveling money."

Lifting his hand, Lord Roebanks contemplated his ruby, red as a concentrated drop of wine. "You must promise to leave tomorrow," he said. One glance at Catch voiced his unspoken threat.

Ascot nodded. "Sunset tomorrow, I promise."

They exchanged rings. Ascot even extended her hand for a shake, but His Lordship's expression made it clear he'd rather pet a cockroach, so she shrugged and let it fall.

"Finish your Muscatel, your Lordship," she said. "Who knows if you'll ever taste it again?"

He sipped, smiling. Tipping back her head, Ascot let it rest against the cavern wall. Catch sidled up beside her. "You're leaving Albright? After all that?" he whispered.

Old cobwebs dangled from the ceiling, twisting in the air currents. "I still need to find my happy ending," said Ascot, watching them.

Catch propped himself next to her, hands in pockets. "I'd prefer no ending at all," he said after a while.

Perhaps he had a point.

Claws scraped stone. Dmitri trotted back into the counting room. "Finished," he slurred. His tongue lolled out the side of his mouth.

"Good." Ascot pushed off the wall. "How's your wine, Lord Roebanks?"

He tilted back the goblet. "Exquisite."

"Pity it's gone, now. Oh, here." As if on an afterthought, she unbuckled the sword belt hidden beneath her skirt and offered it to Jeck. "I'm returning Tonker to you, on one condition."

"What's that?" Jeck asked, snatching Tonker and cuddling it as Scincilla, Maggie, and Jane entered, pink-faced and giggling. Rags-n-Bones walked in on his hands, Moony swinging from one knee.

Ascot smiled. "I'm following Lord Roebanks' example," she said brightly. "If he ever again threatens anyone's life, Jeck, I order you to cut off his head with that sword."

Lord Roebanks turned white enough to hide in a snowbank. Scincilla and Jane gasped, but Maggie's lips curled.

"That is your one and only, very specific, assignment. Do you understand, Jeck?" Ascot met his eyes.

And Jeck grinned. "Perfectly, Miss Ascot." Taking off his head, he saluted her.

CHAPTER TWENTY-NINE:
HAPPILY NEVER AFTER

"Miss Abberdorf."

Go away. Ascot couldn't quite push the words out of her slack throat. Her cheek rested on a flat, rough surface. Blissful comfort, save for the sneeze building in her sinuses. Perhaps if she kept her eyes closed, it would dissipate.

A chill enveloped her left shoulder. "Miss Abberdorf, you must wake."

She opened her mouth to protest and the sneeze burst free. *Frabjacket, I guess I'm awake.* So she shut her mouth and opened her eyes. The familiar contours of the counting room solidified around her. Dmitri lay on the faded rug, reading a thick book by the light of a candle. In the corner, Rags-n-Bones drew a raven on the writing desk with a stick of charcoal. And there was Moony, curled in a furry gray lump on the plank table and lit by a soft pink glow.

Pink? Ascot peered around. The Head Butler stood behind her, holding a basin of water.

Ascot's hand flew to her lips. "They forgot to give you the Muscatel!"

"No. I refused it." He broke the Code of Proper Butlers long enough to give her a reassuring smile. "I can still be of service to Betty Ann. No one knows these cellars better. And perhaps—may it be long off!—perhaps when Betty Ann passes, Moonlight Valley will give Albright another cask of Muscatel and we can leave this world together."

Ascot took her hand from her lips. "I'll make sure of it," she said. After GEL's meddling in their lives, it was the least they deserved.

He nodded gravely. "Thank you, Miss Abberdorf." With a butlerly cough, he proffered the basin. "I believe Miss Maggie left a rope ladder to facilitate your exit over the graveyard wall."

Ascot washed. When she finished, she reached over and tickled Moony's chin until he stirred.

"Murr?" he asked, tongue curling in a backwards "c."

"We did it," she said. "We won everything." She tweaked his ear.

"I always knew we would." Purring, Moony stretched. Dmitri closed his book and Rags-n-Bones put a final flourish on his raven. Ascot dusted off her coat and stood.

"Now it's time to go."

☙

Four people waited in the orchard. Five, if you counted the snorting, red-outlined figure the fourth rode whooping among the apple trees.

A tearful Scincilla threw her arms around Ascot's shoulders. Jane gave her a box of tiny chocolate cakes. And Maggie, always practical, held out a knapsack. "Here. Everything's been washed, and there's cheese and biscuits and, well, you'll find it's pretty heavy."

Ascot's smile felt a bit crooked. She was glad to see them, but . . . She scanned the orchard for a thin, straight line, possibly half-hidden against the trunk of a tree.

"Looking for someone?" asked Maggie.

"Just for somewhere to slip into my trousers and boots," said Ascot, yanking her head around.

Maggie, Scincilla, and Jane started singing while she changed behind an apple tree. Ascot hummed the tune along with them.

"*Ask the moon to fall straight out of the sky . . .*"

"Does this mean you changed your mind, Maggie?" Ascot asked as the last line faded, coming out from behind the tree, dressed in her sensible clothes.

Jane grinned an imp's grin. "You changed all our minds."

"We're going to perform together," burbled Scincilla. "Maggie'll sing, I'll play the harp, and Jane the piano."

Maggie laughed. "If you can win a prince and turn him down, anything's possible."

"Maybe even the moon falling." Scincilla smiled. "Maybe even you and the cap—"

"Here." Ascot thrust out her green-and-gold gown. "I still don't like dresses much, so you may as well have this. To remember me by. Maybe you can use it as a costume."

As she hugged each in turn, Jeck rode back through the orchard. "What, no present for me?" He pouted.

Ascot gave him her pointy-toed shoes. He was delighted.

§

"Ascot," said Moony later, as they stumped through Albright's darkened streets, "since we're not following the book any more, do you think it's all right if I don't wear the boots?"

"Certainly."

"It's just that they're not very comfortable." He fell silent a moment, looking down at them. "What about the sword? Is it all right if I keep the sword, but not the boots?"

He sounded worried. With a snort suspiciously like a smothered laugh, Dmitri shifted the pack carrying his books more comfortably over his back.

Ascot lifted Moony onto her shoulder and helped him pull off the boots. "You do whatever you like," she said. "Live your life, not someone's story."

"That's good," said Rags-n-Bones, swinging off a sign hanging over a tailor's door. "I've noticed that stories rarely feature avocados." Nipper squeaked on his head.

Gaslamps flickered on Albright's street corners, casting a sleepy yellow glow over the silent shops and doll-box houses lining the cobbled streets. The moon, waned a bit past full, shone in the clear sky like a lopsided marble.

They'd almost reached the gate. Was he really going to let her leave without so much as a farewell?

The gate. She'd seen him there first. In fact, if she closed her eyes, she could picture him, hands in pockets, black eye, and expression of indifference.

"Ascot?"

Ascot started. Dmitri waited, staring at her expectantly, tail swishing. How many times had he said her name before she'd heard?

"Are you ready to go?" he asked.

They *had* reached the gate. It hung slightly ajar. She couldn't recall stopping in front of it and didn't want to know how long she'd stood, gawping.

"Of course," she said, ignoring her flaming cheeks. Throwing back her shoulders, she pushed open the gate.

Two figures waited on the other side; one tall and graceful, the other a thin, straight line. Ascot's heart bumpety-thumped.

"Prince Parvanel," she gasped. At the sight of him, her legs wobbled, instinctively attempting a curtsy.

"Good evening, Miss Abberdorf," said Parvanel. He wore a simple cotton shirt and trousers with a gray cloak flung over it all for warmth. Catch looked the same as ever, hands in the pockets of his brown coat, and staring indifferently at nothing.

Stop that, Ascot told her knees, and they straightened. "What are you doing here?" she asked Parvanel.

His smile grew sheepish. Flicking aside his cloak, he revealed a pack on his back.

"You're leaving Albright?" asked Dmitri.

"Why not? I'm not ready to be king yet. Not before I get a chance to be a herpetologist."

"I'm sure you could work in the garden even if you were king," said Ascot. She suspected it wasn't the right response even before Parvanel guffawed.

Dmitri winced. "A herpetologist studies amphibians." He looked to Parvanel, whose laughter was subsiding. "But what about Albright?"

"Now that Lord Roebanks has been reined in," Parvanel's dimples showed, "I think Mother can handle ruling Albright."

"So long as Lord Roebanks never gets a close look at Jeck's sword," muttered Ascot.

"And GEL?" asked Dmitri.

Yes, GEL, after all their machinations, were a worry. But Parvanel shrugged. "She's held them off for two decades. Lord Roebanks will probably help her keep them at bay, at least until he finds another relation to foist on me. And I'll return in a couple years, after I've acquired enough material for a book on amphibians of the world."

"Where are you heading?" asked Ascot.

"Shadowvale, to find a Giant Mung Toad," he replied. "I stole some silverware for pawning."

"Silverware . . . from the castle?" she asked. Beside her, Dmitri closed his eyes.

"Yes. It worked for you!" Parvanel thrust out his chin.

Ever after, Ascot was amazed that she didn't break down laughing on the spot. Instead, she said, "But your Highness, the silverware I took from home was sterling. Albright's plates are probably silver-washed pewter, at best. Virtually worthless in Shadowvale."

He blinked. "Worthless?"

"There's plenty of pewter in Shadowvale."

Even his blond curls seemed to droop. *He knows nothing about Shadowvale,* thought Ascot. *He has no idea what he's getting into. Someone should warn him.*

Although . . . She rubbed her nose. Whatever might be waiting for him, it was better than sitting around the castle with nothing waiting for him. And at least Giant Mung Toads existed, unlike a Happy Ever After that stretched unchangingly on into infinity.

"Here," she said, and pulled Lord Roebanks' ring out of her pocket. "Take it."

Parvanel eyed the ring as he might a stinging beetle.

"I'm with friends, so I'll be fine," said Ascot, flashing a smile at Moony, Dmitri, and Rags-n-Bones. She dropped the ring into Parvanel's palm and folded his fingers over it. "Sell it, if you need funds, but if you don't . . . Would you stop by Abberdorf Castle and give it to my brother, Vlad? He might need to get away from Vincent by now."

Parvanel's expression relaxed into a smile. "Gladly, Miss Abberdorf."

"Thank you." She stepped back. "Good luck finding your Mung Toad."

His smile broadened. "Five feet at the crest, and some authorities say they may grow even larger in the wild." He tucked the ring into his pocket. "I'd never have thought leaving was possible, were it not for you."

He surprised her, and possibly himself, by leaning forward and kissing her on the cheek. His brows contracted slightly as he drew back.

"Good-bye, Miss Abberdorf," he said. With a wave, he started up the white stone road, the one that curved gently to the west, leading by gradual degrees to Shadowvale, that lonely mountainous country where the wind blew shrill and the light shone murky even at the height of noon. Ascot followed him with her eyes as he became a dim shape in the moonlight, growing smaller with every step.

"He's nice," she said.

Dmitri tipped his head. "Having regrets?"

"None whatsoever," said Ascot, glancing at Catch. He remained by the gate, in the same pose as when she'd first seen him, and looked as if he intended to stay there all night.

"Aren't you going to say goodbye?" she asked, telling herself that she was not holding her breath.

"I have something for you," he replied. From the depths of a pocket, he extracted a balled white handkerchief. Its contents shifted between Ascot's fingers when she accepted it, rustling coarsely. She peeled back a corner of the kerchief and black ash snowflakes trickled out, spilling into the breeze.

"My contract," said Catch. "I went ahead and burned it." He examined the sky. "A shame Parvanel left so quickly. There's a pouch of money in my pocket I intended to give him."

"A pouch of money." Ascot let the wind take the rest of the ashes.

"I suppose it's mine, now," said Catch, still studying the moon.

"Lucky you." Ascot waited, but he seemed disinclined to move or speak further. She looked to Dmitri for help, but he just smirked at her. "Well, we're leaving now. Goodbye."

Catch said nothing, so she hefted her knapsack and began walking. He followed, trailing at a distance from Dmitri and Rags-n-Bones. She stopped in her tracks.

"What are you doing?"

"Accompanying you," replied Catch.

"What?"

"Accompanying. Means 'to join, or come along with.'"

Bumpety-thump. "I didn't invite you."

"No point in owning a pouch of money if you have no companions to share it with."

Moony's scratchy laugh broke the following silence. "I could challenge him to a duel."

"No." Ascot sucked in breath until her chest hurt. She held up the kerchief, speckled with black flecks. "He destroyed something he was supposed to give to me. I'll let him stay until he works off his debt."

Catch smiled.

"All settled?" asked Dmitri. "Good. Let's be on our way. I'm sure we'll find time for quarreling on the road ahead."

"We haven't seen a coconut yet." Moony licked a paw thoughtfully. "Maybe they don't live around Albright."

"Perhaps there's some in Moonlight Valley," said Ascot.

"Ooh!" Moony's eyes widened. "Is that where we're going?"

"And do they have avocados?" asked Rags-n-Bones.

"Why not?" Ascot stroked Moony's head as Rags-n-Bones turned cartwheels. She'd only begun to realize how enormous the world was and how little of it she'd seen. Better make a start. She glanced at the lopsided marble moon, set against a backdrop of a billion glittering stars, more brilliant than a thousand lanterns. "Not coming down tonight, are you?" she called.

"Not now and not ever," said Catch, watching her. "After all, you didn't marry Parvanel. Why didn't you believe me?"

"Believe you?" Ascot laughed. "You're a liar."

"Ah, well." Catch shrugged. "Perhaps our journey will make an honest man out of me."

Ascot snorted. *"Ask the moon to fall right out of the sky."*

"Tell a second to step straight out of its time," sang Moony.

Dmitri and Rags-n-Bones took the third line as the party followed the path winding into the woods. Fallen leaves crunched under their feet, and the moon shone overhead, lighting their way. Catch joined in on the second chorus.

ABOUT THE AUTHOR

A. E. Decker hails from Pennsylvania. A former doll-maker and ESL tutor, she earned a master's degree in history, where she developed a love of turning old stories upside-down to see what fell out of them. This led in turn to the writing of her YA novel, *The Falling of the Moon*. A graduate of Odyssey 2011, her short fiction has appeared in such venues as *Beneath Ceaseless Skies, Fireside Magazine*, and in World Weaver Press's own *Specter Spectacular*. Like all writers, she is owned by three cats. Come visit her, her cats, and her fur Daleks at wordsmeetworld.com.

§

**Want to be the first to know about future books
in the Moonfall Mayhem series?**
Sign up at WorldWeaverPress.com/updates for email news on this series. And turn the page to check out other fantasy novels available now.

Shards of History

Shards of History fantasy series, Book One
Rebecca Roland

"Fast-paced, high-stakes drama
in a fresh fantasy world!"
— *James Maxey,* author of the Dragon Age trilogy.

Feared and reviled, the fierce, winged creatures known as Jeguduns live in the cliffs surrounding the Taakwa valley. When Malia discovers an injured Jegudun in the valley, she risks everything—exile from the village, loss of her status as clan mother in training, even her life—to befriend and save the surprisingly intelligent creature. But all of that pales when she learns the truth: the threat to her people is bigger and more malicious than the Jeguduns. Lurking on the edge of the valley is an Outsider army seeking to plunder and destroy her people. It's only a matter of time before the Outsiders find a way through the magic that protects the valley—a magic that can only be created by Taakwa and Jeguduns working together.

"One of the most beautifully written novels I have ever read. Suspenseful, entrapping, and simply . . . well, let's just say that *Shards of History* reminds us of why we love books in the first place."
— Good Choice Reading, *5 out of 5 stars!*

"A must for any fantasy reader."
— *Plasma Frequency*

Heir to the Lamp

Genie Chronicles, Book One
Michelle Lowery Combs

A family secret, a mysterious lamp, a dangerous Order with the mad desire to possess both . . .

Ginn thinks she knows all there is to know about how she became adopted by parents whose number one priority is to embarrass her with public displays of affection, but that changes when a single wish starts a never-ending parade of weirdness marching through her door the day she turns thirteen.

Gifted with a mysterious lamp and the missing pieces from her adoption story, Ginn tries to discover who. . . or *what* . . .she really is. That should be strange enough, but to top it off Ginn's being hunted by the Order of the Grimoire, a secret society who'll stop at nothing to harness the power of a real genie. Ginn struggles to stay one step ahead of the Grimms with the help of Rashmere, Guardian of the lamp and the most loyal friend a girl never knew she had. The Grimms are being helped, too—but by whom? As much as she doesn't want to, Ginn's beginning to question the motives of her long-time crush Caleb Scott and his connection to her newest, most dangerous enemy.

"An exciting new spin on a genie tale. Virginia is a feisty main character who I would love to have as a friend. Captivating!"
— Melissa Buell, author of the The Tales of Gymandrol

"Filled with magic, curses, and mystery . . . a spellbinding journey I couldn't put down."— Kelsey Ketch, author of *Daughter of Isis*

Opal

Fae of Fire and Stone, Book One

White as snow, stained with blood,
her talons black as ebony . . .

Kristina Wojtaszek

In this retwisting of the classic Snow White tale, the daughter of an owl is forced into human shape by a wizard who's come to guide her from her wintry tundra home down to the colorful world of men and Fae, and the father she's never known. She struggles with her human shape and grieves for her dead mother—a mother whose past she must unravel if men and Fae are to live peacefully together.

Trapped in a Fae-made spell, Androw waits for the one who can free him. A boy raised to be king, he sought refuge from his abusive father in the Fae tales his mother spun. When it was too much to bear, he ran away, dragging his anger and guilt with him, pursuing shadowy trails deep within the Dark Woods of the Fae, seeking the truth in tales, and salvation in the eyes of a snowy hare. But many years have passed since the snowy hare turned to woman and the woman winged away on the winds of a winter storm leaving Androw prisoner behind walls of his own making—a prison that will hold him forever unless the daughter of an owl can save him.

"A fairy tale within a fairy tale within a fairy tale—the narratives fit together like interlocking pieces of a puzzle, beautifully told."
—Zachary Petit, Editor *Writer's Digest*

"Lyrical, beautiful, and haunting... OPAL is truly a hidden gem. Wojtaszek [is] a talented new author and one well worth watching."
—YA Fantastic Book Review

Beyond the Glass Slipper
Ten Neglected Fairy Tales to Fall In Love With
Some fairy tales everyone knows—these aren't those tales.
Edited by Kate Wolford

Blood Chimera
Blood Chimera Paranormal Mystery, Book One
Some ransoms aren't meant to be paid.
Jenn Lyons

Blood Sin
Blood Chimera Paranormal Mystery, Book Two
Everything is permitted . . . and everyone has their price.
Jenn Lyons

The Haunted Housewives of Allister, Alabama
Cleo Tidwell Paranormal Mystery, Book One
*Who knew one gaudy Velvet Elvis could lead
to such a heap of haunted trouble?*
Susan Abel Sullivan

The Weredog Whisperer
Cleo Tidwell Paranormal Mystery, Book Two
*The Tidwells are supposed to be on spring break on the Florida Gulf Coast,
not up to their eyeballs in paranormal hijinks . . . again.*
Susan Abel Sullivan

Fractured Days
Shards of History, Book Two
Malia returns home the hero of a war she can't remember.
Rebecca Roland

Far Orbit
Space adventures that harken back to the Grand Tradition of Pulp SF
Edited by Bascomb James
Far Orbit Apogee

Magical Menageries
Edited by Rhonda Parrish
Fae
Corvidae
Scarecrow
Sirens
Equus (Coming 2017)

Specter Spectacular: 13 Ghostly Tales
Once you cross the grave into this world of fantasy and fright,
you may find there's no way back.
Edited by Eileen Wiedbrauk

Wolves and Witches
A Fairy Tale Collection
Witches have stories too. So do mermaids, millers' daughters, princes
(charming or otherwise), even big bad wolves.
Amanda C. Davis and Megan Engelhardt

Bite Somebody
Paranormal Romance
Immortality is just living longer with more embarrassment.
Sara Dobie Bauer

Omega Rising
Wolf King, Book One
Cass Nolan has been forced to avoid the burn of human touch for her
whole life, until Nathan shows up at her ranch.
Anna Kyle

Cursed: Wickedly Fun Stories
Collection
"Quirky, clever, and just a little savage." —Lane Robins, critically acclaimed author of MALEDICTE and KINGS AND ASSASSINS
Susan Abel Sullivan

Campaign 2100: Game of Scorpions
Political Satire Science Fiction
A third party, and an alien, take on a corrupt world government.
Larry Hodges

Murder in the Generative Kitchen
Science Fiction
Does your smart kitchen know you better than you know yourself?
Meg Pontecorvo

Krampusnacht: Twelve Nights of Krampus
A Christmas Krampus Anthology
Edited by Kate Wolford

Legally Undead
Vampirachy, Book One
A reluctant vampire hunter, stalking New York City as only a scorned bride can.
Margo Bond Collins

≈

For more on these and other titles
visit WorldWeaverPress.com

WORLD WEAVER PRESS
Publishing fantasy, paranormal, and science fiction.
We believe in great storytelling.

Made in the USA
Columbia, SC
29 March 2018